TIGERS AND DEVILS

SEAN KENNEDY

Dreamspinner Press

Published by
Dreamspinner Press
5032 Capital Circle SW
Ste 2, PMB# 279
Tallahassee, FL 32305-7886
USA
http://www.dreamspinnerpress.com/

Tigers and Devils
Copyright © 2012 by Sean Kennedy

Cover Art by Catt Ford

ISBN: 978-1-61372-703-4

Printed in the United States of America
Second Edition
August 2012

eBook edition available
eBook ISBN: 978-1-61372-704-1

First Edition published by Dreamspinner Press (March 2009)

For my family:
the one I was born into,
and the one I picked up along the way.

FIRST
QUARTER

CHAPTER ONE

MID-FEBRUARY, the city of Melbourne takes on a different smell. Now it is once again the home of AFL football, it has the smell of hot chips and dagwood dogs, carefully maintained grass, of brand new leather footballs and footy boots. The city becomes noisier on weekends as the sounds of cheering crowds drift down from the Melbourne Cricket Ground, and if the wind is just right they can be heard in suburbs as far away as Northcote or Moonee Ponds.

Melbourne is the hometown of Australian football, its birthplace. The two cannot be separated, even if the game has now spread to other states. The MCG is its Mecca, and the faithful congregate there to watch modern gladiators fight in a savage but beautiful ballet.

My gladiators are Richmond. I have held a member's ticket for the Tigers ever since I was eleven years old. I still have my very first one, when they were paper rather than plastic; my name, Simon Murray, is scrawled across it in almost illegible childish script. My father had come to the realisation pretty early on that I was never going to be an Essendon supporter like him and Mum, and in fact, I copped the blame when my younger brother Tim also turned against Essendon and took up the flag for Collingwood instead.

"It's every man's dream," Dad would tell me every now and again when the beers consumed throughout a game would start to take hold of him, "to have their son support his team. You boys have crushed it."

"At least I don't go for Collingwood," I would reply, as I always did.

"At least there's that," my father would sigh, and he would glare at both of us Murray boys before turning his attention back to the telly.

Mum was far more forgiving. In her mind the less people supporting Essendon the less she had to share them.

THERE was nothing more shameful than being a Collingwood supporter in Patrick Murray's book. The bitter rivalry between Collingwood and Essendon would also flare up between father and youngest son whenever the two teams played against each other.

Me, I'm much more lackadaisical. Team victories always ebb and flow. And if you're a Richmond supporter, it ebbs more often than not so you learn to become very Zen about it all. I would shrug off my family's taunts during the footy season with ease while laughing to myself as I watched them become more and more twisted about their own teams' defeats whenever they occurred.

It became easier for us all when the Brisbane football club formed and the whole family united in hatred. The Brisbane Lions had the distinction of causing the demise of the Fitzroy Lions in order for them to get their own team in the AFL. The Victorian club combined with the Brisbane Bears, and our state hadn't taken it well at all. My best friend since childhood, Roger Dayton, had been a loyal member of Fitzroy. The day the news became official, he burnt his membership card. I remember the solemnity of us, at thirteen, holding a funeral service for the team in Roger's backyard. However, Roger hadn't been able to bring himself to burn his scarf, and to this day it hangs above his bed, much to the chagrin of his wife Fran.

It took Roger a while to settle upon another team to support. The codes instilled in every Victorian child since birth make swapping a team come with more emotional baggage than a Catholic guilt spree. I lobbied for Richmond to be adopted, of course, and was very pissed off when Roger was unable to control his laughter.

In the end, he settled on Hawthorn. We still went to games together, sitting side by side in friendly rivalry, yellow and black by yellow and brown. We would give each other sly digs every now and again, but it never turned nasty between us. It would be what would help sustain our friendship when I got to share my greatest secret with him at the age of nineteen.

IT WAS our second year of uni. Roger was dating Fran, never realising at the time that she would one day be his wife. Roger never thought that far ahead.

It was also a momentous year for me. It was the year that I had my first serious boyfriend. His name was Ian Bevvinson, so of course everybody called him Bevvo. I found him ridiculously hot, but failed to believe that anybody who went by the name of Bevvo could be queer.

At least, I believed that until one night at a uni party I found myself shoved up against a wall with Bevvo's tongue in my throat and his hand down my pants. There had been no questioning of sexuality, and once it began, I made no effort to pull away but responded just as eagerly. Alcohol helped the little courage I had. My first sexual experience with another guy was frenetic, bewildering, and over way too soon. Weak from the expelled energy, my knees could no longer support me and I slid down the wall, trying to pull my pants back up at the same time. Laughing, Bevvo joined me on the floor and finally told me his name.

I was sure this was it. I knew so little about the social etiquette of this world I was now entering. Strangely enough, once the euphoria ended my first thought was of my parents and what they would think if they knew their son had just had his brains sucked out through his dick in a stranger's hallway. That thought faded as Bevvo started kissing me again, and his strong lips, which when parted, gave way to a tongue that tasted of beer and… well, me.

So it was only polite that I returned the favour.

We quickly slipped into seeing each other on a regular basis. And I was heartened by the fact that it wasn't just about the sex, although it was great whenever we had it. It was just that I was extremely lucky, falling into a first-time relationship with someone who wanted the same thing I did. It was what helped me become the person I am today—that I won't put up with anybody else's crap. Sure, you have to sometimes, but I *really* try not to. I knew what I wanted, and Bevvo knew what he wanted, and neither of us were going to endure any sleeping around or drama queening. This would lead to Roger often accusing me of being too picky and Fran countering that just because she settled for less, it didn't mean that I should.

If it hadn't been for Fran, it may have taken Roger longer to accept the truth about me. It took me ages to work up to telling him. I didn't really believe he would turn on me; we had been friends for too long, but you always have that fear in the back of your mind.

Alcohol also helps in the spilling of secrets. And when you say it, it always sounds kind of lame. In the movies and in books there is always some flowery speech and swelling music. For me, it was the sounds of Crowded House playing in the background, beer and nausea fighting for the right to make me vomit, and me slurring, "Hey, Roger, just so's you know, I like guys."

And his reaction?

"Crap, you're in love with me, aren't you?"

I think my laughter at that topped even his disdain at the thought of supporting Richmond.

Of course, that offended him. But once he got over it, he became a little quiet. And things were funny between us for a couple of weeks as he readjusted his perception of me and determined whether our friendship was really now any different than what it had been five minutes before I opened my stupid mouth. Fran, of course, made the comment that now she had a man to shop with. But I was useless in that regard, although my formerly secret love for musicals meant she could leave Roger at home and have a date regardless whenever one rolled into town.

But first loves never stay forever, so Bevvo and I were doomed, although I never thought so at the time. There was no big reason for our breakup, just an eventual drifting apart which probably wasn't helped by both of us being reluctant to tell either of our parents.

You're probably wondering why this is all important. I'm trying to give you a little background information about myself before we get to the meat of this story. To know why I did some of the things I did or why I reacted in certain ways. I'm not hinting that there's some big secret tragedy ahead, just to let you know. But let me fast-forward over the next few years.

I came out to my parents about a year after Bevvo and I split up. My parents had varying reactions, none of them too bad. I was pretty lucky. They still skirt around the issue at times, but I've learnt to live with it. My brother Tim was fine; he'd always thought I was a bit of a freak anyway, and I'd just confirmed it for him. He said that having a gay brother made him seem cooler to some of the girls he was interested in. I don't even want to know if he played that fact up to them so he could get laid in the interest of "proving" his own sexuality. Best excuse ever.

Roger and I continued going to our shared games and still met up on weekends to watch the televised matches. But where there had been our usual manly punches and spontaneous hugs when one team scored on the other, there was now an aloofness on both sides.

To tell you the truth, I think I exuded the standoffishness more out of the two of us, as if, in desperation, I was showing Roger that I wasn't attracted to him by keeping my hands off him. It's funny how coming out makes you repress yourself in other, newer ways. When I finally asked him about it in a fit of drunken self-pity I was surprised to find out he felt my new coldness and reacted accordingly each time.

So, it took a while for us to return to our old selves. I don't think I could even hazard a guess as to when it started getting better. It was all so gradual and in baby steps.

But you know your best friend has entered the stage of über-acceptance when he tries setting you up with other gay guys he's met—no matter how wildly inappropriate for you they are.

After completing my totally clichéd Bachelor of Arts degree with the intentions of writing the greatest Australian screenplay that would revolutionise the entire industry, I soon became realistic and ended up taking a job with one of the various Melbourne film festivals while pledging to write on the side. As of now I've completed twenty pages but had more success publishing film reviews and theoretical essays. A man can dream, though.

Through luck and fortuitous circumstances I ended up becoming the manager of the Triple F Film Festival after a few years. It's not a huge one, catering mainly to independent films (and when I mean independent, I mean *really* independent: you have to have nerves of steel to sit through some of them), but it's amazing the amount of work you have to do all year just to produce a two-week festival in October. Roger says I'm lucky it falls when it does or else it would seriously impede my enjoyment of the final AFL matches and therefore impede his own as well.

So there we all were. Roger and Fran officially had settled down; we had the photos of the wedding and everything to prove it. They despaired of me being fruitlessly single, although it wasn't really through any fault of my own. Okay, scratch that. It *was* my own fault. I tried telling myself that I was busy with work, too busy to have a love life; deep down, I was really a little scared. Roger told me that I was well on my way to becoming the eccentric bachelor uncle who all their kids would think was cool until they became teenagers and discovered I was actually a little bit pathetic.

As you can tell, Roger really knows how to put things in perspective.

But I was happy. Or at least I told myself I was happy. And I probably was really good at fooling myself with that despite the little stab of jealousy rearing its ugly head occasionally as I would see that *look* pass between Roger and Fran— you know, *that* look. I wanted someone to look at me that way, and I wanted to look at them in the way. But I would brush it off and bury it deep, deep within me. The best way to deal with things is to repress them, that's my motto.

I likely would have continued on in that fashion if it hadn't been for one night and one party that I didn't want to go to but Roger and Fran forced me to anyway.

And here is where Declan Tyler enters the story.

CHAPTER TWO

"YOU'RE coming whether you like it or not," Roger commanded.

I ignored him and pretended to be shuffling through my messenger bag, looking for some important documents which in actuality didn't exist.

"I know you can hear me," Roger said unhappily.

"Of course he can."

Without looking up, I knew Fran had returned to the room. We were currently in their lounge, having just had dinner. I had come straight from work, stopping home only to feed the cat and get scratched thoroughly for daring to leave her alone again. I rubbed absentmindedly at one of the wounds on my arm again, causing it to break open and seep a tiny rivulet of blood.

"Gross." Roger noted the obvious.

Fran squeezed in between us, a new bottle of wine in her hands. I hadn't even realised we finished the first and knew that this next glass would have to be my last if I still wanted to drive home. I didn't want to have to catch a taxi home tonight and then back here the next morning to pick up my car, and if I crashed here overnight I would *really* be in the cat's bad book.

"I don't want to go either," Fran told me. "But what can you do?"

"I'm not the one sleeping with Roger," I said. "I'm not beholden to his demands."

"Neither am I, and I *am* sleeping with him," Fran countered, giggling to herself.

"Hey!" Roger protested. "I *am* here, you know!"

Like I said, things have long been back to normal with us now, enough that the casual mention of the thought of the two of us sleeping together no longer made him react like Dracula pulling open the curtains an hour early.

"Pour the wine, hon." Fran threw herself back against the couch and propped her feet on the table.

Both Roger and I reached for the bottle at the same time.

"She meant me, Simon," Roger said, although I knew he wasn't being serious.

"No, I didn't," Fran said, a smirk suggesting otherwise.

"I'm man enough to back down." I held up my hands in mock surrender.

Roger sighed, and I knew he was thinking for the millionth time that it was no fun when we ganged up against him. He passed us our glasses, and we fell into a peace that only broke when Roger murmured, "You're coming, and that's it."

"I don't even know these people."

"That's the point of a party. To get to know new people."

"I don't want to know new people. I get to meet enough new people at work every day." That was true enough, and they more than exhausted my quota.

"There might be some cute guys," Roger said desperately.

I looked at Fran. "Did he just say *cute guys*?"

Fran raised an eyebrow, a trick I wished I could master. "I'm as surprised as you are. I apparently married a fourteen-year-old girl."

"Shut up." Roger sulked. "You know, you *could* help me convince him to come."

"Oh, he's coming." Fran turned to me, and I could see the glint in her eyes telling you in no uncertain terms you shouldn't cross her. "He knows he is."

And that was that. I could hold out against Roger, but Fran got the best of both of us every single time.

"So…," Roger said finally, as Fran drank from her glass. "Friday. Get here by eight. No sense in being the first to arrive."

Fran and I looked at each other, unable to hold in our laughter.

"What?" Roger demanded.

I pushed my empty glass over to him. "One more for the road, Miss Manners."

"WHOSE party is this, anyway?" I grumbled, wrapping my scarf tighter around my throat to protect it from the winter winds everybody claimed blew straight up from Antarctica. I could see the fence of Melbourne Cemetery as we walked along, and truth be told, I would rather be spending the night in there than going to a shindig where the only people I would know were currently in step beside me.

"I don't know," Fran replied, snuggling in closer to Roger for warmth. "Roger knows them."

"I thought you knew them?" Roger asked.

I groaned. "You two have to be shitting me. Aren't we a bit too old to be crashing a party?"

"We're not *crashing*," Fran said. "It's somebody's engagement party. I know that much."

"I thought it was a thirtieth birthday party," Roger murmured.

"Great, just great," I said in an even lower tone of voice, which they couldn't help but hear anyway. "*Is* there even a party?"

"Don't be Mr. Grumpy," Fran warned. "We're saving you from a night of sitting at home and watching your complete box set of *The X-Files* for the twentieth time."

"Or telling kids on Twitter that they need to spell properly." Roger laughed.

I would have given them both the finger if my hand wasn't jammed so far into my pocket and it was too cold to pull it out.

"That all sounds much better than going to a party where we apparently don't even know what it's for."

Roger and Fran ignored me, and the only sounds on the street were our shoes scraping on the bitumen of the road and the clanking of beer bottles in the plastic bag Roger carried. Gradually we could hear music from a distance away, guiding us in like a buoy on the ocean.

"Okay, here's the plan," Roger said. "Synch up our watches, if we're all bored shitless after an hour we sneak out."

That sounded like a good plan to me. I agreed happily. I set my watch a little fast because I already couldn't wait to make a break for it.

"Look at Simon, that's the first time he's smiled all night." Fran sighed as she adjusted the clock on her mobile.

"I can't help it if you're the only two people I like associating with on a regular basis. Or maybe that you're the only two who *will* associate with me."

"Oh, boohoo," Fran said dismissively. "Try to act a little suave at this party, and people might even talk to you this time."

Suave isn't really me. I'm the doofus who normally will end up spilling drinks on somebody or inadvertently insulting the host's partner. Then it's time for a quick getaway and a renewal of vows to never go out again. Until, of course, the next time when Fran and Roger forget about whatever heinous social crime I committed before and force me out again.

We paused before the front door. From the sounds of it, the party was in full swing.

"Do we knock?" Fran asked.

"They wouldn't hear us," I said.

"Doorbell?" Roger suggested.

I sighed and took the initiative. The door was unlocked, and I pushed it open.

"Enter," I told my friends.

They took my lead. In the hallway we unwrapped our scarves and shucked out of our jackets, and threw them upon the bed we could see from our vantage point. It was obviously acting as a coat rack for the night.

Fran and Roger were big fat liars. They instantly found people they knew, mutual friends who I had met only vaguely. From what I could remember we had all come away from the night still uninterested in one another's existences. I circled nervously around the lounge room, the main congregating area. I groaned when I saw the first person I knew properly—Jasper Brunswick. He had worked for the Triple F a couple of years before, and he was a royal pain in the arse. I hadn't been manager at the time, but I was being groomed for eventual takeover. Jasper was one of those know-it-alls who thought he could do everything better, but really didn't want to do the work. I had burned my bridges with him when he drunkenly tried to seduce me one night, and my mouth had fired off before my brain had the opportunity to think of a kinder answer than "No way in hell!"

A cold war began between us and was exacerbated when I had to do some admin work and discovered that his name wasn't Jasper Brunswick at all, but Jon Brown. Yeah, I'm sure you've got him all figured out now.

He was sitting in the centre of the lounge on a red couch that had seen better days. He drew everybody into a circle around him, regaling them with tales about himself and various celebrities he had schmoozed with. Jasper had made a name for himself recently for penning a gossip column for the local gay rag. His ego certainly had recovered nicely since I last saw him.

I immediately slunk into the shadows lining the walls and made a beeline for the kitchen. I needed that beer now and had to find out where Roger had put them. As I did so, I looked at my watch. We had only been here for ninety seconds, and I was ready to do a runner. That had to be a record, even for me.

Sure enough, Roger was in the kitchen. Anywhere there's food and beer, that's where you're likely to find him.

"Roger!" I hissed. "Beer! Now!"

He grinned at me infuriatingly. "Did you see your best mate is in the lounge?"

"Why do you think I need a beer so badly?"

He took pity on me and handed me a bottle. I twisted the cap off savagely and downed half the beer in a few huge mouthfuls.

"Pace yourself," Roger warned.

"We're only going to be an hour, right?" I pleaded.

But it looked as if I may have lost this battle. Roger wore an expression signifying he might be ready to settle in, and Fran could be seen lounging comfortably against the wall, her posture relaxed and her attitude sparkling as she chatted with a woman who had called me a communist at one of Fran's work dos.

I began to formulate whether I had enough money in my wallet for a taxi should the need arise, but the beer started to have an almost immediate effect on me. I'm a true Cadbury kid, needing only a glass and a half to get me going. In fact, even the Cadbury kid could drink me under the table.

"Maybe you *should* sleep with him," Roger said out of the blue as if he had pondered this for the past four minutes.

My spit-take would have put most comedians to shame. "Are you high?"

He giggled like he had already downed a six-pack and it was affecting him already. "I don't know, maybe you should just get laid."

"Does your wife know you talk like this?" I polished off my beer and resolved to take the second one more slowly. I gestured for Roger to hand me another.

"When single *you* are," Roger said, imitating Yoda dispensing advice to Luke, "get *laid* you can. When married you get, *make love* you do."

"Oh, one of the magical gifts afforded to people who can *actually* get married," I said, never one to miss the opportunity to climb up on my soapbox.

"Well, if I had my way you could," Roger said, draping a casual arm over my shoulder. "But you'd also have to find someone first."

I snorted as I opened my beer. "It's not going to be Jasper Bloody Brunswick, that's for sure."

Roger peered behind us to take in the decadent form of Mr. Brunswick draped over the couch with his small crowd of neophytes sitting before him, desperate for some tenuous connection to celebrity. "Yeah, I wouldn't wish Jon Brown on anybody."

"Shut up!" I hissed. "He'll hear you!" The last thing I needed was Jasper Brunswick hunting me down throughout this party because he heard his true name being spoken.

"Do you think if you say it three times in front of a mirror, he appears and slits your throat?" Roger was obviously very amused with himself this evening.

"Are you talking about Jon Brown?"

It was Fran, suddenly appearing behind us and as usual up to speed on everything even though she hadn't been a part of our earlier conversation.

"Fran!" I protested weakly.

She took Roger's beer away from him and drank the remains. "Yes, please, babe, I'd love a drink." As Roger dutifully trotted away to fetch her one, she leaned in teasingly to me and murmured, "Jon Brown, Jon Brown, Jon Brown."

"Simon Murray."

I knew it was Jasper Brunswick from Fran's expression. "Three times and he appears! Watch your throat." She grinned wickedly and slunk off to find her husband.

I took a deep breath to contain myself and turned to face him. "Jasper Brunswick."

His face was flushed, and his pupils were dilated from whatever drugs he had consumed either before or at the party. He leered at me, and I grew uncomfortable under his gaze. "Been a while, Simon."

"Really?" It had seemed far too short to me.

"Mind you, I've done very well for myself since leaving Triple F."

Triple F's full name was actually the Furtive Film Festival but I found it a bit too twee and horrifically earnest, changing it as soon as I took over. Plus, it made the logo look less cluttered. "Why, what are you doing?" I asked innocently.

"Don't pretend to be thick," Jasper Brunswick said, his eyes narrowing as he tried to ready his best insult. "Although it is one of your more endearing traits. I'm sure you've seen my column."

"Column?" Thankfully at that moment Roger passed by and clandestinely pressed another beer into my hand. Three in about fifteen minutes. They would be peeling me off the floor soon enough.

"In the *Reach Out.*"

"I don't read it."

"I find that hard to believe, Simon."

"Yeah, well, it's hard enough to keep up with publications I have to read for work."

"Can I give you a piece of advice?"

Oh, this would be good. I remained silent.

Jasper Brunswick leaned in to me and rested his fingers upon my arm. I could feel them searing my flesh, leaving the permanent mark of the devil behind. "You might want to remain on good terms with the local press. Especially when you want to get coverage of your little festival."

"We already get plenty of coverage," I said firmly, opening my beer so his grip on my arm was shaken off. "In fact, we got a four-page spread in the *Reach Out* last year."

"My column could be very important in helping spread the word further," he insinuated, his breath hot and fetid upon my face. "A few pictures of the distinguished guests and the director of the festival. You can't buy publicity like that."

I winced. "I'm sure you could think of a price."

He faltered slightly and crossed his arms defensively. "Still as cynical as ever, aren't you? I'm surprised you've gotten where you are. No people skills, that's your problem."

"I have people skills," I countered. "Just not the kind of people skills you used to get where *you* are."

He grew even redder. I have no idea if he slept his way to the top, which is what I certainly sounded like I was implying, but to tell you the truth, I was talking more about his snaky schmooziness and brownnosing.

And to my relief, Jasper Brunswick turned on his heel and stalked back over to the lounge room, where he would no doubt find people who would fall at his feet to worship and restore his comfortable sense of superiority.

Roger and Fran appeared from where they had hidden in the pantry. "So he's gone?" Roger asked, looking around like the man in question had the abilities of a chameleon and actually blended in with the '70s-era tiling on the wall behind us.

"He's gone. Thanks for the support," I said dryly.

"I got you another beer, didn't I?" Roger asked, affronted, as if it were equivalent to unsheathing his sword and standing beside me in battle.

Reading my mind, Fran said, "That was Lancelot's main role on the battlefield for Arthur, wasn't it?"

"No," I replied, "it was screwing his wife while his back was turned. By the way, speaking of inappropriate trysts, did you know Roger tried to convince me to sleep with that dickhead?"

"Lancelot?" Fran asked.

"Funny."

"I took it back straightaway," Roger mumbled.

Fran rubbed his back affectionately. "Idiot. Please try to find better conquests for your mates."

"I'm not looking for a *conquest*," I pointed out, shepherding them out into the backyard, where a small fire burned in an old oil drum.

"Last I heard, you weren't looking for *anything*," Fran shrugged.

"Is that a crime?"

"It's certainly not *normal*."

"And what's normal? You guys?"

"Shut up," Fran said, without heat.

"You love us." Roger always got cheesy when he was drunk.

I mumbled incoherently into my feet, an admission of returned love which they could understand without knowing exactly what I said.

Fran hugged me and then pushed me off her. "Now, go away. I want to make out with my husband."

I laughed, not taking any offence, and went off to find a corner where I could hide.

Luck scored me a garden swing in a dark corner that no couple had yet appropriated to mack upon. I settled in and slowly pushed myself, my beer nestled snugly in my hands.

There was a small group standing off to my right, talking loudly. So it wasn't like I was eavesdropping. I wish I knew who they were, because, really, I have them to thank for this whole story. Well, unless you want to give Fran and Roger the credit for dragging me to this party in the first place. But I'm getting ahead of myself. Again. I might as well go all the way back to thanking my parents for having a late-night snuggle one cold winter's night almost twenty-eight years ago.

"The Devils are gonna have another shit year, I'm telling you."

The voices were a garbled mess; beside the gender of each voice I couldn't really separate them into distinct entities.

"Nah, it's about time for them to start crawling up the ladder again."

"You said that last year. There's no way they'll finish in the top eight."

"Yeah, no finals hopes at all. They're wasted."

"They never should have allowed them to merge."

That had been the biggest controversy in the recent history of AFL. To truly make the game Australia-wide (although conveniently neglecting the Northern Territory, but as my father liked to argue, it was a *territory*, not a *state*. My reaction: "It's a bloody big block of land at the top of Australia with people living in it! They deserve some sort of team!") the AFL created a Tasmanian team. But in order to keep the numbers of teams even so that there wouldn't be any hassle in arranging games, they had to sacrifice one of the Victorian teams so they could merge into one (Roger: "It's like bloody Fitzroy all over again!"). We had to say good-bye to the Melbourne Demons, who moved down south and across the Bass Strait to become the Tasmanian Devils.

At the time I remember being horrified at the possibility they might make Richmond merge so that they could be the Tasmanian Tigers, after one of the most famous extinct (supposedly) animals in the world, but we were safe.

So the Devils weren't exactly popular in Victoria, like the Brisbane Lions before them, because they had committed the cardinal sin of taking one of our teams away from us. Problems besieged the Devils from the very start, with two of their key players being injured in their very first season, and although one had gone on to recover, Declan Tyler seemed plagued with injury ever since. It was a favourite source of discussion on both sides of the Bass Strait; we thought it was an act of the gods showing us the merge should never have happened, while the Tasmanians bemoaned the fact one of the best players in the league was doing nothing for them but to sit on the bench and occasionally run out to get injured.

I knew Tyler would come up sooner or later, and it was sooner.

"They've taken Tyler away from us, and look what they did to him."

"I don't think it was *their* fault."

"What are you, a Devils supporter?"

Howls of derision floated over to where I was sitting.

"No, I'm not! Just I don't think they're going to take someone like Tyler and then intentionally injure him so they can't use him at all!"

"They should do *something* with him. All he does is sit on that bench and gather dust. And lard."

"He does not. He's hot."

He *was*, actually. But that's not important.

"Typical bloody woman. Just watching the game to perve at the guys in their shorts."

There was another frenzied protest at such an accusation. I sighed to myself as well. Women and gay guys always get stuck with that image, that they couldn't *possibly* be interested in the game itself—it had to be the guys. I mean, sure, it's a fringe benefit, but when the game is on the last thing you're thinking about is the bodies of the men. You're concentrating on that red leather oval ball and if it will make it between the triad of poles signifying either glory or failure. Not to mention some of the women I've met over the years at games or supporter functions have been the most vocal and knowledgeable proponents of the game.

Those very points were raised between the arguers. I laughed to myself and swore I wasn't going to get involved. But then someone made a comment so wrong I had to butt in.

"It's not even like he was that great a player to begin with, anyway."

"Not a great player?" I made some of them jump when I emerged from the shadows.

I could now make out three men and two women arguing over the oil drum. "You are talking about Declan Tyler, right? Winner of the Best and Fairest for the Devils two years consecutively, a Brownlow Medallist, and winner of the Norm Smith medal *and* the Leigh Matthews Trophy? Yeah, he really sucks as a football player."

"How many Devils fans *are* there at this party?" one of the men asked.

"I'm not a Devils supporter," I said, the disgust plain on my face. "I go for Richmond."

All five of them burst out laughing.

"Hey!" I protested. "We're about due for a final."

"You've been due for over fifty years, mate," the woman closest to me said.

I could feel someone approaching us from behind me and just assumed it was someone else interested in the conversation or a friend of one of the group. "Look, I know Tyler comes across like a bit of an arrogant prick, but you can't say he's not a great player. When he's not injured, of course."

For some reason, everybody's eyes went wide at this point. Puzzled, I raised my hands for any kind of response.

There was the sound of somebody clearing their throat behind me. "Well, thanks for defending my honour."

No way! No way this was possibly happening. I turned, hoping it was just Roger being a dickhead, but I could already tell by the expressions of the rest of the group that it wasn't. Although I had never heard that voice in person, I had often enough on television, usually in news bites or postgame interviews.

Behind me was the man himself, Declan Tyler. And you know how supposedly most people are shocked when they see a celebrity in real life and think they're tiny? Declan Tyler was even taller than I imagined, and had at least a head on me. And I don't think I'm that short, either.

At that moment I wished I had accompanied Roger to his martial arts classes when he went through his obsession with *wuxia* movies. I wasn't any good at any violence or even defending myself *against* violence, should the occasion arise.

"Declan Tyler!" I heard one of the other men breathe in wonder.

"Well, great conversation," I said hurriedly. "Very nice to meet you all."

I managed to escape while the footballer in question was surrounded by the group, of which every member was now star-struck, of course; most of all, the man who previously had been bagging him.

I searched through the garden and the house for Roger and Fran, who were nowhere to be found. Jasper Brunswick was still in his own self-created shrine, and I couldn't help but think that at least Declan Tyler deserved the adoration he was currently receiving, because he actually *did* something, even if it was just kicking a ball around.

Just kick a ball around? What was I thinking? I must have been more agitated than I thought. I was hopeless at confrontations.

I burst through the front door; the yard was empty. They surely wouldn't have left without me. I checked my mobile to make sure they hadn't tried calling or left me a text; they hadn't. I beat the phone in frustration against my forehead, as if I could absorb the information I needed through osmosis.

"Hey!"

I turned around. It was Declan Tyler, coming to punch my lights out. Crap.

"I know krav maga!" I said stupidly.

"Good for you," he said, a confused expression on his face. It wasn't one I was used to seeing on him; on the field he was always in control and stoic. In fact, it seemed to be his default expression. It was like he knew how good he was, and he wasn't going to deny it, which is where I guess my presumption of him being an arrogant prick had come from.

Not only was he a head taller than me, I now saw the span of his shoulders was practically a third wider than mine. He could easily fell me with one king hit. Looking confused gave him more character, it made his boy-next-door looks become even more appealing. He had to lose that gross bit of fluff above his chin, though.

"What do you want?" I asked, still ready to run although it would be akin to a meerkat trying to escape a lion.

He jammed his hands in his pockets. Was he trying to show me that he came in peace? "I wasn't sure whether to thank you for defending my record or yell at you for calling me... what was it again?"

"Arrogant prick," I said helpfully, before I could even think to stop myself.

He grinned. I had walked into his trap. "Most people think I'm either one or the other. It's rare to find someone who thinks both."

"Really?" I asked.

"You sound surprised."

"Well, most footballers are…." I trailed off.

He kept his grin carefully plastered on his face. "Uh-huh."

"… really nice guys," I finished.

"Stereotypes are a killer," he said. "I mean, if I was to go on what you look like, I would say you're a typical arty wanker, what with your cargo pants, your Doc Martens and your all-black wardrobe."

"Ah, but I *am* an arty wanker," I replied. Rule one to survival: always be self-deprecating and get in with insults about yourself before the other party can.

"Where's your beret?"

"That's for Sundays."

Just at that moment, Fran and Roger stumbled through the front gate.

"Where have you guys been?" I demanded, glad that the cavalry had arrived.

"In the cemetery," Roger replied.

"I don't even want to know."

"Not what you're thinking." Fran giggled. "Get your mind out of the gutter."

It was hard to tell who was propping the other up. I think they were really just sagging against each other, and gravity was being their friend.

Some cavalry.

Roger's eyes widened when he realised I wasn't alone. "Are you chatting up a guy?"

I flushed. Roger had just committed a major faux pas. You *never* outed somebody on their behalf. I mean, it's not like I hid it, but you should always be the one to say it yourself. It's just common sense, as it also gives you the opportunity to protect yourself if the situation warrants it.

"No," I muttered.

Roger now looked like an anime character. "Hey, you're— "

Declan shifted uncomfortably and seemed to grow even taller. "Declan Tyler," he mumbled.

"Oh my God, I don't believe it!"

"Who's Declan Tyler?" Fran asked.

Declan looked at her gratefully.

Roger began a spiel listing all of Tyler's statistics, medals, and other achievements.

Fran's eyes got that glazed-over look they usually did where football was concerned.

And meanwhile, for some unknown reason, Declan stood there and listened to it although he seemed somewhat mortified.

"Okay," I interrupted Roger halfway through. "I gotta go. Nice meeting you," I said hurriedly to the very tall and very imposing footballer. I then turned to Roger and Fran. "I'll call you tomorrow."

I was out the gate and a couple of houses down the street when I heard Fran yell,

"Hey, what about your jacket?"

Fuck. There was no way I was going back. I would rather freeze to death. They would have to give it to me at a later stage. I shivered in the cold night air, my visible breath leading me down to Lygon Street where I knew I would stand more chance of catching a taxi.

"Hey!"

I kept walking. I like to pretend that if you don't acknowledge a general yell in your direction, the yeller will just go away. Who's to say they were yelling for me, anyway?

"Simon!"

Even though I had only heard a few sentences from him tonight, I knew it was Declan Tyler again. I steeled myself for the inevitable fist in the face and wished I hadn't left the relative security of my friends. And I mean *relative* security, because I don't think they were capable of doing much on my behalf at the moment except serving as interested, if not terribly accurate, witnesses.

I turned and saw Declan jogging toward me with my jacket and scarf over his arm.

"You need these, you idiot. It's fucking freezing."

To say I was surprised was an understatement. "Uh, thanks," I said, although it didn't come out very graciously. Perhaps more bewildered than anything else. "How did you know—"

"Your friend Fran pointed them out to me when I said I would run them down to you. They looked a bit too drunk to be able to catch up."

"Yeah, they were a bit...." I took my jacket from him. I zipped myself into it, and then took my scarf and wrapped it around my neck. "So...."

"So."

This was awkward. And strange. Very strange.

"So," Declan said again. "You're gay."

Oh, here we go. "Yes. There are gay footballer supporters, you know. I bet there are even gay players."

He began to laugh.

I shook my head, trying not to let my temper rise. "Yeah, well, I'm sure that's funny to you. Anyway...." I turned again, eager to go, but I felt an arm clamp onto my elbow, and I was turned back to face him. Declan was definitely in my personal space now, and he had that look on his face. The look of somebody who was about to lean in and kiss—

I yelped slightly as his mouth closed over mine. I don't mind admitting I was in total shock. The night had definitely taken on a surreal trend. Declan's body pressed against mine, and we shifted backward until I felt the rough bark of a tree against my back. His mouth was firm, and his tongue pressed between my lips until they parted. I was surprised that he tasted like beer, but at the good point, before it becomes stale and a little rank. I know I'm not exactly selling the romanticism here, but I was pleasantly thrilled by it at the time. This was not the kiss of a man who was trying it on, there was no hesitation. His hand curled around the back of my neck to deepen the kiss, and his other hand slipped down my back to hold me in.

I'm not sure how long we stood there for, kissing all the while, but my mind certainly raced through a thousand thoughts. I considered texting my father and brother, but knew they probably wouldn't be impressed with my bragging that I was making out with one of the biggest players in the league. In fact, they would probably be horrified that said player was my way inclined, and it would probably somewhat diminish Declan's abilities in their eyes.

We finally pulled away from each other, panting slightly.

"Stop looking so shocked," he said, grinning at what was obviously a saucer-eyed expression on my face. "See, I *know* there are gay footy players."

I still couldn't formulate words. But this time I went on the attack, and he submitted willingly.

We were sheltered by the low-hanging branches, which is probably why he had been brazen enough to take on such a public display of affection in the first place. There was still a rational part of my mind that knew this stupid for him, as he certainly wasn't out to the public at large. I knew nothing about this guy other than what was published in the AFL Record. I was starting to think I was being stupid as well, but with him squashing me against a tree and claiming my mouth as part of his own, I was too weak-willed to put up any protest.

Car lights flashed in our direction, and Declan jumped away from me. I was disappointed and slightly offended, yet understanding. Quite frankly, schizophrenic.

I could see the look on his face clearly illuminated by the approaching headlights.

He was shocked by his own brazenness, by his recklessness at outing himself. After all, he had a lot more to lose by it than I did. He had no idea of who I was or what kind of person I could be. In his mind, I could already be planning to sell the story to the *Herald Sun*.

I opened my mouth to speak, possibly to reassure him, when we realised the nearing car was actually slowing down. It was a taxi, and Roger was hanging out the back window. "There you are!"

He noticed that Declan was with me and that there was palpable tension in the air. "Is everything okay?"

"Fine," I said. "I take it we're going?"

But Roger was fixated. "Is he hassling you?" he asked, indicating Declan.

"No!" I scoffed.

"Hey, mate," Roger addressed Declan, fumbling with the door of the taxi to get out and confront him. I could hear Fran protesting and see her arm try to yank him back in.

I threw Declan an apologetic look and recognised that I better defuse the situation. Sadly, the best way to do that was just to go and get the hell out of there, taking Roger with me. Nothing like a friend ready to drunkenly defend your honour, thinking you were about to be beaten up when really you had been having one of the best and strangest pashes in your life. Definitely a story to gross out the grandkids.

"Stay, Roger," I growled.

Neither Declan nor I said a word to each other. He watched me get into the taxi. As I belted myself into the front seat, Fran made some sort of apologetic sound, but I was still staring at the man outside my window. Then the taxi moved forward, and I couldn't see him anymore.

CHAPTER THREE

ON THE way home, Roger was still making threats about showing Declan Tyler that he couldn't pick on any of his friends. Fran was berating him, telling him he was acting like a six year old. I was in a state of weirded-out bliss, and confused as all fuck.

Declan was obviously in Melbourne for the weekend because the Devils had just played the Saints at the MCG. He must have known somebody at the party for him to have been there at all. But why, out of all the possible available snogs at the party, had he chosen me? And come to think of it, why had he been so stupid? He couldn't go around kissing strange men all the time, or else his cover would have been blown by now, and I sure hadn't seen him on the cover of the *Reach Out* or *The Southern Star* recently.

I kept thinking of him the next day. There were two lines devoted to him in the back pages of *The Sunday Age* about how he was benched in the Saints game yet again, and nothing at all in the *Herald Sun*. That night on the news there was vision of the Devils getting on the plane back to Tasmania, and although I practically knocked over the television in order to see if I could make him out, all I could see was an indiscriminate mass of male blobs at a luggage carousel.

Roger tried calling my mobile and home phones; I let the answering machines take his profuse apologies, which quickly turned into intense curiosity to discover what I had been talking to Declan Tyler about.

I wasn't trying to punish Roger; I just didn't know what to say. I had never kept anything from him before (barring the obvious, of course), but seeing as I was so bloody baffled myself I wasn't sure if I could make any sense to him about it.

Which was stupid. It wasn't like I was going to run into Declan again. Last night had been pure chance. It was just a drunken pash at a party, and would soon become for me a source of either nostalgia or shame if I ever told anyone.

I went into work the next morning with the aftereffects of the party finally starting to wear off. My second-in-command, Nyssa, came to meet me at the door as I entered.

"Your phone hasn't stopped ringing," she informed me, handing me a pile of messages scrawled on any piece of paper she had at hand including a receipt informing me she had eaten spicy Moroccan soup at The Fitz on the weekend.

Two messages from Roger. One from Fran. One from my mother. Two from film dealers, and another from a tortured artiste who needed to have her hand held through some crisis. I sighed. "Don't they know we punch on at nine?"

"We never punch off," Nyssa grumbled. "Why aren't they calling your mobile?"

Because I had forgotten to switch it back on. I winced and made it my first task when I finally made it into the sanctuary of my office. No sooner had I hung my jacket than my office phone began ringing again.

"Hello," I answered, wishing I had had time to grab a coffee. I desperately needed one. "Simon Murray."

"Why the hell didn't you call me back yesterday?"

It was Roger. The man was nothing but persistent.

"Sorry, Roger. I *meant* to call you back—"

"I was calling to apologise to you, but now I'm thinking *you* should apologise to *me*."

"I said I was sorry, dickhead!" It was so easy to resort back to sounding like a fourteen year old, one of the pros of a long-term friendship.

"Well, I'm sorry too, arsehole!"

I sat down in my chair, grateful for his laughter in response. "You don't have anything to apologise for."

"I was drunk."

"What's new?"

"Shut up. Look, did I just imagine it, or did Declan Tyler try to beat you up?"

I shook my head and was glad he couldn't see my huge shit-eating grin. "No, he didn't beat me up."

"So he *was* there? Fran was trying to convince me I was hallucinating."

"He was there. And I escaped without a scratch." Although there was a very small patch of beard rash on the left side of my chin where he must have pressed too hard while… I stopped thinking about that, no matter how pleasurable it was.

"I'm so embarrassed."

"If it's any consolation, he probably gets drunken idiots accosting him all the time in public."

"Thanks, Simon. Thanks a lot. You sure know how to be comforting."

"You're welcome."

"So we're okay, then?"

I laughed. "Yes. I will extend our friendship contract for another year."

"Good. Speak to you later."

I hung up, determined to get my coffee, but the phone rang again. I knew who it would be. "Hello, Fran."

"Hey, hon," she said warmly. "Have you spoken to Roger yet?"

"I just got off the phone to him."

"Everything good?"

"Of course."

"Stupid boys," she murmured affectionately. "Meet you for lunch?"

"Sure." Our offices were only a block apart, and we had lunches together a few times a week.

"One, at the usual?"

"Yep. 'Til then."

Coffee. Now. I closed my eyes and followed the fumes of the freshly brewed pot to the small closet that served as our kitchen. I filled my cup and said a silent blessing for Nyssa's superior coffeemaking skills.

Nyssa appeared in my peripheral vision. "Agnes King called again. She wanted to move her appointment up to today."

I sighed. The tortured artiste herself. Well, one of many. "Fine. Better to get it over and done with."

Nyssa laughed. "I'm glad you have to deal with her, not me."

"If her doco wasn't so good, neither of us would."

"It's good, and it will be popular." Nyssa leaned in to whisper the next, even though we were the only people in our office. "We need the sales."

"Just maybe make the coffee for the afternoon Irish," I continued.

"Irish and Zoloft-ed up, just for you."

A phone started ringing down the hallway. We both looked at each other, and Nyssa grinned. "That's *your* phone, boss."

"Can't we just pretend I'm running late?"

"Nope. You're definitely on the clock now." Nyssa took her coffee and disappeared back into her own office.

Whoever it was on the phone was pretty insistent. It was still ringing, even though I was giving them plenty of time to reconsider and hang up. I took a desperate gulp of coffee, and my greeting was somewhat garbled when I finally picked up the receiver. "Simon Murray."

"Hello?"

I swallowed properly and repeated myself.

"Uh, hi," the strange voice replied.

Wrong number? Or another soulful artiste? "Can I help you, or do you want me to call in the office psychic?"

A slight pause. "Oh, it *is* you."

"Then you have me at an advantage, as I have no idea who you are."

The man on the other end of the line chuckled. "I would have hoped that I made more of an impression on you."

It couldn't be!

"Uh, Declan Tyler?" I said hesitantly.

"Do you always have to say my surname? You *can* just use the first, especially when talking to me. I know my last name."

Oh, it *could* be.

"Hi," I said in an attempt to be suave.

"We've already said that bit," he pointed out.

A thousand jumbled questions were causing a shorted fuse between my brain and my mouth as I struggled to say something, anything. All I could think was *How? Why? What?* And *Huh?*

"I don't think I said hello," I murmured. "I think I only said my name."

"Then say it."

"Uh, hello?"

"That's it."

He was definitely amused by me. If I had been actively seeking to impress him as part of the first stage of seduction, I was failing miserably.

Best just to be me then, and get it over with. "How did you find out where I worked?"

"I Googled you."

Coming out of his mouth, it sounded dirty. Nicely dirty.

"Simon Murray is a common name." I stared out the window onto the street below. I could see the Flinders Street Station just to the left of me, its gold leafing glinting a bit too brightly in the winter sun.

"Well, when I added the search term 'arty wanker' to it, up you popped." I could hear the smile in his tone.

I couldn't help smiling at myself, and I bit savagely upon my lip as if he could see it from across the Bass Strait.

"Seriously, though. Your name was linked to the Triple F film festival—"

"That's a rhetorical tautology. Like ATM machine."

"Whatever," he dismissed me. "And then I found another article with your picture in it, taken with the Premier."

"He only stayed for ten minutes," I told him. "It was a good photo op or something. Still, any publicity is good, right?"

"It all depends. Anyway, are you going to let me finish?"

"You should know, I tend to rabbit on a lot."

"Why would I need to know that?"

Dammit. He was trying to play it cool. "Well, I don't think it was listed under Google, but you're the one calling me. Finish your damn story."

He laughed again. "So then I found the festival website, and there was your office number and mobile conveniently listed. And your mobile was switched off. So here I am on this number."

"Uh-huh," I said noncommittally.

"That's it," he said, trying to hook me in.

"I guess."

"Come on," he moaned, "give me a break!"

"I'd be looking for a different phrase if I were you, seeing you broke your arm last year and was out for half a season."

He fell silent, and I got my first stab of fear of thinking that I had gone too far. "Uh—"

"Yeah, you're probably right."

I let out the breath I didn't know I was holding. "Sorry. That was bad. Stupid mouth, I said that, right?"

"I don't know. I think it's a cute one."

I could feel the blood coursing into my cheeks. "Thanks," I said inanely. "Do I return the compliment now?"

"Only if you want to."

"I don't know. You're a footballer, do you really need your ego stroked any further?"

"The press and the fans haven't been very nice to me lately, so maybe I do."

"Maybe later. So why are you calling then?"

He paused again, and to tell you the truth, when he spoke he sounded a little nervous. "Look, I'm coming to Melbourne again on Thursday for the game against Essendon. I'll have training on Friday, the game's on Saturday... but would you want to go out for a coffee on Thursday night?"

He had me gobsmacked and speechless again.

"Are you there?"

"Yeah," I croaked.

"I thought the line had cut out for a minute."

"No, I'm here."

"So how about it? Coffee, I mean."

And Simon Murray, the very same Simon Murray who only two days before had been celebrating his single status and crowing about it, and swearing he wasn't looking for anybody, said before the moment could pass, "I like coffee."

"So that's a yes? You're being cryptic. Come on, I promise I'll use cutlery if you leave your beret at home."

"I didn't think you needed cutlery for coffee," I teased, starting to feel a little more in control of my senses again.

"A spoon isn't cutlery? What, do you stir your coffee with your finger?"

"Well, when you promised you'd use cutlery, I was starting to think *you* did."

"Okay, so you're not interested...."

"Interested? Yes, I'm interested," I said, maybe a little too quickly.

"Good." And he *did* sound pleased. "I've got your mobile number. I'll call you."

"Hey, how do I call you?"

"Send up the Bat-signal," he said, chuckling. "Looking forward to seeing you again, Simon."

Before I could answer, he hung up.

Like a clichéd scene in a romantic comedy, I sat in a daze for a little while with the receiver still pressed against my ear and the disconnect tone providing a soundtrack for my state of mind. The sound of a text message coming through on my mobile a few moments later jolted me out of my zombie ways, and I placed the receiver back in the cradle.

It was from an unknown number. I opened it, and it read:

Here's the bat signal.

I saved Declan's number and laughed to myself. I crossed over to the window and watched the people moving on the streets below. I wanted to crank the window open and tell everybody what had just happened, but nobody would believe me. I wouldn't believe me, if I wasn't me.

I wondered if Roger would.

CHAPTER FOUR

THE rest of the day passed in a blur. My mind was definitely not focused on what I was being paid for. Nyssa remarked on my distraction a few times, but I barely heard her. I ended up calling Fran and cancelling lunch, because I knew she would ferret whatever she thought I was concealing out of me. Roger would then kill me if she knew before he did, because she would crow about it endlessly to him (and start another one of his longwinded rants about how friends are supposed to hate their friend's spouse, not become their other best friend).

And Fran knew something was up. I had that certain tone of dorkiness in my voice. She said I sounded too happy.

I had to do laps of Federation Square at lunchtime to burn off the excess energy.

Nyssa said she watched me do the circumference of the building three times before she got dizzy and actually had to go back to work to recover.

On the tram ride home I smiled to myself like a loon and got the usual wide berth that the other passengers afforded to public transport crazies.

I fed Maggie before her yowling threatened a visit by the RSPCA, showered, changed, and drove to Roger and Fran's house.

"It's not Wednesday," Roger said when he opened the door and saw me.

"No shit," I said, and I pushed past him into the warmth beyond.

Fran walked in from the kitchen, and her eyes widened. "Hah! I knew it! Didn't I tell you something was up with him, Rog?"

"Yes, honey," Roger said patiently.

Fran ushered me into the lounge and sat me down—as if I were her child and needed to be lulled into a false sense of security to let slip what I had done wrong at school that day. I took a deep breath and began talking.

"Declan Tyler?" Roger repeated, the shocked look of all shocked looks upon his face.

I nodded.

"Declan Tyler?"

I exaggerated my nod.

"*The* Declan Tyler?"

I did tell you I was nodding, right?

Fran remained impassive, but her eyes were going to and fro between us like she was watching a game at the Melbourne Open.

"*Declan Tyler*, the winner of the Brownlow and Norm Smith Medal?"

"And the Leigh Matthews Trophy," I reminded him.

Roger stared at me, dumbfounded. "And he's going out with *you*?"

"Hey!" Fran and I protested in unison.

Roger seemed to collect himself for a moment, but then was back to dumbfounded and semi-offensive. "No offence, but I mean, you *have* seen the girls they can get!"

Fran frowned, probably envisioning the need to cut off his access to the next telecast of the Brownlow.

"He doesn't *like* girls," I said snottily.

"I know, but he could be going out with a gay supermodel—"

"We get the point!" I yelled, my snottiness turning into extreme prejudice with a license to kill.

"*I* think you're pretty," Fran said soothingly, leaning across and patting my hand.

"Thanks," I replied. "Because pretty is usually what I go for, you know."

So there they sat, my two best friends in the world, and I could have quite cheerfully wrapped them up in a burlap sack at that point and time, weighted it down with some good, heavy stones, and thrown them into the Yarra River to drown.

"Declan Tyler," Roger whispered to himself.

"Is it so hard to believe?" I asked him.

"What, that he's gay, or that he would date *you*?" Roger asked.

"You are such a prick," I muttered.

"I'm just trying to wrap my head around it, that's all!"

"Well, send me a telegram when you do." I stood, but Fran pulled me back down.

"Simon, you know Roger's an idiot. Don't get pissed."

I tried to stare Roger down, but he wouldn't look at me. He knew he was in the wrong, but he was still in shock and incapable of social niceties. Then a thought crossed his mind.

"Do you think he'll take you to the Brownlows?"

I wanted to burst out laughing. Ever since we were kids it had been our dream to go to Brownlow nights. We had gone a couple of times and stood in the audience for the blue carpet trying to get autographs, but we longed for the chance to get inside the actual ceremony and hobnob with the elite of the football world.

"We're going for coffee, that's it. I mean, it's not like he's out."

This made Roger look up. "He isn't?"

"Well, do you see him on the cover of *DNA*? Those dickheads on the footy show trying to cover up their arses whenever he comes near them on the panel?"

"Like I subscribe to *DNA*," he scoffed. "But what does that mean? I mean, for you."

I tried to ignore his question, as I had been avoiding the nagging little voice inside my head asking the exact same thing. "What do you mean, what does it mean?"

"You know what I mean," Roger said.

"I don't know what either of you mean," Fran said, although of course she did.

"Well, if he's not out, that means a lot of sneaking around. What's in it for you?"

"It's just coffee, Rog. I'm not thinking any further than that."

"Well, maybe you should!"

This was getting too soap opera for me. Like *Home and Away* levels of bad. "I thought you guys were the ones who wanted me to see someone? And now that I have a date, you're acting all pissy."

Fran hesitated and then mustered up the courage to say, "We just want you to be careful."

"You have a look," Roger said.

"A look?" Now I was the one who was dumbfounded.

"Yeah, a look!"

"Describe this look."

"I don't know, look in a mirror!"

"Lately you haven't cared about dating." Fran was trying to choose her words carefully. "And now all of a sudden, you look… excited, but trying hard to hide it. You really want to do it."

"And there's something wrong with that?"

"It's just… he's a celebrity… well, as much of a celebrity as a sports player can be." Spoken like someone who didn't know one end of the field from the other. "It's not going to be easy."

"You got that right," Roger mumbled.

I stared them down. "It's just coffee."

But I knew, and they knew, that I was lying. I *was* looking forward to it, too much. I had no more idea than they did about what could happen. All I knew was that I wanted to go and see how it went. I couldn't really imagine any consequences; it was all too abstract.

I DIDN'T hear from either Roger or Declan the next couple of days. My good mood had all but vanished when I met Fran for lunch on Wednesday.

"He cares about you, you doofus," Fran said over her chicken roll. "It's just you two are guys, so you have stupid ways of showing it."

"It's my life," I said childishly.

"And as your friend, he will always butt into it, awkwardly to be sure, and then back off instantly," Fran replied.

"Do you think I shouldn't go on this date?" I asked, half-scared of what her answer would be.

"Of course you should." She fished a bit of scraggly looking shaved carrot out of her lunch and inspected it with disgust. "Just go into it with your eyes open."

I think no matter which answer she had given, I would have been half-scared regardless.

"So what are you going to wear?"

I looked at her, wondering if she thought I had suddenly grown a vagina in the past five minutes. "Clothes."

She sighed. "*Men.*"

THAT night I could barely sleep, and I cursed myself for being so stupid. I was awake at four thirty in the morning, and I pictured myself trying to be cool and debonair over coffee with Declan — and then falling comatose into my latte and drowning before him.

He was a footballer; he had quick reflexes. Hopefully his resuscitation skills would be just as good. I giggled dreamily while I remembered what his lips tasted like and thought that I had to stop such thoughts immediately or else I would never get through the day.

Even the unwashed denizens of the public transport system couldn't stop me from beaming like Pollyanna as I rode the light rail into the city. Nyssa handed me my first cup of coffee of the morning suspiciously.

"Hello, Cheery McCheer."

"Morning, Nyssa."

She watched me closely. "Why are you so happy?"

"No reason."

"There's a reason! You're never this happy! You're surly even when you're happy."

I saw a light cross over her eyes as realisation dawned upon her. I took a step back, thinking she had cottoned onto me and my hypocritical ways.

"You've gotten another job!"

Okay, that stumped me. "What?"

She was now going into full hysterical mode, practically wringing her hands. "I knew it was too good to be true, that you'd stay here forever! You've been headhunted by some larger festival! Or maybe even a studio! I'm going to get a new boss who will be feral and probably make me sign up on a workplace contract, and there'll be no more Bog-off-to-the-Pub Fridays!"

"Did you add Red Bull to your coffee again?" I couldn't help but be amused.

"No!"

"I haven't been headhunted. You know me, I'm too lazy. I would rather be the big fish in the small pond rather than the tiny fish that drowns or is eaten by sharks in the vast deep."

Nyssa collected herself almost immediately, embarrassed at the display she had put on. "You promise?"

I held up my hand and spread my fingers. "Scout's honour."

"That's the Vulcan salute."

I stared at my fingers. "Oh, right. I always get those two confused."

She leant in and glared at me. "Anyway, you're not going anywhere without me, right?"

I gave her a quick kiss on the forehead. "I have it written in my contract."

As I made my way to my office, she yelled after me, "You doing that just makes me *know* something's up!"

I could barely see out of my window because of the sheeting rain outside, but I wasn't going to let anything affect my mood. Besides, I always look better in layers, which is one of the many reasons why I hate it when summer comes around.

As I was on my second cup of coffee, my mobile buzzed with an incoming message.

My plane arrives midday. I have an afternoon training session,

but I hope to be done by 4. See you at 6?

I bit my lip and texted back.

Where?

The reply was almost instantaneous.

I'll pick you up.

That could prove difficult.

How do you know where I live?

I could almost see him shaking his head as he replied:

White Pages online, idiot.

Oh. Well, then.

See you at 6.

His final message made me smile, and I looked up quickly to make sure Nyssa wasn't spying on me.

Looking forward to it.

But I didn't text back. I had to get revenge somehow for the whole idiot thing.

I ONLY managed to make Nyssa even more paranoid when I left the office at four thirty and told her I was calling it a day and she could as well.

"You're going to an interview, aren't you?" she called after me as I ran out the door.

She was kind of right. But I left her hanging in anticipation.

Even leaving early was cutting it fine. I would probably only have forty-five minutes before Declan arrived, if he was punctual. I rushed through my front door, made sure to feed the cat, and jumped quickly into the shower.

I only managed to choose my boxer shorts and wriggle into them before I was stumped. Crap, Fran was right. I should have been thinking about what clothes to wear long before this.

I stood before my mirror and eyed myself critically. Daniel Craig emerging from the ocean in *Casino Royale*, I wasn't. I was too pale, I had skinny arms but a slightly flabby and hairy tummy. My legs were even paler than my chest. I sat down (although fell down might be more honest) on the end of my bed, wondering if I was going to have a panic attack. Who the hell was I kidding? What made me think I could go out with somebody like Declan Tyler, a physical Adonis who was one of the favourites in the annual shirtless AFL stud farm calendars?

Oh crap, I was going to coffee with someone who was in a stud calendar. I clutched my head with both hands.

If it ever got to the point that we would take our clothes off in front of one another, I didn't know if I could be naked in front of someone like him. I mean, with what he was used to seeing in the locker room at least—

My self-pity party was interrupted by my front doorbell being pushed impatiently. I shot to my feet, the panic attack in no way abated. I threw on a pair of trakkies and my faded Tori Amos T-shirt that read with all irony "I don't mind a dirty girl" (my uniform for at-home slouching) and ran into the lounge room.

This wasn't punctuality; this was early with extreme prejudice.

I threw open the door, only to find Roger and Fran standing on the stoop.

"What are you doing here?" I asked, not meaning to be rude but sounding so anyway.

"You are *not* going out dressed like that!" Fran said, her face rigid with complete horror.

Roger sized me up. "He rang up and cancelled, didn't he?"

"No, and *no*," I said emphatically.

"Well, what are you wearing?" Fran asked.

Before I could answer, Roger said, "Are you going to let us in?"

With as little grace as I could muster, I opened the door wider, and they slipped through.

"After your lack of detail over lunch yesterday, I figured you would need help getting dressed," Fran said blithely as she headed straight for my bedroom.

"I can dress myself!" I protested weakly.

"You're as hopeless as Roger."

"I can dress myself," Roger said snottily, sounding exactly like me only five seconds before.

"Oh, hon, you didn't used to be able to," Fran replied sorrowfully as she stood before my open wardrobe and peered hopefully within. "Simon, for a gay man, your wardrobe sucks."

I glowered. "We're not *all* fashionistas or gym bunnies."

"You should be at least one of them." Roger shrugged.

I stared at him. "You know her statement about you and dressing? She's right about that."

"Is that your best comeback?" Roger asked, obviously pitying my lameness on the subject. "Well, maybe your *man* will start choosing your outfits for you."

"He's not *my* man, Roger. He's my… coffee companion."

Roger and Fran could not subdue their fits of laughter. In fact, Fran almost fell head first into the wardrobe. She steadied herself and began pawing through my belongings. "Christ, Simon, do you have anything that wasn't bought from an op-shop?"

"It's my style," was my weak defence.

"Your style says you're cheap," Roger told me.

"And not in the good way," Fran added, sounding muffled from her head being buried as she moved further into the wardrobe.

"Will there be any action with this… coffee companion?" Roger asked, trying not to sound interested.

"I'm not a first date slut."

Roger raised an eyebrow, a quirk I always wish I could master.

"Shut up," I hissed. "Not all the time!"

"Not all the time because there's not many a time," Roger said maddeningly.

"You can talk! You and Fran—"

"And if you ever tell our kids that…," Fran said menacingly.

I crossed my arms defensively over my chest. "Yeah, I'll be sure not to tell your nonexistent children for fear of death."

Fran poked her head out of the wardrobe to stare at me. "And tell me again, why does this guy want to date you?"

"I've been asking myself that all week," I said grumpily. "I don't need *your* help doubting myself."

"Someone wants their ego pumped." Fran moved back out of sight.

"I'm just being honest," I said, even though I knew it sounded like I was begging to get my ego pampered. "I don't get it either."

Roger rolled his eyes, but said nothing. Fran continued rattling coat hangers.

I sighed to myself, now *really* sounding self-pitying.

Fran crawled out of the wardrobe, which was pretty awkward as the bottom of it was filled with crap I was forever chucking in there with an out-of-sight-out-of-mind mentality. She clutched in her hands some items of clothing that I didn't even know I had.

"None of us know why we like the people we do," she said, laying out the clothes on my bed. "I'm sure people look at Roger and wonder how he managed to snag me. But *I* love the doofus. So obviously this Declan guy sees *something* in you."

"*This Declan guy*," Roger mimicked, giving a derisive snort.

Fran glared at him. "So what if he can kick a bloody ball? He's not a god, Roger!"

I tried to avoid their latest spat by examining what Fran had picked out for me. A pair of slightly above-average black pants (sadly, the best I owned), a black button-down shirt and a casual jacket.

"Jesus, Fran, he's not going to a funeral."

"When have you ever seen him wear a colour?" Fran berated him and then turned on me. "Like it or not, we're going shopping one day. You need some colours."

She had also picked out a leather wrist cuff that I didn't even know I owned. I held it up questioningly.

"It's just to give you that funky edge."

"Or maybe he'll think you're into S and M." Roger laughed.

I must have had a look on my face, because Fran ushered me into the bathroom. "Don't listen to him."

As the door shut behind me, I could hear them arguing again. I laughed softly to myself and changed as quickly as possible. When I walked out again, Fran had arranged three pairs of shoes in front of my bed.

"You look good," she said approvingly. "Doesn't he look good, Roger?"

"I can't believe I'm not dating him myself," Roger said obediently.

His wife rolled her eyes and gestured to the shoes. "You only own Cons or Docs. You need a pair of plain black shoes. I'll add them to the must-have list when we go shopping."

"Great. Looking forward to it."

"Well, you're not wearing the green Cons. They're too ratty."

"The red ones look too new!" I protested. "He'll think that I've bought them especially or something."

Roger gave me the once-over. "I don't think so."

"Simon, I love you," Fran said. "But I have to agree with Roger on this one. Nobody would think that."

I self-consciously picked at what was beginning to be a hole in the sleeve of my jacket.

"Docs it is, then," Fran said, having made her decision and pushing the boots towards me.

As I struggled to pull them on, she looked at her watch. "It's almost six. We should go."

I opened my mouth to agree, but was cut off by Roger's protestations. "I wanted to see him!"

"Why? So you could give him the father's speech about looking after his little girl and having him back by midnight?"

"Uh, I'm not a girl, thanks," I interjected.

Fran's eyes narrowed. "You just want to spy on the footballer," she accused her husband.

Roger shifted uncomfortably on the bed. "Well, I was drunk last time I met him!"

"And you threatened him!"

"Maybe I want to apologize."

"Or get his autograph," Fran said suspiciously.

"No!" I cried. "No autographs!"

"See?" Fran asked Roger. "No autographs."

Roger grumbled to himself. "If you were really my friend…."

"Get him out of here!" I told Fran.

Roger stood up and shuffled past me. "Is this all the thanks we get?"

I leant in to kiss Fran good-bye. "Thanks for the help."

"Shopping this weekend!" she instructed.

Already desperate to get out of it, I made noises that were meant to pass for noncommittal, but she wasn't having any of it.

"We have a game on Saturday," Roger reminded her.

"We can shop beforehand." Fran shrugged.

They were still bickering with each other as I shut the front door. I ran back into the bathroom and sprayed some cologne on. Hopefully not too much, I'm never good at judging the right amount. I could smell it on myself and wondered if I should slap some water on to dilute the effect.

The doorbell rang, and I assumed it was Fran and Roger having come back because they had forgotten something. I took my time, lacing my boots, and the buzzer became more impatient.

"I'm coming, shithead!" I yelled.

Yes, I should have known better. For, of course, it was not Roger or Fran.

I threw open the door to find Declan Tyler standing there, looking half-insulted and half-amused.

"Got a pet name for me already?" he asked.

I could only stare at him blankly. "I thought you were someone else."

He looked puzzled. "You were expecting someone besides me?"

Wow, his eyes were really blue. You didn't notice how blue until you were close to him. "Huh?"

He leaned in, and I caught a whiff of freshly washed skin and a faint layer of cologne that smelled far more expensive than my own. "You going to let me in?"

I nodded, my foot still firmly planted in my mouth and feeling heavy. He kicked his boots clean against the welcome mat and stepped into the house.

CHAPTER FIVE

FUCK, he was hot. But something occurred to me in the short space that it took him to cross from my front step to the couch in my living room. What I had mistaken for arrogance before was a carefulness; he moved stealthily and silently, but his every move was guarded. I found it strange, but I didn't comment upon it.

My mother's voice sounded in my head, and like a Pavlovian dog, I snapped to attention and took on the role of the gracious host. "Would you like a drink?"

He grinned at me as he made himself pretty damn comfortable on my couch. "I thought we were going out for a coffee?"

"Uh, yeah, sure."

I could feel him looking me over, and I squirmed.

"You look good," he said, finally.

"Yeah, you too." As if he *never* looked good! I sucked at reciprocal complimenting, apparently. I decided to move onto familiar territory. "How was training?"

That was comfortable territory for him as well. "Good. It's nice to be back on the turf at the G. It feels like home."

There was a wistful note in his voice that I liked to hear. "It must be hard having to set up base in Tasmania."

He scratched absentmindedly at his knee, and the slight padding under his trousers there reminded me that it was currently bandaged up because of his injury. "Well, it's hard being away from home. Even though it's really not that far away. But I miss living here, you know?"

He looked up at me, and I nodded, still feeling a little tongue-tied.

"Are you going to stand there all night?"

I think he meant was I going to sit next to him on the couch. And stupidly enough, although we had already kissed, the thought of being in that close proximity to him made me startle like a jackrabbit on the savannah. "Shall we get going?"

He got to his feet a little awkwardly because of his knee. I didn't know whether to offer to help him up. I hate being such an indecisive bastard.

Of course, he caught me looking at him. "Just a bit stiff."

Was *that* ever the wrong thing to say on a first date. He instantly flushed a little, and I had to bite my lip so I wouldn't burst out laughing.

"Just say it," he pleaded. "I know you want to get it out of your system."

"Say what?" I asked innocently.

He shook his head and moved past me towards the door. I think I took him by surprise when I grabbed his arm and pulled him back to me. My arm slipped round his waist, and I kissed him. Before the party last Saturday it had been a long time between kisses, let me tell you, so I wasn't going to waste any more. Declan responded eagerly, and he shuffled me backward until he had me pinned up against my wall. Tree, wall; I guess he had a thing for pinning.

I broke away when my air supply ran out. I patted him against the chest, thanking him for a job well done, and I could feel the heat from his body beneath my palm.

Believe me when I say that if it were a long time between kisses, it was a long time between other things as well. To feel that warmth of human contact again with someone who wasn't a relative or a friend... before Declan could say anything I kissed him again, except this time I swung him around and pinned *him* against the wall.

He laughed into my mouth, and that was even sexier than his tongue touching mine and that gust of warm air passing from him into me, as if he were breathing for me. I manoeuvred slightly so he couldn't tell just how *much* I was enjoying it, but I felt his fingers slide into the belt loops of my pants and draw me in. The kisses were messy, our breathing was frantic, and our hands were beginning to stray. When the will to live forced us apart again, Declan smoothed down his shirt, which had ridden up, slightly pulling out of his jeans, revealing a tuft of dark hair before hiding it away again. A mad impulse made me want to yank the shirt back up again and tug at the silky hair gently.

"So," Declan said slowly. "How about that coffee?"

I nodded, waiting for him to turn his back so I could wipe my mouth discreetly. From the movement of his shoulders as he jogged down my front steps, I think he was doing the same thing. While he couldn't see me, I let the huge smile that wanted to erupt do so and then composed myself as he fiddled with his car keys to activate the locking mechanism.

That's the funny thing about guys dating. We don't get hung up on the etiquette thing of door opening and seat holding. I mean, sure, we might do it once in a while, but it's really no big deal. Whoever drives, that's up to them. And I was happy to let Declan drive tonight, just in case I needed a drink to fortify my spirits at some point.

I knew it had to be a hire car, as his own would be in Tassie, but he could sense the smirk I concealed.

"What?" he asked. "I just take what I'm given."

"I bet you like the SUV, though. It's a man's man's man's car." I opened my door and jumped in.

He jogged around the side and got in behind the wheel. "You're making fun of me for the car I drive?"

"Hah, you do have an SUV back home, then!"

Declan slammed his door shut and looked at me. "Do I have to answer that?"

"Hey, it would be hypocritical of me to slag you off if you do since I gratefully took a nice little sum of money in sponsorship for them last year."

"You did?"

"Yep."

He looked appeased. "Would it make you happy if I told you it was a hybrid?"

"What makes you think that would make me happy?"

A small smirk tugged at his lips. "You look like you vote Green."

He could tell by my expression that he was right, and he laughed at having caught me out.

"You're not a Liberal supporter, are you?" I asked worriedly. "Because if you are, I have to call it a night."

He looked truly offended. "Christ, my family would kill me if I voted anything but Labor. But we're not going to discuss politics all night, are we?"

"We're going to discuss a lot of things," I told him. I was perfectly serious about the Liberal thing. As Liz Lemon, a personal hero of mine, would say: *That's a deal breaker!*

Declan shut me up by kissing me. It was a good tactic. And I think I had surpassed my own record for the most pash sessions on a first date before leaving the driveway. I was sure that this was either some very nice, very surreal dream or an elaborate hoax that would result in some lame breakfast show DJ jumping out from behind a bush and telling me I had been scammed, with Roger and Fran pissing themselves as they were revealed to be the people who had set it all up.

But nothing like that happened. Not yet, anyway. Declan started the car, and we pulled out of the drive into the night beyond.

Now that he was used to the Tasmanian arctic winds, Melbourne's gave Declan nothing to fear; I was like a dog whenever I was in a car, I always had to have my face exposed to the gale without. I was feeling an ongoing, uninterrupted sensation of happiness. I wondered if this was what Prozac was meant to feel like.

"So where are you taking me?" I asked, realising that we had never discussed our destination.

"My favourite café," he said with a grin.

"Does it have a name?"

"You'll see."

We headed toward the city itself, passing under the iconic cheesestick and ribcage architecture that served as a gateway to the city from the northern suburbs and out past the Docklands. As the streets became more populated, my natural happiness diminished somewhat. I suddenly felt more exposed; until now, whatever Declan and I did was under the cover of trees, within my house, or sheltered in driveways. Now here we were, driving along Flinders Street, where anybody could peer into the car and recognise the celebrity in their midst. Then we would be going to a café. A public café.

I was being stupid. Guys hung out all the time. It didn't mean they were gay. But when you *are* gay, you automatically think everybody knows and wonder if you're safe.

It's not a fun way to pass the time. Mostly you forget about it, but on a first date, boundaries haven't been set. You don't know what the other person is comfortable with, yet. And it doesn't help when the other party is a well-known, extremely closeted sports star.

"What's up?"

"Huh?"

"Well, I haven't known you that long," he said, flicking the indicator light on as he took us off the main road, "but you don't seem like the type to stay quiet for very long."

"Then you *don't* know me very well," I sniped, harsher than I meant.

"Come on, what's up with you?"

"Nothing. Seriously. Nothing."

He chose to accept that obvious lie for the time being, and I didn't want to be the one getting all deep and meaningful before caffeine had even been served.

I could see the ocean come into view before us; we weren't far from the pier where the Spirit of Tasmania berthed. It seemed odd, especially as I didn't think Declan would use the ferry that much, if at all, because he would have flights for all away games paid for him by the club. Better to only spend an hour on the plane than a full night by ferry.

The ferry terminal wasn't such a rocking place at night. I wondered where the hell he was taking me.

He pulled into a car space in front of the pier.

"This is it?" I asked.

Declan unbuckled his seatbelt. "Yep."

Puzzled, I jumped down from the cab and waited for him to come around from his side. He pointed out a coffee cart on the foreshore, which looked lonely and abandoned at this time of night, seeing most of the business people and tourists who would be the main source of custom during the day were long gone by now.

Wryly, I said, "Wow. It's a good thing you're not going out of your way to impress me, on a first date and all."

"A date?" he asked maddeningly. "Is that what this is?"

I should bloody hope so, seeing I've now made out with you three times, I thought to myself, but to keep up the nonchalance, I said, "Well, then, I'm definitely not putting out."

He flushed again. For a footballer, who was probably used to the bawdiness of the locker room, he seemed way too easy to embarrass.

But I wished I hadn't said it. My mouth and my propensity to put my foot in it was one of my less endearing traits. I don't know why I had this need to prove I was tougher than I actually was. It probably made me look just as dumb as the guys he had to work with, all that posturing. But I guess we all do it day to day, to some extent.

"We could go somewhere else," he suggested amiably.

"No," I said quickly. "This is cool."

And it was. I had to admit that I felt more comfortable in the darkness by the water than I would have been in a crowded café on Brunswick or Lygon Street.

As we reached the cart, the owner came out from behind it and treated Declan like an old friend. "Mr. Tyler, you're back!"

"Two away games in a row," Declan said.

"Must get to be a hassle!"

Declan shrugged. "It means I get to come home more often."

"Who'd want to leave this city?" the man asked, looking at me, maybe wanting my input?

I was still wondering if it was a rhetorical question when Declan gestured to me. "Arnie, this is my friend Simon."

"Pleased to meet you." Arnie pumped my hand enthusiastically, like he was about to be my new best friend. "So what do you guys want? Your usual?"

"I'll have my usual. Simon here will have a latte."

I frowned at his take-charge attitude. As Arnie moved back behind his cart, I muttered to Declan, "How did you know I would take a latte?"

Declan shot me that million-dollar smile again. "You look like a latte drinker. Aren't you?"

"Yeah, but…." I shrugged it off.

He stared at me for a moment and then moved closer to the cart to pay for the coffee. Arnie tried to give it to him gratis, but Declan wouldn't hear of it, and I could see he left Arnie a sizable tip.

Not only had the smug bastard picked my drink, he had rightly guessed I would want the largest size available. He handed me the container, which was roughly the size of a laundry bucket. I was grateful, because I take as much coffee as I can, and it would also serve as a convenient hand-warmer against the cold wind coming off from the ocean.

We exchanged good-byes with Arnie. I saw Declan's public face drop for a brief second when he was wished luck for the weekend's game, but he covered it up pretty quickly. Arnie began packing the cart up, and we walked onto the pier, moving out into the darkness.

"You're not playing again this weekend, are you?" I asked to break the silence.

He looked stonily ahead. Maybe he wished I had kept quiet. "Nope."

"They were saying on the news there was a possibility you would."

"You keeping track of me?"

I couldn't tell whether it was an accusation or a tease. His tone was neutral. "It's hard not to," I said evenly. "You watch the news, you get a commentary on all the big player injuries."

He stopped walking and leant against the wooden railing, cupping his coffee in both of his hands. "Well, the media doesn't know everything."

I sipped at my latte. "Okay, so you don't want to talk about it."

He looked at me. "It's not that."

"You don't trust me? You think I'm going to run and tell your story to the *New Idea*?"

There was a faint indication of his smile returning. "Nah, I don't think you'd do that. Besides, the *New Idea* wouldn't care. You'd be better off going to the *Footy Record*."

"How do you know?" I was definitely pushing it, but I was intrigued. "Not the *New Idea* I mean, but you don't know me at all. It's a big risk, it's hard enough dating a guy, but when you take into account how much harder it must be for you—"

"Like I said, I didn't think you'd be like that."

"But—"

"It was just a feeling, okay? No, I don't normally do this, but I just...." He trailed off. "Just... you're one of the few people I've met lately who didn't fall at my feet. Sometimes it's hard to know a person's intentions."

I was gobsmacked. "So it was my natural surliness that won you over?"

He chuckled. "I guess you could say that."

"Wow. Normally it drives people away, not the other way round." I took a huge gulp of coffee to reward myself.

"Maybe you want it to." His tone remained neutral, and he continued to stare out at the waves whipped up by the constant wind.

It was a little too early for him to start psychoanalysing me. "Really."

"Uh oh. You sound pissed."

"Slightly."

"Why?"

"You're making a lot of assumptions about me."

"Like what?" He sounded genuinely perplexed.

"That I look like a Greens supporter. That I'll drink a latte."

"Was I wrong?"

Bugger. "No."

"You're a bit of a type, that's all."

I was starting to get really pissed now. Why the hell was I here when I could be home waiting for the late night repeat of *Forensic Investigators* to come on? "And what type is that?"

"You know. The arty wanker type."

"Are you trying to be insulting?"

He straightened up. "No!"

"You want to analyse types?"

Declan grinned, a surprising move. "You're going to say I'm a typical meathead jock?"

He wasn't, and I had to admit that. "Not really. But you do have the natural arrogance."

"That was the first thing I ever heard you say about me." It sounded oddly nostalgic, coming from him.

"You're fucking weird."

"So are you. That's why I like you."

I was glad it was dark, so he couldn't see *me* flush. "So, you like arty wankers then?"

"I'm not sure as a whole, but I like you."

Definitely flushing now. I took refuge in my bucket-o-coffee again.

"Doesn't take compliments well," Declan remarked. "Noted."

I sighed. "Look, it's just... oh, forget it."

"Yeah, that always works when somebody says that. Spit it out."

I was embarrassed, and I didn't want to show it. "Why me? My friend Roger said you could date anybody you wanted—"

"And he's your friend, saying things like that?"

"He was being honest. It's true, you could date a gay supermodel—"

Declan had to lean against the railing to support himself as he burst out laughing. "Why would I want to do that?"

"Why wouldn't you?"

"You go date a gay supermodel if you think they're so great!"

"I couldn't get near a gay supermodel!"

"Maybe you're not trying hard enough."

Okay, he got me. We both roared with laughter, and I felt the return of that good feeling I had lost once we hit the city. His pinky finger stretched out and stroked the back of my hand. I stood there and let him do it. I wondered briefly if it made me slightly pathetic to find it extremely sexy, but I decided to go with it. I let my other hand wander over, and I linked my pinky with his. We stood there in silence, but both grinning, watching the fishing boats take out to the sea for the night run. I could see why this was one of his favourite places, and I figured he probably came here a lot by himself. And it would have only been at night, when he felt it was his and his alone. So I was touched, rather than offended, that he'd brought me here.

Someone had to say something sometime. "So you really think I'm an arty wanker?"

He shook his head and laughed softly. "Simon, I'm surprised you're not wearing a beret."

"That's what I wear on second dates."

"I thought you said berets were for Sundays?"

I couldn't believe he remembered that. "Sundays and second dates."

I felt his pinky leave mine, and I was shocked at how empty mine felt without his curled around it. This was getting too fast, too quick.

"I look forward to seeing it, then."

Confirmation. But it was a confirmation I wanted to hear.

Although I couldn't resist a little dig. "Who said there would be a second date?"

He was mocking himself as much as me. "What, you could resist this?"

I was slightly worried that I couldn't. But my brain didn't want me to think about it too much at the moment. "When would you next be back in town?"

"Not for another fortnight."

That was too far away. I was already feeling that flush of a new relationship, where you want to hole yourself up with that person, discovering everything about them both emotionally and physically, leaving your friends to send out search parties while you were revelling in your newfound bliss. "I guess there's no possibility of you transferring to another team before then?"

"I wish." There was a hint of bitterness in his voice. I remembered vaguely how he had been drafted out to the Devils as part of their first-year sweetener deal. He had done all the requisite PR, but everybody who followed footy on any level could tell he wasn't happy about it.

"What, you don't like Tassie?"

"I love Tassie. It's a beautiful state. But it's not my home."

I tried to imagine leaving Melbourne, but I couldn't. As Arnie had said before, who would want to? There were a multitude of reasons why it was the city with the largest pattern of migration in Australia, not the other way round. Sometimes you had to really search to find a person born and bred in Melbourne, because it seemed like every new person you met was a refugee from another state.

"You miss your family?"

"Yeah. Of course I do."

"Do they know—" Coded speak once again.

"About me?" He paused, to toss his coffee cup into a nearby bin. It seemed he could have been a basket baller had his football career not taken off. He indicated my cup, silently asking me if I had finished with mine. I shook my head. "I think my mum does, but I'm not sure. Nothing's ever been said, anyway. But that's it. What about you?"

I thought of my family. And how they didn't really talk about it, but seemed to accept it as best they could. "They know."

"They okay about it?"

"In their own way. We'll see what happens if I ever bring a guy over to meet them."

"You haven't ever done that?" He sounded surprised.

"Fuck, no! I don't know who would be more freaked — them or me."

"Why would you be freaked?"

I sipped at the dregs of my coffee. "Maybe I'm not as out and proud as I like to think I am."

Declan stared down at his feet. "At least you're out."

I felt sorry for him. I wasn't comfortable with the feeling. But the thing was, I could understand him. "Hey, I'm an arty wanker in an arty wanker industry. I think the only thing gayer would be working at a fashion magazine. It's harder doing what *you* do."

"I'm not looking for justification," he mumbled.

"I know you're not." I shrugged, turned, and aimed for the bin. A gust of wind caught the coffee cup and it rattled onto the wooden slats of the jetty. Declan dived after it like he was on the field, scooping it up deftly and handballing it into the bin.

"Show off!" I laughed.

But he looked happier again.

"Let's go for a drive," he suggested.

"SO WHAT do you do when you can't play?" I asked as we drove through the back streets of the city.

Declan kept his eyes on the road ahead, trying to avoid a near-collision with the 86 tram. "What do you mean, what do I do?"

"Well, they always make you fly over even though you can't play. Why?"

"For one thing, I like it, because I come back here. Secondly, it's meant to be for team morale. You know, to keep the whole team together. So that I can help the assistant coach."

"Sounds like they're training you up to become Captain."

He sounded distant. "Nah, I don't want to be Captain."

"Why not?"

"Too much attention."

And that was the crux of it, I guess. What he wasn't saying was that it would bring him even more public scrutiny. At the moment everyone thought of him as a great footballer who happened to be shy. If he were Captain, he would be interviewed almost every day; the media would probe more into his life. I wondered, not for the umpteenth time, where this was going and how we could manage to keep seeing each other, if indeed it was what we both wanted. Which it looked like we did.

"You're being quiet again," Declan said.

"You're not exactly talking my ear off yourself."

"What are you thinking about?"

"Coffee," I lied.

"Shit, you must have an addiction."

"Better that it's caffeine than crack." Once the words were out of my mouth I realised that joking about drugs in sport probably wasn't the best thing. Change the subject, quick. "So, what suburb did you grow up in?"

"Glenroy."

"Are your parents still there?"

"Yeah, they like it there."

"I bet you they've kept your room like a shrine."

He didn't say anything, but his eye twitched.

"They have!"

"Well, it's not like I'm ever going to go back to it."

"My mum has a shrine dedicated to Essendon," I said. "It's very sad."

"So says the Richmond supporter!"

"Hey!"

He laughed, pleased with himself. "Come on! Richmond?"

"We have *history* behind us, matey. Unlike your team, which was only created through the dregs and pity of another."

"Ouch." He whistled cheerfully. "Got me there."

I began to sing the Richmond theme song softly to myself. "*Oh we're from Tigerland... BOM BOM BOM BOM!*"

"Stop it," Declan growled.

"*A fighting fury, we're from Tigerland—*"

"I'm warning you!"

What was he going to do? "*If we're behind, then never mind, we'll fight and fight and win—*"

"Keep dreaming, and maybe it *will* happen one day." He laughed, looking back in the rear view mirror.

"We never weaken till the final siren scores! Like the tigers of old, we're strong and we're bold—"

"Don't do it," he pleaded.

That was just like waving a red flag at a bull. *"Yes we're from Tiger—"*

If he hadn't been driving, he would have blocked his ears at the anticipated bellow that always came at this point of the song.

"YELLOW AND BLACK!"

"That's it!"

"Yes we're from Tigerlaaaaa—"

My final word become a strangled yelp as he swerved to the side and deftly swooped into a parallel parking spot.

"This'll shut you up," he said menacingly. In one fluid motion so quick I could barely even make it out, his seatbelt was unbuckled and flung over his shoulder, where the metal lock almost smashed the driver's window. He was half on top of me, pinning me uncomfortably against the door, the armrest digging into my back. I laughed, and he *did* shut me up by plastering his mouth hungrily against mine. I managed to pull my right arm out from where it was wedged between the seats and ran it up his back, bringing him in closer to me. My other arm was stuck between the dashboard and his neck, and there wasn't anything I could do about it. He was pretty bloody strong.

But you should never underestimate someone who has the adrenaline of passion inside them. I surprised him by pushing against him, and this time he was pressed against his door, with me squirming around on top of him. His arm was now in the position mine had been in before, but the other one was free enough to travel down and cup one of the cheeks of my arse.

Roger was right. I *was* a first date slut. And I proved it by pulling away from him and grinning lasciviously. While he was trapped under me, I ran a finger along his side and then across to the front of his jeans, scraping beneath the fold and connecting with the zipper. Declan stared up at me, looking slightly dumbfounded, but he sprang into action when I started pulling his zipper down.

"Wait a minute!"

Dishevelled, he pulled away from me, retreating as far into his corner as he could go.

I slumped back into my own. "What?"

"We're just... going a bit too fast!"

Wow. I had never heard *that* from another guy before.

"Uh, okay," I said. I sat up and tugged at my clothes to straighten them out.

"You're pissed."

"No," I said, and I wasn't really. Just confused.

He sat up and straightened himself. "I'll take you home."

What, home already? Something was wrong now, but I heard myself saying robotically, "Sure."

Declan threw the car back into gear, and we pulled out of the space just as easily as we had swung into it.

WHEN we got back to my house, I didn't invite him in. I don't think he was expecting me to, and I really don't think he wanted me to either. I was already trying to figure out in my head what had gone wrong, but I couldn't come up with an answer that seemed logical.

"Thanks for the coffee," I said, pulling on the handle to open the door.

"Listen," Declan said urgently, and he leaned across to me, putting his hand over mine. "Don't go away mad. I meant what I said, I do want to see you again."

I couldn't think of what to say. "Cool."

"Cool as in cool, or cool as in whatever?"

"Cool as in cool," I replied. Coolly, no doubt.

Declan sighed and gave me a brief kiss.

"Good night," I said. I jumped out of the cab.

He watched me from the driveway as I unlocked my front door and entered my dark house. I didn't turn the lights on, but closed the door behind me and crossed to the window to look out into the yard.

Declan sat there for a few moments, the engine running. I was hoping that I would hear the engine switch off, and he would come and knock on my door. But he stared stonily ahead at the house. Maybe he was waiting to see if I would come out again.

Then he drove off, and I made my way to my bedroom in the dark.

CHAPTER SIX

TO THINK that I had been stupid enough to entertain the thought that I might have woken up in the morning with Declan Tyler beside me!

Instead, what I got was the cat staring at me, waiting for me to open my eyes so she could begin her wailing for her breakfast.

"Morning, Maggie," I mumbled.

Her plaintive cry was a shock to the system. I stumbled out into the kitchen and got tripped by her three times before we reached her bowl.

She was silenced by the food produced for her. If only people could be so easily pleased.

At least it was Friday. I would only have to stumble through one more day before the promise of the weekend would arrive. A game with Roger on Saturday—which reminded me, I had to try and get out of shopping with Fran. I wondered if she would accept the fact that this relationship was over before it began and that I was too depressed to go shopping for clothes I would now never wear? I had a vision of myself—a male, modern Miss Havisham, sitting in my lounge room in my mouldering second-date clothes. I kind of liked that image.

When I got into the office, Nyssa jumped on me immediately. "How was the interview?"

I wasn't with it that morning. "Interview?"

"Don't play dumb. For the new job!"

I sighed. "There's no new job, Nyssa."

"You say that now!"

"Uh-huh. I'll say that later as well."

I holed up in my office. I would like to say that I distracted myself by working like a demon, but I mainly stared out the window a lot and took the occasional phone call. I got messages from both Roger and Fran, asking how the date went, and I ignored them. I couldn't talk to either of them about it yet, not when *I* didn't even know what had happened!

I should have known I couldn't escape them at work, though. At ten my phone rang, and when I picked it up Fran was on the other end.

"Oh, so you *haven't* been murdered, and we don't have to call the police."

"Morning, Fran."

"You could return a person's phone call."

"Technically, it was an SMS."

"Same thing."

"Not really."

"Why didn't you *text* me back, then?"

I hesitated, and it made a long enough pause for her to jump back in.

"Simon, what's wrong? Didn't you have a good time?"

I began to bite at my thumbnail. "At the start, yeah."

"What happened?"

"I can't talk about it now." I ripped the free edge off and winced as part of the cuticle came with it. "Can you make lunch?"

"I can at one, if you don't mind a late lunch."

"Yeah, I can do lunch at one."

Her voice entered super-serious mode. "Simon, are you okay?"

"Yeah, of course, yeah. See you at one."

Fran didn't sound like she believed me, but at least she hung up. Probably to ring Roger to tell him something was up and she was going to sort it all out, so he was not to call me because he'd stuff it all up. For that I was grateful, because I didn't want to have to talk about this twice; one of the benefits of being friends with Fran. It was hard enough having to do it once.

FRAN kissed me on the cheek before she sat down. "Okay, tell me everything."

I sipped at my Coke and wished it was wine. But I couldn't go back to the office with alcohol on my breath or Nyssa would assume it was a drink to celebrate my new job or whatever she thought it could be at this moment.

Reluctantly, I started giving her the details as we ordered. Fran had the linguini; I had a calzone. While waiting for the food to arrive, I got to the point where contact occurred in the car. I grew a little red as I tried to get away with the barest details. "Anyway, I was kissing him, and I... reached *down*—"

"Down where?" Fran asked innocently.

"*Down.*"

"Oh, *down.*"

I hated her right then. "It's not like I managed to get it out... my hand was on his zipper... but he kind of freaked out and said he would take me home."

"Huh," Fran said thoughtfully, but not helpfully.

I looked to her for elaboration.

"Did you ask him why?"

I leaned back as the waiter arrived with our food. Once he was gone, I leaned back in. "No, not really."

"No, or not really? Stop being so vague."

I cut into my calzone savagely. "No."

"And I suppose he didn't volunteer any further information?"

"Just that it was too fast."

"*Men,*" Fran sighed, not for the last time in her life. "It's hard enough being a woman and dating a guy, I can't imagine how much worse it would be when there are two guys in the equation not communicating with each other."

I mumbled an incoherent reply.

"Maybe he's more traditional than you. And by that, I mean less slutty."

I almost choked on my food. I gulped at my Coke and tried to gain back some of my dignity. "I am not a man ho!" I don't know where this reputation came from, seeing I had fewer relationships and hook ups than either Fran or Roger before they found each other and settled into coupled bliss.

"Maybe to him you are."

"He's a footballer! They're supposedly all sluts."

Fran grinned. "Apparently not all of them."

"Can you think of any other reason he would fob me off like that?"

"You said you had kissed him a few times, right?"

The room seemed to grow warmer as memories of us in my lounge, against the tree at the party, and in the cab of his SUV swamped me. "Yeah, a couple. Why?"

Fran seemed lost in thought. And then it occurred to me.

"Oh, he was lying, wasn't he? Maybe he just doesn't find me attractive."

Fran hastily hid behind her hand and giggled.

"He just gave me a mercy pash, thinking that would be enough."

Still smiling, Fran began to dig into her food again. "Oh, Simon."

"What?"

She paused with a forkful of linguini in midair. "Wasn't it just the other day you said you hadn't suddenly grown a vagina?"

I realised I was starting to sound like a maudlin chick flick character.

Fran nodded to emphasize her point and swallowed her pasta.

I stared disconsolately at the clichéd checkered tablecloth under my plate.

"Did he kiss you goodnight?" Fran asked.

"A very brief one."

"On the lips?"

I nodded. "Yeah. It was on the lips."

"That's a good sign."

I tried not to hope too much. "Is it?"

"If he didn't kiss you, but said he'd call you, then you'd be in trouble."

"Yeah, but I got a *brief* kiss and a promise to call later."

"But yours was on the lips. That makes it different, Simon."

"Unless he was just trying really hard to fool me so I wouldn't ask any awkward questions."

Fran wiped her hands on her napkin and stared at me. It was the stare she sent right through you, that made you squirm and made you know you couldn't lie because she would catch you out and make you pay. "It sounds like you almost want it to be a kiss-off."

I shrugged.

That only threw her into persistency mode. "Do you like him?"

I met her gaze and knew that resistance was futile. "Yes." That one little word came out against my whole will. "What I know of him at the moment, anyway."

"That's a start."

"So what do I do?"

She patted my hand and let hers rest above mine. "You just take it as it comes, hon. It sounds like it's going to be hard enough with him being in the limelight. You can't make it more difficult for yourselves by second-guessing everything."

"So what you mean is I'm going to have to talk to him."

"I know that's a hard concept for you. The whole opening-up thing."

"I'm doing it right now, aren't I?"

Fran laughed. "Yeah. To the wrong person!"

She asked me to share sticky-date pudding with her. Feeling somewhat cheered, I had no trouble being convinced.

I CONSIDERED catching the tram the two stops back to the office, I felt so bloated with food. But I walked it off and was in a much better mood when I walked back in the door.

"Long lunch," Nyssa commented.

"Lots of things to talk about," I said vaguely.

I noticed the horrified look on her face, but decided not to reassure her again. Girl is too paranoid.

I wondered if Roger was going to call me regardless. I knew Fran would have called him as soon as she got back to work so they could swap notes. She probably would have told him to lay off me for the moment. Roger, if he did what he always did, would listen to her for a day, so I was expecting him to grill me once he had me cornered at the footy tomorrow.

Like I really wanted to discuss my love life when watching Richmond get thrashed once again. That's just letting salt be poured into your open wound.

As I settled back into my chair, Declan crossed my mind again. To try and get him off it, a futile attempt I know, I busied myself by starting to go through some DVDs delivered that morning. They were potential entries for the festival, and there was a reek of desperation and hope about them. The desperate ones always got to me the most.

I knew how they felt.

Halfway through a heartfelt and achingly amateur documentary about schizophrenic teens forming a garage band, which managed to check every box for guaranteeing a hit among the liberal-minded audience that always attended our festival, my mobile buzzed with a message.

Far from being the cool, calm, and dispassionate person I hoped I would be, I almost did the Snoopy dance of suppertime joy when the screen informed me it was from Declan.

Hope things are okay between us.

Okay, so a flutter of hope sounded in my heart. Shut up.

I pondered over what to write back. This was the best I could do:

They're fine. Good luck with the game tonight.

I tapped the mobile against my lower lip, staring out the window and watching the crowds scurry in and out of Flinders Street Station as I waited for his message.

A few moments later, it came.

I'm glad. And thanks.

I couldn't help but be me, though.

I'm only wishing you luck because you're not playing us.

His response was quick.

I wouldn't expect anything else from you.

I laughed.

Wise move.

While waiting for his response, I entertained the possibilities that could arise from the first time our teams met each other on the field. When we couldn't even figure out the sex thing, how would we tackle actual combat? Football was even more sacred than fucking.

Declan became serious in his next one.

I really want to talk to you. If I could, I would come and see you before I leave, but our flight is immediately after the game.

I replied that I would definitely see him the next time he was in town.

His next message managed to make me feel more confident.

I'd like to talk to you before then.

I thought I would give him a glimmer of hope.

You know my number.

There was no hesitation.

I do. Talk soon.

So he wasn't dumping me, but I still had no idea what was going on with him. I wondered where he was exactly at this point of time. At the locker room in the MCG? Sitting on the field watching his teammates train without him? Maybe they were noticing him texting a lot and teasing him about finally finding a girlfriend.

Even just the thought of that and of him playing along with it as natural cover made an irrepressible bitterness well up inside me. I pushed it down as much as I could, and tried to focus on the good, but came up empty-handed and had to distract myself with work instead.

Nyssa eventually returned to haunt my doorway about four in the afternoon. She looked at me expectantly, half-fearful as always that for some reason this would be the Friday that I would expect us to work all the way through to the normal quitting time. And that divine light in her eyes would go out, possibly forever.

"Yes, Nyssa?" I asked, as if the boss never thought of quitting early to go to the pub and must be reminded of these things even though he can think of nothing else.

"So, it's Bog-off-to-the-Pub day, Simon."

I closed my diary with a resounding thump. "So it is! Get your coat!"

Nyssa clapped her hands excitedly like she was six years old again. Slightly disturbing to think of her as a six-year-old girl getting excited over the prospect of beer.

I checked my mobile for the fifth time that hour to see if Declan had texted me. He hadn't. That was fair enough, I mean, it was getting closer and closer to kick off time. Already, crowds were starting to make their way down to the G, last-minute ticket sales would be going fast, and beer and chips would be selling like… well, beer and chips.

We hopped the tram to take the short ride into Fitzroy and headed for The Napier.

Fran was already there, Roger was on his way, and the usual crowd was assembling. We pushed tables together out into the mosaic-tiled back room and ordered the first round of drinks. As the patrons got rowdier and the music got louder, Fran leaned in to me. "I can tell something's happened," she said, her voice low and warm in my ear.

"He texted me," I muttered back.

"In a good way?"

"I think so," I replied.

Fran leaned back into her seat, studying me. "You have that look again."

"I'm not getting my hopes up," I assured her.

I don't think she believed me. I'm not sure *I* believed me.

Luckily, Nyssa blundered into the conversation as she sat back down with roughly eight packets of chips crushed against her chest. "Are you talking about his interview?"

"Not again, Nyss," I groaned.

"Interview?" Fran asked, immediately beginning to open the chips.

"Nyssa's paranoid," I said quickly.

"I am not!" Nyssa objected, shoving a salt and vinegar chip into her mouth. "Just because I suspect things a lot doesn't make me paranoid."

"You're not seriously leaving the Triple F?" Fran asked.

"No!" I yelled, partly because I was frustrated and partly because the music had gotten louder.

"Bit defensive," Fran said.

"I told you," Nyssa replied. "He's being secretive about something."

"He's a smitten kitten," Fran teased, and then she screamed when I kicked her under the table. "What are you, five?"

"What are you, the town crier?" I shot back.

Nyssa stared me down. "That's it," she said slowly. "I thought you were planning to leave. But the phone calls, the lunch rendezvouses—"

"That isn't a word," I interrupted her.

"What is the plural of rendezvous?" Fran asked. I'm sure she was really interested.

"Rendezvous is both singular and plural," I said, trying not to sound like Grammar Boy.

"Those French are so smart," Fran mused, rubbing her ankle. "Two for the price of one."

"Anyway, Nyssa, those calls and rendezvous? Are mainly with her." And I pointed at Fran.

"You're fooling around with my wife?"

Roger had finally appeared. He whacked me over the head as he manoeuvred around the table to sit with the woman in question.

"Only on Thursdays, hon," Fran said, kissing him hello.

"And Mondays," Nyssa said. "Oh, and Wednesday as well."

"I told you, you were a manwhore," Roger said to me.

"Ha ha." I frowned, trying to shake it off. After all, it's not like he knew what had happened yet.

Roger yelped when Fran kicked him under the table.

"What was that for?" he cried.

"Because it's your shout," she said grimly.

"Alright, alright." He knew when he was beaten, even though he wasn't sure why his shin was suddenly bruising. "Come and help me, homewrecker."

I got to my feet and followed him back out into the main bar.

"You know," Roger said, leaning against the counter, waiting to be served. "I wish for once you would tell me something before you tell Fran. You've known me longer, remember?"

"I can't help it if you don't work in the city a few offices away from me," I said, placating him. "It's really easy to catch up with her."

"Yeah, and I live so far away from you," he pointed out.

"I do want to tell you things, she just gets to you in the meantime. Besides, you're not a fag hag." The word rankled on my tongue; I had never liked it. "Female companion. Gossip girl. Something."

"Whatever." Roger was approached by the barman, and he placed his order.

"Do you really want me to tell you everything?" I asked, leaning in closer to him and lowering my voice. "You want all the details? Of how I tried to blow him, and he wouldn't let me?"

Roger jumped as if he'd been scalded. "You couldn't be a little less vulgar?" he asked primly. He was acting like he had just escaped from a BBC classic drama, with Elizabeth Bennett waiting beneath a weeping willow for his return.

"See? You can't hack it."

"I can so," he said petulantly. "Just try me."

I hadn't wanted to be vulgar. It's really not me. But it was fun to test Roger. Like most guys, he's easy to gross out when you describe any guy-on-guy action to them. It's my opinion they usually act so grossed out because they're too scared to think about if it actually happened to them, they might enjoy it. I'm not saying everyone's a latent queer, but when the juices start flowing sometimes you might not care about who's on the other end of your dick. But I wasn't even sure if I truly believed that either.

"Okay. To put it simply, I tried to go down on him, he acted like you are at the moment, and then he drove me home."

Roger frowned. "Maybe he's not really gay."

"Oh, come on!"

"Maybe he's… confused."

Bloody Roger. Now he was helping to plant the seeds of doubt in me, something I could do very well on my own. Maybe it *was* true! This kind of thing happened all the time, although usually to kids in first-year Bachelor of Arts courses. They turned bisexual for a few months and then quite as happily slid back into heteronormativity when selection for second-year units came around and thus causing true bisexuals to be lumped in the same category with unicorns and other mythical creatures.

"Or maybe he's just never done it with a guy," Roger suggested helpfully.

I think that was even more unbelievable. Declan Tyler, one of the current gods of the AFL, unable to get a date?

"You're making me feel worse," I told him.

"Sorry," he said cheerfully.

"This is why I like talking to Fran."

Roger scratched at the end of his nose. "What kind of guy turns down a blowjob?" he asked, just as the barman returned with our drinks.

Not realising it was a rhetorical question, the barman answered, "No guy would."

"You got to have standards, though. You wouldn't just take one from anyone, right?" Roger asked him, completely forgetting he was discussing sex with a total stranger.

"Dude, I would take a blowjob from Mr. Squiggle, if it was going free."

I shook my head. "That's just sick."

"Calling it as I see it."

As we made our way back to the table, Roger giggled like a schoolgirl. "Even *I* thought that was going a bit too far."

I could only shake my head, too dumbfounded and too grossed out to even formulate words.

"You took your sweet time." Fran frowned as we sat with them again.

"We just found out the barman would take a blowjob from Mr. Squiggle if he could."

"That's disgusting!" Fran and Nyssa said in unison.

"But would he take it from the blackboard?" Nyssa asked thoughtfully, chewing on the lemon from her gin and tonic.

Fran just shook her head and found solace in her beer.

Roger nudged me and pointed at the television set up in the corner. It was hard to hear what was being said above the music and the general hubbub of the pub, but it displayed a familiar face.

Declan. In the locker room at the MCG. He was sitting in a blue suit with a Tassie Devils tie closely knotted at his throat. He didn't look too happy.

Fran had now noticed as well and was showing interest that had nothing to do with the game.

"…Tyler," I could hear the reporter say, "once again benched due to injury but supporting his team in the best way he can. So, Declan, when do you think we can see you out on the field again?"

"I'm not sure," Declan said evenly, not really looking at either the camera or the reporter. "We're really just taking it one week at a time and hoping that I won't have to go in for another surgery."

"Because that just means more time out of the game, right?" the reporter asked.

"Exactly," Declan replied.

The camera swung away from him again to focus on the reporter. Fran, Roger, and I exchanged looks. Luckily Nyssa had been distracted by someone she knew coming over and asking her if she wanted to play pool.

"The man looks good in a suit," Fran said, finally.

He did, but I kept my mouth shut.

"I look good in a suit," Roger huffed.

Anybody could look good in a suit. Even I could.

"Biggest waste of fucking money," came a voice not far from us.

We turned around. One of the local oldies was leaning up against the wall, his stubbie in his hand. He drank from it with disgust, although apparently it was with what was on the television rather than the taste of the beer.

"What's a waste of money?" Fran asked politely.

"*Fran*," Roger hissed, "don't engage the crazy man."

Too late.

"That Declan Tyler," the man said, as viciously as if he was invoking the name of Beelzebub himself.

"What's wrong with him?" I asked defensively, finding myself now brought into the fray.

"All the money they forked out for him to get him released into the draft so the Devils could pick him up, and he's been benched ever since!"

I opened my mouth to speak, but Fran got in there before me. "Are you a Devils supporter?"

The old man laughed derisively. "No way! I haven't forgiven the AFL for selling Fitzroy up the river!"

"Me too!" Roger declared, happy to find a like-minded individual and totally forgetting he had earlier dismissed him as crazy.

"Is that why you went to Hawthorn so quickly afterwards?" I asked him.

"Shut up!" he snapped back.

The man was still staring at the telly. "That Tyler's a sham. Makes me think that all his awards were just a fluke. Maybe he did himself in deliberately so he wouldn't eventually be found out. Best thing for his career."

"Hey!" I said. "Anyone who wins all the awards he did, plus the respect of players and umpires alike, is no sham! He's just been cursed by injury, and given time, he'll probably be back to form soon enough!"

Fran and Roger stared at me, openmouthed, surprised by my impassioned delivery.

The old man sized me up. "You his manager?"

"No," I said coolly. "I just believe in credit where credit is due. Everyone bitches about Tyler, but they all wish he was on their team."

That made Fran and Roger lose it, and I shook my head slightly for my unheralded double entendre.

"The only team I would want him on is Fitzroy," the man said. He leaned in to Roger. "You're a disgrace to the memory of your team!"

Roger sat up fully. "Hey, wait a minute!"

But the man disappeared into the main bar.

"They've been gone for almost twenty years!" Roger called out. "You have to let go sometime!"

Fran dug at me with her finger. "And you! What was that all about?"

"What?"

"Flying your flag for Declan Tyler!"

"Credit where credit's due, remember?"

"I'm not a traitor," Roger mumbled to himself.

Fran grinned smugly at me. "You *are* a smitten kitten."

"Shut up," I said. "It's your shout."

CHAPTER
SEVEN

THE Devils lost that night and the next morning it was all over the papers that Declan Tyler should have been playing, as if he was singlehandedly the saviour of his team and they were dying without him. They didn't care about his injuries, and I thought for what was really the first time how hard it must be to *be* him. The old man's words from the Napier kept coming back to me; it was like Declan could never win. What would happen when he returned from the field, and his injury was too bad for him to start over again?

His previous record would be tarnished, people would feel justified in saying that he was like a beginner in poker, with a run of good luck that never had the test of time to show his true worth as a player. If he *did* come back, and the Devils started winning again, it would only set him up for a greater fall when they would inevitably come down again. It seemed like too much pressure to me.

I wondered how Declan felt. Maybe he didn't even read the papers anymore because he didn't want to read what they said about him. I tried calling him on his mobile, but it was switched off, and I didn't know his landline as it was a silent number and he hadn't given it to me yet. Luckily Fran had imbibed a bit too much at the Napier and called off our shopping date, so I was still in relatively good spirits when I met Roger in town for the game despite not being able to reach Declan.

Roger was in a mood. He wasn't wearing his Hawthorn scarf, and I could tell he was still dwelling on the whole traitor thing.

Of course, my Richmond scarf was wrapped securely around my throat in preparation for the cold winter wind that always blew through the MCG and seemed to make a beeline straight for you.

"You look a bit naked for a football game," I said lightly as I approached him under the clocks of Flinders Street Station.

Roger stared at me grumpily, and we began to walk, melting into the crowds heading for the G. We cut through Federation Square and down like we were heading for Parliament Gardens, to where the new gates were for the plebes like us that didn't have gold passes or corporate boxes.

"So, seriously, Rog, where's your scarf?"

He gave me that look which, to his mind, meant I should shut up. But always contrary, I took it as a please-press-the-issue glance.

"Did you do something to piss Fran off, so she's punishing you?"

"I just didn't think it was cold enough to wear a scarf today, okay?"

We edged into the queue for our gate, the crowds awash in divided loyalties of yellow and black, and yellow and brown. "Are you kidding? Even the penguins are wearing mittens."

"Drop it," he warned.

You *never* tell me to drop it. It's impossible for me. And Roger *knew* that. "You're taking to heart what that crazy old man said?"

"No."

"Bullshit."

"Well, didn't *you* take what he said to heart? You went riding up on your big white horse to defend Declan bloody Tyler—"

"What, are you pissed you didn't do the same for Fitzroy?"

He glared at me. "You don't understand."

"Fitzroy's dead, Rog. Just because some old man in a pub can't accept it, doesn't mean you have to go the same way. You want to be without a team for the rest of your life, yelling at younger footy fans across the bar?"

"No," he mumbled.

Our queue remained at a standstill. Funnily enough, the queues for the rich were nonexistent.

"Hold my spot," I said, like he wouldn't.

"Hey, where are you going?" he yelled after me, but I ignored him.

I found one of those family-business stands like you see at weekend markets, where some bored fifteen-year-old was manning it, obviously forced into child labour in order to earn his pocket money for the week. I picked up a Hawthorn scarf and handed it over with the money. He snapped his gum and looked at the Richmond scarf around my neck.

"Trying to hedge your bets?" he asked.

"No, I'm trying to be nice to a friend."

The kid looked unimpressed. I refused the bag he tried to stuff it in and then jogged back to where Roger had barely progressed in the queue.

"What are you doing?" he asked.

"Don't say I'm never nice to you," I muttered, throwing the scarf at him.

He looked down at it as it lay coiled in his hands, like a dormant snake, almost as if he thought it might bite. "What's this for?"

I jammed my hands into my pockets. "For you to wear your colours with pride."

"But I already have a scarf."

"Yeah, but you're not wearing it today, idiot. Now put it on. Seriously, even just touching it seemed to burn my hands, so you can't make me suffer for nothing."

Roger grinned. "Do I have to hug you?"

"No. A simple thanks would suffice."

"Thanks, mate." He punched me on the arm affectionately.

"You're welcome." I shook my head and rubbed my arm as he wrapped the scarf around his neck and threw the tails over his shoulder. "There, that looks more like my football buddy."

"Now I have two. Does that make me a super-special fan?"

"Only if you get your wife to sew them together into a super-special scarf."

We both chuckled at the thought of Fran actually sewing.

"Well, maybe her mum can do it for you," I suggested.

"She can't sew for shit either. But her dad can."

"What?"

"Yeah, from when he was in the Navy. They had to know how to sew to repair their own uniforms. Fran said back when she used to go to school it was her father that always did their mending."

"Wow. I can't picture that." And seriously, if you had ever met Fran's dad, you wouldn't be able to either. The man had the handgrip of a steel-jaw trap. A needle would get lost in his meaty paws.

Our queue finally started to move, and we made our way into Mecca. As usual, we were in the nosebleed section—the one where you get vertigo just from looking down and seeing the building drop away from you down into the faraway oval.

"I think these seats are even worse than the last ones we had," Roger said. "If that's possible."

I grunted my agreement, and he suddenly perked up.

"Hey, do you think if you-know-what continues happening with you-know-who, you might be able to score us better tickets?"

"Roger!" I hissed. "Shut up!"

He looked hurt. "I didn't mention any names."

"Yeah, well, you're still no Mata Hari."

"Who?"

I considered strangling him with his new scarf, but decided against it. One of the teams from Auskick were playing on the field, and the crowd was suitably oohing and aahing for the little kids as they were able to do what very little of us could; that is, touch the hallowed ground of the G.

"Do you think we'll ever see one of your kids down there one day?" I asked Roger.

He looked horrified at the thought of there being a kid in his future. But I saw the little smile he tried to hide as he stared at his knees and then looked back at me. "Maybe we'll see yours before mine."

I scoffed at that for many reasons. Logic was never part of Roger's repertoire.

"Hey," he said instantly, "there are plenty of ways it could be possible—"

Thankfully, my mobile rang. "Hold that thought."

My smile could not be hid when I saw Declan's name pop up on the screen. "Hello?"

That voice, starting to become so familiar to me, came through loud and clear. "I'm not interrupting anything, am I?"

"No," I said honestly. "Perfect timing, actually."

Roger's eyes narrowed.

"I just rang to wish you luck for today."

"Really?"

He laughed. "Only because you're not playing us, of course."

"Of course."

"I still want to have that talk with you, you know."

Yikes. "You know, normally when someone says something like that, I dread it."

"Not in this case?"

"Okay, a little bit. But looking forward to it more than any other time."

"You're so quick with the compliments, don't strain yourself." Declan snorted. "I was thinking we should make a bet for when the Tigers play the Devils."

"Oh. Really?" A thousand and eight possibilities ran through my mind, and I bet Roger could tell just what I was thinking by the way he was looking at me.

"A carton of beer. Good beer. Not the cheap shit."

Fuck. That wasn't one of my thousand and eight possibilities.

"Of course," Declan said slyly, "I think the loser should help the winner drink it."

Aha! That was more like it. "Sounds good."

"Anyway, I'll let you get back to the game. I'll speak to you soon."

"Yeah, good. You know how to reach me." I felt like slapping myself in the head as soon as I said it.

Declan chuckled. "You're on speed dial."

Cheesy. But I liked it. And I had a sneaking suspicion he knew that I did.

"See you, doofus," I said, and I let him go.

Roger's mouth was hanging open. "*See you, doofus?*"

"What?"

"No wonder you're always fucking single."

I couldn't believe Roger was critiquing *me* on *my* romantic etiquette.

"Seriously," Roger said. "You need help."

"This from the man who once called his wife Frangipanidellasqueegymop?"

"Hey, I was drunk. And it was cute! It was from *Strictly Ballroom*."

"Yeah, it was used as an *insult* against that character."

Roger opened his mouth to try and defend himself once again, but luckily at that moment, I was saved from certain death by the roar of the crowd as Hawthorn ran out onto the field. I couldn't believe he still really thought that *Fran* thought that was cute, but as he said, he was drunk at the time. And he didn't know her well enough back then to properly interpret the expression on her face, although, one would think that now they had been together for almost six years that he would have cottoned on to what bad impressions he may have given on their first meeting.

From where we were sitting, the players appeared as very small yellow and brown specks on a green mass. But that didn't matter to Roger, as he was out of his seat and jumping up and down like a man possessed.

Of course, I did the same a minute later when black and yellow blobs appeared on the opposite side of the green. All thoughts of romantic rules and regulations were quickly forgotten about in the face of the game.

RICHMOND lost, of course. Because they were playing Hawthorn, it wasn't by much. Not that that really means a thing. Despite my loss, I was still strangely happy, and Roger couldn't help but miss it as we made our way back to the tram stop to take us home.

"So, aren't you going to tell us?"

"Tell you what?"

"You know what."

I did know what, not that I was going to admit it.

"Declan Tyler called you at the game, didn't he?" Roger asked.

We paused at the kerb while waiting for the little man to turn to green, and we raced across the road as we could see our tram coming in the distance.

"Yes, he did," I admitted.

"And?"

"And what?"

"This is like pulling fucking teeth," Roger hissed. "How did he seem?"

"Fine."

"Just fine?"

"Uh-huh."

"No mention of why no-no on the blow?"

I stared at him, trying to make sense of what he had just said. It finally hit me a moment later. "No, gross, Roger!"

Roger shrugged. The tram rumbled up beside us, and we clambered on, opting for seats at the back. I stared out the window while Roger continued to press for details. "So what did he call you for, then?"

We passed under the lights of the French end of Collins Street, and the tram seemed aglow from within before it fell back into shadow under the edifice of Parliament House.

"To wish me luck for the game."

Roger looked appalled. "That's dangerous, that is."

"Why? I did the same for him when he played on Friday."

"You *never* wish another team luck!" Roger leaned forward, his earnest expression becoming intense. "It's like betting against your own team in the office pool. You *never do it*."

There was really no way I could refute that. I mean, I never bet against Richmond in the office pool, but it didn't seem like I would be adding to their woes if I wished another team luck in a game the Tigers weren't involved in.

"You must really like him," Roger said solemnly.

"He's okay," I said flatly.

Roger chuckled to himself. "Hah, you really, really like him!"

Watching my best friend morphing into Sally Field was disturbing to say the least.

"Just admit it," he provoked me.

"It's too early to say one way or another," I shrugged.

He knew I was lying. I knew he knew I was lying. But the bonds of friendship meant that he couldn't question me about it too much right at this point of time. But all gloves would probably be off after the second date, and he would come in at me with a right hook.

I HADN'T been home for very long when another game of message tag began.

Guess we're both losers this week, then.

I managed to multitask by responding while feeding Maggie and pulling a beer out of the fridge:

As long as we're losers together.

He must text like a demon.

But what happens when one of us wins?

That looked pretty doubtful at the moment, for either the Tigers *or* the Devils.

Then we'll try not to lord it too badly over the other one.

I grinned to myself as my fingers flew over the keys. *Maybe some comforting will be involved.*

This time he took a little longer to respond.

I like the sound of that. Even better than the beer.

Bloody mixed signals in light of the incident on our first date. It was probably why he hesitated.

Just have to make sure our differences don't tear

us apart like any other doomed romance.

Declan obviously had no shame in acting like a sap or a geek:

To quote INXS, they can never tear us apart.

I wished I was at that stage. But it always took me a while. Like it took me a while to reply to that last message:

Yeah, well, to quote Aimee Mann, you're with stupid now.

I could almost hear his laugh through the tips of his fingers.

Stuck with stupid, more like.

I couldn't help but laugh myself:

For a while, at least.

His reply was brief, slightly insulting, but also sweet:

Goodnight, stupid.

As was what seemed to be my regular sign off now:

Goodnight, doofus.

As I closed up my phone again, I could hear Roger's indignant words replaying for me: *"No wonder you're always fucking single."*

Maybe I was getting ahead of myself, especially as some things with Declan were still obfuscated by his actions, but perhaps I wasn't going to be for much longer.

CHAPTER EIGHT

"SO, WE need to have that talk."

And that was how it started. It was Tuesday, and I had just gotten in from work.

Monday night I had come home from having to endure a meal with the family to find Declan had left me a message on my answering machine. I was disappointed he hadn't tried to reach me on my mobile, but it wouldn't have been easy trying to field his call at my folks' house either. I had thought it too late to call him back as he would probably be training the next morning, and he must have been because he didn't call me at work.

"Hello to you too," I said. "And that sounds really ominous. You might want to tone it down a little."

"Sorry," Declan replied. "I just wanted to clear up this… thing between us. And, uh, hi."

I nestled the phone between my ear and shoulder awkwardly as I spooned Fancy Feast into Maggie's bowl. "So you've noticed the… thing?"

"How could I *not* notice the thing?"

"Well, you were doing a good job of avoiding it." I threw the can back into the fridge and made my way back into the lounge room.

"So were you."

"I was the injured party. Of course I had to wait for you to bring it up." I collapsed upon the couch and used the arm as a shoe lever to prise the sneakers off my feet. They fell noisily upon the carpet.

Declan was silent.

I sighed. "So talk to me, Dec."

Somehow, all it took was this affectionate shortening of his name. "I just couldn't do it right then."

I hated myself for letting that part of me sneak through, but I guess like any human being I needed that reassurance. "Was it… me?"

He laughed, and I felt like he had just skewered me with a meat fork. "Wait," he said quickly, "I wasn't laughing at you. It's just, I was going to say it's me and realised how clichéd it sounded."

Relieved, I agreed with him. "Yeah, it would've."

"But it is me. It's stupid, and I'm embarrassed to tell you."

"Is that why you wouldn't tell me on the night?"

Declan paused. "...it's just that you want everything to go right on the first date—"

"I shouldn't have been so stupid to—"

"No, shut up for a minute. We had a great night and believe me, I wanted things to go further."

I wanted to scream *Then why didn't they?* but I bit my tongue.

He stopped again, and I waited for him to continue. He didn't.

"Dec? Are you there?"

"Yeah, I'm here."

"Well, I'm listening."

"I still feel bloody stupid."

"Well," I said, trying to sound wise. "We're not going to get past it if you don't tell me, are we?"

"It was the night before a match," he said finally. As if that explained *everything.*

I waited for him to elaborate, but he didn't. "And?" I prodded him.

"Oh, come on! Surely you've heard about pregame superstitions."

It finally dawned on me. And I burst out laughing.

Now it was *his* turn to be butt-hurt.

"Hey!" he protested weakly.

"It is a *bit* stupid," I told him.

"You don't get it."

I tried to be fair. Hey, I'm that kind of guy. Sometimes. "No, I do. But it's all a bit arbitrary, isn't it? I mean, just because your coach tells you it probably builds up your stamina or something—"

"Well—"

"I mean, I'm sure I recently read somewhere that they did a study, and they proved that sex before a game has no effect upon your ability to play it—"

"Oh my God, will you stop?"

Cowed, I fell silent.

"Let me get a word in, huh?" Declan asked.

"Shoot," I said. And couldn't resist adding, "After all, you're not playing tomorrow."

He sighed. "Are you always like this?"

"Please don't ever ask Roger and Fran that. They lie a lot."

That elicited a chuckle out of him. "So the answer is yes. You're impossible, you know that?"

"I thought you were about to defend yourself?"

Back to serious mode. I wondered how he was sitting. Was he lying down, like me? Or was he upright, perfectly postured, conditioned into being so after years of rigid sportsmanship? I wished I could see him right now. Talking over the phone was fun, but I would rather have been needling him in person.

"I know it's got nothing to do with how you'll play the game," he said hesitantly. "It's just that the very first coach I had told me that, and it became a superstition for me. Like the guys who wear the same socks every game and don't wash them until the end of season."

I winced. "At least yours is more hygienic."

"Yeah, believe me, you don't want to be around them when they pull those fuckers off after a game."

"Can I ask you something?" I picked at a stray bit of fabric on the couch arm nervously. "Without you hating me?"

"That doesn't sound good."

"You're not playing at the moment, so why does the superstition still stand?"

There was a long pause before he answered. It seemed like days that we sat there in silence with me beginning to sweat thinking that once again I had crossed the line.

"I'm still part of the team, aren't I?"

I nodded and remembered he couldn't see me. "Of course you are."

"Then, it still stands."

"Then I apologise for jumping you."

The warmth was evident in his voice. "If I remember rightly, I jumped you."

"That's *right*, you did."

"You know, maybe I should come up a day earlier than usual next time."

I squirmed with anticipation at the thought, my dick starting to feel heavy. "That could be good."

"I'll see what I can arrange."

I couldn't believe that was still almost two weeks away. That's when it hit me. I was entering into long-distance relationship territory. As if it weren't hard enough maintaining a relationship with someone in the same city, I had decided to throw in the towel and see someone who had an entire sea between us.

We said our good-byes, and promised to speak again soon. I should have been happy that everything had been sorted and things were right between us. But truth be told, I was now feeling a little… sad.

WHEN I had been to dinner at my parents' on Monday night, Mum for some strange reason had decided to ask while serving the mashed potatoes whether I happened to be seeing anybody at the moment.

My dad's fork clattered against the plate as he dropped it, and Tim leaned in wolfishly to take delight at whatever might happen next.

Even though my normal world was pretty much upside down and all over the place at that point of time, I played it safe. "No."

Dad picked up his fork again, and Tim leaned back into his chair with a disappointed expression on his face.

I thought that would be the last mention of my love life for the evening, but for some reason Mum had a bee in her bonnet about the issue.

"But why not?" she asked as she sat herself back down.

"I'm too busy at the moment, Mum," I said, using the same old excuse as always. "I can hardly fit in everything I have to do for work, to do anything else."

"Got enough time to hang out with Roger and Fran twenty-four seven," Tim grumbled, obviously hoping he could goad me into making this family time a controversial one. "Got enough time to go see *Richmond* play."

I glared at his obvious attempt to remind Dad of another reason that I was a thorn in his side. "Yeah, doofus, they're my best friends. I have to see them occasionally."

"Are we going to eat?" Dad asked uncomfortably.

"So you have enough time to see friends, but not a *boyfriend*?" Tim asked deliberately. I wondered how many beers he'd had before I turned up.

I used my peripheral vision to see how Dad was taking this. His knuckles were kind of white as he clenched his fork and used it to shovel peas into his mouth.

"Why are you so interested?" I asked Tim.

"It's what families do, they ask shit," Tim replied.

"Timothy!" Mum cried, whacking him over the hand with her fork.

He winced and waved his fingers. I laughed.

"Boys," Dad said. "Act like adults."

"Tim has a new girlfriend," Mum said, desperate to keep the conversation flowing.

"Another one?" I asked. "What happened to the last one?"

"Got bored," was his laconic reply.

And they think *my* kind is promiscuous.

"We're going to have her over for a barbecue in a couple of weeks," Mum continued.

"Uh-huh," I said, already trying to come up with an excuse for why I couldn't attend.

"I just thought if you were seeing someone you could, you know, bring them."

It's funny how she resisted saying the word "him" like his gender could be mistaken for the other one by any listener. Still, you had to give her an A for effort, at least.

"Sorry to disappoint you," I said, really hoping this would be the end of it.

"I'm not disappointed," Mum said kindly. "Just it would be nice if you did. Like your brother." It was nice that she meant it. Or apparently meant to mean it. Or hoped to mean it, or was at least practising. Okay, that was a lot of "ors."

But if my brother was meant to be the epitome of coupled bliss, I was glad I was… whatever I was at that point of time.

"No one will have him," Tim sniggered over his meal.

I rolled my eyes, but kept silent. There was no use fighting it.

"I'm sure somebody will," Mum said.

"Pass the gravy, please," was Dad's response.

I did so and tried to imagine Declan being exposed to this situation, having Mum's earnest pawing at him to see if he was suitable husband material coupled with Dad steadfastly trying to ignore his gender and Tim trying to provoke any kind of reaction he could get out of him. Of course, it could be totally different as it would be *Declan Tyler*. Maybe they would just sit in openmouthed awe and express shock at his inclination to like dick, because that just wasn't meant to be possible with people like him.

I couldn't even begin to imagine Declan meeting my folks or me meeting his. It seemed even more impossible than me going out with Declan in the first place. So, really, stranger things *had* happened.

After dinner Tim sidled up next to me. "So you're really not seeing anyone?"

This amount of interest in my love life was really unnerving me. "I said so, didn't I?"

"Jesus, you're the most boring gay guy I know."

"Aren't I the only gay guy you know?" I asked.

He started reciting a list, and I zoned out.

I came back to the real world just in time to hear him say, "I mean, you should be getting *some* action. It's unnatural. You must have carpal tunnel just from jerking off."

I went back to my happy place in which my brother refused to be so… so *himself*.

And not long after that I begged off coffee and dessert, citing work that needed to be done before the morning. As I drove home I wondered if I was being too hard on them. After all, I guess they were trying in their own way although Dad could afford to be a trifle more accommodating.

But in the end, they were what they were, and I was what I was. Somehow we would meet in the middle.

I'VE never done the long-distance relationship thing. I mean, I've found it hard enough doing the three-suburbs-away relationship thing. But it really hit me hard over the next couple of weeks what was what I was doing. Declan and I spoke every day, getting to know one another, but somehow it still didn't seem real enough because we weren't actually together. You can find out a hell of a lot about a person by speaking to them for hours on end, but without the added intimacy of being able to see their expression or touch them, all the subtle intricacies of contact and closeness were nonexistent. We may as well have been pen pals, and I wondered how it was that people could fall in love over the Internet. Maybe I just didn't get it.

All I wanted to do was see him. But their next two games weren't in Melbourne: one was a home match and one was in Darwin to try and popularise the game in the far north.

It felt like I was in a relationship, but with none of the advantages. And yet I was happy. I would have been happier if I could see him, but that's what you get for falling for an interstater.

Luckily, work was busy. Nyssa seemed to calm down when she saw that I wasn't going anywhere, especially when I commissioned a local documentary maker to film the events of the festival. Her name was Alice Provotna, and she took her work very seriously. She had started trailing around us with a camera to get some behind-the-scenes footage. I became more adept at hiding around corners and behind stacks of film and tape canisters while Nyssa treated it as if it was her audition reel for *Neighbours*. I was only too happy to push her in front of the camera and let her take the limelight, as I continually berated myself for thinking this was a good idea.

Fran had already become an on-air victim when she wandered over bored one day and found herself having to reenact a scene with Nyssa where we discovered one of our major sponsors had fallen through.

"Wow, that's really… bad," she said flatly, staring right at the camera.

"Bad?" Nyssa gasped like a Victorian heroine finding a ghostly nun upon the belltower of her Gothic mansion. "It is an *abomination*! This could well be the end of our festival!" She turned her back on Fran, now becoming a modern-day soap star, about to begin a lengthy monologue while not at all facing the person she was speaking to.

Fran looked at me, bewildered.

I said, "Oh, don't worry. We will find someone else."

Honestly, I don't know who sounded more robotic.

"That's going to be one exciting documentary," Fran said as we fled to the safety of my office.

"I'm wondering if it's too late to pull the plug."

"It would be an *abomination* to do so," she teased.

Luckily Alice wasn't around all the time. We couldn't afford to keep her on call, for one thing. We arranged a series of important dates for her, and the office returned to some sense of normalcy for a little while at least. Nyssa and I ran all over town in a series of endless meetings to pick up more sponsors. I don't think there was one building on either Queen or Elizabeth streets that we weren't in at some point, and we still had Collins and Bourke to cover. At least it meant the fortnight began to pass quickly, and Declan and I were soon making plans to meet in person once again.

"SO, THE Devils are in town this weekend," Roger said nonchalantly as we drank beer on his back porch, waiting for Fran to get home from work.

"Yeah, I think so," I replied, just as nonchalantly.

Roger's eyes narrowed over the neck of his bottle. "So, you're not seeing Declan, then?"

"Maybe. Depends if he has the time." I'm such a liar.

"You fucking liar."

He knows me too well.

"Well, his schedule is pretty tight," I said defensively.

Roger smothered his laugh.

"Oh, grow up!" I glared at him, to no avail.

"Seriously, are you seeing him?" Roger asked, trying to contain himself.

"Yes."

"Aha. So when are we going to see him?"

That was almost enough to make me panic. "*You* see him? Why would you be seeing him?"

"Well, you're going to have to do the meeting-the-friends-thing sooner or later."

I hesitated. "We haven't discussed that."

"At all?"

I shrugged. "It hasn't come up."

No repressed laughter at that line; Roger was now in serious mode. "Really?"

"That's what I said."

The thing was, we talked every day. But there were certain topics we navigated around. Like what we were going to do if this became really serious, how aspects of his life would affect what we could do together as a couple. We hadn't even gotten to do the fun things new couples did yet, like spend days in bed with the only interruption being the delivery of pizza.

Okay, so I had a bit of a one-track mind at the moment, but how could I think any further about the heavy stuff?

"You don't think you'll ever introduce us to him properly?" Roger actually sounded a little hurt.

"Of course I will," I said to assuage him.

"But will he do the same with his friends?"

I frowned and couldn't disguise it before Roger noticed.

"He won't?"

I shrugged. "I don't know yet."

"But—"

"Rog," I said calmly. "Drop it for now."

"But—"

"Please." My tone was firm.

He wasn't happy, but he nodded. I wondered how long it would be until he brought up this potentially painful subject again. Somehow I didn't think it was that far away.

Fran emerged from behind us with a quiet tread that she often used to her own advantage. "Okay, who died?"

Roger accepted her kiss and rubbed the small of her back. "What?"

"You two are being very quiet. What's going on?"

"Nothing," we replied in unison.

Fran shook her head. "Fucking liars, I hate it when you do that. I need a beer."

"Make that two," I said, shaking my bottle at her.

I could see the concern in her eyes, but I smiled slightly to try and alleviate it.

It didn't work, of course, but Roger stuck to his word for the rest of the evening, and as a consequence, the subject of Declan Tyler was not referred to at all.

"GOOD news," Declan said.

He was talking to me on his Bluetooth as he drove himself to the Hobart airport for his flight to Melbourne.

"I could use some," I said gloomily, remembering the strained atmosphere at Roger and Fran's the night before.

"Why, what's wrong?"

"Nothing," I said quickly.

"Come on."

"Just work. So tell me the good news."

"I've arranged to go back later than the rest of the team, so I have a couple of extra days in Melbourne."

That *was* good news. If I was involved, of course. But I had to play it cool. "Do you have a party or something?"

"Or something," he replied. I could hear the gentle prodding in his voice. "I thought you might have liked to see me a bit more."

"Yeah, it'd be cool."

"You're a cold bastard, you know that?" he asked, although once again there was laughter hidden behind his angst.

"You know I want to see you, so don't play dumb."

"Why not? Aren't footballers dumb?"

"Only to wanky arseholes."

There was a pause as I heard his indicator activate and then switch off. "Look, I'm almost at the airport. I have training, but I should be done by six again. Mind if I come over at about seven?"

"Sounds good."

"Do you have food in your house?"

"No, I don't eat. Of course I have food in my house."

"Well, I could bring food. Save you from cooking?"

"Who said I was cooking?"

"That's why I said—"

I laughed. "I could try subjecting you to what passes for cooking from me."

"Shall I bring takeaway, just in case?" he asked.

"Thanks for the vote of confidence."

"Gotta go, Simon. I look forward to both you and your attempt at cooking."

I grinned and closed my mobile. Then I immediately rang Fran at work to gain ideas of what would be both palatable and easy enough to make so that I couldn't possibly fuck it up.

FRAN had suggested pesto; I didn't want to admit I was uncomfortable with the idea of garlicky morning breath just in case *something* happened. And Fran being extremely smart and prescient, guessed it without me having to try and arse about bringing it up indirectly and moved on to Indian. Then she discounted Indian in case of unwanted effects upon the gastric system.

And not once did she tease me for my attention to every detail and possible scenario.

"You do know once you've gone out for a while, you stop caring about all this stuff, right?" she asked me.

"Yes, but in my defence, I remind you how much Roger tried to hide all his faults from you when he first started going out with you."

"He didn't hide them well." She snorted. "Hey, Simon, you going to let me in on whatever you two were fighting about before I came home yesterday?"

"We weren't fighting."

"Well, something happened."

"He didn't tell you?"

"No, and he was remarkably resilient at refusing to let me get it out of him."

I wondered if he was actually worried that she might have told him off for trying to pierce my temporary shield of obliviousness.

"It was nothing, really."

"One of you will crack sooner or later and tell me."

She was right about that.

In the end, it was decided I would make stir-fried veggies and tofu with rice.

"It's nice and simple," Fran said. "And you've made it before, so you can't possibly screw it up. Plus it probably fits in with whatever crazy football diet the coach makes them stick to during the season."

I hadn't even thought of that. It was a good point.

"It's just going to add to him thinking that I am a crazy, wanky, greenie, hybrid-driving hippie," I complained.

"Has he seen your bomb of a car?" Fran asked in disbelief. "Greenpeace arranges a protest every time it leaves your driveway."

She had a point. I would have to make sure Declan took a drive in it soon enough.

I LEFT work early again. It's good to be the boss sometimes. Nyssa was past suspecting me of going for interviews although she tried to grill me for details once more about what I was up to. I told her to be grateful she was also leaving early, and she wisely collected her coat in silence and followed me out the door at a quarter to four.

"Fran said something about you being besotted with someone," she unwisely said as we were waiting for the lift. "Who is it?"

I counted to three in my head before saying nonchalantly, "You know, I think there's a pile of filing that you could probably be doing—"

"She was probably teasing, after all, you don't go out," Nyssa said quickly, punching the elevator button once again in the hope that it would arrive immediately.

"I think so," I agreed. We got into the lift without further incident.

On the way home I stopped off at Safeway to pick up ingredients for the dinner. A bit of wishful thinking perhaps, but I also picked up a pack of condoms. Better to be prepared than unsafe or sorry. I lugged everything back onto the tram; I suppose I could have gone home and picked up the car and backtracked, but really, it was just as easy to do it this way.

It was just past five when I got home. Declan would still be at practise, so I had plenty of time to start chopping the veggies, put the rice in the cooker, and get a quick shower before starting to piece everything together. I had never been so organised and time-efficient before.

He sent me a text telling me he was on his way just as I was finishing dressing. I ran into the kitchen and began heating the wok. Now the nervousness began settling in. It had been two weeks since we had last seen each other, and I was filled with both anticipation and fear of the moment he would cross back over my threshold.

But I didn't really have time enough to think about that at the moment, thankfully. Between Maggie wanting to be fed, timing when the tofu should be added to the veggies so it wouldn't fall apart, and then having to scoop some shit out of the kitty litter tray because she knew company was coming and wanted to mark her territory before their arrival, I was running around and starting to work up a sweat. Flustered was not a good look on me.

I had just mixed vegetable stock and corn starch together when my doorbell rang.

"Fuck," I whispered. I looked down at myself and realised I was covered in corn starch. I dusted myself quickly and tried to walk calmly to the door. How bloody domestic. Maggie jumped onto the couch arm, an expectant glare on her face as she was cognizant of the fact that the normal peace of the house was about to be disrupted.

I peered through the burglar-hole. It was Declan, and he looked as good as he always did. There was no bag hanging on his shoulder; maybe I had been too presumptuous in buying the condoms. I shook that thought out of my head and opened the door.

"Hey, you," Declan said, grinning at the sight of me.

"Hi," I said, as concise as usual with him. I moved aside to let him in, and he closed the door behind him.

I found myself suddenly enveloped by him as he drew me in. "Hey," he said again.

"You already said that."

"What the hell are you covered in?"

"Corn starch."

"You trying to be Jamie Oliver?"

I was going to make some crack about Nigella and fellating cucumbers but couldn't because he was kissing me. And I suddenly became a hell of a lot more relaxed. I leaned further in to him; I could almost feel the muscles of his stomach through the layers of clothes between us. This time it was me who stupidly said "Hey," when we pulled apart.

He didn't say anything. He just gave me another kiss.

"I thought you were bringing food?" I asked, pointing out his hands, that although now full with me, had been empty before he entered.

"I didn't want to insult your culinary skills," he said, still holding me close. "I thought if we needed to, we could order pizza."

"Good call," I approved.

"Whatever you're making, it smells good."

"Stir-fry. Hey, wouldn't pizza be on the banned list during the season?"

He winked at me. "What the coach doesn't know doesn't hurt him."

I guess that could cover a lot of things. Such as knowing that his star player was currently pashing his sorta-boyfriend at the moment.

Declan had become distracted by Maggie, who instead of treating him like an invading enemy had suddenly become wildly enamoured of him and desperate for his attention. I knew how she felt.

"I don't think you've formally introduced us," Declan said. I liked how he bent down to pet her while still keeping one arm around me.

"Maggie, meet Declan," I said, although Maggie was now too enraptured with her new find to care anything about me and what I might have been saying.

"Hey, Maggie," Declan cooed. He instantly found her weak spot, scratching behind her left ear. She was now his for life, although he was momentarily in her bad books for letting her go and turning his attention back to me. "So, did you call her that because it was close to 'moggie'?"

I bit the inside of my lip, knowing he was about to give me shit. "No, she's actually named after a character from George Eliot's *The Mill on the Floss*."

Declan smothered his laughter.

"Oh go on, give it to me."

"Do you know what my family's cat is called and why?"

"No idea."

"Socks. Because it looks like it has socks on its feet."

"So I named my cat after a literary character. Is that so bad?"

"No, it's just something I like about you."

"Pretension?" I asked grumpily.

"That's not the way I would put it. Stop being so defensive."

There was nothing negative in his tone of voice, so for once in my life I listened to somebody else. "It's a good book. All about how we try to make our own free will, but sometimes catastrophes are thrown in front of us and our lives become determined by them."

"It sounds heavy. Is there at least a happy ending?"

I winced. "Maggie drowns. Along with the brother she only recently reconciled with."

"Oh, for fuck's sake," Declan laughed. "Let's eat."

We moved into the kitchen, and Maggie followed, winding herself around Declan's legs. He tripped and fell against me, and I grabbed him.

"So much for the reflexes of a professional footballer."

He gave me a playful shove and bent down to scoop the cat up out of harm's way.

I added the stock mixture to the wok, and a satisfying cloud of steam erupted from it.

"Do you always cook?" Declan asked.

I shrugged. "I try to get out of it as much as I can. Living by myself, it's mainly a diet of takeaway and toasted cheese sandwiches. Do you want a drink?"

"I brought beer," Declan announced. He grinned when I looked at his empty hands again. "I left them in the car."

"Stupid place for them," I told him.

"I'll be right back."

He jogged back to the front door and disappeared outside. Maggie watched him go fretfully and looked back at me.

"You too, huh?" I asked her.

She replied in the affirmative by jumping from the stool Declan had placed her on and hovering over by the door watching for his return.

"Yep, you too," I murmured, now throwing the tofu into the wok.

Declan moved like a cat in more ways than one. I didn't even hear his tread when he returned and placed a cold bottle of beer against my hand. I ran my thumb along the raised glass on the neck that formed a familiar image.

"Beer from your home state, huh?"

He twisted the cap off his bottle and lobbed it perfectly into the bin. "Yep. Is it okay?"

"I like Cascade. Although probably more for the Tasmanian Tiger than anything else."

Declan grinned. "Why aren't I surprised?"

"Come on, you can tell me. Have you ever seen one while driving around late at night?" I twisted the cap and threw it towards the bin, and was pleased that I made it.

It turned out, that like Roger, he could raise one eyebrow. "Have I seen an extinct animal in the suburbs of Hobart while driving in the dark?"

"*Supposedly* extinct," I told him before taking a swig of the crisp malty goodness.

"No, I haven't, but if you throw a stone in Hobart you'll more than likely hit someone who will claim they have seen one."

I reached behind me into the cupboard, pulling out two plates. "I think it's possible they could still be out there. Aren't there areas of wilderness that no human has stepped in?"

"Not around where I live," Declan said dryly. "You might have to venture out a little further."

"You've never wanted to do it?"

"I take it you would?"

I nodded and set down my beer so I could start serving up dinner. "Sure. Trekking into the hills, going further than most people ever have into the wilderness, and then being rewarded with one undeniable look at a thylacine in its natural habitat."

Declan grinned knowingly. "And you would never tell. You would keep it a secret, because you know if you didn't, even though it would bring you fame and fortune, especially if you had photographic evidence, letting the world know would mean their refuge would be destroyed by people wanting to find out more about them. It would be best for you to just let that tiger fade back into the forest and remain a myth as it continues to survive and build its numbers."

Damn. He had me pegged. And he could be poetic when he wanted to be. "It would be the right thing to do." I was now becoming uncomfortably aware that this conversation could be serving as an allegory for something else altogether.

Declan put his beer down and moved behind me. I was half expecting a cuddle, but he took the plates of food off me and delivered them to the table. I fumbled in the cutlery drawer and produced two pairs of chopsticks. I grabbed our beers and joined him.

"What would you do?" I asked him.

He took a deep breath and sat down. He looked up at me and smiled. "Seeing as the last time we had anything to do with them, we wiped them out, I wouldn't want to be responsible for anything like that happening with a new lot." He reached for his beer.

I clinked my bottle against his and smiled stupidly at him.

"What are we drinking to?" he asked.

"Whatever."

"That's specific. How about, wherever this takes us?"

We clinked the bottles together again and picked up the chopsticks to start eating.

Declan handled his deftly, sending them out across his plate as if they were warriors seeking prey. Despite years of use, I still occasionally used mine as a spear rather than a utensil.

"This is really good," Declan said appreciatively.

"It's not *that* good," I said. "You don't have to butter me up."

He winked suggestively at me, and I quickly downed another mouthful of beer, which was thankfully beginning to work its magic upon me.

"This was exactly what I needed after training," he continued. "They're testing me out to see whether I can return to the field this week."

"Do you think you will?"

"*I* think I can. But of course, I've been thinking that for the last month, and they still haven't put me on."

I stabbed at a piece of tofu. "Well, they don't want to damage the goods after getting you back."

Declan shrugged. "I guess it's always a problem, that line between what a player needs and what the coaches decide is best."

I thought it was interesting, his use of the word *need*. In the normal world, a worker wishes to be put out of commission for a little while in order to enjoy a holiday away from the strain of the office; but to somebody like Declan, where work also happened to be his passion, he must have felt, and continued to feel, pretty close to bereft being kept away from it for so long.

His easy going expression slipped a little as he drank his beer, thinking about the possibility he might not get what he wanted — *needed* — next week. Then it was gone again, so fast I wondered if I had imagined it.

"Are you still in any pain?" I asked.

He shook his head. "It's a bit sore sometimes, but not painful. I think it's rusting from inactivity more than anything."

"I doubt it's inactive. I've seen you on the sports report."

"Have you really?" He grinned at me.

"Hey, I can't help it if your ugly mug pops up every time I'm trying to find out the lineup for Richmond's next game."

Declan laughed. "And here I was thinking you kind of liked my mug."

I shrugged. "It's okay. As mugs go." I then laughed and stared down at my plate.

There was the sound of movement underneath the table, and I felt his foot pressing up against mine. It was a comfortable weight.

"So's yours." Declan began eating again.

Wow. I was beginning to like hearing these sly compliments. I froze as Declan's foot crept up underneath the cuff of the right leg of my pants. He had kicked off his sneaker, and I could feel the warmth of his stockinged foot against the hairs of my leg. He continued eating with an innocent expression on his face as his foot began rubbing towards my knee. I tried to collect some vegetables between my chopsticks, but my aim was unsteady and a small pile of onion flew across the table to land close to Declan's beer. He grinned, but kept his momentum.

I swallowed a mouthful of beer to steady my nerves and was disappointed when Declan's foot withdrew. I tried to think of something to say to fill the sudden silence, when his foot was back against my skin. Except this time there was a difference. It was skin against skin. He had shucked his sock off, and I was now feeling the direct heat from his body transferring to mine. It was also having effects upon other areas of my body. He kept the foot in place, maybe just enjoying the simple contact.

"So," I said, trying not to let my voice crack.

Declan put his chopsticks down and looked at me expectantly.

"It's Wednesday," I said weakly.

He nodded, not giving anything away.

"You're not playing until Friday."

"Yep." Funny how that one little word sounded so full of promise.

"So your superstition won't be in effect until tomorrow."

"No, I guess not." There was a small smile playing upon his lips. I wanted to kiss it off him.

My curiosity got in the way of passion. "How does that work exactly? I mean, does the superstition kick in at midnight, or is it just in the general timeframe of the night before?"

He looked adorably confused at my sudden change of tone. "Uh, I don't know. It's just a superstition. There's no logic to it."

"But there must be a time frame, right?"

"I guess… probably just in the vicinity of the evening before and the day of the match."

"Huh." I sat back thoughtfully.

"Does that answer your question?"

I think it did, because the next thing I knew I had launched myself at him, and he was trapped in his chair as I squirmed up against his body, gripping his face in my hands as I kissed him. His arms pulled me in closer, and I noticed how they strained against the material of his shirt. I was no lightweight, but I bet he could pick me up and throw me across the room like a javelin. I crouched over him like a cat with a mouse, but suddenly I was pulled onto his lap. That was more comfortable.

Our kisses grew more heated and desperate; dinner was forgotten. Well, we had almost finished anyway. Declan's hand crept under my shirt and rested against the small of my back. While my mouth was still occupied with his, my brain stupidly went into overdrive as it realised that *this was it*. It was going to happen. And all those idiotic insecurities that normally came with any time two people are first intimate with each other came flooding over me. Especially with Declan. The guy was going to have an amazing body; he was surrounded by astounding specimens of masculinity every time he met with his colleagues, and mine could never compare.

But then I saw him staring back at me.

And saw that he wanted me.

There was an unmistakable hunger in his eyes, and he was eyeing me appreciatively. I didn't really understand it, and it didn't settle my insecurities completely but I managed to get over that bump in the road.

Without speaking we rose as one and stumbled out of the dining room, through the lounge, and paused as Declan realised he didn't know where the bedroom was. I took the initiative and pulled him with me, still clutching him.

We sagged against the bookcase in my room; Declan's hands were starting to pull my shirt up my body, but I pressed against him, inhibiting his actions. This time it had nothing to do with the insecurity of being naked before him. I was now desperate, close to the edge, and unable to hold on much longer. He gasped as I ground against him, searching for friction. I found it, and his gasp turned into a guttural moan as I locked into him and began getting us off.

"Simon…" he moaned, and I liked hearing my name said that way.

I pulled his lower lip between my own and then released it to lick along the side of his neck. I let my mouth rest against the hollow of his throat; Declan threw his head back. His hands came to rest on my arse as he helped me continue to thrust against him.

Declan swore to himself, his breathing becoming more hoarse. I raised my head again, as I wanted to see his face in this most unguarded of moments. He bit his lip, and closed his eyes; I kissed him, and they flew back open. His breath erupted from him in a hot rush into my mouth, and he sagged against me. I bucked against him slowly, letting him ride out his release. As he sighed contentedly and his breathing steadied, I kept eye contact with him and started thrusting again. He held me tighter, his eyes never off me until I cried out and fell against him. He continued to hold me, and his hands travelled up my back, rubbing softly. I buried my head in the crook of his neck as postorgasmic bliss gave way quickly to *Oh fuck, what have I done?*

We didn't speak. The only sound in the room was both of us breathing heavily; we leaned against each other, sweating and dishevelled, unwilling to let go. Waiting for a second round.

SECOND QUARTER

CHAPTER NINE

"IT'S past midnight," Declan murmured in the dark.

"Are you going to turn into a pumpkin now?" I asked, giving his horrendous soul patch a slight tug.

"Oww," he moaned, grabbing the offending fingers and holding them tightly.

"Hey!" I protested, and then I moaned as he then began sucking on them slowly. As much as I didn't want to, I withdrew them and smacked him lightly on the top of his skull. "Hey, pumpkin boy!"

From the small amount of light coming through the window, I could see him looking offended. "What?"

"So, it's midnight."

"Oh yeah. No more playing."

"I thought you said it was only the evening before?"

He chuckled. "You're insatiable."

"I didn't hear you saying no any time."

"But I feel pretty exhausted and a little bit sore now."

So was I, but just knowing he was here in my bed with me could almost get me going again. I kissed him slowly and tenderly, and he responded eagerly.

"Christ," he moaned. "What the fuck are you doing to me?"

"It's reciprocal, believe me."

Five hours ago, I had been wary of taking my clothes off before him. Now I never wanted to put them on again. We lay skin to skin against each other, sticky, sweaty, happy.

"I never asked you before," he said. "But I was hoping I could stay the night. Is that okay?"

I laughed and nuzzled his shoulder, the hair on his chest tickling my chin. "Yeah, I guess so."

He looked over his shoulder at the pile of messed up and crumpled clothing next to the bed. "I really need to wash those so I'm somewhat presentable when I go to my parents' tomorrow."

"You at least brought clean socks and jocks, though?" I asked.

"Yeah, but I didn't think you were going to make me mess my jeans," he complained.

Dirty pillow talk is so hot. "Sorry. Couldn't help it." I didn't want to leave the bed, but I scrambled over him. While my arse was up in the air I received a resounding slap on it. "Hey!" I cried out.

Declan laughed. "Where are you going?"

"To put these clothes in the wash."

"Do you have a dryer?"

"I live in this city, don't I? You can't survive here without one."

You seriously couldn't. Melbourne had long had a reputation for being the city that experienced all four seasons in one day. You could never rely upon the weather report.

He grabbed me around the waist. "Maybe I don't want you to leave."

I retaliated by digging him in the ribs. "Stay in bed, do my laundry. What am I, your maid?"

He spoke directly into my ear, his warm breath an invitation. "You can be whatever you want."

"Hold that thought." I ground against him, and he moaned, but I slipped out of his grasp and deftly scooped up all of our clothes in one move while heading out of the bedroom and towards the laundry.

"Tease!" he yelled after me.

As I made my way through the lounge, Maggie watched me disapprovingly from her position on the couch. She had been locked out of the bedroom during our shenanigans, and she was not happy.

"Sorry, baby," I whispered. I gave her a quick rub behind the ear, and her tail twitched dangerously.

In the small laundry behind my kitchen I threw the clothes in the washer, chucked in the powder, and slammed the lid shut as quickly as possible in order to race back to bed. When I turned around, Declan stood behind me. In the full light, he was even more fucking hot and beautiful. Declan Tyler. Naked in my laundry.

"Now that's even better than your calendar shot," I said, before I could censor myself.

"You've seen my calendar shot?" He grinned, looking slightly bashful.

"Dude, it was splashed over every newspaper. Why the fuck did they make you wax though?"

Now he really *did* look bashful. "Apparently women like a smoother body."

"They don't know what they're missing."

"Please, let's stop talking about the calendar."

"Why?"

"It's embarrassing. I didn't even want to do it in the first place." He moved closer to me and took my hand, leading me back to the bedroom.

"Why not?" I asked. "It was for a good cause."

Back in the bedroom, he pulled me onto the bed and lay on his back, using my shoulder as a pillow. "I wasn't comfortable doing it, being on display. But it was when I was first starting, and I didn't feel like I *could* say no."

"But you can say no now?"

"I'm in the position where I can, yeah."

"Bet they were disappointed."

"I make a donation to them every year instead of doing it."

I found myself stroking his hair as we lay looking at the ceiling. "I bet you sales have plummeted."

He laughed. "I remember you saying a while back you didn't think my ego needed to be stroked."

"I also told you that I tell the truth."

"So would you do it?"

"What?"

"Pose in a calendar for charity." His hand travelled down and rested upon my knee.

"No way."

His thumb caressed the flesh of my knee. "Hypocrite."

"Nobody would buy a calendar with me in it."

Declan rolled over, resting his arms upon my chest. "I would," he said.

"Great. I would sell one copy."

He kissed me. "Nah, I'd buy a few."

Fuck, I was ready for him again. "Shut up. Or else I'll make you defy your superstition."

But his fingers were travelling down my body, a trail of desire leaving my mouth dry. "I thought I said evening, didn't I?"

My eyes rolled back in my head, and I managed to grunt out, "As long as we make it clear—"

Declan silenced me by arching up and kissing me again.

Afterwards we showered, and I threw the now-clean clothes into the dryer. Declan helped me strip the bed, and we remade it with fresh sheets before falling beneath the covers dead with exhaustion.

"Goodnight," I whispered, but there was no answer from him because he was already asleep.

THE sun was glaring in my eyes, I rolled over to find Declan's side of the bed empty. I know it sounds really girly, but I wanted to wake up with him. Although disappointed, I wasn't acting stupid enough though to wonder if the previous night's events were all just a dream or fevered fantasy. I pulled on a pair of trakkies and a hoodie and padded quietly out to the lounge.

Maggie was sitting in the window, looking out into the garden. I peered through the blinds and saw that Dec's car wasn't in the driveway. Puzzled, I looked around to see if he left a note but there wasn't one.

Strangely enough, the table had been cleared, and the dishes were stacked neatly in the sink. I sure as hell hadn't done it, so I could only assume he had.

I went through the motions of starting a pot of coffee, wondering what it all meant. If he was doing a fuck and run, he wouldn't have cleaned up. But he would have left a note if it wasn't. None of it made any sense.

Of course, it did five minutes later when I was morosely sipping at a cup of coffee and heard the sound of a car pulling into the driveway. Maggie mewed a warning, and I petted her absentmindedly as I stood behind her to look out into the garden once more.

It was Declan. He jumped out of the cab of the SUV and reached back in to pull out a couple of brown paper bags. I hurried back to the table and sat down again, trying to look nonchalant. I heard him fumbling at the front door with keys, and he stumbled through trying to balance everything.

"Hey," he said cheerily, catching sight of me. "Morning. You sleep like the dead, you know that?"

This was true.

He noted my expression and asked, "Did you think I had abandoned you?"

"No," I scoffed. But neither of us was fooled.

Declan made his way over to me and dumped the bags on the table. "I bought breakfast." He leaned down and kissed me. "You're not a morning person, are you?"

I cleared my throat so it wouldn't sound rusty. "Not really. Do you want a coffee?"

"Sure, thanks."

We moved together throughout the kitchen, me making him a cup of coffee, him finding plates and utensils. It was all bizarrely domestic and easy going. In fact, Declan was acting right at home, as if he had been doing this with me for months instead of it being a new experience for him.

"I found this great little café just down the road," he said, sounding a bit muffled as he was investigating the cupboards. "You probably already know it. The Tin Man."

"Yeah, it's a good place. Good muffins," I nodded, realising I didn't really know how he took his coffee.

He was on the ball. He swept past me on his way back to the table. "White with one, thanks."

As I poured the milk and stirred the coffee, Declan pulled open the bags and started placing containers on the table.

"Wow, you went all out," I said appreciatively, joining him at the table.

He had. Turkish bread, omelettes, muffins, hash browns, bacon, and mushrooms spread across the table. Being an athlete, he had the appetite to match, but he also had the table manners of a girl who had attended finishing school.

Declan grinned, noting I was watching him. "They make us attend etiquette classes, in case you were wondering." He was starting to make me feel like trailer trash as he deftly smeared his Turkish bread with butter and nibbled at it daintily.

"Boy, they're really taking it seriously."

He shrugged. "There's been too much trouble with other teams. They think if they enforce manners classes and public relations training that things will improve."

"It can't harm it, can it?" I began piling omelette onto the bread and sawing away at it. "But you've always stayed pretty much out of all that kind of crap. The partying and that, I mean."

He shrugged. "It's not my thing. Oh, it was as first and I got a bit carried away with it but it didn't take me long to see we can act like fucking idiots when we get on the piss in a big group."

"Anybody can."

"Yeah, but they think they can get away with it, because most of the time they do. The clubs always manage to cover up about 90 percent of their indiscretions."

I looked at him thoughtfully and swallowed before speaking. "So what made you so sensible?"

He grinned. "Because my mum would kill me if I acted like a fuckwit. She almost had to."

"And all the other players don't have mothers?"

Declan shrugged. "I guess some of them don't listen to theirs."

I couldn't decide if that was cute or slightly Oedipal.

"Anyway, I'm not the only one. A lot of them are really good guys."

"Like Abe Ford?"

Abe was the captain of the Devils, and from what the papers said he and Dec shared a fine bromance.

"Abe? Abe's one of the best. The best, actually."

I was already slightly jealous.

"What time do you have to leave for work?" Declan asked.

I looked at the clock above the fridge. "Shit, in about half an hour."

"I have to go to Etihad for a team meeting. I can drop you in the city."

"That buys me a little more time," I said, reaching for a muffin.

"I'm going to grab a shower if that's okay."

"Sure." I stood up, still holding the muffin. "Come with me, I'll grab you a towel."

He followed me back to the hall, where I opened the linen cupboard and passed him what he needed.

"Don't you need a shower?" he asked.

"Yeah, but you can go first."

He reached out and stroked my arm. "Aren't you a greenie? Shouldn't we conserve water and share?"

That… was a pretty good idea actually. To save time, I stuffed the muffin in with the other towels and followed Declan to the bathroom.

"SO WHAT are your plans for the rest of the day?" I asked as we headed towards the city.

Declan glanced into the rear view mirror as he changed lanes. "Meeting, practise, press conference, dinner with my parents."

"Wow, that's pretty packed."

"I'd like to see you tonight," he said regretfully, "but I promised my folks I'd see them."

"You could always come over after," I said, trying not to sound too eager.

"I don't think I could resist you if I came over tonight," he replied in all seriousness.

That bloody superstition.

I tried to laugh it off. "Yeah, I'm pretty irresistible."

His hand rested briefly on my knee between the changing of gears. "You are."

I stared out the window, hiding my smile.

"And tomorrow I have the game," he continued. "But remember how I told you I was trying to stay on another day or so? I managed to arrange it."

I looked back at him. "Really?"

"Yep."

We had now entered the city and were making our way down Flinders Street.

"That's great," I said, because I couldn't really think of any other way to express how bloody fantastic I thought it was.

We crossed down to Elizabeth Street, and it was only a matter of moments before we were at my building.

"I'll call you before then," he said. "But I'll be seeing you Saturday. If you're free, of course."

"I think I should be," I said, my mind too muddled to remember if I had anything planned or not. Richmond was playing away this week, so there wasn't a game to go to.

"Well, pencil me in," he said with a smirk.

"I'll *ink* you in," I told him.

I almost had door-to-door service as he pulled quickly into an emergency bay just down from my building. As car horns started honking between us, I threw him a quick look.

"I had a great night," he said.

"Me too. I can't wait for Saturday." I realised that might have sounded a little sleazy, so my mouth did its usual trick of letting my foot insert itself. "And not just for the sex part. Just because I like seeing you."

"I see you've been working on your compliments." He chuckled.

I wanted to kiss him good-bye, and I got the feeling that he wanted to as well. But there was no way we could. I grabbed his hand quickly and squeezed it gently. He smiled and stroked his thumb over the back of my hand.

"Bye, Simon. I'll call you."

"Bye, Dec."

I got out of the car, and he sped off in an effort to stop the honking of the impatient drivers behind him. I watched his SUV slow down at the traffic lights and then execute a hook turn as he turned past Flinders Street Station and continued in the direction of Etihad Stadium and out of my sight.

I COULD almost have believed that the previous night *had* been a dream. The work day continued on as normal, except for Roger and Fran being ushered into my office by Nyssa. Roger didn't even work in the city, so I knew that a special trip had been made on his behalf.

"What are you doing here?" I asked bluntly.

"Boss needed someone to deliver stuff to Bourke Street, and I volunteered," he said without an ounce of shame. "So I thought I would take up lunch with my wife and best friend."

"You hate delivering stuff," I replied. It was true; he always tried to get out of it because he couldn't be bothered signing out the work car and dealing with the paperwork that followed.

He shrugged. "I also wanted the goss."

Fran, his partner in crime, giggled.

"There is no goss," I said, slamming the manila folder I was holding shut and chucking it on my desk.

"Liar," they accused in unison.

"That's cute," I snarled.

"Come on, your fake bad mood is showing," Roger said good naturedly. "Come to lunch. My shout."

His shout? Man, he really wanted to know.

"Never turn down a free meal," I said reluctantly.

"That's my boy," Roger grinned.

He didn't really get his money's worth; I skimped on a few of the details. But that was the Roger *Reader's Digest* version I was giving, pretty light on the graphic smut. I was sure that Fran would try to get those gaps filled in for her own Special Extended Mix later on.

"So," Roger said, mouth slightly agape. "It could be getting serious, then?"

Fran slapped him gently. "The man went out *especially* and bought him breakfast the morning after. It's the sensitive guy way of getting flowers for another guy."

I liked her spin on things. Roger huffed to himself. "I would have thought that would have been *beer*."

"I said *sensitive* guys, Roger."

"Sensitive is such a dirty word," I said. "It makes him sound... *wrong*."

"Well, you can be a sensitive guy sometimes," Fran said casually.

Roger burst out laughing. "Simon?"

"Who came home with a second Hawthorn scarf because of him?" Fran pointed out, and Roger fell silent. Her "hah!" sounded like one of true vindication.

I shifted food around on my plate with the fork and pretended that I wasn't there.

"So, what's next?" Fran asked, undoubtedly happy for me.

"He's arranged a couple of extra days off this week in Melbourne, so I'll see him this weekend again."

"Cool," Fran said, and she did look very pleased for me.

Roger, however, scowled. "And after that?"

I pointed my fork at him. "We had a deal."

"A deal for that *day*," he pushed.

"No, I believe the words I used were *for now*."

"And how long does that specify? A day? A week? A month? Forever?"

"It means *for now*," I said stubbornly. "Until I decide."

"You can't have it that way!"

"Says who?"

"Me!"

Fran's eyes were darting between the two of us like she was at the Australian Open. "So, is this what you guys were fighting about?"

"No," we answered at the same time.

"Wow, you aren't at all transparent."

Roger and I glared at each other. I had a bad feeling this issue wasn't going to die between us. And quite frankly, I was pissed off that he was taking up arms for me over the matter. I was an adult; I had made the decision to take this relationship as it came. It wasn't up to Roger to start making judgements on what was right or wrong for me.

I threw my fork down upon my plate and stood. "I've got to get back to work."

"Simon—" Fran said, but I shook my head and laid some money next to my plate to cover my part of the bill.

"See ya," I said brightly, too brightly, and left the restaurant without looking at either of them. I heard Fran call my name once more, but I continued on back out into the street and made my way back to the office.

I hadn't even been able to look Roger in the face. I was so angry that I was scared about what might have happened if I did.

EVERYONE always says they want you to be happy. Then when you become happy, they resent it in some form or another. They nitpick to make you feel uncomfortable and question everything.

I wasn't stupid. I knew what I could be committing myself to by continuing to see Declan. But the guy was really growing on me, and that was an understatement. Roger's constant needling of me made me feel like hating him, but I could never *hate* Roger. I could be as mad as hell, and hold a mean grudge, though.

The truth was he only questioned things I didn't really want to think about at this point of time. I wanted to revel in this newfound happiness before reality managed to crush the spark and grind it into the ground with its usual steamroller antics.

Nyssa was out to lunch when I made it back; the sign on the door said somebody would be back in an hour. I still had twenty minutes of relative peace if nobody called me. I left the sign on the door, grabbed a Coke from the fridge, and turned on the television in my office. I managed to find a news update, and as always in our fair country, it was centred on sport.

As I had been expecting, Declan's face flashed upon the screen. He was sitting beside his coach, Scott Frasier, with a bank of television and radio microphones before them. The backdrop to their table was the Devils logo. Declan's face was set in stone as Frasier talked for him.

"…with the full go-ahead from the doctors, we are pleased to announce the return of Declan Tyler to the game this weekend."

Even through the television screen, I was almost blinded as the reporters' flashes went off in conjunction with the appearance of a smile on Declan's face. I felt happy for him and wished I could have been there to tell him so. He was getting his dream back.

I got out my mobile to text him and offer congratulations, but it sprang to life in my hand as someone was calling me.

It was Roger.

I grimly pressed Reject and had no qualms doing so. For the moment. I navigated the menu to start writing my message, when the screen disappeared with Roger trying to call me again.

Reject. Once again.

This time he got the hint. I fired off a quick message to Declan and grinned to myself as I heard the unmistakable sound of a received message being picked up by the microphones at the press conference. Declan remained still. Maybe he was anticipating a slew of such messages. Of course he would be.

The office phone rang. I startled slightly and pondered who it could be. It obviously wasn't Declan; he was still talking to the reporters. I couldn't risk picking up in case it was Roger; we both might say things we would really regret later. Best to let it go to the messenger service.

But there was the sound of Nyssa's keys in the door. "Can you get that, Nyss?" I yelled.

"Sure!" And I heard her picking up the phone with her usual cheery greeting.

Moments later she had stuck her head in the door. "Fran's on line two."

I tore my eyes away from the screen, where stock footage of Declan in his pre-injury days was running. I couldn't help but notice the now-familiar roll of his hips was taking on a new significance to me. "Can you take a message?"

Luckily for me, rather than jumping to the conclusion that I was fighting with my friends, Nyssa noticed the television and rolled her eyes at my inability to stop watching football long enough to speak to Fran. "Okay."

"Thanks." I knew I wasn't fighting with Fran, but she would be playing the dutiful wife and trying to sell Roger's better points to me in an effort to make me forgive him. And I couldn't really listen to that right now.

On the screen, Declan was running in slow motion, and then they faded back into the press conference. He and Frasier were now standing and making their way back to the change rooms while the cameras and their flashes ineffectually tried to capture their every move.

I switched off the television and suddenly felt very lonely.

HALF an hour later, a text arrived from Declan.

Still can't believe it's finally happening.

Funny, I thought the same thing, although for different reasons.

It was only a few seconds before another came through.

Wish I could see you tonight. But you know the rules. Looking forward

to Saturday. I might even watch the Richmond game with you.

Guiltily, I thought of Roger. But it wasn't like they were playing Hawthorn this weekend anyway, so it wasn't guaranteed that we'd be watching it together. Even though we almost always watched *some* football game on the telly with each other every weekend.

My mobile buzzed again, impatient with another message.

Speak of the devil, and by that I didn't mean Declan. It was from Roger.

Are you avoiding me?

I thought about it a minute and then sent a terse reply in the affirmative.

He didn't respond. I think he got the message.

It didn't make me feel any better though. I chewed at my thumbnail, stared out the window, and waited for the work day to end.

CHAPTER
TEN

I TOSSED and turned most of Thursday night, thinking of Declan at his parents' house and wondering what they really knew about their son and his private life. I couldn't help but try to imagine what they might think of me if they ever met me, which if truth be told, seemed to be a moot point anyway. And I wasn't sure if that was merely the moment or the whole of the unforeseeable future.

When I wasn't thinking of Declan, I was thinking of Roger; how I felt justifiably pissed off and also slightly ashamed of how I had reacted to him.

Roger and I never fought for long periods of time, but I had never felt so resentful of him before. There are times when you have to suck it up and let your friends do what they have to do, even if you know it's the wrong course of action to take. Fuck knows I had done it with Roger before. I had said my piece initially and then kept my trap shut until it was time to help him pick up the pieces.

That was what I needed for him to do for me right now, but he wouldn't grant me the same favour in return.

As I got off my tram at the corner of Collins and Elizabeth streets, I saw Fran on the opposite side of the road heading up from Flinders. She must have caught the train rather than the tram, which she only ever did if she was running late. I wanted to run over and catch up with her, but my feet failed to move. I watched her disappear within her building and made my way to my own.

Nyssa was biting at her fingernail and studying an unruly file full of papers when I walked into the office. "Hey," she said without looking up. "Alice Provotna called. She wants to film you today."

I groaned. "It's not on the schedule."

"She won't be able to make it Monday, so she's coming today."

"But there's nothing for her to film today, really."

Nyssa slapped the file shut. "Well, she'll get a realistic depiction of the office, then."

"Nice."

"Oh, and Roger rang. He wants you to call him back. It sounded urgent."

I managed to stop myself from making a dismissive huff and just nodded before walking into my office.

THE day passed relatively smoothly, although I was a bit troubled by the fact that Roger never called back again and that Fran didn't even try once. I know that I had taken the step of ignoring them in the first place and it was extremely hypocritical for me to be upset when they started doing the same, but I now felt that as I supposedly had the moral upper hand I couldn't cave in.

Yeah, I know. You don't have to say it.

The interview with Alice Provotna was a perfunctory one, at least on my end, and I was glad of it. It was a series of questions dealing with how it could take all year to plan for a festival that only took place for a couple of weeks towards the end of the year.

Basically, it was me justifying my job. Seeing as I had to do a performance review with the board every year, I felt I could do it by rote.

I knew my answers would be sliced into sound bites and probably used as voiceovers with different bits of footage throughout the doco so I made sure they were serviceable and tried not to sound too bored. Alice tried not to look too bored as she hovered over her camera and asked her questions.

Declan sent me a brief text during lunch, and I wished him luck for the game. Even his text sounded preoccupied and stressed about what might happen that night. He sounded like a man staggering under the weight of expectation, and I wished there was something I could have done for him. But there wasn't anything I could do.

By the time of our customary knockoff for Bog-off-to-the-Pub Fridays, I was ready to call it a day. As Nyssa hovered in the doorway, I waved her on.

"Can't make it tonight," I told her. "Tell the guys I said sorry."

She slumped into the chair opposite me. "You're not coming?"

"Can't. Sorry."

"Why not?"

I started throwing things I didn't even need into my messenger bag, so I wouldn't be hooked by her imploring look. "I have things to do."

"Yeah, like coming to the pub," she asserted. "You *never* miss the pub on a Friday."

"Well, I have to today."

"But why?"

"I told you, I have things to do," I said. Vaguely.

"What things?"

"Give it a rest, Nyss."

She glowered, her light eyes suddenly seeming dark. Which was kind of scary. "Are you fighting with Fran?"

Wrong person, but close. "No. Why?"

"I saw her on the street during my break. She seemed remarkably vague about you when I said something."

Great. Now Nyssa thought she was a private dick. "I'm not fighting with Fran."

"Is this about your secret boyfriend?"

I knew I must have been turning red, because I could feel the heat rising in my treacherous face. Even though this had nothing to do with Declan! Nothing!

Well, not directly.

"I don't have a secret boyfriend," I lied. Unsuccessfully, I'm sure.

"Uh-huh." Private Dick Nyssa saw right through me.

I couldn't even use him as an excuse because then Nyssa would probably say something to Fran and Roger about it at the pub, and the last thing I needed was them thinking they were being ditched for the boyfriend. Nothing stirs up bad blood between the friends and the partner like being dumped in a blatant display of favouritism.

So I trotted out Old Faithful. "Of course, you *could* do one more ring-around of the sponsors—"

Nyssa gathered up her bag. "Gotta go if I don't want to miss the tram."

At this time of day, there was one every six minutes. "Have a good weekend, Nyss."

The slamming front door was her reply. Great. I was losing friends at a substantial rate, and I only had myself to blame.

Rather than breaking out the world's tiniest violin to play an ode to myself, I turned off all the lights in the office and locked the doors behind me.

I WAS just getting off the tram and walking towards my house when a message sounded from my mobile.

Opening it, I saw it was from Roger.

You're not even coming to the Napier? No balls, Simon.

Ouch. I was definitely pushing it too far. I hoped my response would come across as somewhat conciliatory.

I just can't handle it tonight. I'll call you tomorrow.

There was no reply from him.

I kicked off my boots as soon as I got inside and sought sanctuary within my bedroom. Maggie was stretched out upon the bed; I fell upon it next to her and buried my face in her fur.

I woke up unexpectedly in the dark; Maggie had in the meantime fled for safer ground. I stumbled groggily into the lounge room and turned on the Devils and Bombers game. It was only the pregame banter, so I called Maggie and realised she was on the chair behind me. Once she was fed, I grabbed a beer and collapsed onto the couch.

"…the eagerly awaited return of star midfielder Declan Tyler."

My body sprang into action unbidden, sitting me up and pushing me forward as if that distance of two extra inches would allow me to see the television more clearly.

The footage switched to Declan in the change room, togged out in the Devils' orange and green guernsey as he nervously batted a football between both of his hands.

Someone spoke to him off camera; he nodded and moved towards another player and they started handballing between themselves.

"That is a man who is holding the entire weight of a team's hope on his shoulders," said one of the commentators. "Let's hope it isn't too much for him."

His colleague did the faux wince to camera. "If anything, Tyler has proved in the past he is more than capable of supporting his team. It's his body that's the problem."

I don't know, I thought it was an exceptional body. For altruistic reasons, of course.

"Tyler is probably the most injury-prone player in the past decade of AFL," the first commentator agreed.

The footage switched back to Declan. The team was now in a circle with coach Scott Frasier in the middle. It was time for the pregame litany of *go out there and win*.

No *do your best*. They were Devils; they had to act like such. Blah blah blah. It would have perhaps been more inspiring if they weren't so close to the bottom of the ladder.

"Let's hope he remains injury-free tonight," commentator two said in his overly ingratiating tone.

I hoped for Declan's sake he would as well.

THEY rested him at halftime.

Declan kicked two glorious goals over the first quarter, but by the start of the second the strain on his body was starting to become apparent. The commentators were very pleased with themselves having predestined a potential tragedy unfolding on the ground they could talk about endlessly.

"What was meant to be Declan Tyler's night of triumph has quickly turned into one which we've seen all too often before," the annoying one said, his arch smile threatening to split the screen in two.

It was official before the third quarter even began. Declan was out of the game, being rested upon the advice of the team doctor. Although he hadn't done any further damage to his knee, it was obvious to everybody that he couldn't play on.

"We brought him back too soon," the team doctor said on camera. The footage cut back to the two commentators of the game, who shook their heads with seasoned perfection.

As the third-quarter siren sounded, the cameras cut away to a dejected Declan sitting on the bench, staring blankly out onto the ground where his teammates continued to play without him. I just knew that would be *the* picture all over tomorrow's sport pages in the papers, with some pithy caption designed especially to twist the knife in further, rather than a photo of his body stretched triumphantly as he booted in one of his two goals.

I wanted to call him, but I knew I couldn't. And that was when it hit me for the first time; a girlfriend probably would have been able to do so, with no questions asked. But a male, who wasn't an immediate family member? That would just look strange. Mind you, a girlfriend would probably already be at the field, doing the loyal partner thing.

The footballer's wife. And I was no Posh Spice.

Devil's advocate always nagged at me, though. If I were Declan (don't laugh), Roger would certainly be calling me at this point of time, and we weren't fucking. But I guess that's always the guilt and the secrecy of the gays masquerading as straight.

It was too late at night for my thoughts to be this heavy.

In the end, the Devils lost again. As they walked off the field, the reporters attacked them in waves, most making a beeline for Declan. Stony-faced, he mumbled brief answers that gave very little away.

"Declan, how do you feel after tonight's game?"

"Crap, of course."

"Declan, do you think you'll be able to play next week?"

"It's up to the coach."

And that was the last bit of footage they showed of him. The Devils seemed to restrict entry to the change rooms, because there was a crossover to the Bombers' victory song in their room, and that was where the camera stayed for the rest of the broadcast.

If I had to find a bright side, at least my parents would be happy.

I stayed up a couple of hours after that, just in case Declan called. He didn't.

I WAS woken by the ringing of my mobile at about half past two.

"Hello," I mumbled, still in that stage between coma and the shot of adrenaline you get when your phone goes off in the early morning and you automatically expect some form of tragic news.

"Simon, sorry to wake you."

It was Declan. I immediately sat up. "Dec, hey. Stupid question, how are you?"

His voice sounded slightly shaky. "Yeah, not so good."

"I wanted to call you earlier—"

"I wish you had."

Damn. I should have done it.

"I only just got out of the debriefing with the coaches and the doctors."

"What did they say?"

He hesitated.

"What is it?" I could now feel the worry starting in me.

"Do you mind if I come over?"

"No, of course not."

"Cool. I'll see you soon."

I closed my mobile and sat there groggily for a few moments. I stumbled back into the lounge and turned on the heater as it was freezing in there. I wasn't sure if either of us wanted coffee, but it felt good to be going through the motions by making a pot anyway. With the sound of the water hissing through the grounds in the filter and then spitting into the carafe, I sat on the couch and promptly fell back asleep.

I woke again at the sound of Declan knocking on the front door and the smell of freshly brewed coffee perking up my senses.

Declan still looked just as unhappy as he had on the television. "Hi," he said. He sounded like saying one syllable required too much exertion for his body.

I pulled him into the house and into my arms while simultaneously kicking the door shut with my foot. He didn't shy away from my hug; in fact, he welcomed it.

Instinctively, years of living with my mother kicked in. Obviously if you're upset, you need food.

"You must be hungry," I told him. "I could make something. I also put on coffee, if you want coffee. Do you want coffee?"

He gave a slight laugh. "Coffee would be good."

It was three in the morning. Coffee might not be good. But hey, it wasn't exactly like I had Horlicks in the house. We weren't ready for our seniors' cards yet.

Declan sat down on the couch, his long legs stretched straight out in front of him, which I realised was in order to take pressure off his knee. However, I was also concerned by the fact his hands remained jammed deep into his pockets in a defensive position.

"That must have been a long meeting," I said amiably as I prepared our drinks.

"Yeah, they wanted to go over every possible scenario," he replied glumly.

I handed him his coffee. "Do you want a cushion or something to elevate your knee?"

He shook his head and took a grateful gulp from the mug. "I'm wearing a compression bandage, thanks."

"Is it uncomfortable?" I sat beside him.

"No, you get used to it pretty quickly. Feels weirder when it's off, once you're used to it."

"Bet you won't be saying that once you get it off."

He gave me a small, tired smile. "Probably not."

"So what did they talk to you about for so long?" I wasn't sure if I should be prying, but I hoped he felt like he could tell me to shut up if he wanted me to.

Declan wrapped both hands around his mug, using it for warmth. "Just plans. Plan A, Plan B, all the way through to Plan Z, Part Four. All the possible ways to fix me and all the possible contingencies should they fail."

"Sounds fucking clinical," I couldn't help but say.

"You got that right," he sighed. "It is. They were sitting there talking to each other, rather than me. As if I didn't have a say in it."

"I bet you didn't put up with that."

He bit his lip and looked even more defeated. "To tell you the truth, I did. I was so fucking miserable by that point I didn't care one way or another."

That did it. I put down my mug and swung myself over to his side of the couch. "Scoot." He leaned forward and I squeezed in behind him, my legs uncomfortably splayed on either side of his. He leaned back into me, and I wrapped my arms around him.

"So, what's Plan A, then?" I murmured into his ear.

Declan's hands rested over mine. "Intensive physio. I'll probably be off for another couple of weeks before they decide to try me out again."

I kissed the back of his neck. "Don't let this get you down too much. I know it's easy for me to say that, but getting depressed will make it worse."

"It *is* easy to say," he agreed, but he didn't sound mad. He leaned his cheek against mine, using the crook of my neck as a pillow.

"I wish there was something I could do for you," I said, feeling as helpful as a calculator in an English exam.

"You are," he murmured.

It was a big concession to make, and I didn't ruin the moment by trying to get further clarification. Even though my legs were aching, I closed my eyes, and found sleep wanting to take me as Declan's body warmth seeped through into my own. I was vaguely aware of hearing a slight snore come from him before I probably added to it.

I JERKED awake with a massive leg cramp that had me leaping over Declan and almost causing him to fall to the floor. He mumbled something incomprehensible as I jumped around in the middle of the lounge room, hissing a litany of *fuckfuckfucketyfuckfuck.*

Declan shakily got to his feet and approached me. "Left or right?"

"*Fuckfuckfuckrightfuckfuckfuck!*"

He couldn't help grinning as he grabbed my hip with one hand to keep me in one spot and then ran his other down my calf. I leaned on his shoulder, trying to resist the urge to start jumping around again as pain shot up and down my leg. He began rubbing my calf gently, and I think it was probably the psychological effect of his ministrations more than anything else that made me calm down as I started to feel my muscles relax.

"You trying to beat me in the bad leg stakes?" Declan laughed, his second hand now travelling down my leg to begin working in unison with the other.

"Yes, my night cramp is jealous of your million dollar injury," I said, embarrassed I had made such a spectacle of myself. Way to go to, drama queen.

"Feeling better?" he asked, looking up at me.

I nodded. "Thanks." I helped him back to his feet.

"I just realised," he said slowly. "I haven't done this tonight yet."

We kissed, long and deep and hungry. But there was no denying we were too tired to take it any further.

"Better late than never," I murmured.

And I realised I really needed to pee. I ran to the bathroom without another word. When I finished and came back out, Declan was in my bedroom and undressing. I hung back for a moment and couldn't help but perve as his clothes fell away until he stood there in only his boxers and began turning down the bed. I walked around to jump in beside him.

"You have too many clothes on," he complained.

I let him pull my T-shirt over my head, and he kissed my shoulder. His hands tugged at my trakkies until they were caught around my feet, and I gracelessly kicked them out the side of the bed.

"That's better," he said with a smile.

My body tried to suggest I was ready for action but sleep was more insistent for both of us, and I don't even remember how the bedside light got turned off.

THE sun was warm upon my face, and Declan was even warmer curled up beside me. We stayed in bed the whole morning, sometimes with coffee, sometimes playing around and the rest of the time napping from our exertions.

At one point while Declan was asleep I ran out onto my front lawn, knowing that the paper would have been delivered. I kicked the offending object until it was concealed underneath a bush, where its articles on Declan's short return to the field would not be seen by him.

The rest of the day stretched before us beautifully, and the night promised even more. I stretched blissfully when I woke again around midday and watched Declan as he slept. The lines of stress on his face from only hours before seemed to disappear during down time.

I ran my thumb gently over his lower lip, and his eyes opened.

"Sorry," I said, not having meant to wake him.

"'s okay," he said. He looked over my shoulder at the alarm clock. "Shit."

"We've still got the whole afternoon."

He grabbed me quickly before I could defend myself and rolled over onto me, grinding me down into the mattress. "As much as I would love to keep you in here all day, I think I have to prove I like you for more than sex."

I shook my head and laughed. "I'm not a girl."

"Come on, let's go and grab some lunch, and then I'll watch the Richmond game with you."

I wondered if it was such a good idea, as undoubtedly his injury would be brought up yet again to be dissected by the commentators during lulls in today's game. "Wow, you *must* like me."

He looked down at me seriously. "I do."

I kissed him. "Just so you know, the feeling's mutual."

He moaned as I continued kissing him. "Don't start again or else we'll never leave."

More kisses. "Would that be so bad?"

He pushed me against the pillow. "What would Richmond say?"

I pushed him back. "You're right. Get off me."

Declan now seemed to be practicing passive resistance as he sagged against me and became dead weight. "Nah, I've changed my mind now."

"Bastard." I struggled against him, but he was too heavy for me to budge him.

Which you know, it's not *that* bad a thing to have Declan Tyler naked and on top of you, but it does start to make breathing slightly difficult after a while.

He took pity on me and rolled off. "Shower, then a late lunch and watch Richmond get slaughtered again."

You never know, it could be Richmond's day. After all, it seemed to be mine.

WE HAD just showered and were getting ready to go out when both of our mobiles rang within seconds of each other.

"Scott," Declan said unhappily. He had been hoping to get through the day without a call from his coach.

"Roger," I said, almost as unhappily. I was not ready for the talk that we needed to have. Especially now.

I left Declan in the bedroom to have privacy while I took mine into the study and closed the door so we wouldn't be heard in the background of each other's calls.

"You picked up," Roger said, sounding surprised.

"Yeah, I meant to call you before this."

"Oh."

Silence. Apparently now that we were talking, we had nothing to say.

"Look, I'm sorry," Roger said, finally.

"It's okay," I mumbled.

"Not really, it's not," he replied. "Just, as your friend, I get to be concerned for you, okay?"

I made some kind of noise of agreement.

"How about if I come over, bring some beer, and watch the game with you?"

Oh fuck. There was no way this situation would end well.

He could sense the hesitation in me.

"What the fuck, Simon? Are you still really that mad at me?"

"No," I said quickly. "It's just... Declan's here."

"Oh."

Funny how that one little word, one syllable, two letters, could mean a thousand different things.

"Look, he's just really upset because of what went down yesterday, so today probably isn't a good day to do the meet-the-friend thing."

"Yep."

Fuck, *he* was pissed now. The tables had turned. "I'm sure you saw what happened at the game last night, Rog. He's... not in a great state."

Maybe I was exaggerating a little. But with things still unsorted between me and Roger, and with him being free and easy about his opinion on my new relationship, I couldn't guarantee a thermonuclear-free day if the three of us got together.

"Roger?"

"Yeah, fine. That's cool, if that's what you want."

And just like that, my needle swung back into the red zone. "Hey, it's not like when you and Fran first got together you didn't disappear for the first month or so, and I never gave you any shit for it."

I had him there, and he knew it. But he wasn't going to let it go.

"Like I said, Simon, fine."

"Fine. Speak to you soon."

And I hung up on him.

It wasn't a good thing to do, but with the way things were heading in our conversation one of us was going to do it in the end. Might as well be me. I childishly turned my mobile off so that if Roger tried calling back, which I doubted he would, he wouldn't be able to get me. And if he rang the landline, there was always the answering machine.

I opened the door to the study and listened to ascertain whether Declan was still on his call. It was dead quiet in the house, so I walked back towards the bedroom.

Declan was sitting on the bed, all vestiges of the carefree aura he had had all morning wiped away. He was back in his defensive position, staring at the floor.

"Hey, what is it?" I asked, sitting beside him.

He sighed heavily. "You're going to kill me."

"I doubt that. Why, what have you done?"

"I have to leave for Hobart. This afternoon."

Okay. Not a killable offence, but one which would make my day a whole lot less pleasant. "You're kidding."

"I wish I was. I'd try to wrestle my way out of it, but they've hired a special private jet that flies at a low altitude so there won't be any further pressure on my knee."

That's when it finally hit me that I was dealing with a totally different world. A world where no expense was spared to protect a million-dollar investment, which is what my boyfriend was. I had joked before with Declan, calling him the million dollar baby, but the truth was he was *more*. He earned about one and a half million annually just in salary from the club. I had no idea how much his endorsements and sponsorships would be worth, but they would be even more than that. He was important enough that special planes were now being hired to ferry him home with as little inconvenience as possible.

I tried not to hyperventilate audibly and to laugh it off. "You would think they would rather keep you safe in Melbourne, instead of shuffling you back and forth."

"Believe me, *I* would prefer it."

I kissed him, with a hint of desperation I really didn't want to show.

He looked at me, and although I wanted to look away I couldn't. "I'm sorry, Simon."

"Dec, it's not your fault."

"But I promised you—"

"I think there are larger issues here than a thwarted dirty weekend."

I regretted saying that, because he looked disappointed that I had reduced it to *that* when it meant so much more to me. Now it was my turn to apologise. "I'm sorry, that was stupid."

"See, you *are* upset."

"Of course I am!" I admitted, deciding that honesty was the best policy. After all, look at the problems caused by concealment last time we were together. "But not at you. Just upset because we see each other intermittently, when normally any other couple would be in each other's pockets getting to know each other for the first month at least."

My conversation with Roger couldn't help rearing its ugly head. "But this is our situation, and we can't feel shitty about it. We just have to enjoy *when* we see each other."

"I'm enjoying seeing you," Declan said. "If it wasn't for this fucking jet, I would have told them to piss off."

I nodded. "So, when do you have to go?"

He winced. "Now," he said regretfully.

Fucking typical. I nodded.

To soothe the pain, he kissed me. And for a few seconds, it almost worked. But as he pulled away, the feeling of shittiness returned.

I watched him zip up his bag, and he flung it over his shoulder. I could tell he wanted a quick getaway, and in essence I agreed with him because there was no use in prolonging what we were both unhappy about.

At the front door, he reached for me. "I'll call you when I get home."

I nodded. "Fly safe."

"You know what they say," he said, opening the door, "you're more likely to die in the car on the way to the airport."

Wow. They say couples start to look like each other. At that moment, he *sounded* like me. That was the end of conversation between us for now. We kissed, and it felt like the last time for a long time. Then he was gone, obscured by the tinted windows of his hire car. He pulled out of the driveway, and I was left standing on the veranda.

The morning had started out so promising. Now I only had the inevitable defeat of Richmond to look forward to for the afternoon.

CHAPTER ELEVEN

THE unthinkable happened.

In the third quarter Richmond came from thirty-one points down to muster an unbelievable rally, and with the game in overtime they were only three points behind. New recruit Farid Al-Hanin managed to intercede the ball and drive it down toward the goals with the entire Richmond fan base on his side, trying to harness control over the ball with the power of thought and will it into a six-pointer, Al-Hanin gave a mighty kick, and it soared perfectly between the two centre posts.

I gave such a mighty scream, Maggie fled for the sanctuary of the bedroom. I believe I shrieked gratitude to every god and goddess I could think of. Al-Hanin's name became instantly sacred to me, as it probably did to every other Richmond fan nationwide. Richmond had won their first game of the season.

I just wished Roger or Declan had been there. It felt a bit lonely not being able to share it with anyone.

On a rare but venerable high, I decided to take the bull by the horns. I jumped in my car and drove to Roger and Fran's house, tooting my horn triumphantly whenever I saw somebody with a Richmond sticker on their bumper. They, of course, hooted in reply.

I wondered if this was an omen that things might be turning around—I could only hope. Declan would return to form, Roger and I would patch things up, Richmond would win the Grand Final (next season, I was no fool to believe it was possible this year), and I would win the lottery so there would be no embarrassment between Declan and I when it came to paying for dinner.

My dreams were quickly dashed when Roger opened the door and glared at me. "What do *you* want?"

Ouch. "I came to talk to you."

He looked out beyond me, perhaps surprised I was alone. "Where's your *boyfriend?*"

Huh. That was an entirely new side to him. I counted to three in my head before answering so this wouldn't get any worse. "Probably somewhere over the Bass Strait by now."

"What happened to your date?"

"Are you going to let me in?"

"We're not your second best, you know," he said childishly.

I decided to call his bluff. "Okay." I turned my back and stomped back toward my car.

"*Hold it!*"

That certainly wasn't Roger's voice.

I turned to see Fran whacking Roger over the head, and he howled in righteous indignation. "Let him in!"

Roger rubbed the back of his head. "Get in here, you dickhead."

"Ask him nicely!" *Whack!*

"Simon, would you like to come inside?" Roger asked, a forced tone to his voice.

"Why, thanks, Roger, that would be nice," I replied as I climbed back up the porch steps.

As he moved away from the door to let me through, and I pushed between him and Fran in the narrow hallway, I was given an extra special greeting in the form of a slap upside my head from his lovely wife.

"Ow!" I cried, now reflecting Roger's gesture from earlier as I rubbed the offended area.

Fran glared at me. "*That's* for ignoring me the other day on Elizabeth Street."

"I didn't see you until the last minute!" I protested. "And then I was stuck there trying to decide what to do—"

Her unchanged expression told me I was digging my grave even deeper. "I gave you *plenty* of time to come after me."

"It didn't seem that long," I said sheepishly, and I received another whack for it.

"You hurt my feelings," Fran said, and her tone of voice made me feel what could have been the guiltiest I ever had felt in my life.

"I'm sorry," I said in all honesty. I was now rewarded with a hug.

"Hey, my feelings were hurt too!" Roger said.

"Because you hurt mine in the first place," I reminded him, pulling away from Fran.

"Well," he replied defensively, "you hurt mine *again* after that."

"Oh for fuck's sake," Fran muttered. "Just hug and make up like normal people."

Pushed into it, we did so; although "normal people" was also pushing it.

"Just letting you know, I'm still upset," Roger pointed out, his elbow digging into my ribs as we embraced awkwardly.

"Same here," I replied, rubbing at my side unhappily and *accidentally* stepping on his foot.

We pulled apart, and the three of us now stood in the cramped hallway, all looking uneasily at one another.

"So, how about a beer?" Roger suggested, falling back on old faithful for backup.

I nodded gratefully.

Fran clapped her hands together. "Finally! Something we can all agree on!"

"HE LOOKED *crushed* on the news," Fran said, reaching for another handful of chips.

We were on the back porch, despite the cold, staring out into the yard which was desperately in need of a mow. Fran and Roger usually liked to wait until one of their more industrious relatives decided to do it for them.

"The picture on the front page of the *Sun* was even worse," Roger pointed out. "Extreme closeup, looking like he was about to cry, and that new name they've given him—"

"What new name?" I asked quickly, feeling dread gnawing at my guts in anticipation.

"You haven't seen it?" Fran asked.

"I hid my newspapers," I admitted.

Fran and Roger exchanged glances.

"He was miserable enough," I said defensively.

"Well, he's probably seen them now." Fran grimaced.

"Show me."

She sighed. It was clear she didn't want to but knew she would be pressured into it eventually. She disappeared into the house and was back just as quickly, her arms full of the morning's papers.

"*The Age* was kinder, as per usual, but the *Herald Sun* loved it."

The Age was nicer, with just a picture of Declan looking devastated.

The *Herald Sun* had the more emotive picture. Roger was right. Declan looked like he was about to cry as he sat alone on the bench, away from his other team members.

The headline crowed *HERE WE GO AGAIN! THE TEMPORARY DEVIL.*

"Fuck." It wasn't the most coherent response I could have given, but it certainly summed up my feelings enough.

The Age's account was straightforward, giving the facts with a few statements sprinkled in from the coach and doctor; the *Herald Sun* was given to hyperbole, lamenting about Declan's performance in comparison to his salary, how the fans were disappointed in him and turning against him even more now that they had "received another slap in the face," and how Declan might also quite possibly have contributed to the problems in East Timor through his downright suckiness.

I tossed the tabloid aside. "What can you expect from a paper that publishes Andrew Bolt's columns?"

"Not much," Roger said, and he clinked his bottle against mine.

Fran smiled at us proudly, as if this simple act had resolved all grievances between us. And she was probably right. It didn't take much.

"When do you think you'll see Declan again?" she asked.

I shrugged. "It's all up in the air. Depends what they're making him do in Tassie."

"It sucks," Fran said passionately.

"I know," I said, my tone completely opposite to hers. It was too tiring to feel that much at the moment.

"No, it *really* sucks," Fran repeated with emphasis. "If that was me, all I would want is Roger there to make me feel better. I bet you that's what Declan wants."

"Roger?" I asked, to deflect having to think about it.

Luckily I was out of reach from her slapping hand. "You, you idiot."

"Oh."

"Don't *oh* me."

"You're pushing her," Roger mumbled, passing me another beer. "And you know what happens when you push her."

I had never pushed Fran, although I had seen Roger do it plenty of times; the results weren't pretty. I had to head her off at the pass. "Fran, we've only been seeing each other for about a month. And of that month, we've seen each other maybe four days. I don't think I'm the beginning and end of his world just yet."

"At the start of a relationship, where every emotion is turned up to eleven? I doubt that," Fran countered. "And what, you're trying to tell me you don't speak practically every day? I know you're long-distance, but I bet you're finding ways to overcome it."

"What are you saying, Fran?" I asked derisively. "That I should jump on the plane and go to Hobart?"

She folded her arms over her chest and looked considerably pleased with herself.

"Finally, he gets it."

Roger snorted, and I turned to him. "Is she serious?"

"You know her."

I did, and she was way past serious. I sputtered almost incoherently as I tried to make her see sense.

"Fran, that's *crazy*."

"Why?"

"There are lots of *whys*."

"Name some."

Oh great, a quiz. I looked at Roger again; he stared at the long grass at the bottom of the steps like it was growing before him. He wasn't going to be any help.

"Fine. Work."

"Make it a two-nighter. Fly out today, fly back Monday morning."

"Maggie."

"You know we'll feed her, Simon."

This was getting harder. "The cost of the ticket."

"I know you always have money stashed away. You're a good saver. It's like your one responsible quality."

This was true. Fuck it, she did know me too well. "That's for emergencies."

"This *is* one."

"It fucking well isn't!"

Fran glared at me. "It would prove to Declan that you really care about him. He probably needs that right now."

"I could prove that with a phone call."

"Guys are such *arseholes*," she muttered.

Roger and I were both stunned.

"Fran!" Roger protested.

She jumped to her feet and towered over me. It was pretty impressive and intimidating. "You know what, Simon? There are two reasons you don't want to do it. You're lazy, and you're chickenshit!"

And with that barb, she thundered off into the house, slamming the door behind her for good measure.

In the eye of the storm, Roger and I compared wounds.

"Lazy and chickenshit?" I practically whimpered.

"Well, she had the lazy part right," Roger said.

"And the chickenshit!" we heard Fran yell from inside.

"Does she have a bionic ear or something?" I asked.

"Shit, mate, you *know* she's psychic."

I put my beer down and headed in to the house. Fran was only just a couple of feet inside the door. She didn't look at all apologetic for her behaviour.

"Why am I chickenshit?"

"So you're accepting the lazy part?"

"Just answer me, Fran."

"You know why you're chickenshit. Because if you do this, you'll be showing him a part of yourself you hate showing. That you care. You do it enough to us sometimes. That day when Roger came in with the Hawthorn scarf, I almost thought he was lying and that he'd bought it himself. We know you love us, but you like to pretend you're all aloof and unreachable. That's what makes you chickenshit. Getting on a plane will show Declan how you feel, and you'd hate to be that transparent."

"I don't know how I feel yet," I said, still bleeding from the wound caused by the sword she had stabbed me through the stomach with.

"Don't lie." Her tone indicated it was a warning. "We can all see it. Even Nyssa knows you're up to something, although she hasn't quite figured it out yet. Why are you so scared of showing that you like someone?"

I didn't know how to answer without sounding like I was throwing a pity party. But that's the thing when you grow up feeling different to everyone else. And I know when you're a teenager *everybody* feels different and alien to the other people around them, but there seems to be an added dimension when you're queer. It's because for that period of time you're more isolated than anybody else, and you truly think you *are* the only one of your kind so you create fantastic barriers and defence strategies for yourself to survive. And when you get older and realise that you can take them down, it's an internal *and* eternal struggle to do so. Fear is the best de-motivator in the world.

So all I could do was stare at her. Fran returned my stare, her eyes showing a sadness that made me feel even worse.

"Jesus, Simon," she said finally. "You can't go on like this."

There was still that part of me battling madly against everything she was saying, this logical Vulcan inside me that was coming up with a thousand reasons why this was impossible. But Fran's sad face combined with knowing Declan was unhappy pushed me over the edge.

"Get me your phone," I instructed her, even though my mobile was in my pocket. If I had to pay out for a short notice ticket she could at least pay for the phone call.

She hugged me, almost crushing my ribs in the process. "I love you, Simon."

And as her reward, I mumbled, "I love you too."

It made her cry. Jesus. "I'm so happy," she sobbed. "This is a beautiful moment."

"Would you like a tissue?" I asked.

"Don't ruin it," she warned.

The door opened, and Roger stepped in to see this strange little tableau. "What the hell is going on?"

AND that is how I found myself on a six o'clock flight to Hobart. I barely had enough time to rush home, beg for Maggie's forgiveness, throw some clothes together in a bag, and run back out into my front yard where Fran and Roger sat waiting in their car. They had followed me back home so they could drive me to the airport. Fran was overflowing with excitement, imagining the gay romantic comedy she was writing in her head. Roger was amused by the fact I was actually doing this crazy thing, and I was sure he would be bringing it up for years to come: *the day Simon went wildly insane for love*.

On the way to the airport, it dawned on me. "I don't know his address."

That put a dampener on Fran's plans. "What?"

I repeated myself.

"How can you *not* know his address, Simon?" she practically shrieked.

"Uh, because he lives in another state, and I've never been to his house because of that very reason!"

She drummed her fingernails on the steering wheel, thinking furiously. "Right. Call him."

"And say what?"

"That you want his address, stupid!"

"For what reason?"

"To send him flowers."

"No way!" Roger and I said together.

"Fucking men," Fran fumed. "Just do it!"

Too scared to raise her ire any further, I opened my mobile and called Declan.

"Hi," he said warmly as he picked up. "I was just about to call you."

"What's your address?" I blurted out.

Fran and Roger groaned at my finesse.

"What was that noise?" Declan asked.

"Trolls," I replied casually.

"Have you been drinking?"

"Just a little bit."

"You're not driving?"

"No, Fran is. She only had one beer."

"Oh. Where are you going?"

"I'm asking the questions." I was getting a little panicked. "What's your address?"

He gave it to me, and I scribbled it down. "Can I at least ask why?"

"I'm sending you flowers."

"Wow, you *are* drunk."

"What, you don't like flowers?" I could hear Roger snigger behind me. "Fine, it doesn't have to be flowers. They have those things online where you can send cartons of beer or boxes of freckles and caramel buds. Would you rather have beer and caramel buds?"

"*I'd* like beer and caramel buds," Roger murmured. I ignored him.

"Really?" Declan asked, sounding slightly dubious. "If I were you, I wouldn't be using my credit card so freely while under the influence."

"Fine. Fine, I'll choose it. And you'll probably get something really crap."

"Simon, are you okay?"

It was a question I should have been asking him. But if I spoke to him for much longer, I would give the game away. Fran had already drummed into me this was meant to be a surprise. She was my romantic counsellor, apparently.

"I'm fine. See you."

I hung up on him. And turned off my mobile so he couldn't call back.

"You could have handled that a bit better," Fran said.

"I was about to crack."

"*That* happened a long time ago," Roger muttered as he stared out the window.

I HAD to wait an hour for a cab from the Hobart airport. I wasn't going to risk attempting public transport.

It was in the taxi, with the buzz of the beer finally wearing off, that I started to have doubts about what I was doing. Hobart was a small town, with roughly two hundred thousand people in comparison to Melbourne's four million. Declan would be even more recognisable here than back home. And there I was, a guy, arriving on his front door step.

If there was a doorman, should I cover myself up by claiming to be Declan's cousin? Or would that be even more suspicious?

The beer buzz was now heading into paranoiaville.

The apartment complex Declan had given me the address for was in Battery Point, which seemed to be a rather pretty, perhaps blatantly touristy maritime village. You could tell back in the convict era it was probably a hardened seaport, but now it was gussied up and yuppified and more likely to sell patchouli oil and vegetable-based soaps than seafood. I tried not to be too judgemental about it all as I stared up at the fancy seven-storey building before me and entered the lobby.

There wasn't any doorman, but it seemed that after a certain time of night the interior doors were locked. I found myself in a small alcove before the main lobby and a wall with all the apartments listed with a buzzer next to each.

There went the surprise. I pressed Declan's number and waited.

A fuzzy-sounding Declan answered. "Simon? What the hell?"

"Uh, surprise?" I said, just as confused as him. "How do you—?"

"Wave to the camera," he instructed me wryly.

I turned to see the small squat box, attached to the wall, following my every move. I did as he said and gave a small wave. A buzzer sounded, the interior door swung open, and I had access to the lobby.

I scratched at my wrist unhappily as I rode the elevator to Declan's floor. This was a mistake. A huge mistake.

I was still contemplating heading back downstairs and getting a ride to the airport, even as my feet took me to Declan's door. I knocked with a heavy heart, and the door swung open to reveal Declan with a huge smile upon his face. He pulled me in and crushed me against his chest as he kissed me.

"What the hell are you doing here?" he asked again, breathily.

"Like I said," I was still trying to catch my own, "surprise."

"I TAKE it you're not mad, then?" I asked groggily as we lay in bed.

"Fuck, no," he laughed. "It's the best surprise I've ever had."

Now starting to feel the cold, I pulled the doona up over us. "Fran and beer helped me decide."

"When I finally meet Fran, I'm going to give her the biggest kiss she's ever had in her life."

"Roger and I might be unhappy about that."

"Fine, does she like wine?"

"She's Italian—are you kidding?"

He rolled over onto his side so he could look at me properly. "Seriously, I feel so much better. I hated leaving you today. I want to kidnap you and keep you here for a week rather than two days."

"It's not kidnapping if the victim wants to be kept." I yawned.

"I guess not. But when I say a week, I really mean a month."

"Is that all?"

"Don't get cocky."

I pressed against him. "Bad pun."

"DEC?"

"Yeah?" he murmured.

"I was worried about coming here." Half asleep, and in the dark, as usual it was easier to be more forthright.

"Why?"

"Because this is your territory, and it's a much smaller town—"

"I'm happy you're here."

"But it could be a problem—"

"Didn't you hear what I said?"

"I did, but—"

"Simon, no buts. Not right now."

"Okay." I didn't say anything about *his* bad pun.

It seemed as if Declan had his concerns as well, but he was pushing them away. It was easier to exist in our little bubble, as if the world around us didn't exist. It felt safer, but it was illusory. Which I guess is why we liked being with each other so much. It was like we could go on perfectly together if the rest of the world just didn't get involved.

"SIMON?"

"Yep."

"I'm going to sound like a fucking idiot for saying this—"

"Then don't say it," I laughed.

"Just—you and me, that's all there is, right?"

I struggled up onto my elbows to look down on him in the dark. "What?"

"Don't get insulted."

"I'm too confused to be insulted right now. What are you asking?"

"You're not seeing anyone else, right?"

Okay, I was *slightly* insulted now. "I find it hard enough to get one partner, let alone juggling more than one."

"Don't get pissy. I want to make sure we're—"

"Were you seeing anyone else?" I asked, scared of his answer.

He must have heard the tinge of panic in my tone, as he sat up. "No!"

"Okay, so it's just us. That's sorted."

"Hey—"

"Dec, just leave it."

"No. I didn't mean to insult you, Simon. Just—"

"What?"

He drew his knees up to his chest, and picked uncomfortably at the bandage.

"What, Dec?"

"I've been a bit paranoid about it since... well, the last guy I went out with."

"He cheated on you?"

"Well, yeah."

"*He* cheated on *you*?" I asked incredulously.

"Yeah, it happens, Simon."

"But to *you*?"

"Will you stop saying that?"

"I'm sorry, I'm… shocked as hell that somebody would cheat on *you*."

"I don't get you sometimes. You seem so unfazed by me, unlike the rest of the public, and then there are just some times when you say things like that." Declan thumped his knee in frustration, and I grabbed his hand so that he couldn't do it again. "As if I'm special. Simon, I'm just like any other guy. And sometimes that means you get cheated on, and that fucks you up."

I slipped my arm around his waist. "I'm sorry. But you *are* special. People are always going to see you differently. And although it really doesn't matter to me that you're Declan Tyler, god of football—"

He laughed weakly.

"—sometimes I will be amazed if someone does something against you. And not just because you're Declan Tyler, god of football. But because you're Declan Tyler, guy I like."

He kissed me. "Good answer."

"I can be surprising sometimes."

"HERE, babe. Coffee."

My eyes sprang open. Did I just hear what I thought I heard?

I wasn't sure. I rolled around and found a mug in my face. I sat up, and Declan handed it down. He then climbed in beside me, holding his own.

I sipped at my coffee in silence, wondering if I should say something about what had been said. There was an awkward air hanging between us, and Declan drummed his fingers against his mug.

"So—" I began.

"Too soon, right?" he asked.

Relieved, I laughed. "I didn't imagine it!"

"You thought—"

"You called me *babe*," I laughed. "*Babe!*"

"Okay, you don't like terms of endearment."

I took his mug off him, and set both of them next to the bed. He looked at me quizzically as I pulled him over onto me and kissed him. "Oh, *babe, babe, babe*," I teased, covering his face with kisses.

"Okay, I get it. I won't say it anymore."

"Don't you dare stop it," I warned him. "Just, not in front of anybody else. I have a reputation to consider."

"You?"

"Yes. Me."

"Sure thing," he said, grinning. "*Babe.*"

FRESHLY showered and caffeined up, we moved into the kitchen. In the daylight and not as distracted by Declan's charms, I now got to see exactly what kind of apartment I was in.

I felt like I was in a *Modern Home* layout. Dec had opened the blinds, and I was greeted by a picture-postcard view of the harbour and Mount Wellington rising up just behind it.

"Like the view?" Declan grinned.

"It sure beats my view of Mr. Grimmauldson's veggie garden," I said wryly, watching the boats bob upon the waves below me.

"Mr. Grimmauldson might argue with that," Dec replied, filling the coffee machine.

"I could stare out there forever."

"You *do* look slightly hypnotised."

"This isn't the penthouse, is it?" I asked.

Declan scoffed at me. "There's no penthouse in this complex."

It sure seemed like a penthouse, but I was only comparing it to my own weatherboard shack in North Brunswick.

Declan's lounge room was tastefully and sparsely furnished. A faux-vintage coffee table sat upon a large dark rug. Two expensive leather couches sat at opposite ends to each other, facing a large entertainment unit.

But there was something vital missing.

"Where's your telly?" I asked.

He moved beside me and picked up a remote control from the coffee table. The entertainment unit slid open to reveal a huge plasma television that was practically half the size of my lounge room wall at home. "Holy fuck," I breathed. There may have been angels singing hallelujah as well. "I'm bringing my DVDs here."

"You're easily pleased," Declan murmured, nuzzling my neck.

"Do you have surround sound?" I asked, still distracted.

He laughed; it felt soothing against my skin. "Yes. I actually had the subwoofer inserted into the bottom of the couches. You should feel the Death Star blowing up in *Star Wars*."

Puzzled, I grabbed his head and gently turned it so I could look him in the eye. "I thought *I* was meant to be the geek? That's even geekier than anything I've ever said in my life."

Declan looked pleased with himself. "I guess I like surprising *you* every now and again."

The coffee machine began hissing, letting us know the coffee was ready. I gave him a quick kiss and jogged over to start pouring.

"You know, the fastest I ever see you move is when you're going after coffee," Declan remarked.

"At least I'm consistent that way," I said, pulling the milk out of the fridge.

His fridge was well-stocked. "You must have a maid hidden somewhere," I murmured.

"What was that?" Declan asked from the lounge.

"Nothing," I called back as I shut the fridge and turned my attention back to the coffee.

We both froze as a knock came at the door.

"Dec! Open up!" a loud, deep voice reverberated through the wood.

I looked at Declan, sure that I had turned pale.

Declan, however, looked as relaxed as he had moments before. "I think it's time you met some of my friends," he said casually.

CHAPTER TWELVE

MEET his friends? Was he joking? Shouldn't I be acting like someone in a bedroom farce, hiding under the bed or shimmying down a drainpipe outside the window? I doubted I would be able to shimmy down a drainpipe—I would be more likely to hang on grimly for a few seconds before losing my grip and plunging to my certain death seven storeys below.

"Dec—" I said feebly.

"Hey," he said, crossing over to me. "It'll be fine, trust me."

Of course I trusted him, but I needed to be given a debriefing first, in which it would be outlined what I could and couldn't say, how to act, what to do…

"Simon!" Declan said, taking me by the arm. "It's Abe, he's cool."

And of course, I knew who "Abe" must be—Abraham "Abe" Ford half of the inseparable team of Ford and Tyler. Friends on and off the field, but Declan sure hadn't told me that he was part of the in-the-know list. Or was he? Why couldn't he just fucking tell me?

He kissed me again, and he was so cool about it I had to assume Abe knew. I took a deep breath as Declan left me and jogged to the door to open it.

The instantly recognisable form of Abe Ford walked through, looking like he owned the place or was at least was comfortable enough here to treat it as a home away from home. He slapped palms with Declan, and even though I was on the verge of a nervous breakdown, I was still amused by the hypermasculine bonhomie between them.

"I bet you smelled the coffee from downstairs," Dec said.

"We were too lazy to make our own," Abe grinned.

We?

"Hey, Lisa," Declan said, easily kissing the woman who followed Abe into the apartment. She gave his arm a quick rub, and my guts turned to rubber.

"Morning, Dec," she said, casually shortening his name, which up until this point of time I had stupidly assumed I was the only one who did.

By now Abe had turned around to see me standing like a stunned mullet in the kitchen, using the coffee machine as camouflage, hoping that my black clothing would blend chameleonlike against its plastic. He pointed at me and looked back at Declan. "Who's this?"

Lisa's eyes widened, but there was a glossiness to them that showed she was both surprised and delighted for some unknown reason.

I wondered whether to introduce myself or let Declan do it and therefore give me some clue about the role I was meant to act out. Declan beat me to it.

"This is Simon."

Nice and nondescript. Noncommittal. Brief. Thanks, Dec.

But this condensed introduction seemed to signify a lot more to the people now unexpectedly sharing the kitchen with me.

"Simon!" Abe said, crossing behind the counter to grab my hand and shake it furiously. "I assumed it was, but it's good to meet you!"

He had barely released me before I was getting my very own kiss from Lisa.

"We've heard so much about you," she said, smiling as she pulled back to have a proper look at me.

"Uh, hi," I muttered, wondering what the hell was going on.

"Believe me, he usually talks a lot more than this," Declan said wryly.

"Relax, Simon," Abe said, throwing open the cupboard doors as he searched within them. "No bikkies, Dec? What kind of host are you?"

Lisa was the one who really took pity on me. "We know Dec's dirty little secret."

Her tone of voice proved that she didn't think it was either dirty or little at all.

"These are my friends." Declan shrugged, sounding both apologetic and happy about it all.

"Why don't you run downstairs, Abe, and get some biscuits from our flat?" Lisa suggested.

"Me?" he asked.

"You're the athlete, mate, not me. Count it as part of your training."

He put on a good show of being annoyed by it, but he wasn't fooling anyone. "Be back in a minute."

"Bring back the good stuff," Lisa called after him. As the door shut, she turned her attention back to me. "You said he was cute, Dec," she said approvingly, "but he's *really* cute."

She was either a flatterer or a pathological liar. My ego wanted to believe the former.

"Told you," Declan agreed.

"And you two look very cute together," she continued.

Desperate to deflect attention, I asked her, "How do you take your coffee?"

"Oh, and *modest*," she teased. "No wonder you like him. White with one, thanks."

She was very friendly from the get-go, wasn't she? You couldn't help but like her. Lisa was casual, smart, and able to put you at ease within moments of meeting her. She reminded me a lot of Fran. Which made me think that if they ever met each other, they would probably collide. Or take over the world together.

"What about Abe?" I asked.

"What about him?"

I stared at her, and Lisa laughed. "Black with one."

"I'll be right back," Declan said, and he disappeared into the bedroom.

I watched him go, wondering if I was wearing that beseeching *don't leave me alone with her* expression. She might have been friendly and casual, but I didn't want to be pressured into giving the first encounter tell-you-my-life-story speech just yet.

She sidled around the counter and leaned in to me confidentially. "Dec must really like you."

I handed her a coffee. "What makes you say that?"

"Because he wanted to introduce you to us so quickly. You've been going out, what, a month or so?"

"About that," I agreed reluctantly, not sure where this was headed.

"Believe me, he normally takes a few months, even longer. If he introduces us at all." She must have read the expression on my face. "Oh, don't worry, it's not like he's a male slut or anything. He's practically a celibate hermit compared to other footballers."

I finally found my tongue. "It's your use of the word *practically* that worries me. Especially in context of other footballers' sex lives."

Lisa snorted into her coffee. "Point taken. But what I'm trying to tell you is he *really* likes you."

I sized her up. "Now that's starting to sound like a warning."

She shrugged. "Maybe it is. Do you like him?"

This conversation was really going into uncomfortable territory for me. "Of course I do."

"*Really* like him?"

"You're sounding like an American high schooler. It's not like he's given me his letterman's jacket."

"Yeah, but I *know* Declan. I don't know you. I *know* he's serious."

"And I don't have to justify myself to you." Okay, probably not the best reaction to give to one of Declan's best friends within minutes of meeting them, but I felt cornered.

And when you're cornered, you go on the defensive, if not the attack.

She set her mug on the kitchen bench. "Maybe not. But I've seen other guys latch onto Declan for their own agendas, and he's gotten badly burned for it. It's not going to happen again."

"I don't have an agenda," I said honestly.

She relaxed slightly. "You know what? Dec told me that although you hide a lot and laugh things off, your face is an open book. And he's right, you can't hide anything."

You would think I shouldn't like her after this interrogation, but I still did. At least she was honest, and I always respect that. "Does this mean you'll give him the friend approval?"

"From me, yes. Abe will be another thing entirely."

I groaned. "Fantastic."

"Relax. He's not dense. He'll be able to see how much you like Declan, even if you try to deny it."

"Dec knows you're interrogating me, doesn't he?" I asked her.

Lisa grinned. "Of course he does."

I held up a finger. "Just excuse me a moment."

I heard her giggling into her coffee as I fled from the kitchen to find my wayward boyfr… partner… whatever word doesn't sound naff.

Declan was lying on the bed, his hands intertwined on his stomach, staring up at the ceiling.

"Bastard!" I hissed, jumping on top of him.

He looked me over appreciatively. "You don't seem too worse for wear. She must like you."

I grabbed him by the wrists and pulled his arms up over his head. "Like I said, *bastard*."

He tried to reach up to kiss me, but I held him down. He squirmed beneath me. "Hmm, this is nice."

"Nice? *Nice?*"

It turned out his captivity was just a ruse. Before I knew it, I was flying through the air, Dec was out from under me, and in seconds had me trapped beneath him.

"Get off me—"

"Say please."

"You have *guests* in the next room!" I reminded him.

"One little word."

"Declan—"

"Wrong word."

I sighed heavily. "Please."

I was rewarded with a slow long kiss. I arched up beneath him, and he pulled my arms behind his back. It wasn't that comfortable, to tell you the truth. I teased him by slowly thrusting my lower body against his, and he moaned into my mouth.

Which was when I took advantage of his temporary distraction by throwing him off me and jumping to my feet.

He fell against the bedside table. "Fuck, my knee!" he cried, hugging it into his chest.

Games were forgotten immediately. I threw myself down beside him. "Oh, Dec, fuck, I'm so sorry—"

Immediately my back was against the floor, and Declan was back on top of me.

"Gotcha."

"Motherfucker!" I wheezed, out of breath as Declan was slowly squeezing the air out of my body while he used his own to restrain me. "You can't use your injury—"

"Who said?"

"It's not fair!"

"Awww," he teased.

I sagged against the floor, all energy expended. "Fine," I said with an air of martyrdom. "Do to me what you will."

"That's a tempting thought," he said mockingly. "But there are guests in the next room."

"Then get off me—"

Distracting with the kissing again. He was a master of that.

He stroked the side of my cheek with his thumb. "I guess we better get back out there."

I nodded, although I kind of was happy where I lay.

He helped me up to my feet, and we made our way back to the kitchen.

Lisa grinned at us as we entered. We *did* look a little mussed up, but we also hadn't been gone long enough to be accused of doing the deed so at least there wasn't that particular embarrassment.

"Did he punish you, Dec?" she asked innocently.

"I think we punished each other enough," he said, deadpan. "Is Abe still not back yet?"

He arrived only a couple of minutes after. "I couldn't find any biscuits. So I ran down to the milk bar."

Lisa rolled her eyes. "They're in the tin. That's marked *biscuits*."

They squabbled good-naturedly between themselves as Declan made fresh coffees for everybody, and when we were all seated together was when the true interrogation began.

"So you work for a film festival?" Abe asked.

I nodded as I took a bite of a Granita. "The Triple F."

"Do you like it?"

"I love it. Of course I complain about it all the time, but it's a great job."

"It must be a big responsibility," Lisa said.

"Well, it's really only me and my assistant who plan and run everything. That's why it takes a whole year for us to arrange it."

"Are you like most people who work in the industry?" Abe asked. "Do you have a script hidden under your bed?"

"About three, actually. All unfinished."

"Why?" Lisa asked.

I laughed derisively. "Because they're pretty shit?" I admitted. "Sometimes I think I'm a better critic or film festival organiser than one of the creative types. I guess somebody has to do it."

"I doubt they're shit," Declan said softly.

"*You* haven't read them."

"I'd like to," he persisted.

Abe snorted behind his hand.

"What?" Declan asked dangerously.

"Dude, you are so gone."

"Abe, baby," Lisa said, laying her hand upon his arm. "Don't forget Dec has as much on you as you do, or will, on him."

Declan nodded satisfyingly, and Abe was suitably cowed.

I could feel Dec's knee pressing against mine, and I smiled. And then I felt the pressure of his hand resting upon my thigh. I almost jumped through the ceiling, but when the moment was right I slipped my right hand down to close over his.

I doubted either Abe or Lisa could miss it, but they politely refrained from teasing us about it. I just hoped that when Fran and Roger were given the same opportunity they would be as polite.

After coffee, Lisa and Abe made plans to have lunch with us. As soon as the door shut behind them, Dec and I were both running back to the bedroom, peeling off our clothes. We had enough time to fool around (which we did), have a nap (which we did), and shower (which we did), before going down to Lisa and Abe's apartment. Declan told me in the lift that it was purely by coincidence that they had ended up buying in the same complex, but that it was good to have his best friend living only a few flights down. I couldn't help think as much as I loved

Roger and Fran, I was glad there was at least a suburb between us. They were close enough but far enough at the same time. I also wondered if it *was* true, as rumour had it, I was an antisocial bastard.

"So where shall we go for lunch?" Abe asked, rubbing his hands together in anticipation of a meal.

"Go?" I repeated stupidly. "We aren't eating here?"

The three of them laughed, as if I had said the stupidest thing ever said by a member of the human race.

"About the only thing either of us can make is toast," Lisa told me.

"Yeah, we even have to rely upon Dec for our coffee," Abe agreed.

"As you saw," Declan reminded me.

Abe and Lisa began having a heated discussion about what they wanted for lunch; Declan sensed my hesitation and pulled me aside.

"Hey, what's up?" he asked.

"Are you sure you want to go out?" I asked hesitantly. "In public?"

He studied me for a moment, and said, "That's what you're worried about? If people look at us, all they'll see are a group of friends out for lunch on a Sunday. Nothing more."

I wasn't sure if it was that simple or if maybe I had just become too paranoid on his behalf. But when I thought about it, from the average person's perspective if they saw us all out they would be too blinded by the sight of Declan Tyler and Abe Ford to pay much attention to either Lisa or myself.

"Okay," I nodded, "if you're sure."

Declan smiled at me. "Sure I'm sure."

They sure sounded like famous last words to me.

"YOU'VE been quiet ever since lunch," Dec told me as we lay together in bed after a simple dinner of toast.

"No, I haven't," I lied, burying my head further in the crook of his shoulder.

"Well, you weren't your normal sarcastic self," he pushed.

I remained silent. Lunch had been fine, but I couldn't help admitting to myself I had been left with a somewhat bittersweet feeling. Perhaps slightly more bitter than sweet.

We had walked the short distance from their apartment complex to the Salamanca Place markets, and after wandering around the stalls for a while, where I bought a very touristy resin statue of a thylacine for Fran and Roger we decided upon a local café for lunch. Abe and Lisa were great company, and over the course of the afternoon I found myself growing to like them even more.

Lisa especially took me into her confidence, I guess because she sensed a kindred spirit in someone who knew what it was like to go out with a man who was regarded as a god by the public at large. I could tell there were little nuggets of wisdom she wanted to impart, and to tell you the truth, I wanted to hear them, but they couldn't really be discussed with the men in question at the same table. I guess it would wait for some day in the future when we got a moment to ourselves.

Like when we went shopping for dresses for the Brownlow ceremony, right?

Anyway, Dec was right. I wasn't entirely myself. I was in hypervigilant mode, making sure I kept a respectable distance from him so that no outsider would be able to guess at anything untoward between us. I was on the lookout for people with cameras, especially as we had some fans approach the table from time to time asking for autographs. Both Dec and Abe politely declined requests for photos, as it was their day off, but invited them to the next training sessions, which were open to the public, and they could get their photos taken then. Those etiquette classes were paying off.

But I never felt fully relaxed; I was putting on a show. And I think my discomfort hung in the air between us all. By the time we got back and Abe and Lisa said their good-byes and hoped they would see me again soon, I felt drained. Dec and I watched a movie on his giant screen and fooled around a little on the couch, he made dinner (well, toast, we weren't particularly hungry), and we went to bed disgustingly early because I had to be on a flight at five in the morning.

"Simon?" Declan asked again.

I rolled over onto my side to look at him. "I'm fine."

"Don't lie," he said, an edge to his voice now, which he tried to alleviate by adding, "please."

I played with the small tuft of hair that served as his right sideburn. "It was just… lunch."

"What about it? Did you not like Abe and Lisa?"

"No!" I said quickly, to stop his fear on *that* point. "I like them a lot, and it'll be great to see them again. I think *I* fucked up at lunch."

"You weren't yourself, but you didn't fuck up."

"You all probably think I'm an idiot."

"I will, if you keep thinking like that."

"Why were you so okay about going out in public, when you're the one who needs everything to be kept so private?"

Declan sighed. "There's a difference between going out in public and going *out* in public."

Funny how that one word emphasised summed up everything.

"You have to stop worrying so much," Declan said. "We can still go out, I mean, shit, Abe goes out one-on-one with other guys all the time, and he never has his sexuality questioned. If we go out with a guilty air, *that's* what'll make people suspect. And I don't want to make us scared so that we can never leave the house together. That's not what I want for us."

"But we have to be careful."

"We *were* careful," Declan assured me.

"Maybe I'm just feeling guilt because I'm the one doing the bad thing."

Declan suddenly sat up, and I found myself face down in the pillow. "Shit, Simon!"

I sat up. "What?"

"Don't you ever fucking say that again!"

"What?" I asked, truly confused.

"*The bad thing*," he spat.

I hadn't even realised what I'd said and how it could be construed. "You know that's not what I meant."

"Maybe on a subconscious level you did."

That hurt, so I stupidly struck back. "Hey, I'm not the one in the closet!"

Even in the dark, I could see his face fall.

It was the worst thing I could have said, and I told him so immediately. "I'm sorry, that was stupid."

He shook his head sadly. "Hey, it has to come up sooner or later."

"I know you have to be, because of the industry you're in. I understand it on every logical level. Believe me."

"Well, I don't want you to start thinking shit like us being a bad thing because of it," he said sadly, staring at the doona that was shoved up between us.

"I don't," I said honestly. "Hey, look at me."

When he didn't, I took him by the chin and made him. "Dec, I *don't* think we're a bad thing. I'm in this because I really like you, and I want us to go further. I think we've got something, don't you?"

"Yeah," he said just as truthfully. "I do."

"So we're going to have some issues now and again, but we'll get through them."

"And this is just the first one."

"Probably just the first of many," I said cheerily.

He could only laugh at that. I gently pushed him back down upon the mattress and draped my arm over his chest. He wrapped his around my shoulder and placed his free hand upon my arm, stroking it gently. "I could get used to you being here."

"I would rather have you in Melbourne."

"Well, that's true. I'd rather *be* in Melbourne. Guess it's going to be like this for a while."

"I think you're worth it," I said, glad we were in the dark so he couldn't see me.

"Only think?" he teased. "I *know* you are."

I wished I could be as sure about my worth to him as he was. To me it seemed as if the scales were tipped heavily in my favour as to who was winning out more.

"Are you sure I didn't fuck up?" I asked.

"I'm sure," he said, sounding sleepy. "And I'll tell Abe and Lisa, even though I don't think it's a problem. They really liked you."

I still felt troubled and stayed awake far longer than he did.

When the alarm went off at four, I dressed silently in the dark. Declan tried to rise, but I kissed him and pushed him back down.

"I'm calling a taxi," I told him. "You have those appointments in a few hours, get some more sleep."

"I'm driving you," he protested, but I shut him up in the best way possible with my mouth on his.

"You know I'm right," I said.

He groaned. "I don't want you to go."

"I don't want to go, but hey, real life calls."

"Please let me drive you."

"Get some sleep, babe."

That new magic word between us seemed to placate him. "Fine. Call me when you get to work so I know you got back safe."

"Yes, Mum."

"Shut the fuck up." He laughed tiredly.

And that was how I left Declan, falling back asleep in the bed I wished I could have stayed in with him. I picked up my bags, closed the door behind me, and called for a taxi as I walked to the lift.

I was glad Fran had forced me into doing this, but once again I didn't feel all that happy at the end of it. I wondered if I would have been better off staying in Melbourne over the weekend, but then reminded myself of all those moments with Declan in which our relationship seemed to solidify and become even stronger, and I realised I shouldn't wish it away.

But I still locked myself in the tiny tin toilet while miles above the Bass Strait on the flight home and tried not to cry.

CHAPTER THIRTEEN

I MUST have been exhausted, because after catching the shuttle from the airport into the city and walking to the office, I promptly fell asleep in my chair while staring out the window. I hadn't even switched the lights on.

Nyssa came in to switch on the light, emitting a small scream when she saw me sitting there, which jolted me awake.

"You scared me!" she cried. "And… you looked kind of dead."

I *felt* kind of dead.

"Why are you in here so early?"

"I wanted to get here first," I yawned.

"Then why were you asleep?" Her eyes narrowed. "Are you checking up on me?"

"It's not review time, Nyssa. I got here early, and I was tired."

Nyssa frowned. "You're getting weirder and weirder lately. Do you want a coffee?"

"I love you." I smiled at her.

"Funny how you never show that when it *is* review time."

"I don't get to make the budget, you know that," I yelled after her. "Otherwise you would be making double!"

"Triple!" she yelled back. "I'm worth it!"

I chuckled and did the old yawn-and-stretch. My phone rang, and I yelled to Nyssa that I would get it.

"You didn't call me," came the accusatory voice.

"I fell asleep as soon as I got in here," I said.

Declan didn't sound impressed. "I was flicking through all the news channels, trying to find out whether your plane had crashed."

"Bullshit."

He laughed. "Okay, I'm ashamed to say I just got up."

"Well, you better get a move on. Your first appointment's at ten."

"Wasn't it you who was calling *me* Mum this morning?"

"Call me later," I told him.

"*I* will. And hey?"

"Yeah?"

"In case I didn't say it enough, thank you for coming over here. Seriously."

"Any time."

"Don't say that. I'll hold you to it."

I was smiling to myself as I hung up the phone. Nyssa placed a mug before me, examining my unusually happy expression with suspicion.

"Okay, who were you talking to?"

"Nobody."

"You're looking like it must have been somebody."

"Wrong number."

She gave an exasperated sigh. "Screw triple. I should be getting quadruple."

I took a sip of coffee and gave a long, contented groan. "With this coffee, yes, you should."

IT DIDN'T take that long for Roger to call me.

"You had lunch with *Abe Ford*?"

I instinctively sat upright in my chair as my spine turned to icy steel. "How did you know that?"

"The net," he replied. Could it have been anything else?

My spine was now trying to work its way out through my throat, no mean feat.

"Where exactly?"

"Did you really?" he asked again.

"Roger, where?" I repeated, ignoring the wheedling in his voice. My spine had now worked its way out of my throat and found the nearest bridge to jump off, and my heart was planning to follow.

"*The Mercury* online," he sighed.

The Tasmanian newspaper. This was not good. I quickly brought up their site. I couldn't see any lurid photos splashed on the main page of us enjoying yuppie pub fare, so I barked to Roger, "Which section?"

"*Seen About Town*."

Ugh, society column. The haven of the rich and the bored. I clicked upon its link.

"What are you doing reading that?"

"Fran told me."

"What was she doing reading it?"

"To see if you were mentioned."

I shook my head, slightly miffed with my friends and at the loading speed of the web page. When it finally came, I could let loose a small breath of relief. There was no picture, just a two-line blurb:

Salamanca Place: Devils Declan Tyler and Abe Ford, dining with

Ford's girlfriend Lisa Jacobs and unknown friend.

So nothing too salacious. In fact, it could even be as an assumption I was Lisa's friend. But still, it was the first time I was mentioned in proximity to Declan in the press. I wonder how he felt about that, seeing as I was close to hyperventilating.

Still, *unknown friend?* Could I feel slightly miffed about that as well?

"Simon, are you there?"

"Yeah."

"Well, tell me."

"What?"

"What was Abe Ford like?"

And it was like we were fourteen years old again, discussing the private lives of the football gods of the time, wondering what they ate, what they drank, where they went, and what movies they might like. For once I was able to satisfy Roger's fantasies and give him the details he had always wished to know in the past, about one of the players in the present. He took them all in hungrily, even down to whether Abe Ford had a lemon or a lime in his Corona.

Pretty soon though, it turned back to the old argument.

"So Declan introduced you to his friends, and *we* still haven't met the guy?"

"You insulted him at a party and offered to fight him," I reminded him.

"Yes," Roger admitted shamefacedly. "But we still haven't *formally* met."

I decided to throw him a lifeline. "Well, next time he's in town, I'll have you and Fran over for dinner." Declan had already suggested it when I told him Roger was desperate to make up for his less-than-stellar performance at the party. "It's only fair," he had said. "My friends got to judge you. Yours have to return the favour now."

"No," Roger replied grandly. "We'll have you!"

I couldn't believe my good fortune. "Okay, that's even better. I won't have to cook."

"And neither will I!" Roger laughed.

I couldn't help but join in. "Fran would kill you if she heard you say that."

"Just don't tell her."

"You know she'll know anyway, but you owe me."

"No, *you* owe *me*. I still can't believe you had lunch with Declan Tyler and Abe Ford on Sunday."

"I know they're gods on the field, Roger, but when you meet them you realise they're just people."

"Yeah, when you *meet* them. What's the use of having a friend who's dating a superstar of the game if you don't get any fringe benefits?"

"You sound like *you* want to date him," I pointed out.

"Very funny."

"He doesn't even play for your team." I paused. "Literally *and* figuratively."

"Once again, funny. Doesn't mean I can't appreciate his talent."

"You're sounding gayer than anybody else I know at the moment."

"Fuck off, *unknown friend*."

I hope that didn't start to stick as a nickname.

"HELLO, my *unknown friend*."

So much for that. Declan obviously sounded okay; better than me, at least.

"You saw it?" I gulped.

"No, I'm psychic," he replied tinnily. It was a bad connection. "How did you see it?"

"The friend network."

He understood immediately. "Ah, yes, Roger and Fran."

"Are you okay?"

Declan sounded confused. "Yeah, why wouldn't I be?"

"It's not very *discreet*, is it?"

"It didn't say you were my boyfriend."

I nodded and realised he couldn't see me.

"Are *you* okay with it?" he asked.

"Yeah, yeah, I'm fine."

"You don't sound it, Simon."

"I guess I'm being jumpy for *you*."

"I thought we agreed you'd try to stop that."

"I know. I'm fine."

He didn't sound so sure, but he let it drop.

"How did your appointment go?"

"I'm starting more intensive physio this arvo. They want to try and avoid surgery until the end of the season."

"What, so you don't miss any more games?"

A bitter note crept into Declan's voice. "I could hardly miss any *more* games, could I?"

"I know. So it's better this way, right?"

"The one good thing is I'll have to come to Melbourne for the surgery."

"And recover here?" I asked hopefully.

He laughed finally. "You'll probably have to fight my mum for that honour, though."

Like *that* was ever going to happen. Still, at least I might get to see him a little more. I couldn't believe I was wishing surgery upon Declan so he'd be trapped in the same city as me. I *sucked* as a partner.

The sound of somebody clearing their throat came from the doorway. I looked up to see Fran, standing there with a cheeky look on her face. I wondered how long she'd been eavesdropping.

"Are you free for lunch?" she asked.

"Fran?" Declan asked from the other side of the country.

"You guessed it," I agreed.

"Tell her I hope I'll see her in a couple of weeks."

I relayed the message back to her and had to laugh when she gave a totally self-conscious little giggle. Declan had no idea of the effect he had on people, even people like Fran who didn't know one end of a football from the other.

"I think that meant 'cool'," I told him.

"I better get going, and so should you. I'll speak to you soon."

"Bye, Dec."

Maybe a bit more formal than I would have liked after the weekend we had just spent, but we had an audience. I hung up, and Fran leaned in and punched me on the shoulder.

"Smitten bloody kitten."

"So, ARE you happy that I made you go?"

Fran looked particularly smug as she took her last bite of pizza and patted her mouth with her napkin. I screwed mine up and threw it at her.

"Just admit it."

I took a sip of my Coke and made a face. "Fine. I'm happy you made me go. And Declan thanks you."

Her face took on a slightly dreamy expression. "Really?"

Feeling slightly impish, I added, "He said he was going to give you the biggest kiss you've ever had in your life when he sees you."

There was that starstruck giggle again. You would think Fran was suddenly crushing on my boyfriend, the way she was going. "Really? Well, Roger might have something to say about that."

"The way he is at the moment, I would think he would be jealous *he* wasn't getting the pash."

"Oh, I know! He wouldn't shut up about Abe Holden on the phone."

"Abe Ford."

"Holden, Ford, whatever. I knew it was some kind of car."

I laughed, wondering what Abe would make of the casual dismissal of his name.

"What?" Fran asked, looking at me suspiciously.

"Nothing."

"You've changed," she mused.

"No way," I scoffed.

"You have. Sure, you still *look* like the same cynical, wannabe hard-hearted Simon Murray—but there's too much smiling and real laughter sneaking out every now and again. You know what?"

"What?"

That smug smile again. "You've become one of *us*."

"*Us* what?"

"One of those awful, gross people in love." She rolled her eyes to great effect.

"Oh, bleh!" I so didn't want to be *that*.

"It's true, Simon."

"You lie."

"No, *you* lie."

"I am not in *love* with Dec." Even to me, that sounded hollow.

"You so are."

"I *like* him. In fact, it's a very *strong* like which has the potential to go further—" A bread roll hit me square in the forehead. "Fran! Fuck!"

"That's what you get for lying."

I'm not sure it was *technically* a lie. And although I knew I could be *falling in love* with Dec, I wasn't sure if I was there yet. It was all too early, and besides, if any admittance of love was to be made it should first be done to the man involved and not one of your best friends.

She looked at me smugly, as if she could read something in my face I wasn't aware of myself. I hate that. She shrugged casually and poured herself another water. "I wonder if this came from a river in Egypt. You would know!"

I ignored her.

"I HAVE to go to this bloody barbecue this weekend."

"Will it be that bad?" Declan asked.

As usual, we were not together physically; we were connected only by signals that bounced off towers and satellites. I lay in bed with Maggie; Dec was in his own bed, which I could now picture, seeing as I had actually been in it. If we were in a movie they would have shown us on a split screen to give the illusion of togetherness.

But in real life he couldn't feel any further away.

"I'm considering throwing myself under a tram to get out of it."

"Not a train?"

"No, I don't want to *kill* myself. Just maim myself slightly."

"Well, I don't want you *killed* or even *maimed*. Just suck it up and go."

"What, to see my brother's latest squeeze pretending to be the last in a long line of squeezes? Hoping to be the Annette Bening to his Warren Beatty? And the rest of my family ignoring the fact I'm queer so they can keep on pretending one day I'll bring home a pretty girl?"

"I thought you said your mother was starting to come around to the idea of you eventually bringing home someone with a penis."

I choked back my laughter. "Okay, maybe Mum. But Dad and Tim... never. Well, Tim only for the controversy."

There was a big fat elephant in the room we were avoiding: the fact I *did* have a "squeeze", and there was no way, given his profession, that he would ever be coming to a Murray family barbecue.

"Maybe you can take Roger and Fran along to help save your sanity," Declan suggested.

"I've subjected them to enough Murray events," I shuddered. "This one I'll have to suffer on my own."

"SO, YOU'RE the gay one?"

I almost choked on my beer. Tim laughed, Dad stared at his feet, and Mum hovered over the table while looking suitably confused and harried at the same time.

"Yeah. Changed my name by deed poll and everything," I told her.

"Huh?" She didn't exactly get it.

Her name was Gabby Spencer, and I think deep down she really meant well. She knew it was politically correct to show the fag that she was really down and all with him… as long as he didn't kiss another fag, hold his hand, or breathe in front of her. My brother, of course, was besotted with her. For now.

"Sausages?" my mother asked breezily.

I had to cough behind my napkin to stop from bursting into hysterical laughter. Tim wasn't so subtle.

"So what do you do?" Gabby asked me, leaning in as if we were the best of friends about to disclose confidences to one another.

"Do you mean sexually?" I whispered back.

"Oh, gross!" Tim said.

"What's gross?" Dad asked of Tim, not having heard me.

"Simon's about to—"

"The weather report's on, dear," Mum told Dad, to avert a crisis.

Dad's eyes lit up, and he disappeared into the lounge to see the tail-end of the nightly news. Tim and I snickered together at this old habit you could set a watch by, a brief moment of camaraderie between us that would disappear soon enough.

Tim murmured something into Gabby's ear, and that brief exchange ended up being the only direct conversation we had the whole night.

Once the food was devoured, Dad went in to watch the news channel, Tim and Gabby were lost in their own little world (which was verging on the inappropriate, at least for the dinner table), and of course nobody was helping Mum clear up so I had to take up the slack.

Mum's lips pursed unhappily as she scrubbed away at the grill. The atmosphere in the room would have made a New Age-ist run for some cleansing crystals, but I had to stick it out.

"What's wrong, Mum?"

"Nothing, Simon," she lied through taut, grimaced lips.

She was never good at lying; it was just that Dad and Tim were too oblivious to anyone's feelings but their own to ever pick up on it.

"I know something's bothering you." I snuck a quick peek out the kitchen door to make sure Tim and Gabby were still going at it in the dining room and Dad in the lounge. The enemy camps were still in their respective positions; Tim was copping a feel under Gabby's cardie.

"Just leave it."

I shrugged. "Okay." And counted to five in my head.

Mum was just like Roger, although she wanted to have stuff wheedled out of her she would snap far quicker if you feigned nonchalance.

"It's just that you sat here, a few weeks ago—"

"In the kitchen?"

"Don't start! In the dining room," she fumed. "And you told me that you weren't seeing anyone."

This again? Was she trying for some Mother of the Year award? Had she been brainwashed by an Aussie chapter of PFLAG?

"I wasn't," I said feebly.

"Are you now?" she asked.

I couldn't answer her. It would just lead to more questions.

So now another woman was giving me *that* look, which suggested she could read far more on my face than I would ever say out loud. She and Fran could start up a support group. And then maybe they could let me in on their little secrets that they shared about me, and if only I knew them I would be able to sort out my life once and for all.

"I would just like you to talk to me."

That caused a long-smouldering ember within me to suddenly light up. "Like you did to me when I first came out?"

She turned her attention back to the grill. "I had to take time to digest it all."

"Six years?" I asked incredulously.

"Well, I'm sorry I'm not perfect!"

Here it was, the guilt trip to make me feel bad because everybody else had caused me to feel like I was less than them. And it worked, I *did* feel bad. But I had to continue standing up for myself; nobody else in the family was going to take up my cause.

"I'm sorry, but *I'm* not perfect either."

"Your *brother* talks to me."

I thought of Tim groping his girlfriend at the dinner table. "That must make you so happy."

"Yes, it does! He at least tells me who he's seeing, what he does at work and on the weekends, and what he wants to do in the future. I have no idea what's going on in your life!"

"Because none of you have ever shown any interest lately. So I don't bother."

It sounded harsher than I meant it, and I was horribly rewarded with the sound of a sob escaping from her. Here was one person in my family finally talking to me in a normal way, and I was tearing strips off her for it.

"You're so hard to talk to," she whispered. "I wish I could."

"So do I," I said truthfully.

"Why is Mum crying?"

Fucking Tim! I threw the tea towel at him from where he lounged in the doorway. "Get out of here!"

"Calm down, arsehole!" he yelled. "I just came to get beer."

I yanked the fridge door opened and shoved two cans at him. "Here."

"I need one for Dad too!"

I practically threw the third at him. "Get!"

Thankfully he did so.

"You should be nicer to him." Mum sniffed.

"I should be a lot of things," I fumed. "Maybe he should be nicer to me."

"I saw Fran at the Plaza today," Mum said suddenly, ignoring my last comment.

Fran? What did she have to do with all this?

"Oh," was all I said, wondering if Fran had recently taken out life insurance.

"I asked her if you were seeing someone, and she fudged her way around it, but I could tell she was covering up for you."

I sighed. "It's complicated."

"Everything always is with you," Mum said tiredly. "Even when you were a kid. Nothing was ever simple."

I wanted to rail against her for turning it all back to her and making it somehow why *she* should be pitied. Because obviously I was so hard to raise. But here was someone in my family trying to talk to me about my private life for the first time in years, and I felt a sudden rush of affection for her. Maybe it had taken her a while to come round naturally, or maybe she had finally realised that this wasn't a phase or a choice I had made to continually make her life difficult. For the first time it felt like she was on my side.

"He's in the closet," I said. "And I have to respect his privacy."

"Oh," Mum said, giving up on the grill and letting it fall like a doomed ocean liner beneath the water in the sink. She turned her attentions to the kettle and switched it on. "I thought maybe you were too embarrassed to bring him over here."

"No," I lied, for her sake, while trying to imagine Declan here. It would be hard enough if he wasn't *Declan Tyler*, to put up with my brother's pointed digs and my father's silences, but his celebrity would bring a whole new unwelcome angle to it all.

"Like I said, it's for his privacy."

"That's a hard way to live," she said, not knowing how astute her comment was.

I said nothing, and I think for once Mum sensed that she should let the subject drop.

"Maybe we can talk some other time," she suggested.

And it suddenly didn't seem so bad to think about that happening. "Sure. Some other time."

"IT'S good that your mum is starting to show some interest," Declan said. "It gives me hope that maybe my mum will be fine if I tell her outright, rather than keeping her guessing."

I couldn't help but notice the *if*, not *when*, but I repressed it. I had called Dec as soon as I had gotten home. Abe and Lisa were over, but he had excused himself to take the call in his bedroom.

"You never know," I replied. "Do you ever think about telling her?"

There was a long pause. "All the time," he said sadly.

Trying to sound as lighthearted as possible, I said, "Well, mine sounds practically ready to adopt you, and she doesn't even know who you are yet."

This made him laugh. "It's always good to have a fallback position. By the way, Abe and Lisa said hello."

"Say hello back."

"I will."

"I suppose you have to get back to them."

"I suppose so. So no chance of you flying down here for the rest of the weekend?"

I laughed, but it was nice to hear the longing in his voice. "Not enough frequent flyer points."

"Just as well I'll be up next weekend, then."

"It's the only thing helping me hold on," I said as melodramatically as possible.

"Bastard," he chuckled. "Oh, also, all the guys are coming over here tomorrow night, so probably best neither of us call."

That took the wind out of my sails a bit, although the logical side of me understood the necessity of laying it all out on the table to avoid any awkward scenarios. "Uh, okay."

He hesitated. "You're not upset, are you?"

"Fuck no," I said hurriedly. "I'll speak to you Monday."

"Okay. Have a good night's sleep, babe."

"You too, Dec," I said, unable to return the term of endearment. It was lucky Fran wasn't around to conk me with another bread roll.

As I tried to fall asleep I could hear my mother saying, *That's a hard way to live.*

"Shut up, Mum," I murmured, and finally slept.

CHAPTER FOURTEEN

"SATURDAY night?" Roger asked.

"That's the plan, if it's okay with you guys. He's back in town this weekend for the game."

"How did I get roped into cooking?" Fran demanded.

"Your husband," I told her.

"Thanks, you dobber," Roger groaned.

"Gee, she never would have guessed it," I pointed out. I tried to make peace with Fran. "I'll come over and help you, of course."

"Thanks, Simon, that would be nice. But I'll also make sure Roger does his fair share as well."

I chuckled, and Roger threw a cushion at me. We had left the porch to come in and seek sanctuary at the fire. It was a typical winter Melbourne's day; the Antarctic winds were in full force as they tore through your skin and bone to reside in your marrow.

"I wonder what I should make," Fran mused.

"Whatever's easy and good," I told her.

"You do make the best pasta," Roger agreed.

"Pasta?" Fran wrinkled her nose. "I can't just make bog-ordinary pasta for Declan!"

"Sure you can." I patted her hand gently. "He needs to be introduced to how good your pasta is."

"But I should be cracking out the Jamie Oliver's or Bill Grainger's—"

"Who wants that, when they could have a Francesca Dayton original?"

She sighed. "Fine. But at some other time I *have* to try something new."

"Okay."

"Bloody pasta!" she muttered to herself. "…maybe lasagne."

I grinned. It seemed this night was going to be okay after all.

THE rain never let up that weekend. Declan flew in on Friday morning for a game that night, and once again he was told he couldn't play at the last minute. He spoke to me briefly on the phone, but was short and snappy and very un-Declan-like. He called me again two minutes later to apologise, but had to get off the phone straightaway to attend a press conference.

I hoped after the game he might turn up on my doorstep, but he texted me in the wake of the Devils losing another match to say that he was tired and was going to crash at his parents' but he would see me at dinner the next night.

So I was starting to get some nerves about dinner, but when I went around to help Fran prepare the food she managed to put me at ease by just being herself. She had decided to go with lasagne and had even made her own sheets, cranking them out by hand.

"You didn't have to go to so much trouble," I told her.

"It's no trouble at all," she smiled. "Make Roger go out and pick me some basil. I'd send you, but you'd come back with grass."

"I'm not that bad," I protested. "I know what basil smells like, so I'd be able to find it just through that."

"After pulling up all my plants by the roots. On this one, I'm still going to trust Roger," she laughed. "I'd go with you on anything else, hon."

I shook my head, and when Roger next ambled through the kitchen he was quickly dispatched to cut basil. Fran and I worked industriously for the next couple of hours, making garlic loaves from scratch and struggling with the blender to create chilli, cashew, and parmesan dip for munchies before dinner. Roger managed to avoid most culinary activities, but was very good at getting us drinks. By the time we had everything prepared I was pleasantly sloshed and Fran acted as surly bartender with a heart of gold, suspending my drink privileges at least until Declan arrived.

"Drunk is not going to look good on you when he turns up," she said wisely.

A quick shower and a change of clothes helped sober me up, and the elation of alcohol turned back into the frayed nerves I had been feeling beforehand. I hid in Fran and Roger's spare bedroom for a while, until Fran knocked at the door.

"Are you okay?"

"Yeah, fine, yeah."

She frowned. "You sure sound it. Are you that scared we're going to fuck it up?"

I glared at her. "Please."

"*That* sounds more like you."

"It's always nerve-wracking to introduce the friends, you know that."

She sat next to me on the bed. "I hardly know, you always try to get out of it for as long as possible. Usually until they're out of the picture, and there's no point anymore."

"It's not because of you guys."

"Is it because of them?"

I sighed. "Partly. But mostly because of me."

"What about you?" Then it struck her. "Oh, *that* again."

"*What* again?"

"Showing anyone your feelings about them. We've seen you cry at Disney films or RSPCA commercials, but if there's an actual human involved you may as well be a robot."

"I'm not *that* bad."

"Okay, *slight* exaggeration, but pretty damn close."

We sat in silence for a moment, and Fran suddenly nudged me. "Is it Roger?"

I didn't want to admit it. "He's been acting a bit funny lately. Only a bit."

"He's jealous," Fran admitted.

I turned to look at her properly, shock obviously evident on my face.

"Oh, *come on*," Fran said, exasperated. "He's never really had to put up with you going loopy over someone before. He's always been the alpha male in your life, and all of a sudden Declan Tyler has made you change your mind about everything."

"You make it sound like I've become a mindless drone."

"No, just that you've become part of a couple. Although *you* probably still think that's all about being a mindless drone, when all it means is that someone is now extremely important to you, someone equal to your friends, if not on a different level altogether."

I've always hated that distinction being made between how much you care for people, but you do fall victim to that mentality. "I've always known you two are more important to each other than I am to you, so why can't he accept that?"

She took my hand. "Not more important. Just different. It's like there are two separate ranking systems. You're number one on the other system. It's not about Sophie's bloody Choice."

I leaned over and whispered into her ear, "I'd choose you."

Fran laughed and pushed me away. "You are such a liar."

I grabbed her hand back, and kissed her knuckles. "Thank you."

She shook her head, smiling. "Just go easy on Roger. You can both be stubborn shits, but this is just as new for him as it is for you."

"Why isn't it for you?"

Fran looked at me as if the answer wasn't already obvious. "Because I'm a woman. We're smarter about these things."

Rather than try to defend my sex, I just accepted it as truth. She pulled me up, and we made our way back to the kitchen.

WHEN there was a knock at the door, Fran pushed me out of the kitchen. "You answer it. It'll give you time to make out a little before you bring him in."

I could hear Roger snort behind me as I made some sort of protestation. Finding myself now alone in the hallway, I covered the short distance to the front door and pulled it open.

Declan was dressed in black jeans and a dark purple shirt that managed to cling in exactly the right places. I wondered if my tongue was hanging out like a character in a Loony Tunes cartoon.

"Hey," he said, moving in to kiss me. He tried to hug me at the same time, but it was awkward as his hands were full with beer and other things I couldn't exactly make out in the dark. I tried to compensate with grabbing him by the hips and pressing him against me. The beer bottles clanged together with enough noise to alert the neighbourhood to our presence, but we ignored it.

"How were your folks?" I asked politely as I closed the door behind him.

He looked a bit surprised that I asked, but he nodded. "Good. They were glad I was staying with them, I usually tend to sleep around—"

I burst into laughter, and he looked mortified.

"Not in that way, doofus! I meant around other friends' houses."

I pushed him against the hallway wall and penned him in with my body. "I hope not other 'friends' like me."

He went to kiss me, and I teasingly ducked my head so it blocked him. "Not like you. But I always like it when I stay at your house the best."

I looked up. "Yeah, my sleepovers *rock*." Before he could answer, I kissed him again. The beer bottles slipped out of his grip, and we fumbled between us so they wouldn't fall.

"We better get these inside," he murmured.

We composed ourselves, and entered the lion's den.

Fran and Roger tried to look like they weren't waiting for us to enter, but they didn't pull it off in the slightest. As I entered the kitchen, they practically ran up to me to be the first in line to meet Declan Tyler™.

Declan seemed to be wearing his best *face the scrum* expression, not surprising seeing their first meeting had been less than auspicious.

"Fran, Roger, this is—"

"Declan, Declan Tyler," Roger said, grabbing Declan's hand and pumping it furiously.

"Hi, Roger," Declan said, amused.

"Roger, Roger Dayton," Roger replied, not hearing his name already being mentioned and feeling he had to introduce himself.

Fran pushed him aside and managed a handshake, although she found it difficult to pull her husband's paw out of Declan's. "Hi, Declan. I know we've already met, but it's nice to see you again."

I could see Declan falling prey to her charms immediately. "You too, Fran. Whatever you're making, it smells delicious."

Fran giggled. "Simon helped. A little bit."

"Hey!" I protested.

She ignored me, of course. "Now, Simon mentioned something about you owing me a kiss—"

Declan laughed, Roger perked up, and I groaned inwardly.

My boyfriend scratched at the back of his head bemusedly. "I guess I did say that." Fran was starting to look a little bit like Miss Piggy eyeing Kermit. Then she laughed and pulled back. "The sentiment's enough. I see you brought beer. That'll do."

I swear for almost a second Dec looked disappointed. So much for trying to avoid the footballer slut image, but I was amused. He handed over the beer to Roger, who also looked relieved, although you could almost believe he was slightly disappointed that his wife hadn't been kissed by Declan Tyler as well.

"I knew you'd have coffee," Declan said, "but I also brought you a special Tasmanian blend to try," and he fished out a large silver bag that I had seen him buy at Salamanca but had thought nothing of it at the time, especially seeing as Abe's addiction for caffeine was almost as bad as mine.

"That's really lovely of you," Fran said, touched.

Roger was more pleased with the beer, of course. I could see him itching to ask Declan a million questions about the AFL, but he was really trying to be on his best behaviour and treat Dec as the normal human being he was meant to be.

Once the dip had been consumed, Roger became more like his usual self. He started to ask everything he wanted to know, and Declan humoured him.

Fran was up to her old tricks of making sure everything was running smoothly. She pulled me out into the hallway and asked how I thought it was all going.

"Fine, don't you think so?"

She held up a finger as she cocked her head and then yelled into the kitchen, "Roger, don't ask that!"

"You are such a multitasker," I said admiringly.

"I know," she grinned. "And for the record, yes, it's going well. You two are disgustingly cute together."

I gave her a quick kiss. "Gross. But thank you."

No sooner had we stepped back in, Fran managed to get Roger away from the table by claiming they needed to grab more firewood, and Declan and I were left alone for the first time since he first walked in the door.

"Okay, is it unbearable?" I asked.

Declan took a swig of his beer. "Roger? Nah. I've met worse. I bet you once this night is over, he'll get past the glamour of it all and see me as just another schmo."

"Man, I hope so," I said.

He gave my hand a brief squeeze. "You'll see."

"Fran's probably reading him the riot act right now."

"I like them both. They're like a crazier Abe and Lisa."

I laughed. "You got that right." I thought of my friends with great affection and how *easy* it could be to get used to this. As Declan stood to clear some of the debris on the table, I came up behind him and hugged him close. His hands closed over mine and he leaned back to take my kiss. I cheekily arched a finger and teased his nipple through the fabric of his shirt, and he breathed heavily into my mouth.

"God, not here—"

I let him go, and he sat down quickly, his face red. "You are such a bastard," he said shakily.

I bent down and kissed him again. "You *are* staying over tonight, yeah?"

"I think you're definitely going to have to put out, yes."

"Perfect night," I sighed, and I fetched us fresh beers from the fridge. I had just sat back down opposite Declan when Fran and Roger reappeared. The lack of firewood in their hands proved that their excursion was the ruse I expected. Declan self-consciously adjusted the front of his shirt slightly, and I grinned to myself as I imagined him stripping out of it later.

"No firewood?" I asked innocently.

"We've run out," Fran said smoothly. "I should have realised. But I think it's time for lasagne!"

Roger took his seat at the foot of the table again while Fran busied herself with the oven.

"Fran does the best lasagne," I told Declan.

"Not as good as my mum's," Fran said self-deprecatingly, placing the gourmet extravaganza in question on the table before us as artwork.

"I don't know," I said, "they're pretty much on par."

"Yeah," Roger said, taking a swig of his beer. "Maybe you'll try it one day, Declan."

Everyone froze uncomfortably for a second or so.

Declan broke it by smiling and saying quietly, "I hope so. But for now, I can't imagine anything tasting better than this."

Fran rested her hand upon his arm briefly, and as she walked away she shot a glare at Roger only I noticed. Roger was too busy peeling the label off his beer bottle, a nervous habit that he had never seemed to grow out of. It also made me feel slightly wary something wasn't quite right with him.

We started serving ourselves, and a huge bowl of garlic bread was passed around.

Fran and I had decided the no-garlic rule only existed for the first two weeks of a relationship, so now I was home free and I made sure I loaded up my plate with the offending foodstuff.

"Oh, this is *good*," Declan said appreciatively after only the first bite.

"I told you," I said while Fran looked pleased with herself.

"So, what are your intentions with Simon?" Roger asked out of the blue.

The question obviously took Declan by surprise, as he started coughing.

"Roger!" Fran exclaimed.

I stared my best friend down, trying to decipher *his* intentions. But his face might as well have been carved from stone, and as such, was unreadable.

"I assure you," Declan said smoothly, or just as smoothly as he could when a mouthful of food has gone down the wrong way, "that my intentions with Simon are completely honourable." He was trying to be casual and a little bit fun, but judging by Roger's sudden change in body language it wasn't going to go down well. Like that mouthful of food.

"Sure," Roger said. "But you're not *out*, right?"

Declan shook his head and laid down his fork, drawing his own battle line. "Only to a few people. But publicly out? You'd already know that if I was."

Roger nodded. "Well, Simon *is*."

"I know."

"Roger," I said calmly, although my voice scraped like unsheathed steel.

"No," Declan said gently. "He wants to ask some questions. Let him get them out."

Fran didn't look as amiable. She looked as if she was going to slash her husband's throat with the spatula. A dull one, crusted with melted cheese, to inflict as much pain as possible.

"So what does that mean?" Roger continued.

"What does what mean?" I asked dangerously.

"Well, it seems like Simon is sacrificing a hell of a lot," Roger said, still speaking to Declan rather than to all of us. "What about you?"

"I know he is," Declan agreed.

"Do you really?" Roger asked. He had now finished his beer and was pouring himself a glass of wine. Strangely enough, he started politely pouring everybody else a glass as well.

"I know it's hard for him—" Declan began.

I interrupted him, mad as hell and upset that he was being made to justify himself. "It's a decision *I* made. I'm not going into this blindly, Roger."

"And it's not something my own friends haven't pointed out to me," Declan said.

Now I turned on him. "What?"

"Abe and Lisa said—"

"I thought they liked me?"

"They do!"

"But they talked to you about this—"

"Of course they did! What, Roger and Fran have never said anything about this?"

I fell silent, as he was right, and felt the gentle pressure of Fran's hand upon my shoulder. Strange that she should be the one trying to comfort me in this emotional shitstorm—shouldn't it be Declan?

"See?" Declan asked.

"What you're asking him to do is squeeze back into the closet with you," Roger said. "And he shouldn't have to, not when it took him so much to come out himself. He shouldn't have to go back."

"Rog, shut up," I warned him.

"I'm your friend, so I get to say this!" he shot back. "We want to see you happy! And this situation is only going to get harder and harder! I mean, how long can you go on like this?"

"We're taking it as it comes," I said, sounding unconvincing to everyone in the room.

"Declan?" Roger asked, obviously trying to see if he could get more out of him. "How long can it go on like this? You going to give a big speech on your retirement day? Or just let it leak out gradually after that? You're only twenty-seven. You could still play professionally for at least another six or seven years. Does Simon get to wait around for that long, hiding in the shadows, pretending he doesn't exist to the outside world?"

This was all starting to sound a bit melodramatic for my taste, but Declan was staring down at his plate.

"No," he said softly, "maybe not."

"But that's my fucking decision," I said. "And I think it's worth it."

Declan looked up at me and smiled. But it didn't reach his eyes.

"This was meant to be a nice dinner," Fran murmured.

"Yeah, thanks, Roger," I said bitterly. "You've really made a good impression."

"Hey," Declan said. "He's trying to be a good friend."

"Don't defend him!"

"Someone has to. He's going to be copping it from Fran when we leave."

Fran said nothing, but her mutinous eyes declared Roger was living on borrowed time.

"What about the Brownlow?" Roger asked.

It seemed like the stupidest thing he could have brought up at this point of time, and Fran and I stared at each other in confusion. When I looked at Declan, however, I could see he knew what Roger was getting at.

"It's coming up in a few weeks," Roger prodded him.

Declan nodded.

"Do you have a date?"

Declan sighed and folded his arms defensively against his chest. "Yes. I do."

I should have expected it. Because I knew I would never be going to it. Yet hearing that affirmation hurt, especially because we hadn't had the opportunity to discuss it between ourselves. For him to explain it all and let me in on his plans.

"Who?" I asked, trying to keep my tone light.

"My sister's friend, Jess. The same girl I took the year I won."

"Does she know you're gay?" I asked.

Declan nodded. "We have an understanding. She's a friend. She likes to help out every now and again when I need a date for a function."

"Wow, that closet's getting a little full," Roger murmured.

"Shut the fuck up!" Fran hissed at him. "You've said enough!"

My chest felt tight from trying not to explode. I didn't know whether I just wanted to yell at everyone or go off somewhere and either scream or cry until this tightness went away. I wondered if this was what it felt like to have a heart attack; I was surprised I was still breathing normally. I managed to somehow get to my feet and stammer out, "Yeah, look, I think I'm going to go."

"Simon," Fran said desperately.

Roger stood up to follow me, and I glared at him. "Don't."

All it took was that one word to stop him in his tracks.

I gave Fran a quick kiss. "Thanks."

"I'll call you tomorrow," she said.

The last thing I wanted to do was speak to anybody, but I nodded. I didn't want her to think I was going to ignore her again like last time.

Last time.

This was all becoming a bit too frequent and repetitive for my liking.

As I stumbled out into the hallway, I heard Declan make his apologies to Fran. He even said good-bye to Roger, although it was a terse one. I was fumbling with my car keys, trying to open the door when he came up behind me.

"Hey," he said tenderly.

"I'm sorry," I said.

"What for?"

"Just, Abe and Lisa—"

"This has nothing to do with Abe and Lisa—"

"But they were so nice to me, and my friends attack you—"

"Fran was perfectly lovely. Roger… well… he was trying to defend *you*. I can't be pissed with him for that, although I can be pissed off in a lot of other ways."

"Stop sounding like you're on his side—"

He took my keys off me and unlocked the door himself. "I'm on *your* side," he said, passing the keys back.

"Well, I'm on yours, so I can be pissed off for you."

"Good thing we're on each other's sides, then," he mused. "Because it'll be hell if we start in on each other too."

Damn, he looked pretty in the moonlight. Okay, technically, it was the fluorescent glow from a streetlight. But he still looked pretty.

"We have to be," I told him.

"Can I still come over?"

I wanted to kiss him, out on the street, under the light, but I knew I couldn't. "Like you had to ask."

"After that in there, I thought it was best."

"See you back home."

I felt his hand briefly on my hip, but it was gone just as quick. I got into my car and looked up to see Fran standing on the front porch. She gave a small wave, and I gave her one back. Then I savagely threw the car into reverse and got the hell out of Dodge.

Declan wasn't far behind me; I was only getting out of my car when he pulled into my driveway.

"I'm calling for pizza," I told him. "Strangely enough, I'm starving."

He grinned. "Me too. It must be because of that huge lack of food we got to eat."

Maggie was surly when I got in the door. I fed her, ordered pizza, and let Declan fetch me a beer. We didn't speak much, it wasn't until the pizza arrived and we were finally getting food into our bellies that we started to talk.

"This is in no way as good as Fran's lasagne," I told him.

"I have to agree. But it's warm, and I'm hungry, so pass me another slice."

My phone rang, and I could tell from caller ID it was either Fran or Roger. I let the answering machine get it and turned it down so I wouldn't have to listen.

"You're going to have to talk to him sometime."

"Not tonight. Probably not for a while."

"Just don't freeze Fran out. She doesn't deserve to get caught in the middle."

"I won't," I replied. "But she'll be in the middle anyway." I put my plate down, suddenly not hungry anymore.

"Hey," Declan said simply, and he put his plate down as well. He pulled me over to him, and I sank against his warmth. His arms came around me, and as much as every inner demon within me screamed to resist, I let myself go limp and closed my eyes, taking comfort in him and feeling soothed. I felt my anger fade away in those moments I lay there, while the soft steady thump of his heart close to my ear calmed me out of my natural skittishness. Was this what love was like? The mere thought of the word made me want to yak like a cat with a hairball, but even though I could now put a word to it I still couldn't say it. I didn't know what I thought I would lose, but everything around us seemed (or felt) precarious, and I didn't want to tip the balance any further when we seemed to have found a moment of calm in the eye of the storm.

THE real talk, of course, happened under the cover of darkness in the bedroom.

"She's pretty," I said.

I could sense Declan wanting to say "who?" and pretending he didn't know straight away what I was referring to, but he just sighed and said, "Yes."

"She looks good on you," I pressed further.

He gave a short laugh. "Jess isn't a suit."

"I remember her vaguely from all the photos of you in the papers when you won the Brownlow."

"I guess anyone couldn't help but miss it."

"Why does she do it?"

"Because she's my friend."

"There isn't anything more than that?"

He hesitated before replying. "I wonder how Roger knew."

I sat up, finally, sensing we wouldn't be sleeping for a while. "Knew what?"

"He made that comment… about how crowded the closet was."

It dawned on me. "She's gay?"

He motioned for me to lie down again. "Yeah."

I slid back down, and we recommenced cuddling. "So it's a relationship of convenience?"

"It's not a *relationship*. We just help each other out."

"But doesn't that make her family think that you're a couple?"

"It's amazing what people won't ask when you act deliberately vague about it all."

I just thought they hadn't crossed the right people. I seemed surrounded by those who wanted to know everything about you in excruciating detail as soon as they were formally introduced.

"But it's been two years since you won the Brownlow—"

"Jess gets the feeling we're considered to be an on-again, off-again couple. It helps I live in another state."

I dug my chin into his shoulder. "So you're on again for the Brownlow?"

"You can't go there alone. That would be a hell of a way to stand out."

I thought of the blue carpet ceremony, which had been introduced in the past decade, a crass offshoot stolen from American award shows, where the footballers and their girlfriends had to parade like cattle. The girls would have to name-drop their designers, and the boys would be stumped when it came to remembering where they hired their suits. Turning up without a girl would be tantamount to career suicide and endless speculation. "Yeah, it sure would."

"In a better world, I'd be taking you."

I laughed. "And I'd be taking advantage of the free booze."

Declan lifted my chin so I could see how his eyes were pleading his case for him. "You're not pissed off?"

"At the world maybe," I admitted. "But not you."

He kissed me, and his hands began wandering south. I threw back my head and moaned softly as his mouth travelled down to the hollow of my neck.

"Dec...."

He looked up. "Yeah?"

"These *favours* you and Jess have... how far do they go?"

"Huh?"

"Like in a few years, you're not going to be harvesting your sperm for her children are you?"

"Simon," he said tiredly, "you're really going to have to learn to be quiet when someone is trying to seduce you."

My body agreed, because in a few seconds Jess and her possible future spawn were the last thing on my mind.

CHAPTER FIFTEEN

"I WAS thinking...." I heard Declan murmur through some fuzzy part of my brain.

"And I was sleeping," I groaned.

I felt my head shoved down into the pillow, and I struggled out from under his hand. "Okay, okay, I'm awake! *Now.*"

Satisfied, Declan rolled over, half onto my chest, which he tapped with his finger.

"Oww," I said pettily.

"Baby," he said, and it wasn't a term of endearment.

I yawned and tried to give him my full attention. "What were you thinking?"

He looked a bit apprehensive, which I didn't like at all. It usually means bad things are coming your way. "I was considering… buying some real estate."

Huh. Okay, I certainly wasn't expecting *that* revelation. "You already own an apartment."

"Yeah, in *Hobart*. I was thinking of buying something here."

My own mortgage was crippling me; I couldn't even comprehend how someone could get or even *want* two. "How can you afford it?"

Declan suddenly was extremely interested in a button on the doona cover as he said softly, "Well, I've already paid off that apartment."

I tended to forget he was Mr. Moneybags. "Ooooookay."

"Look, I don't drink, I don't do drugs—"

"Are you *sure* you're a professional footy player?"

"Simon," he said in all seriousness.

"Sorry. Continue."

"So I've always been good with my money."

"Please don't tell me you have investments and stocks. I can't go out with somebody who has that."

A little smirk tugged at the corner of his lips. "I have investments and stocks."

I began pummelling him with the pillow. "That's it! We have to break up!"

He defended himself easily by grabbing the pillow and whacking me soundly. "My brother-in-law is an accountant! They know how to do these things!"

"Okay," I said. "But why here?"

"Because I don't have an *anywhere* here. I split my time in Melbourne between here, my folks' house, friends' houses, and hotel rooms paid for by the club. I have enough money that I could get a mortgage and buy a second place. I mean, I'm going to need one when my contract ends."

"But that's a while away."

"Only one more season. It was a three-year contract."

"So you want to come back and play in Melbourne?"

He nodded. "It's always been my plan."

"But will the Devils let you go?"

"After the amount of money they paid for me, and the little return they got for it?" he said, sounding for a moment like one of the many whiners who wrote in to the papers or called talkback radio to rant about his injuries. "I think they'll be glad to get rid of me. Especially as they'll then be able to tell the press it was a mutual understanding."

I leaned my forehead against his. "After the op, they'll be singing a different tune. They always do. Then it will be about how they saw you through the hard times, and it was all worth it."

He gave me a sweet kiss. "Thanks. But I still want to come home."

I imagined Declan here permanently, and it was a nice prospect. We wouldn't be continually split and doing a part-time long-distance relationship. I pushed away Roger's nagging voice with all his doubts from the night before. "Any other reason?"

He smiled ruefully. "I have to admit, you have a bit to do with it."

"How?"

"Well, if I have my own place, people will expect me to be there. No more keeping up the pretence of staying with friends or having to fulfil expectations of being on tap at a big, fancy hotel. It means we would see each other more often."

But there would still be pretence involved. I couldn't say that, though. "Sounds good to me. Where would you buy?"

"Somewhere you'd hate," he grinned. "The Docklands."

I did groan slightly. The Docklands were even worse than where he was currently living in Hobart. Once again he would buying into a waterfront that had been yuppified out of its previously sleazy state into a preprepared secure community with no charm.

"Oh come on," Declan protested. "We all can't be bohemians like you in North Brunswick. Which, you do know, is becoming more gentrified every year."

"I guess you need the security," I admitted grudgingly.

He scoffed at this. "I'm not being mobbed on the streets."

"No, but I could imagine why the Docklands would be more appealing to you."

"Nice views too. You liked my view in Tassie."

"It was the view *inside* that sold me more."

He shook his head. "Nuff-nuff."

I laughed, but conceded defeat. "Hey, if it means I'll see you more, I'm not complaining."

He whacked me again with the pillow. "Come on, it's too nice a day to stay inside. Let's go out."

Out? Into the fresh air and sunlight and… outside?

"We'll go for a run on the beach. Perfect cover."

A *run*? He was thinking of making me *exercise*?

He laughed at the horror obviously etched across my face. "Surely you must have something you could wear?"

I DIDN'T think I looked the part of jogging companion. True, I had trakkie daks, but those combined with my Cons and a faded "No Blood For Oil" longsleeve from a protest during my uni days didn't exactly sell me as someone who would be out running with Declan Tyler.

"You'll do," he said, trying not to laugh.

I left him to finish dressing as he continued to towel his hair dry. I fed Maggie, and on my way out of the kitchen was reminded of the light flashing on the base of the phone. Roger's message. Or it could be Fran. I sighed dramatically and pressed the button to listen to it.

"Hey, Simon, it's me," said the life of the party himself. *"I just wanted to ring and apologise for what I said. You know I meant well, although Fran says it isn't an excuse. Can you call me back? Oh, and if Declan is still there, I'm sorry, mate. Hope you don't hold it against me."*

"You have to call him back," Declan said, coming up behind me.

"No, I don't." I pushed the delete button a little more firmly than I intended. "It's not that simple."

"It would be if you called him now. Leaving it will make it worse."

"Later," I told him. "We're going for a run." I almost shuddered; I couldn't believe I could say that so casually and still live.

Declan shook his head sadly. "You are such a stubborn shit."

He sounded like Fran when he said that. She sure didn't kiss like me like he did, though.

DECLAN looked the part at least. His trakkies were formfitting and tucked neatly into his four hundred dollar sneakers. He wore a singlet under his lightweight longsleeve, ready to be discarded once he worked up a sweat. A baseball cap was pulled low on his brow, and large wraparound sunglasses were in place to hopefully obscure his features.

Together, we were *one of these things is not like the other one*.

We drove a little further down from St Kilda Beach, where there would be fewer people and the sand wouldn't be a minefield of discarded syringes. Declan grinned at me easily before he started stretching to loosen up. I stood still, wrapping my arms around myself to try and ward off the chill winds, watching him perform some arcane sacrificial rite.

"You have to loosen up first," he instructed me. "Or else you'll feel it more later."

There were so many places one could go with that comment, but I asked, "You're not *seriously* expecting me to run, are you?"

"I thought that was the point," he said amiably.

"I thought *I* would just find a café and read the paper while you got your jollies pounding the sand," I replied.

"Then *you* thought wrong," he said sternly.

Declan had suddenly gone from boyfriend to the PE teacher from hell in all of twenty seconds. Cowed, I began imitating his stretches. My muscles began protesting almost immediately. He swung his leg easily over a park bench so he could bend over and flex his toes. I struggled to do the same move and almost fell over.

"You're just acting up," he scoffed.

Unfortunately I wasn't, but I wasn't sure I wanted to admit to it and shatter his fantasies.

Declan clapped his hands together. "Let's go!"

I could hear the blood pounding louder in my ears than the actual crash of the waves against the sand. I thought of strokes and heart attacks, of the medics being summoned to the beach and being mentioned in the papers as "and friend" again, with a photo of Declan looking concerned, but distant. Immediately I was panting, and wishing for a shark to suddenly grow legs and waddle out of the surf to eat me and put me out of my misery. In fact, I would have willingly thrown myself into its mouth.

Declan jogged easily, not having even broken a sweat at this stage, his long lean legs propelling him forward with seemingly no effort. I had to yank at the waistband of my trakkies as they kept threatening to slide down and trip me over. The sand, damp with the tide, kicked up divots as I ran. Declan's feet skipped over the surface: Jesus walking on the water.

"Time to pick up the pace!" he called over his shoulder.

Pick *up* the pace? I was already at full speed.

He sprinted away, his firm arse acting as a beacon to lure me further. I stopped, bending over with my hands on my hips, trying to catch my breath back. Declan quickly blurred to a vague shape in the distance while I hacked my lungs up. Once I could breathe again, stars still shimmering in my vision, I began walking, so that if he returned he could see that I hadn't given up completely. A few other joggers passed me by in both directions, and I was embarrassed by an elderly couple who had to walk around me as I was slowing them down. Their extremely fat golden retriever still breathed far easier than I did.

After some time, a jogger in the distance revealed himself to be Declan. He was sweating a bit now, as he ran back towards me. I smiled at him sheepishly; to show off, he continued to run backwards in circles around me as I walked.

"Didn't have to worry about this undercover thing too much, did we?" he asked. "I turned around, and you were nowhere to be seen."

"All part of my master plan," I said innocently.

He shook his head. "Why don't you go and get coffee, and I'll meet you back there? I'm just going to run a bit further."

"Sure." Anything to get me out of the exercise regime.

Declan started sprinting off again, and this time it was my turn to shake my head at the thousand and one better things that could be being done with this time. I headed towards the café across from the car park. After ordering two lattés to go, I headed back to the beach, a little way down from the main thoroughfare of people and parked my butt on the sand with a dune as my backrest.

The natural athlete that was Declan Tyler™ didn't waste any time in covering the ground that had taken me a good while to cross. And instead of plonking himself down next to me, he took a few moments to stretch once more.

"You're so fucking professional," I teased. "When are they hiring you to do a workout DVD?"

"Piss off," he ragged back, stripping off the longsleeve and throwing it in my face. "You have the stamina of a chronic invalid with emphysema, and you don't even smoke. You should be ashamed of yourself."

As he finally sat beside me, I asked in a low murmur, "Would you rather have a jock boyfriend who could run with you?"

He took his coffee and shook his head. "If it's not you, no."

I tried not to be distracted by his golden shoulders, even when relaxing they were bunched with toned muscle that I could never hope to achieve. These were the same arms that held me when I slept, I marvelled. "Would you rather I became a jock?"

Declan laughed. "Then you wouldn't be Simon."

That *was* a scary thought.

"Would you rather have an arty wanker boyfriend?" It was now apparently Declan's turn to play the game.

"No," I said honestly. "I like the differences between us."

We watched the waves, and their wake inched closer towards us as we sat in comfortable silence. I could tell he wanted to put his arm around me as we watched the ocean, sitting there like any normal couple. I wanted to put my arms around him as well, and let his head rest in my lap. The few people that passed us paid little, if any, attention to our presence. Maybe we *were* too paranoid, but Declan's celebrity helped foster that. Mind you, we were sitting on the beach on a typical Melbourne's winter day—it wasn't like we were sitting al fresco at a café on Brunswick Street where all the sensible people would be.

As it always was with us, our time together ended too quickly. Before we even realised it, it was time to drive back to my place and for Declan to shower and pack before heading out to the airport.

"Call Roger," Declan said as he kissed me good-bye.

"*You* call him," I said childishly.

He shook his head and kissed me again. "Speak to you soon."

The house seemed empty without him in it. I turned on the stereo, loud, to fill the leftover space.

I DIDN'T call Roger back, of course, although he tried three times that afternoon. I did answer when Fran's mobile number displayed on caller ID, but it was Roger's voice through the earpiece so I hung up immediately. A few minutes afterwards I received a text from her saying that she hadn't put him up to it, and would I please call her at work tomorrow?

I had an early night after checking in with Declan, who had arrived home safely and was preparing to go out to dinner with Abe and Lisa. "Wish you were here," he said breezily, and I found myself feeling horribly lonely.

So I was determined that I wouldn't be stupid and shut Fran out again just because Roger was being a dick. She sounded surprised when I called her at exactly a minute past nine.

"I haven't even gotten a coffee yet," she said ruefully. "Have you?"

"Yep, and it's wonderful."

"Bastard. You must have gotten in early."

"I did."

And then the awkward pause. I slowly turned in my chair to watch the crowds still streaming out of Flinders Street Station below me. It was always surprising how many people seemed to be late for work every day. Of course, I was making a gross generalisation—maybe they all didn't start at nine. But I was sure a fair few of them were late.

"Simon?"

"Sorry, I was distracted. What did you say?"

"Just, I'm not sure if I should bring up Saturday night or whether we should just pretend that nothing happened."

"I don't think I can pretend *nothing* happened."

"Meet me for lunch?"

It was a busy day for me, but I had to agree so she wouldn't think I was pissed with her. "Sure."

"Great."

"Fran?"

"Yeah?"

"You're not going to try and bring Rog, are you? In some misguided attempt to set things right?"

She took a deep breath. "Hon, I'm not stupid."

I shouldn't have doubted her. It was dim-witted of me. "Okay. See you at one."

"YOU'RE lucky I didn't turn up with a camera crew," I said easily as I sat before Fran.

She grimaced. "Alice Provotna again?"

"Yeah, I've got meetings all day. She thinks they'll be interesting. Our definitions of that word are *not* one and the same. And she seemed to think this was a business lunch."

"Thank God you put her off. How did you convince her?"

"I told her you were my mistress," I teased.

"Hopefully not on camera, just in case any of my family ever get to see it."

"What, you don't think we'd make a great couple?"

She raised an eyebrow. "My family would *agree*."

"Well, knowing your husband—"

"Hey!" she warned.

I put up my hands in surrender. "Sorry. I had to get one cheap shot in."

Fran shrugged and picked up the menu even though I knew she had already chosen what she wanted before even arriving at the restaurant. "I'll give you *one*."

"All the rest will be earned, though."

"Let me just say though, Simon, he *is* really upset."

"Boo fucking hoo."

She glared over the top of the menu. "I said only *one* cheap shot."

The waiter took our orders, and I could no longer hide behind my menu-shield. It was time to come out swinging. "So, *he's* bloody upset? It can't be all about him. He attacked *us*."

"I know, but he knows he's screwed up and now he wants to fix it."

"And I want to lick my wounds for a little while."

"Get Declan to do it, and maybe it'll speed up the process."

I glared at her.

"It's a joke, Simon. We used to be able to do that."

I took a sip of my water, something to distract me so that I didn't blurt out a friendship-ending insult. "Well, I'm not feeling very funny at the moment."

"You have to forgive him sometime."

"I *know*, Fran. We've been friends for over sixteen years. This isn't the end of it. But I need some time at the moment. I just can't pretend everything's hunky-dory just because he's feeling guilty and wants it stopped."

She nodded. "It's just he's my husband. So I have to defend him."

Dammit, her bright eyes were getting to me as she was sincerely trying not to cry. "I know, Fran. But how you're feeling at the moment, that's what I feel about Dec. I have to defend him because of what Roger said."

She reached over and took my hand. "I get it. How is Dec?"

"*He's* fine. Defending Roger as much as you are, surprisingly enough."

"That's why I like him." Fran gave a delicate sniff, trying to compose herself. "He's very fair-minded."

"Maybe too much," I agreed. "I'm still trying to find his faults."

"He has them," Fran laughed softly. "We all do."

"I guess he did try to torture me yesterday with the run on the beach."

Fran began to choke. I pushed a glass of water towards her, and she hurriedly took a gulp. "You… *run*… beach?"

"I didn't last very long."

"I bet. Still, I wish somebody had had a camera," she said in awe, as if I'd just told her I'd spotted a Tasmanian tiger loping along with Declan.

I grinned at her and suddenly felt the empty space at the table that was Roger. Even when he wasn't here, he was still between us.

"No matter what happens, or as long as it takes," I said, "let's not let it affect us, Fran."

She frowned. "You're scaring me with a sentence like that."

I sighed. "Maybe I'm being melodramatic. But I just don't want *us* to fight."

Fran twisted her napkin into a little stress ball and smoothed it back out to begin all over again. "We won't. But sooner or later, if things aren't resolved, we probably will."

On that ominous note, our food arrived. For the rest of our lunch hour together the subject of Roger was studiously avoided.

HOWEVER, it was the first thing Declan brought up when he called me later that night.

"No, I haven't spoken to Roger. But I did speak to Fran."

"I guess that's something, at least."

"She doesn't want us to fight, but she thinks that the longer things go on like this between Roger and I, the more our friendship will eventually get pulled into it as well."

"She's right," Declan said, refusing to sugarcoat it.

I sighed. "I know. But I'm so pissed off at him at the moment I can't even look at him. I'm scared I'll just punch him out."

Declan laughed. "You?"

"Hey!" I protested. "I can be pretty scrappy when I want to be."

"I just hope you punch better than you jog."

"Yeah, well next time you see me, just try me."

"*Now* you're getting kinky on me," he teased.

"Would you like me to be? I'm surprisingly good at tying knots. It was the only way I got any peace when Tim was about eight."

"I would be too scared you would have a perverse fit and leave me for hours while you go catch a movie."

"Sounds like *you're* heading into fantasy territory, not me."

He ignored that. "Seriously, Simon, call him."

Back to *that* subject. "In a couple of days. Give me time to cool down." Desperate to change the subject, I went for the mundane to replace it. "So what did you do today?"

He sounded a bit hesitant. "I, uh, had physio, a team meeting… and then I went to get measured for a suit."

"Oh?"

"Yeah. For the Brownlow."

"Oh." Realising I was quickly heading into a territory of jealous in which I didn't want to stray, I tried to sound light as I asked, "What colour?"

"What colour?"

"Yeah. The suit. What colour?"

"Normal, traditional black."

"You know, you could try something different."

He laughed. "Trying something different gets you noticed more. That's what I try to avoid, remember?"

I remembered the premiere night of the Triple F last year when I had worn an emerald green suit purchased from an op-shop on Sydney Road. There was a reason why Jess was going to the Brownlow instead of me.

Damn. I had let the silence go on for too long.

"Hey, Simon?"

"Yeah?"

"We didn't really talk about it, before I left. About the Brownlow."

"What else is there to know? I thought we covered it all."

"I just wanted to say… the whole damn thing has been crushing me. For the past couple of weeks I've been discussing plans with Jess, and I wanted to tell you, but to tell you the truth, I was scared to."

"Why?"

"Because it isn't the way it should be."

His voice pained me, it was low and passionate and heartfelt, and I hated we could only be so open with each other when we were so far apart physically.

"I know, Dec."

"I should be making these plans with you, trying to talk you out of whatever crazy thing you would be trying to wear—"

"What do you think I would try to wear?" I asked, interested in spite of myself.

"Probably something bright purple or one of those old-fashioned coats that make you look like a vampire from one of those Anne Rice books before she found religion."

Hmm, purple. Or a Victorian coat? The man knew me, it seemed.

"I wouldn't do that to you at the Brownlow," I teased him. "Maybe at the premiere night of the Triple F."

He laughed. "That's probably normal dress at that event."

Sadly, he was correct.

"I knew you would say you would understand," he continued, "but I know it still hurts."

"It does, a little bit," I admitted. "But like you say, I understand."

"I guess I just thought if I didn't talk about it then I wouldn't have to confront it with you."

"Yeah, that always works."

"Anyway, I'm sorry about it."

"Don't be. Just talk to me from now on," I told him.

"I promise. And hey, thanks for setting up that segue. How about you do the same with Roger?" he asked, not at all subtly.

"Good night, Dec."

"Night, babe."

Damn, he did the *babe* thing again, beating me to the punch. It would have sounded daft if I had repeated it back to him, so I just had to let it be. For now.

THE next few days were filled with continual pleas from Fran and Declan to give in and speak to Roger. I, of course, let those pleas fall on selectively deaf ears. Until Roger turned up at the office.

It was close to five, Nyssa had already left because of a "dental appointment." I had locked up and was coming out of the lift when I ran right into the friend I was currently kind-of-feuding with.

"Hi," Roger said, kind of dopily.

"Yeah, hi," I replied, just as dopily.

"I, uh, came in to pick up Fran but thought I'd try and catch you as well."

That irked me. "How nice to be your afterthought." I started walking through the lobby doors and out onto the street beyond.

"Hey!" Roger protested, not that far behind me. "In case you've forgotten, I *have* been trying to talk to you."

"And in case *you've* forgotten, I've been ignoring you."

"And how long is that going to go on for?"

"I don't know. As long as I feel like it."

We had reached the intersection of Swanston and Collins, where I normally caught my tram. The streets were already packed with people rushing to go home.

"Where are you going?" Roger asked as I stopped to wait for the pedestrian light to cross over the tram tracks.

"Home."

"I said I would give you a lift."

"And I'd rather catch the tram."

To tell you the truth, I was feeling a little perverse pleasure in tormenting him. It was payback for how I felt on Saturday night, dishing it back to him. He looked genuinely hurt that I was refusing after days and many overtures to try and deal with the problem.

"Fucking Declan Tyler," he fumed. "We never used to fight like this, until *he* came along."

"*He* isn't the problem," I said pointedly.

"Oh, and I am?"

"That's what I was implying."

The pedestrian crossing started beeping, and we all swarmed over towards the island in the centre of the traffic. There was no sign of my tram yet, but I hoped it wouldn't be too long.

"You can hate me right now," Roger said, "but there's a part of you knows I'm telling the truth, and you don't want me bringing it up because that means you'll have to think about it some more. And that will destroy this little Disney fantasy you've currently got in your head."

Fuck him. I knew it wasn't a fantasy life; I was the one goddamned living it. All I could do was stare at him coldly.

"Got nothing to say?" he asked.

Thankfully, I could see my tram at the next stop, slowly making its way towards ours. "Thanks for your support," I said. Not the best comeback ever, but there was enough venom in my tone to press the point.

He leaned in to me so he wouldn't be overheard by the other waiting passengers. "Good luck watching your boyfriend preen with his beard on TV next week."

Wow, that was remarkably bitchy for a straight man. I didn't say anything, and Roger stood there staring sadly at me for a moment before walking away.

I can't say I thought there was an air of finality about this confrontation, but as I got onto the tram and watched him through the window as he made his way to Fran's building I certainly felt like things would never be the same between us again.

But I'm melodramatic that way.

Later that night when Declan rang I let it go to the answering machine. Despite me telling him that we should talk, I didn't think I could share how empty I felt right then.

In the morning when he called again, I would fob him off and say that I was tired after work and slept like the dead and be evasive about answering questions about Roger. I was a hypocrite, and all I wanted to do was Rip van Winkle my way out of this whole mess which I had just made worse.

CHAPTER
SIXTEEN

AND suddenly, September was upon us.

Only the most important month in the AFL calendar. The Brownlow Ceremony takes place the same week as the Grand Final, and the two teams competing in the final usually don't attend because the coaches want them concentrating on the game at hand rather than falling prey to one of the biggest booze-ups of the year.

This meant that Declan was freed up; as the Devils were near the bottom of the ladder they were effectively out of the semifinals, and he could spend more time in Melbourne preparing for the ceremony and finalising the details of the surgery he would have just before Christmas.

Having him around more was a salve for me, as Roger and I hadn't spoken since our confrontation on Swanston Street. Declan was disappointed that our estrangement was being taken this far, but he knew he couldn't budge me to do anything about the issue. Likewise, Fran was experiencing the same thing on her end with Roger, and as she had foreseen in our lunch together just after that disastrous Saturday night, it was beginning to affect *our* friendship. Although we pretended otherwise, we just happened to become more and more busy at our respective workplaces, and our lunches became less frequent.

"You know, you don't look so good," Declan said one day.

"What?" I asked, distracted by a packet of coffee beans that refused to open.

"You look all pinched, as if you've just sucked a lemon."

"Gee, thanks."

"You've got to go and see your friends."

"And you have got to sit there, shut up, and look pretty."

"Don't be an arsehole." He threw the newspaper at me, and it went way off its mark, crashing uselessly to the floor.

"You better not go back on the field with a throw that wide." I noticed his weapon of choice was the real estate section, with glaring red circles marked around listings of apartments with prices that were more than five times that of my own home.

"Good way to try and change the subject," Declan grumped.

I finally managed to get some beans into the grinder and hit the button to pulverise them into oblivion. "What was that? Sorry, can't hear you over this!"

He resorted to giving me the finger.

"Really mature," I scoffed as he scrambled out of his chair to grab the newspaper again. He gave me a look which more than let me know who he thought the mature one out of the two of us was.

Work was becoming really busy, so I wasn't exactly lying to Fran when I used it as an excuse to fob her off yet again. It was only a month until the Triple F began; Nyssa and I were scrambling with last-minute deals to grab sponsors, finalise dates and screenings, and deal with a change of one of the venues. Somehow I didn't mind it as much, because I knew that most nights I was coming home to Declan. I was becoming *domesticated*. Normally that might have made me baulk at the thought, but scarily enough it just made me give a Cheshire Cat grin.

The Brownlow threatened to deflate my mood, but I tried not to give in to it. Only a few nights before the actual ceremony, Declan came over and told me something I wasn't expecting to hear.

"Jess thinks the two of you should meet."

I sank onto the couch. I think I would have been less shocked if he said the Pope was coming over for dinner. "What? Why?"

He shrugged laconically. "Maybe she wants to prove her gay status to you so you won't feel that she's trying to steal your man."

"She didn't say that!" I spluttered.

"Not in so many words, but it was what she implied. Although she did chuck a fit when I told her you thought she wanted to harvest my swimmers."

I whacked him on the shoulder. "You didn't!"

He couldn't keep it up for much longer and burst out laughing. He clutched his shoulder, wincing slightly. "You have a mean right hook when you want to."

"Yeah, ask Tim sometime." Why did I keep saying these things? It wasn't deliberate, but it hung in the air like a dying firework between us.

"So you'll meet her?"

"Why *does* she want to meet up?"

"Because she's my friend. And she just wants to clear the air between the two of you."

"There's no air to clear."

"Well, it will make her feel better."

I opened my mouth to say something, then thought better of it and quickly shut it.

Declan, of course, didn't miss it. "What?"

"Nothing."

"Bull. What were you about to say?"

"Just…." I sighed. "Did she meet with your other partner when she went to the Brownlow with you before?"

"No," Declan admitted. "But then, she didn't have to."

"Why?"

Declan coloured slightly. "Because he was already going to be at the ceremony."

I'm pretty sure my mouth dropped open. "He was a footy player?"

"Yes. What, do you think I'm the only queer in all of AFL?"

Statistically, of course he wouldn't be. But it was also hard to imagine that there could be more, to reconcile against the stereotype we had all been conditioned to believe. And certainly the presence of gay players wasn't exactly advertised, much less acknowledged.

"Don't ask me who it is," Declan said. "He's extremely closeted. He would hate other people to know."

"Is that why you broke up?"

Declan nodded and looked away.

"Is he also the one who cheated on you?"

He sighed. "Yes."

Righteous indignation on his behalf burned through me. "That's not very closeted of him, is it?"

"Well, it's easy to fuck around on the sly," Declan said bitterly. "It's much harder to try and have a relationship."

"Why did you stick around?"

"I really don't like thinking about it."

"You can talk to me. You *should* talk to me."

"I don't like thinking about it because it reminds me of what I put up with at the time," Declan said, finally looking at me, and I didn't like seeing the pain reflected in his eyes. "It doesn't make me think very highly of myself." He paused and dropped my hand. "Or what you might think of me."

"Hey," I said, grabbing his hand back, and with my free hand rubbing the back of his neck. "I think *very* highly of you."

"Yeah?"

"Yeah. We all do stuff we're not proud of when we're with other people."

"I think at the time I didn't know I could have anything better."

Boy, had I been there. "You think I haven't done that as well? Everybody does. It's what human beings do in the fucked-up name of love."

"I thought I loved him. Looking back, I know it wasn't."

I burrowed in closer to him. "He didn't deserve your love."

That moment would have been the perfect time for either of us to say those words to each other. I could tell he was thinking it as well, but the moment passed, and a new, nagging thought came to my mind.

"Dec, can I ask you something?"

"Of course."

"It may make me sound like a dickhead."

His gentle snort made me laugh. "That's never stopped you before."

"Yeah," I admitted, "but I don't like looking like a dickhead in front of you."

"Really? Then you should stop being one."

"Fuck off. And stop bringing up Fran and Roger."

"I didn't even mention them."

"I know what you were getting at."

He pulled me down so my head rested in his lap, now a therapist's couch. "Come on, tell me what's troubling you."

Where to start? Besides the fact that he had reminded me, although I didn't *need* reminding, of the Fran- and Roger-shaped hole in my existence.

"Why me?"

"I thought we'd already covered that?" Declan asked, confused.

"No, not in relation to Jess."

"What, then?"

"What do you see in *me*?"

He sighed. "This is an old argument, and I hate repeating it."

"Well, you keep spilling little secrets every now and again, and they throw me for a loop. When I think about the guys you've had, and what you *can* have, I have to wonder, what was it about me?"

Declan groaned and shook his fists in the air before taking a deep breath. "You seemed interesting. Different to everybody else I knew. Plus, you had a mouth on you. You weren't shy about saying what was on your mind."

"You mean I was a mouthy bastard." Not exactly the basis for mutual attraction I'd hoped to hear.

"Yeah. But I like that about you. I told you before, I'm not used to getting that kind of honesty from people most of the time. Especially strangers. Usually it's only my family, Abe, and Lisa."

"I guess I can kind of understand that."

Declan grinned and stroked the side of my cheek. "Plus, you're hot."

My face grew warm. I was embarrassed, because I really couldn't believe *that*.

He pulled me up so that we were face to face. His breath was warm against my neck as he sucked on it lightly. "You look even hotter when you're mortified."

I made some strangled noise of disbelief, and he pulled away to look straight at me. "Hey, I find you irresistible and sexy. So shut up, and believe it."

I didn't want to play the self-esteem card *again*, so I let it slide. His hands rested upon my hips, and his right thumb coaxed its way under my shirt to stroke the skin beneath it. "And the more I got to know you, the more I liked. So if you're making me do this, you have to tell me, what was it about me?"

"Where to start?" I leaned my forehead against his. "You were totally different to what I expected."

"And that was good?"

"You defied my own prejudices."

He laughed. "You sound like such a wanker."

"I *am* a wanker, remember?" I paused. "Plus, you were hot."

"Dickhead."

"I think you must have really nice parents," I said, out of the blue. It was a surprising statement, even to me, and I was the one who said it.

He gave me a strange look. "What makes you say that?"

I shrugged. "Because you're such a good guy. Face it, Dec, you're in a sport where if you're good you get treated like a god. And there are a lot of guys that let it get to them, and they believe it. Your parents must really keep you grounded."

"Thanks," he said. "I guess they do."

Wow, another awkward silence. Because I suddenly realised that I would really like to meet his parents and see who had brought Declan into the world and made him the person that he was. And I think he would have liked them to meet me.

But it wasn't possible, blah blah blah.

"So," I said, desperate to break the silence. "Jess, huh? When?"

WHEN turned out to be the actual night of the Brownlow.

Do you want to know what one definition of bizarre might be? Driving to your closeted boyfriend's pretend-girlfriend's house to watch them prepare for a faux date. This was a time when I really needed my friends to help me. I tried calling Fran's mobile, but it was switched off. They were probably at a movie. Or maybe they had found a new best friend already. Nothing would surprise me anymore.

I wanted to speak to Roger so badly, but seeing as this whole Brownlow controversy was the reason why we weren't talking any more to begin with, I didn't expect I would find a sympathetic ear in him. That only left Nyssa, and she didn't even know for certain I was dating somebody so there would be too many land mines to navigate before she would be able to focus on the problem at hand.

So that found me on a stranger's doorstep, still wondering whether I should just turn around, go home, and hide under the bed.

Unfortunately, the decision was made for me. Somebody must have heard my car in the driveway and was opening the door as I stood there equivocating.

The woman who answered the door was my age, relatively short, with blonde bobbed hair that suggested she should be posing against Art Deco furniture and doing the Charleston with a long cigarette holder dangling from her artfully drawn lips.

"Simon?"

"That's the name on my birth certificate," I said perkily.

She opened the screen door to allow me in. "I think you need a drink."

"That would be great." And that was perhaps the finest introduction I had ever been part of in my life.

She ushered me into the lounge. "Oh, I'm Jess, by the way."

I shook her hand. "I kind of figured." No need to say I had Googled her the day before and felt my gut drop at the pictures of her with Declan over the years. They made a lovely couple, and a few pictures had captured them looking at each other with a familiarity which probably argued a long-term relationship to those not in the know.

"Dec's still getting ready."

Oh shit, compliment time. "You look great, by the way."

And she did. She was practically sewn into a dark green dress that accentuated all her curves. She looked sexy, but not slutty. *That* probably couldn't be said for some of the girls attending tonight.

"Thanks," Jess said, sounding pleased. "I find it fun, kind of like playing dress-ups. But only for one night! I'm much more comfortable in a hippie skirt or jeans."

Damn it, she *was* nice. So the irrational part of me couldn't blame her for what we were being subjected to even though I really, really wanted to. "I have to admit I would hate getting all tuxed up."

"I know," she replied, with a twinkle in her eye. "I've seen the photos of the way you dress when I Googled your arse."

"Why would you Google *me*?"

She pulled a vodka bottle out of the freezer. "To see who it was that Declan can't shut up about."

I froze in place, not knowing how to reply.

Jess giggled mischievously as she started preparing glasses with garnish. "Why don't you go and check up on him while I finish these? Third door down the hall."

I fled before I could get any more embarrassed.

As I opened the door to the spare room, I found Declan struggling with a bow tie.

He smiled when he caught sight of me in the mirror. "I thought I heard you. What do you think of Jess?"

"I like her," I admitted.

He laughed. "Did it hurt to say that?"

"Shut up! You need help?"

He immediately surrendered. "Yes. I hate these damn things. How do you know how to do them?"

"Just one of my many unexpected talents." I moved over to him, and started expertly folding the material until I had one perfect bow tie against his neck. Just as I straightened it, he kissed me and I willingly let myself be caught up in it. I had one fleeting thought of how cruel it was to see him looking so good when he would be doing so on someone else's arm, but I let it be washed away.

"It should be you," Declan whispered, reading my mind.

"I don't think I could outrun a whole auditorium of footy players if I went as your date," I said. "You would have to leave me behind in order to save yourself."

He shook his head. "You're so noble."

"You're lucky I am. Because you look so fucking good tonight I want to tackle you and tear you right out of that tux."

He groaned. "Don't start. I don't need another reason not to go."

"I bet you dominate the first few rounds of voting."

"That'll be all I'll dominate," he grumbled.

"Then you concentrate on the free drinks," I replied, remembering that his latest spate of injuries had happened in the fourth round. It was going to be a long night for him.

"Good idea, look for the silver lining," Dec said, giving me a tired smile. "Let's get back out to Jess."

I nodded and followed him back to the lounge. Jess had poured the drinks and handed them to us. We toasted together to the eventual winner of the night and drank hurriedly.

"The chauffeur just rang," Jess said easily, the word rolling out of her like she was used to dealing with one every day. "He'll be here in about twenty minutes. Time for another round, I say."

I agreed, perhaps a bit too quickly. I caught Declan looking at me and said, "Don't worry, Officer. It'll be my last until I get home."

Jess grinned. "Good to see *one* footy player takes the 'drink responsibly' sponsorship of the game seriously."

"Hey," Declan warned; an empty threat.

"So what are you doing tonight, Simon?" Jess asked as she started pouring various spirits into the shaker.

"Well, I'll check out you guys on the blue carpet special, and then I should probably do some paperwork I neglected over the weekend."

"I have a full ticket to the Triple F, you know," she said.

"You do?" I asked, surprised.

"Yeah, I had one last year as well."

I was impressed. "A regular? I feel bad I didn't recognise you, we have so few."

She laughed and began shaking the mix. "I didn't go to any of the premieres, just the regular screenings. With my partner Robyn."

This, of course, piqued my interest. "So Robyn didn't want to see you glammed up tonight?"

Declan gave a warning cough, and Jess threw a tea towel at him.

"Sorry," I said. "I shouldn't have asked."

"Don't listen to him," Jess said, pouring the drinks. "Robyn's gone out drinking with her friends. She always gets upset this time of year because she has this irrational fear Declan and I will get really drunk, accidental penetration will occur, and his magical penis will instantly cure me of my lesbian ways."

Even *I* wasn't that paranoid. Was I? "Wow, are you sure *she's* a lesbian, if she thinks you can be cured by dick?"

Declan gave another warning cough.

"Dec, stop doing that!" Jess cried, handing me one of the glasses and giving Dec one with a complimentary side order look of admonition. "Robyn obviously just isn't as capable of coping as Simon is."

"I think he just hides it better," Declan said.

"*He* is in the room," I reminded him.

"Do you just hide it better, Simon?" Jess asked, sipping gingerly at her drink.

Emboldened by the alcohol, I nodded. "Probably."

"So you are jealous?"

"*Jealous* isn't the right word. It's not that strong a feeling."

"What is the feeling, then?" Declan asked.

I felt like I was on the witness stand. "Bittersweet disappointment."

Jess clinked my glass with her own. "Can't tell you're an Arts grad."

We laughed, and it seemed to settle the mild tension in the air.

"By the way," Jess said confidentially, leaning in to me a little. "I don't see Dec as a potential sperm donor, despite his obvious genetic pedigree."

It was now my turn to look at Dec.

He refused to meet my eyes, looking instead into his glass.

"Don't kill him," Jess giggled. "He's too much like a brother to me."

"You are *dead*," I warned him.

"He would be the perfect sample though," Jess mused. "I mean, he's good looking, athletic, smart, and has all those nice-guy characteristics... if he was a woman... well, I don't know, Simon, maybe you *would* have competition from me."

"If he was a woman, you could have him," I said.

Declan was colouring visibly over his drink, but was mercifully saved by the honking of a car from outside. Jess ran to the window and peered out. "Shit, it's the car! He's early!"

We all downed our drinks and congregated by the door.

"Are you all right to drive home?" Declan asked me.

I nodded. "Scout's honour."

He frowned, looked me over, and obviously decided I passed muster. "Okay. Drive safe." He leaned in and kissed me.

"Aww," Jess said mockingly. "That's so cute."

"Shut up," Declan winced as he pulled away from me.

"Don't worry, I'll take care of him," Jess declared as she opened the door and threw her keys into her bag.

I followed them out, shutting the door behind me. As I turned back to say good-bye, they were already walking down the porch steps, arm in arm, like the king and queen of the school ball heading to their limo. Fucking picture perfect.

As the chauffeur opened the back door of the car for them, Jess turned back and waved. I gave a halfhearted one back. Declan then turned and gave a subtle two fingered salute. I nodded and watched the chauffeur jump back into the front and the car glide away.

I sat on the steps for a few minutes, before the cold drove me back into my car, and I headed home.

WITH Maggie on my lap and a beer in my hands, I tortured myself by watching the blue carpet special before the ceremony itself. I knew that I didn't have anything to worry about with Jess, now I'd met her, but I could still haunt myself with the what-ifs as I watched my boyfriend take a date other than myself out for the night. And I'd get to watch it all on high-definition television, with a running commentary from the vacuous himbo and bimbo combination they hired every year to do the preshow fashion spiel.

I let the parade of the who's who of footballers and their girlfriends and wives unfold before me. I couldn't help but grin with a sense of affection as Abe and Lisa appeared on camera. Abe looked suave and confident in his black priest-collar tux while Lisa matched him in a gown that wouldn't have looked out of place at a Hollywood premiere in the 1940s. They stood out among the previous interviewees, who had made some stunningly bad choices, including someone from the Dockers who had obviously been trying to bring the parachute pant back into vogue.

Roger popped into my head yet again as I remembered the very first time we had gone down to the Crown complex to be part of the crowd watching the entrance to the ceremony. We were only sixteen and had snuck into the city by telling our parents that we were staying over at each other's houses. Surprisingly enough, despite being surrounded by about six cameras stationed to catch all the action on the carpet, we never once wound up as part of the broadcast. Our parents, watching at home, were totally oblivious to our being there.

I wanted to pick up the phone and call him, as I had been wanting every day for the past fortnight. Like I had only scant hours before, but this still wasn't the right time.

And suddenly there he was. Declan Tyler, on screen. With perfect girlfriend Jess.

"Are you disappointed coming here, knowing that there is no way you can be in the running for the medal?" the himbo was asking rather insensitively as I turned up the volume.

Declan took a second to compose himself by licking his lips slightly, a move I now recognised instantly as being one of either nervousness or restraint from saying what he really felt. "No, not at all. It's a night to come here with all the guys, putting aside rivalries, and celebrating the mateship in the sport instead."

Wow. What a perfect sound bite.

"Do you think you'll be in the running next year?" Himbo asked.

"Who knows?" Declan replied as the camera swayed over his right side to take in Jess. She stood there, arm in arm with him, looking every inch the supportive girlfriend. "I hope to be playing enough to be in contention, that's for sure."

"And what do you think, Jess?" Bimbo asked. "Do you think he'll be able to do it?"

"Of course," Jess said smoothly. "I have every faith in him. Next year we'll see Dec on the field, and with his usual form."

Man, they could have even fooled me. And I was the one who had Declan in my bed every time he was in town.

"And what are you wearing tonight, Jess?" Bimbo asked.

Jess flared out her gown slightly, so that it shimmered on camera. "A local designer, Heather Marlson."

"And you, Declan?" Himbo asked, in a tone that suggested that Declan, like any real man, would probably have no idea.

Which of course, Jess helped perpetuate by stepping in. "He would probably just tell you it's a tux, but it *is* by the same designer."

Declan gave a self-deprecating shrug of the shoulders, and all four on the carpet laughed as if they were at the end of a *Scooby-Doo* episode.

Maggie suddenly gave a little sneer from my lap, and I rubbed behind her ear proudly. "Good girl."

I SAT through the whole three-hour ceremony with more gusto than past years, mainly because I perked up every time Declan appeared on screen. He dominated the voting in the first three rounds, with the most votes for each. Of course, everybody knew that wouldn't last. The fourth round was when he got injured, and after that his name didn't show up on the scoreboard again. Abe made quite a good showing, being the highest-ranked Devil player, but he wasn't in serious contention for the medal either.

If you've never seen a Brownlow ceremony it can be like watching paint dry, even if you're the most passionate football fan in existence. Players are awarded points per game and per round by the umpires, based upon their decision of who has been the best and fairest of the game. Take into account that there are eight games per round, with sixteen teams, and twenty-two rounds per season... that's a *lot* of counting you have to sit through. It's kind of like listening to a really long Bingo game. But I watched until the credits rolled and got to see Declan one last time as he solicitously helped Jess out of her seat and they walked over to Abe and Lisa. I felt one last little stab of jealousy. *Hey, they're meant to be my friends now as well!*

I shook it off.

"That's that, then," I said to Maggie. She opened her eyes and looked up at me languidly, probably thinking for the millionth time that her human was completely stupid. "Time for bed."

She followed me into the bedroom, knowing she would be able to sucker me into giving her one of the kitty treats kept on the bedside table. Of course I acquiesced and could hear her crunching it in the dark as I drifted off to sleep.

I WAS woken abruptly by someone climbing in to bed with me.

Groggily, I flailed about, on the verge of panic until I heard a familiar voice say my name.

It was Declan.

"Fuck, you scared me." I leaned over and switched on the bankers' lamp. He was sitting on what had become *his* side of my bed, still struggling to pull off the white shirt that had come with his tux. I had no idea how he'd managed to get his pants off without me hearing him.

"Sorry," he slurred.

I had given him a key ages ago, but he had never had cause to use it like this, at this hour of the morning. I wasn't used to someone letting themselves into my house when I was asleep. My heart was still pounding furiously; I could hear its thud in my ears.

"Let me help you with that," I said, and I managed to deftly pull off the shirt and the singlet beneath it in one move.

"You're good at that," he said rakishly.

"Wow, you really got into the free booze, huh?" I asked, amused as I had never really seen him this plastered before.

"It was there," he said, his eyes at half-mast. "And I was thirsty."

He fell back into bed with a heavy sigh and tried to cover himself with the doona. It twisted around his legs, and I had to get them sorted.

"I thought you were going to crash at Jess's tonight?"

"Turn off the light," he moaned. "It's too bright."

I did so, and as I settled back upon my pillow he rolled over to use me as one. His breath reeked, and I knew he would feel the pains of a major hangover in the morning.

"How did you get here?" I asked.

"Robyn drove me," he murmured. "Only too glad to get rid of me. She hates me."

"Who could hate you?" I teased. I felt Maggie jump up upon the bed and snuggle between our feet.

"Robyn. Because of my magical lesbian-curing dick."

I laughed so hard, his head almost rolled off my chest. "I don't think it's done too good a job of curing Jess so far."

"Only 'cos we haven't done it."

All I could do was laugh again. "You've got tickets on yourself."

"It cured you, didn't it?"

"Well, I'm not a lesbian, so I guess it must have."

"There you go," he said, sounding very satisfied with himself.

"I wish I was recording this," I told him. "You would be so embarrassed in the morning if you heard it."

"As long as I'm here in the morning," he yawned. "This was where I wanted to be all night, so that's why I came here."

There was a deliciously gooey feeling in my belly, damn it. "I'm flattered."

"I love you," he whispered.

I was stunned, unable to breathe or think.

"Did you hear me?" he asked, suddenly sounding not quite so drunk.

I couldn't say anything. All I could think was that this wasn't the time—as I had told Fran what seemed like *years* ago now, first declarations of love should not be spoken lightly. And definitely not while drunk. I wondered how I could say all that without hurting his feelings when I realised he had fallen asleep.

I lay there for ages, his breath warm against my chest, thinking that I had fucked up again.

CHAPTER
SEVENTEEN

IT WAS impossible to rouse Declan in the morning. He moaned incoherently as I brought in a glass of water and some painkillers and told him I was leaving for work. He pulled the pillow over his head, and I could only laugh and leave them beside him.

But I still felt guilty as I remembered his last words to me before falling asleep. I tried to think about something else, anything else, on the tram ride in to work, but it was continually nagging at me in the back of my mind. I had no idea how it was going to come up, and how Declan was going to react to my lack of response once his hangover wore off.

He and Jess had made the newspapers, of course. Their shining, smiling mugs leered at me from the paper of the guy sitting across from me. It was nice to see, however, that Lisa was voted one of the best dressed of the night.

The morning passed pretty uneventfully as I waited for Declan to call, but my direct line never rang. However, Nyssa passed through a call that made me sweat with dread.

"Simon, Jasper Brunswick on line one."

I almost fell off my chair.

"Nyssa, take a message."

"He said it's urgent."

Jasper Brunswick? *Urgent*? Oh, this couldn't be good.

"Isn't that the same jerk who used to work here before I did?" Nyssa asked, her voice extraordinarily loud through the speaker.

"One and the same," I said through gritted teeth.

"He's not trying to get a job here again, is he?"

"He'd think it was beneath him now," I told her.

"Good," Nyssa said, satisfied her job wasn't in danger. "So, shall I put him through?"

I groaned. "Fine."

There was a slight squawk through the speaker as Nyssa changed lines. "Putting you through now." Her usually charming tone to clients and sponsors was not to be heard; she obviously still saw Jasper as a potential threat.

I picked up the handset. "Simon Murray."

"Simon, Jasper Brunswick."

"So Nyssa told me. What can I do for you?" I asked, trying to affect a casual tone although I was intrigued despite myself.

"Well, Simon, it's more what I can do for you." His voice was somehow even oilier over the phone than it was in person.

"Is this about a piece on the festival again? Because I'm pretty sure your editor has already lined up an interview."

"No, Simon. In fact, this is much more of a personal matter."

My skin crawled. He surely wasn't bringing *that* up again, was he? I should have given Nyssa a timeframe in which to come in and save me. "Oh?"

"Yes. As I'm sure you're aware, my column—"

I was pretty sure that I had told him that I never read his column, and that was the truth, but of course Jasper was never one to allow the truth get in the way of his own agenda. "Uh-huh."

"No need to sound snobby, Simon. I told you, I'm calling as a friend."

I winced. "Actually, you never said *that*. And, really, we're not friends."

He sighed. "Fine. As ex-colleagues then."

"I'm more comfortable with that."

"I'd be nicer to me if I were you."

"Stop dicking around, and just tell me what you want."

He hesitated.

"Jasper—"

"My column likes to tell secrets."

"Yeah, I thought that was the point of a gossip column."

"It's much more than a gossip column, Simon."

What? Was he trying to say that it was actually biting social commentary? I let it slide. "Okay. But what's that got to do with this call?"

I could hear his pause for obvious dramatic effect. "One thing I've never stooped to doing is to out people. That's their own decision to make. And I've had quite a few people tell me recently that you're off the scene."

A small rivulet of sweat suddenly ran down my neck and through my shoulder blades. "I was never *on* the scene," I pointed out as calmly as I could.

"So you say. But these people say that the guy you're seeing, well, he's definitely not in any way *out*, and it could be quite detrimental for him to be so."

Feeling like a character in a noir movie, and just as desperate, I said hoarsely, "Is that a threat?"

"So you're not denying it?"

Fuck. If I were in a noir movie I would have been dead before the second act, I was so green at this. "You haven't given me a name to deny."

Good. Regained some ground there.

"I don't think I have to. I can hear it in your voice." Jasper sounded smug. "I have to say, you're a dark horse, Simon. I didn't think you would be able to pull someone like that."

"And as usual, the gossip you're talking about is unsubstantiated and full of crap," I said, not the finest comeback imaginable.

"Don't get so defensive. I told you, I don't out anybody."

"Then why are you calling?"

"To let you know that no secret ever remains that way. You're not as careful as you think you are." He paused so he could get me with his next comment. "And to get confirmation. Just to let you know, if it does come out, you're fair game to me. I'll publish everything I can get on you and your footballer."

"Thanks for the call," I said snidely.

"Just trying to be a friend," Jasper said, sounding hurt. And damned if I couldn't even tell if he was being honest or not anymore.

"Thanks, *friend.*" I hung up the phone.

Now I was off the call and could let the façade drop, I actually shivered. My body felt overheated, and my shirt was sticking to my back. I wanted to call Dec, but paranoia had settled in, and I was entertaining the idea that Jasper had tapped my phone to confirm who my next call would be to.

This could not be happening. And it was my fault, because I knew Jasper Brunswick. He could find entry into our lives because of me. I was suddenly scared of what Dec might think.

Nyssa stuck her head inside the door. "Did he want his old job back?"

I looked up at her. "Nyss, I'm not feeling well. Will you be okay if I go home?"

Nyssa looked at me with concern. "You're sweating."

"It must be a fever," I lied.

"I can handle things," she said.

"You're my trooper, Nyss."

I felt her eyes upon me as I grabbed my bag and coat and hurried out the door.

DECLAN looked almost as sick as I felt. But his panic had the unfortunate effects of a hangover mixed with it.

"Well?" I asked him, anxious to get an answer. What I really wanted him to tell me was, yes, I was paranoid and everything was going to be fine.

"I don't know," he said finally.

"What?" I asked, dumbstruck.

"What do you want me to say, Simon? *I don't know.*"

"You think this is my fault, don't you?"

If it were possible, he looked even more perplexed. "Did I say that?"

"Not in so many words, no."

"*You* must think it's your fault, if that's what you're getting at."

"Well, I do know the guy. Unfortunately."

"That doesn't make it your fault." He held the bridge of his nose, willing away the pain in his head.

"You say that, but do you mean it?"

Exasperated, he dropped his hand. "Are you trying to make me mad, so I *do* blame you?"

I threw my hands up in the air. "I want some kind of reaction out of you!"

"You want me to panic?"

"Something!"

He took a deep breath. "I don't want to panic. The guy never even said my name."

"He said 'footballer', you don't think that's close enough?"

Declan was silent.

"Dec...."

"He said he wasn't going to do anything about it, right?" he asked.

I nodded.

"Then there's nothing to worry about."

"But other people told him. What if *they* tell?"

"From what you've told me of this guy, his *few people* could just be one person."

"I wish I knew for sure."

Declan looked at me sadly. "I've made you so fucking paranoid, haven't I?"

"I was paranoid a long time before I met you," I told him.

He tried to laugh, but it was halfhearted. "Look, we can't go crazy. If other people know, although I really have no idea who unless there are spies on this street who have bugged this house, they haven't told anybody else."

"For all we know."

"If they told someone who wanted to out me, it would have been done by now. Unless you think they're so evil they're waiting for the perfect moment."

"I don't know what to think," I admitted.

"And when *I* said that, you got shitty."

"I'm sorry."

We sat there, just staring at each other across the table. We both felt compelled to say something, to break the silence but words were having difficulty forming naturally.

Finally, Declan said, "You didn't have to come home from work just to tell me."

"Christ, Dec, aren't you at all worried?"

"Of course I am!" he hissed, but sat back and calmed down. "There's nothing we can do."

"I just don't want you to end up blaming me."

"I won't," he replied.

I wanted to believe him. But I didn't know what I could believe at that moment. I tried to shift the atmosphere in the space between us into a lighter one. "Well, I now have the benefit of an unexpected day off."

I waggled my eyebrows, hoping to get a laugh out of him, but he just gave a tired smile.

"I told my parents I would meet them for lunch. I better get ready." He stood up, and moved around me to head to the bathroom. He rested his hand briefly on my shoulder, nothing else, before leaving the room.

I sat there and listened to the water starting to run through the pipes.

THE distance that seemed to have popped up the instant I got home only increased as he got ready to go out. He packed his bag, which meant he wasn't expecting to come back today. I didn't say anything; just accepted it. I didn't want to turn into Scarlett begging Rhett not to leave her, as it would be far too camp and melodramatic for my liking. It was far more likely he had to get away and mull over it, like he had with our awkward first date.

It didn't make me feel any happier or secure, though.

He said he'd call me that night, but he didn't. I felt miserable the next morning and called in sick to work, ignoring the sound of panic in Nyssa's voice and her reminder the festival was only a month away.

I called Roger. I don't want it to come across like I only called him because I was desperate. I missed my best friend, and I wanted to talk to him. I wanted to have all this bullshit between us cleared up, but I still had the nagging feeling he was right and what was happening with me at the moment would only prove his suspicions. And I didn't want Roger to be right because that would mean further trouble ahead for me and Declan, and probably even me and Roger again.

Roger didn't call. And I didn't hear from Declan either.

The next morning found me back at work, practically dragging my bag along the ground being Charlie Brown on suicide watch. Nyssa was relieved to see me turn up, and there was a hell of a lot of work to be done so I was easily distracted from thinking about the disaster my life seemed to be at the moment.

I could have almost cried when Fran called me.

"Hey," she said, and that one word in her usual warm manner would have made me cry if I were afraid I wouldn't stop.

"Hi," I replied. "It's good to hear your voice."

"Yours too, hon. Can you do lunch?"

Almost as if life was back to normal.

She hugged me when I entered the restaurant, and I clung to her for a little while longer than I normally would have. She was nice enough not to say anything about it, and we sat down.

"I'm sorry I haven't been in contact," she said. "But, you know—"

"Nothing for you to be sorry about. I guess it was easier to let things slide for a while."

"It wasn't easy," she said, and the tone in her voice made me back up.

"You know what I meant."

She nodded. "When you were being the stubborn shit, it was easy to blame you for the awkwardness between us. Now Roger's being the stubborn shit, it's easy to blame him."

Oh. "You heard my message, then?"

"Of course I did."

I wanted to ask her so much, but I didn't want to put her in the middle again. "I might go for a calzone."

"You always go for the calzone."

"Not always."

She snorted, laid aside her menu, and changed tracks. "You can ask me."

"What?"

She shook her head. "Don't play dumb, although you try to do it so well. You can ask me about Roger."

I relented. "What did he do when he heard the message?"

Fran sighed and began pouring water while we waited for our other drinks to arrive. "At first he was happy, really relieved you had finally come round. Then he had time to think about it and got shitty it took so long."

"Oh."

"Now he's decided to play the arsehole and avoid *you*. Even though he still talks about you incessantly and worries about you. You should have heard him the night of the Brownlow. *Oh, I hope Simon's okay. He's probably not dealing with it too well.*"

I smiled faintly. Fran could always do a good Roger impression, greatly exaggerated of course. "I tried calling you that day."

She sipped at her water, trying to hide a slightly guilty expression. "I know. I ignored it."

"I thought so."

"Well, I was trying to be the good wife! But I had to be the bad friend to do it."

"I understand."

"Don't try to sound too magnanimous there, Simon. A lot of this is your fault."

"I know." I wasn't trying to rile her up; I was just admitting the truth. It didn't stop her from looking at me suspiciously, though.

"How were you that night?"

"Better than I thought I would be, surprisingly enough."

"Really?"

"Yeah, but maybe that's all because of context."

"What context?"

I filled her in on the phone call with Jasper, and how I hadn't heard from Dec since. Fran grasped my hand sympathetically, only dropping it when the food arrived and she could no longer have her arm across the table.

"No wonder you look so frigging miserable," she murmured. "I'm sorry, Simon."

"It's not your fault."

"I know, but it's what a friend's supposed to say."

I nodded.

"I think Dec has the right idea, but, I mean, Jasper Brunswick could just be trying to get info out of you. He doesn't know for sure."

"He probably does now."

"But he told you he wouldn't print it."

"Can I trust him?"

Fran shrugged. "I wish I knew. When does the *Reach Out* come out, pardon the pun?"

"Every Thursday."

"I guess you'll find out tomorrow. Maybe that's why Declan's in hiding. He's just sweating it out."

"I wish he would speak to me. This is the second time he's done it, just run off and hid. I guess it's his thing."

"Here's a thought: have you called him?"

I squirmed in my seat under her unflinching expression. "No."

Fran groaned, her head in her hands. "What the hell are we going to do with you?"

"I don't want to look like I'm pushing him. He's gone into hiding for a reason. Maybe he needs some alone time without me bothering him. Maybe it's the way he copes."

"And maybe he wants you to run after him a little. So he knows you give a shit."

"I *do* give a shit. He knows that."

Fran looked like she was going to start beating her head against the table. "Why do I try to give you advice? You never bloody listen!"

"Fran—"

"No, seriously! I tell you to call Roger before it blows up into something bigger, and you let it go to the point where he's too upset with you now *you* can be bothered. *And* you're going to do the same thing with Declan! You're a fucking idiot."

Wow, that was harsh. But maybe true.

Who am I kidding? She was right. If Fran's eyes were lasers, I would have been a smoking pile of ash by now.

"Well?" she demanded.

"I promise you, I'll call him. And I won't give up on Roger. I'll call him again."

She sighed with relief. "Thank you! Now, do you want to share tiramisu after we eat?"

I did.

WITH the righteous fire of Fran's wrath burning within me, I sent Nyssa to lunch once I got back. Alone in the office, I felt some of that fire leave me, but I knew I had to pick up the phone; maybe not in the service of earning my paycheck, but at least to try and salvage my personal life on two fronts.

I called Roger first. His mobile went to message-bank, which wasn't a surprise. He was usually hard to get at work anyway. I left a message saying I hoped we could catch up soon.

The ball was in his court again. I wondered what the shelf life of payback was.

When I called Dec he answered almost immediately.

"Hi," he said. "I'm glad you called. Hang on a minute."

I could hear him moving, and the unmistakable sound of a door shutting.

"Hey, I'm back."

"Where are you?"

"Still at my folks'."

"Oh."

"How are you?"

"Fine," I said. "You?"

Oh yeah, this was going great.

"Better."

"Better as in you weren't fine?"

"I had a minor panic attack, yeah," he admitted.

"Well, why didn't you call me?"

"I knew you were already stressed enough."

"To be honest, you stressed me out even more by disappearing and not talking to me," I said in a measured tone.

He sighed. "I know. I'm sorry."

Silence fell.

"Am I going to see you before you go away?" I asked.

"Of course you are, don't be stupid."

He and the rest of the Devils would be leaving the Monday after the Grand Final to go on their end-of-season trip to New Zealand. It was a tradition that every club followed, and more party-hard destinations such as Las Vegas were now frowned upon after a few cases of questionable behaviours and stomach pumpings hit the press.

"Well, I didn't know what to think when I didn't hear from you."

"I said I was sorry, Simon." He sounded tired.

"Look, I didn't call you to berate you. I just wanted to know you were okay."

"I'm fine."

"And I wanted to know if *we* were okay."

"We are."

"Good. I'll let you go then."

"Hey, wait a minute."

"What?"

"We're okay."

"You said that already."

"I wanted to repeat it."

"I—"

"Shit, someone's coming. I've gotta go. Call you later."

The line disconnected, and I stared at my phone, willing him back onto it. I hung up just as I heard Nyssa coming back into the office and went to meet her and make a much-needed cup of coffee.

CHAPTER
EIGHTEEN

DECLAN sent me a text message later on that said

One more night here. I'll see you tomorrow if that's okay with you.

His choice of words troubled me. Since when did he feel he had to ask permission to see me? I had a feeling this fallout from Jasper Brunswick's phone call would be with us for a while.

Roger didn't call at all. I wasn't expecting him to, really. I wondered if he would even tell Fran I had attempted contact again, but knew that with Roger being Roger he wouldn't be able to keep it to himself. So I could at least give myself the satisfaction his time in the dog house would probably be lengthened.

Declan's car was already in the driveway when I got home from work the next night. It was nice to see the lights on in my house as I trudged through the growing darkness, and even nicer to think that there was somebody in there waiting for me.

Especially when they've prepared food for you. I could smell the garlic before I even stepped in the door.

"Hey!" Declan greeted me as I entered and peered around the corner of the kitchen.

"Hey yourself."

He jogged over to greet me, surprising me with a bear hug and a passionate kiss. "Hope you don't mind that I cooked for you."

"Are you kidding?" I asked, pleased that he seemed to be more like his old self. "I never turn down a free meal."

"Don't know how *free* it is, most of the stuff came from your cupboard."

"It's the thought that counts."

He looked at me earnestly. "It's part of my apology for being a jerk the past few days."

"That was you being a jerk? You need to step up your game, man," I said with far more joviality than I had felt within that specified timeframe.

"I mean it."

"I know." I rested my chin on his shoulder. "You *did* make me worry."

His hand rested upon my back as if he were trying to settle me after the fact. "We can take on Jasper Brunswick," he laughed softly.

"Jesus, a four-year-old could take on Jasper Brunswick," I said, rolling my eyes. I sniffed the air. "So what did you make me?"

He pulled back to look at my reaction. "Comfort food of the highest order. Macaroni cheese and mashed potato."

"Hopefully neither of those come from a packet?" I asked, as they probably would have if I had been cooking home alone.

He looked offended. "The macaroni cheese is Fran's recipe." He pulled me towards the stove, and it took a couple of seconds for it to dawn on me.

"Hold on, Fran's recipe?"

"Yeah, she gave it to me."

"When were you speaking to Fran?"

Declan looked at me quizzically. "I've *always* been speaking to Fran."

I wasn't sure whether I should be happy about them getting along or suspicious about how that reflected upon me when my own dealings with my friends had been so fractious lately.

Distracted momentarily by checking the contents of the oven, Declan turned back to me, caught sight of the expression on my face, and sighed. "Okay, it's time to come clean."

Oh, *here* it comes. "What?" I asked warily.

"I've also spoken to Roger."

I felt like I needed to sit down; instead I turned around and reached for a beer from the fridge. "Right. Why?"

"He wanted to apologise to me himself for what happened at dinner that night," he replied. "Got one of those for me?"

I took a swig to calm my nerves and grabbed one for him. "When?"

"A couple of weeks ago."

"And you're only telling me this now?"

"I figured it would piss you off." He studied me carefully, while twisting his beer open. "And I guess I was right."

"You should have told me," I said.

"Yeah, obviously."

"But I'm glad he had the balls to tell you that himself, at least."

"Well, he's had the balls to tell you too."

"Don't start on that again."

He held up his hands in mock surrender. "Okay. Tonight's about us."

"That sounds better."

"But just let me say one thing," he murmured quickly. "Keep trying with him. Even if he's being the stubborn one now. Don't you think, especially in light of this Jasper Brunswick crap, we need our friends? Especially those in the know?"

He was wearing me down. And holding the Jasper Brunswick card over me was low, but it worked.

"You could be right," I conceded begrudgingly.

He tapped his bottle against mine. "I love it when you say that."

"Don't get used to it." It was an empty threat, and we both knew it.

"You know, the phone's just over there, while I finish up here—"

"Let a man eat first," I protested.

"You always have an excuse."

I snuck up on him and hugged him from behind. His back was warm and broad, and I snuggled into it unabashedly. "*This* is a pretty good one."

"Yeah," he chuckled. "It's not bad."

"I HAVE something else to tell you," Declan declared while we were eating.

"Good something else, or bad something else?" I asked cautiously.

He scratched his chin mockingly, his eyes glinting. "You'll probably think it's both."

I laid down my fork and put up my fists in a defensive stance. "Okay, tell me."

He laughed, reached over, and pushed my hands down. "I made an offer on an apartment yesterday."

I had just taken a sip of wine and had to swallow the mouthful with some difficulty. "Details?"

"It's in the Docklands, great view of the water, security entrance—"

I didn't want to do the vulgar thing, but I had to ask. "How much?"

He named a figure which would have taken me over ten years to earn. In fact, longer. I gulped more wine at just the thought of that. "What do you think?" he asked.

"Uh, wow."

"I don't think 'wow' is a proper reaction."

"Well, I'm happy if you're happy."

"Also not a reaction," he pointed out. I could tell he was starting to get a little pissed off.

"No, really. I mean, it's *your* apartment, Dec. And if it means you have a place to anchor you in Melbourne a little more, then I'm over the fucking moon about it."

"Yeah?"

"Yeah!"

"Then you'd be happy to know they accepted the offer?"

Okay, there was no way I could finish this wine just yet without winding up with it spilled embarrassingly all over me or the table, so I put the glass down. "They did?"

"Yep." He looked very pleased with himself.

I leaned across and kissed him. "Congratulations."

"Thanks."

"When do I get to see it?"

"Soon, hopefully. I can show you the pictures and everything after dinner."

"You are such a real estate mogul," I teased. "You'll have the orange section of the board bought out in no time."

"I hope you like it," Dec said. "I mean, I hope you'll be spending a lot of time there."

"I guess my humble home on Old Kent Road fades in comparison, huh?"

He gave me a little wink. "Not at all."

DECLAN jumped back into bed, brandishing a manila folder, and immediately spooned into me again. "I paid for the quickest settlement offer. I should be able to get the keys in forty days."

"Wow, that's fast." Everything still seemed pretty surreal to me. I couldn't believe in little over a month Dec would have a permanent space here, even though he would still be spending the majority of his time in Hobart. I also had to admit, despite what I said about it being an anchor to keep him in Melbourne, I was disappointed as it meant my house wouldn't be the lure for him that it used to be.

He started laying photos out on my chest, proudly showing them off as if they were of his kids. "Look at that view."

"Doesn't have the mountains like your place in Hobart does, but it's still pretty spectacular."

"It looks even better in person."

"Can't wait to see it."

"Plus there's also three restaurants on the ground floor, a minisupermarket, and a residents-only gym."

"There's a gym?" I asked in awe, even though it would most likely be the last place *I* would frequent.

"Yeah, with a pool and a steam room."

"A steam room, huh?"

"Get your mind out of the gutter," he chuckled.

Porny fantasies and the reluctance to show an interest in something so obscenely bourgeois aside, the concept of this apartment was beginning to grow on me.

Declan gathered up the photos, tossed the folder aside, and took up one of his favourite positions, which was using me as a pillow. My arm began falling asleep immediately, but I wouldn't dream of moving it.

"I also bought an extra car space next to my own, for any, uh, *visitors* I might have," he said.

"Your parents?" I asked, playing dumb.

He reached up and flicked me across the temple. "Yes. They're coming for really long visits."

I remember reading once in an online article about space-starved New York City that such an act like the one Dec had just made was tantamount to buying an engagement ring. And okay, so we were in Melbourne, but it still was a nice feeling.

"I even made sure there wasn't a no-pet policy in case any visitor who wanted to stay awhile had to bring their feline companion along."

Holy shit, this *was* like an engagement. I kissed the top of his head. "You thought of everything."

"I'm going for another viewing on Saturday. Would you like to come?"

"Sure. But aren't you going to the Grand Final?"

"I'm going to go to the apartment beforehand. Abe and Lisa are probably also going to come, and they want to see you."

It burned slightly that they would all be going off to the final together, and I would have to trudge off home. Dec and I had avoided talking about it, a kind of unspoken agreement that we both knew it was impossible for me to go in any guise with him as he would be going with the rest of his team and their girlfriends.

But he knew I was thinking about it, because he murmured sleepily, "Call Roger."

That oft-repeated mantra continued to echo in my head as I closed my eyes.

I CALLED Roger the next day and left a message. Would you be surprised he didn't call back?

I drove by their house the next night. Their lights were on, and I could see shadows moving behind the curtains. He and Fran were unaware that there was a stalker in their midst. A stalker who was too shit-scared to leave his car and actually confront his demons by knocking on their front door and demanding his oldest and best friend speak to him; a stalker who rather feebly just put the car back into gear and drove away.

Nyssa was *busy* on Friday afternoon. She was never too *busy* on Bog-off-to-the-Pub Fridays, and I knew she was still meeting Fran and Roger at the Napier, but had to fob me off so I wouldn't try to come. I thought about firing her for not showing loyalty to her superior, but decided I would need evidence first. And I really couldn't be bothered stopping off at the pub on my way home and peering pathetically through the coloured windows to try to make out the vaguely discernible shadow puppets of my friends.

Dec didn't stay over Friday as he was drinking with the boys, and the Grand Final traditional breakfast was held the next morning. But on Saturday I caught the tram into the city and then hopped off at Southern Cross Station to walk across the bridge into the Docklands.

It seemed like the last time I was here, the Docklands was still a black hole, devoid of life. Now it was a bustling minimetropolis, and I couldn't help but wonder about Declan's privacy issues. It seemed there were far more people about here than there were on my quiet street. Maybe it was because there was a sense of anonymity in crowds, and that's where he felt safest. But I could only imagine that it would get worse here at night when the restaurants and bars started getting more business, although he would have the benefit of undercover private parking in his building and a discreet entrance.

He was waiting for me where he said he would be, just down from the lobby doors, sitting on a sandstone wall and lazily swinging his legs. He was wearing a closefitting cap and sunglasses that managed to obscure most of his facial features, along with the casual disguise of cargo pants and a plain long-sleeved top. He jumped off the wall when he saw me, and we exchanged greetings with a carefully maintained distance between us.

"Hey," he said.

"Hey," I replied. I resisted adding *bro* to maintain the façade of our rampant heterosexuality.

"You ready to see it?"

"Sure."

Crap, it was killing me. Let me have some whine with my cheese, but a so-called normal couple would have been able to kiss and hug each other instead of this coded bullshit we had to adopt. As he swiped us through the lobby with a security card, I wondered whether even without the secrecy built around our relationship, if we would feel comfortable with such a public display of affection. When it came down to it, I honestly didn't think I would be. And I wasn't sure if it was fear or just the fact that I was reserved to begin with.

Okay, fear. I knew a lot of it was fear. But I hated admitting it, even to myself.

Could someone who was gay suffer from their own form of homophobia? Or was it merely common sense and practicality combined with a desire for self-defence and protection?

All I knew was that whenever I met up with Dec my natural response was to want him in my arms, and it was too early in the morning for me to be having a philosophical debate with myself.

"You're being very quiet," Declan observed as we waited for the elevator.

Obviously he couldn't hear the voices in my head, which was a relief. "Enjoy it while you can," I said wryly.

"I like your babbling. I'm used to it. It scares me when I'm with you, and I suddenly realise I can hear something else in the silence."

I smiled at him. "Arsehole."

The elevator sounded its arrival. The doors slid open, and we stepped within. Back within our own personal bubble, Declan gently took my face in his hands and kissed me.

Sense and practicality quickly left me, and I responded quite happily in return, but I didn't get so lost that when the elevator began slowing down, I forgot to pull away.

"You better hope there are no cameras in here."

"Only in the lobby," he responded.

"You *do* think of everything," I said in awe.

"Believe me, the money I'm forking out to live here, you get to ask these questions."

"I wonder if you have any famous neighbours."

"I didn't ask."

"Like, imagine if there's a knock at your door one day, and it's Cate Blanchett asking for a cup of sugar."

The elevator doors opened, and he led me down the hall. "Doesn't she live in Sydney?"

"You own property in two states, why wouldn't she?"

"I promise, if Cate wants a cup of sugar I'll get her autograph for you."

"Bugger that, I want her reenacting scenes from *Elizabeth* in your loungeroom."

Dec laughed, and we came to an abrupt stop at the end of the hall. A large window looked out onto the water. This place was so swanky, even the halls had views.

Unlocking the door, Declan posed like a model on some game show. "Ta da!"

I walked through, and it was like I was hanging over the ocean. As his apartment was on the corner of the building, his windows took up half the walls of his lounge and kitchen area. "Holy shit," I breathed.

"No view of Mount Wellington, but it's pretty fucking good," Dec said.

"You're not kidding," I murmured. "Wow."

"So you approve?"

Suddenly I was ready to forget my ingrained sense of loyalty to the proletariat and sign my soul away. "Fuck yes."

I walked over to the window and leaned against it. I could almost believe I was suspended in air. The wind carried the salt off the waves, and I could smell it even through the glass. Declan came up behind me; I could see his reflection. I turned, and he waved the keys at me.

"Come out onto the balcony."

I followed him. We leaned against the railing, the water far below us. The wind was fresh and strong. I closed my eyes and breathed it in.

"I'll miss you while I'm gone," Declan said suddenly.

I opened my eyes and looked at him. "I'll miss you too."

"I feel pretty shitty, running off to the Grand Final today, and then leaving tomorrow. This is the last time I'll see you for a couple of weeks."

"Hey," I said reassuringly, "it's the way it is. It's cool." I was just glad he was saying it, because I knew I never could have brought it up out of fear I would sound whingey and clingy.

"Really?"

"Yes. Really."

"It'll be better when I get back. Off season, and I'll have more time here."

"Plus, you'll be incapacitated, and you won't be able to run," I said, in reference to his operation. "That helps."

He laughed. "Bastard."

"I look forward to making you chicken noodle soup and mopping your fevered brow."

"You would make me soup?"

I winced. "From a packet, probably."

"Hey, if I'm getting operated on, I want the real thing."

"What about if I get Fran to make it and then pretend it was me?"

"The way you're going, I seriously doubt you'll be speaking to Roger by then."

"Hey!" I protested. "I'm talking to Fran!"

"Yeah? Well, I want soup made from scratch. By you."

Time to change the subject while I still was able. "I could just imagine lying out here all day and reading. Why would you ever want to go inside?"

Declan shook his head, knowing what I was transparently up to, but letting me get away with it for the moment. "Because there isn't enough room for a bed?"

"There is for a banana lounge."

"I'll have to invest in one then."

"Make sure it's big enough for two," I said with a glint in my eye.

He looked at me, and the air between us was growing serious again. I could tell he wanted to say something, but he was holding it back. I wasn't sure if it was the moment, but I *wanted* to say it, what I had wanted to tell him ever since the moment I had procrastinated over a couple of weeks ago.

"Dec—"

We were saved—or cruelly interrupted—by the security buzzer as it sounded within the apartment. "That must be Abe and Lisa," he said, giving my arm a quick squeeze before going to let them in.

For fuck's sake. Would I ever be able to get it together?

I wasn't left pondering this rhetorical question very long as Abe and Lisa made it up in record time. We exchanged greetings; Abe shook my hand and gave a manly hug and back slap to Declan, while Lisa kissed us both.

"This place is amazing," Abe said. "Two waterfront apartments, Dec. Good to know where *your* salary is going."

"This puts my little place in St Kilda to shame," Lisa agreed.

"I like your place in St Kilda," Declan told her. "It's close to the beach and the Espy, and that's all you want."

She shrugged affably. "Not if you like your view to be of the next complex's wall."

"Don't worry, baby," Abe said. "When I get traded, we'll buy a place like this."

"You want to get traded as well?" I asked.

Abe nodded. "Melbourne's home."

"I bet you the Devils will hate to lose both of you."

"They won't have any choice when contracts are up," Lisa said, sounding less than sympathetic towards the club.

"Maybe we should buy in here so Dec can never escape us," Abe said, with a devilish glint in his eye.

"Fuck no, I'm meant to have classy neighbours," Dec laughed. "I've heard Cate Blanchett is buying in."

Abe feigned a punch to him, and Dec sidestepped it gracefully.

"I only meant Abe, of course," Dec told Lisa. "I know *you're* classy."

"Too bloody right," Lisa replied. "And just to show how classy I am…." She began burrowing into the large tote bag she was carrying and produced a Frij bag.

Abe rolled his eyes at Declan, and they both laughed with the easy camaraderie of friendship that gave me a pang for Roger again. Lisa produced four plastic cups and a cheap bottle of champagne that was still chilled. "Let's drink to your new abode!"

Declan did the honours; the pop of the cork sounded like a gunshot in the empty apartment and reverberated around the stark walls. The contents of the bottle were shared amongst the four large cups, and we toasted the apartment and drank, all making faces at the cheap taste.

Abe looked at his watch and said regretfully, "We better get going."

He and Lisa began talking amongst themselves, pointedly looking in the other direction to give Declan and I some privacy. Dec pulled me aside into the hall.

"I hate rushed good-byes," he said. "And I hate having to say it here like this, instead of when we actually should."

I nodded. There was nothing more I could add to that. I recalled what I had been about to say on the balcony and wished I could say it now, but the presence of Abe and Lisa stopped me. It shouldn't have, but it wasn't an ideal moment.

"I really like the apartment," I said lamely.

He leaned in and kissed me. I hugged him close and whispered, "Hurry back."

Dec smiled at me. "I will."

He pulled away, and all I wanted to do was pull him back.

Declan clapped his hands together. "Let's go and see how real footballers make it to a grand final."

Abe laughed, and Lisa shook her head, rolling her eyes at me for my benefit.

We locked the apartment behind us and walked through the Docklands precinct.

Declan was starting to get really excited over the thought of living here, although I think it was the thrill of having a home in Melbourne again that was more appealing to him.

We parted ways at the junction of the station and Collins Street. Abe and Declan thought they would be better off walking down to the MCG and remaining barely unrecognisable rather than risk jumping on a tram and being hemmed in by other AFL supporters and detractors. Lisa baulked at the idea and insisted that they would have to piggyback her most of the way.

"Don't let the hobbits kidnap him in New Zealand," I told Abe.

"I won't." He grinned, bumping fists with me by way of farewell.

Lisa grabbed me and hugged me. I held onto her for a little longer than I would have normally, pretending it was Declan's hug by proxy. "We'll catch up soon, okay?"

"Sure."

Declan and I awkwardly bumped fists, in the same fashion I had with Abe.

"Take care," I said.

"Call—"

"Roger. Yes, I know, Oprah."

He winced. "You could at least call me Dr. Phil so I feel secure about my masculinity."

Abe guffawed, and Lisa punched him on the shoulder lightly.

"If you're going by Dr. Phil to prove your masculinity, I would still stick with Oprah if I were you," I scoffed.

"Bye, Simon."

I waved them off and watched them turn and leave, disappearing down Collins on their way to cut across to the G at Elizabeth. My tram came quickly, and as it rattled down the middle of the street I craned my neck to catch sight of them once more. The three of them waved at me through the window, looking comfortable together, like Athos, Porthos, and Aramis. I waved back and remembered in the story that there were eventually four musketeers.

I hoped that would be the same with us one day.

WHEN I got home, I checked my answering machine immediately in the hope that Roger had left a message.

He hadn't.

Before I could lose my nerve, I picked up the phone and called his number.

The answering machine swung into action. Again. "You've reached Roger and Fran. We can't take your call, so let us know who you are."

He *had* to be home. It was half an hour to the Grand Final, for Christ's sake!

Unless... he had *gone out* for the final. It was inconceivable, but it could be possible. Or maybe he and Fran were holding a huge barbecue with all of their new friends...

"Uh, hi," I said, my voice barely above a whisper. "It's me. Again. Look, I know when I was pissed with you, you knew that it wouldn't be forever. Just as I know now, when you're pissed with me, that it's not going to be forever. So I hope it's sooner rather than later that we do the inevitable and talk. See ya."

I think that is what's called *laying it all out on the line.*

This would be the first time since I was twelve years old that I would be watching the final without Roger. I was pretty sure the fact wouldn't be lost on him either, and I guess I was hoping for a last-minute miracle, like one from a really bad Christmas telemovie where everything comes all right in the end.

I was still thinking that during the pregame entertainment, and into the first quarter.

At halftime I was losing hope. The beers were going down smoothly though, and my lunch of a large packet of cheese and onion chips was more than satisfying. I caught one brief glimpse of Declan on the telly, sitting in one of the VIP boxes with the rest of his team as they watched the game unfold below.

I fell asleep before the end of the game and was awakened by the phone ringing.

Hoping it was either Dec or Roger, I stumbled over and answered it, trying to sound like I wasn't recently brought back from the dead.

"'ello?"

"Hey, mate! How are you? Did you watch the game?"

The voice sounded familiar, but I couldn't quite place it. "'o's this?"

"Very funny. Are you drunk?"

It clicked into place. "Tim?"

You have to understand my surprise here. Tim hardly ever called me of his own volition. The only way I could have been *more* surprised was if it had been my father.

"Of course it's bloody Tim!"

"Uh, how are you?" I asked politely.

"Good, good. That's why I'm calling, actually."

"Oh?" Because he was good?

"Yeah. Guess what?"

This was Tim, my guess could be anything. "You need bail?"

He laughed. "Yeah, right. No, I was ringing up to tell you that Gabby and I just got engaged."

If I didn't have such a good grip on the phone I would have dropped it. "What?"

"Yeah, I proposed to her after the final."

"Did she say yes?" I asked, dumbfounded.

"Of course she did, arsewipe. Or else I wouldn't be ringing you up to say we're engaged, would I?"

"Oh, of course. Well… congratulations."

"Thanks, bro. Who would have thought I would have gotten married before you?" He paused and chuckled. "Well, of course, you can't."

"Thanks for reminding me," I said dryly.

"You would also have to be seeing someone first."

All I could think was *I hope I'm not best man.*

He didn't make the offer, and I was relieved. "How did Mum and Dad react?"

"Way more excited than you."

I knew I better muster up some energy. "No, really, Tim, I'm very happy for you. Have you set a date yet?"

"We're giving ourselves a year."

"That's probably sensible. You know, giving yourself enough time to plan and save, and all."

"Yeah. I mean, I wanted January, but Gabby insisted on a year."

"You were ready to get married that soon?" I wondered what it was about Gabby that she managed to become the Annette Bening to his Warren Beatty. But then, people might think that about Simon Murray when it came to trying to find a reason for Declan liking me.

Tim laughed good-naturedly. "When you know, you know."

I think it was the only time I have ever heard my brother say something unrelated to football I could actually agree with, except I couldn't tell him that. It was his moment, anyway; I was happy for him to have it.

I wanted to ring up Roger so I could share the news and the *what the fuck?* reaction. Declan wouldn't be able to understand the bizarreness of this new development in my family history, as he wasn't a part of it. But in the end I thought I had harassed the Daltons' machine enough this weekend.

My mother called about ten minutes after Tim got off the phone, and she sounded drunk with happiness at the prospect one of her sons was getting hitched. Especially as this had the universal meaning to mothers everywhere of the promise of grandchildren to follow.

"There's just one thing I'm not happy about," she said.

That's another thing about mothers. There's *always* something they're not happy about. "That your favourite son is being taken away from you?"

"No, not that," she said haughtily. And then added as an afterthought, "and I don't have a favourite."

"What, then?"

"Well, he didn't ask you to be his best man."

"Why should he?"

"Because you're his brother."

"But we barely associate with each other. His best man should be one of his bogan best friends."

Mum sighed. "It's *tradition*, Simon."

"Whose tradition?" I asked. "And it's his wedding. He can do what he wants."

"But—"

"Seriously, Mum. If he's not fussed, and I'm not fussed, why are you?"

"Because people will think it's odd you're not—"

"*That's* what you're worried about?"

"I just also want my two sons to be brothers to each other occasionally."

"That's not going to happen if I'm forced to arrange his buck's night."

I could tell Mum was getting agitated. "Simon—"

"Let it go, Mum. Just be glad it's happening for one of your sons. Don't worry about the minor details."

She wasn't happy when she got off the phone, and I knew it probably wouldn't be the last time I heard about this issue. The engagement ring hadn't even been placed on Gabby's finger yet, and somehow I was already being sucked into the drama.

THE sound of a message coming through on my mobile woke me the next morning.

I'll call you when I get to the land of the long white cloud.

I smiled and stretched out with a mighty yawn. Rather Declan shooting the rapids and bungee jumping in New Zealand than me. Well, he probably wouldn't be bungee jumping, the bosses wouldn't want him doing anything that could jar his knee. Besides, they would probably be touring the pubs more than anything else.

My Sunday passed uneventfully, reading the papers and doing some planning for the festival, which involved a lot of talking on the phone with Nyssa. I kept listening out for the beeping of call waiting, expecting Declan and hoping for Roger, but we remained undisturbed.

While I was making cheese on toast for dinner, the phone finally rang. I picked up, nursing a finger I had burned on the grill. "Hello?"

There was the sound of an intake of breath, and then Declan said, "Simon?"

"Hey, you arrived safely then?"

He took a deep, shaky breath.

"Dec? What's wrong?"

"I'm still in Melbourne."

"Why?" Worry began to build in me. He didn't sound like himself at all, like he was trying to hold it together but was teetering on the brink of total meltdown.

"I'm at St. Vincent's."

"What happened? Are you okay?"

"Yeah, I'm fine…." He broke off, and sniffed.

"Dec—"

"Can you come here?" he asked, his voice shaky. "My dad's had a heart attack."

CHAPTER NINETEEN

I FOUND Declan in the garden in the middle of the St Vincent's Hospital complex. He was in a secluded corner, mostly hidden away by hedges and large trees, sitting on a wooden bench and staring dully ahead of him.

I wanted to hold him, but we weren't in a private enough space. Declan put an end to any internal rationalisations I was having though as he saw me and jumped up, pulling me into him. I wrapped my arms around him, and he burrowed his head into my shoulder. I could feel him shake slightly as he tried to control his breathing, but the tears took over and all I could do was stand there and let him cry. When he finally calmed a little, I manoeuvred him over to the bench and sat beside him.

"Are you okay?" I asked stupidly.

He tried to smile at me, but failed. "Better now you're here."

"Is there an update on your dad?"

"He's still in surgery."

"Christ, Dec, what happened?"

He took a deep shaky breath. "I was at the airport, waiting for the rest of the team to arrive when my sister called me. I jumped into a taxi and got here as the ambulance was bringing him in. Apparently he just keeled over at home, right in the hallway—"

He broke off and wiped his hand across his eyes.

I looked around to see if there was anybody in the vicinity, then inwardly berated myself for doing so. If a guy couldn't comfort another visibly distressed guy in the grounds of a hospital, then when would it be okay? I put my arm around his shoulders, and he leaned in to me.

"I'm so pissed at myself," he said suddenly.

"Why?"

"Because I was up there with my family, and we're all stressed and crying, and whenever I managed to stop thinking about Dad for one second, all I wanted was to see you."

"You can't be pissed off with yourself for that," I told him.

"Why not? I should be thinking of my dad," he argued.

"Because we're human. And when we're upset we want comforting. So we turn to the person we want for that comfort."

He didn't answer.

"Are they all still upstairs?"

"Yeah, my mum told me to go and get some air and walk it off. I think I was driving her crazy."

"Do you want to go back up there?"

He looked at me. "But I just dragged you all the way out here—"

"Like I care. And like I wouldn't want to be here to help you." I rubbed his arm in what I hoped was a comforting gesture. "Besides, I'll stay here. And if you need to, you can come down again and talk to me."

"What, you'll stay out here?"

"All night, if I have to," I replied honestly. I would have done anything to help him feel the least bit better; besides, he called *me* to come to him, not Abe, not Lisa.

"And you wonder why I—" He stopped and looked away.

"What?"

He changed track awkwardly. "One other thing I was thinking about when I should have been thinking about my father… I thought, what if that had been me in his place? All I would want is you to be there, but you wouldn't be, because my family doesn't even know about you."

"It's okay."

"No, it's not. And that's not fair, Simon. It's not fair to you or to me."

A tiny rivulet of sweat caused by fear ran down my neck. This was sounding dangerously close to a breakup speech. "You already have enough on your mind, Dec. Don't start worrying about stuff that hasn't even happened."

"I bet my father didn't think his Sunday afternoon included a heart attack," Declan said bitterly.

"Probably not. But still—"

"I'm in hospital *next month*, Simon. If we go on like this, the best you can probably do is come in as a 'friend' of Abe and Lisa's without incurring too many questions from my family. That's not good enough."

"And we'll worry about that when the time comes. You have to concentrate on your dad—"

He cut me off by kissing me, hungrily and desperately. His breathing was laboured, and his cheek was wet against mine. His lips stopped working and rested upon my own, but he remained locked in position, not wanting to let go. I traced along his jaw with the edge of my knuckle, gently, not shying away from his intense stare.

And even though it was probably the worst moment to do so, the words came rushing out of me which should have weeks ago, because I knew how fucking *true* they were. "I love you."

He pulled back, his eyes wide. "What?"

"I know this isn't the time to say it—" I started feebly.

"Say it again."

I looked at him steadily, without hesitation. "I love you."

Declan laughed and, if I was reading him right, looked relieved. "You don't know how many times I've been hoping to hear you say that."

I couldn't believe it had been so difficult to say, but now all I wanted was to hear it from him.

He didn't keep me in suspense. "I love you too. But you already knew that."

"It's not that I didn't back then, it was just—"

He kissed me. "I know."

"You should really go up and check on your family," I said, although there was a selfish part of me that wanted to keep him down here after such a huge moment between us.

"Yeah, I should." He kissed me again and then stood. "I hate to send you away, but go home."

"I want to be here for you," I told him.

"Thank you. But you've already done it, more than you think."

Looking at how much calmer he appeared now than he had five minutes ago, I had to accept that. "You'll call, right?"

He nodded. We kissed once more, and I hated letting him go.

I watched him walk away with his hands jammed in his pockets. I became aware that our little corner of the garden was not as concealed as I had first thought, but the space was empty and night had fallen while we were talking. I stared at the tall building above me; all the lighted windows of rooms in which miracles and tragedies were currently taking place, and hoped that for Declan's father, it would be the former.

I'm not sure how long I sat there, but a teenager walking past me jolted me out of my daydream. He scowled at me, and I scowled back, wondering what his problem was; but inwardly berated myself because he probably had his own drama to deal with in being here. I reluctantly stood, and headed for the car park.

BACK home I was restless and anxious, wondering how Declan, his father, and his family were. It felt strange to have so much emotion invested in a man who didn't even know I existed, and although I knew it was because my ties were to Declan's well-being more than anything else, I still hoped they were all coping.

I ended up falling asleep on the couch and was woken by a text message coming through.

Dad conscious. Still waiting to hear from doctors.

That was good, at least. I sent back a quick reply and set my mobile's alarm to wake me in the morning. I couldn't be bothered getting up and going to bed.

When the alarm started sounding, I got up as if in a daze, fed Maggie, had a shower, and stumbled out the door. I tried to read the paper on the tram but couldn't concentrate. Just as I made it through the doors at work a new message came in from Declan.

Didn't want to wake you. Dad is pretty out of it, but docs say more of a warning than anything else. Keeping him in for obs for a few days. Staying at mum's as she needs us, but will call you.

So, what a difference a night makes. Declan had thought his world was crashing around him only twelve hours ago, and now things were looking up again. Despite sleeping badly, I also felt reenergised and surprised Nyssa with a cheerfulness that was hardly ever my habit on a Monday morning.

It wasn't to last.

At about two in the afternoon, Nyssa came into the office with a bewildered expression. She had the PM edition of the *Herald Sun* in her hand.

"What's up?" I asked.

"I think the secret you've been keeping has just come out," she murmured. "No pun intended."

She laid the newspaper before me, and I felt my stomach drop when I saw the headline.

AFL STAR IN SECRET GAY SHOCKER!

And there, plastered to the left of the sea of print was a box in which a series of photos of Declan and I in the gardens of St. Vincent's Hospital appeared. They hadn't left anything to the imagination—one of us hugging, one of us kissing, and finally one of me sitting on the bench alone.

"So what's the story?" Nyssa asked.

I couldn't move; I was rooted to the spot with a sense of dread. "Looks like they've already got it."

HALFTIME

From the Herald Sun, 1 October

AFL STAR IN SECRET GAY SHOCKER!
By Peter Van Niuewen

These exclusive photos, given to the *Herald Sun* by a sharp-eyed member of the public, reveal that one of the most well-known stars of AFL is allegedly in a secret homosexual relationship.

It will undoubtedly come as a shock to fans of the Devils that midfielder Declan Tyler, a past Brownlow Medallist, appears to be gay. These photos, however, will dispel any doubts.

They were taken in the grounds of St. Vincent's Hospital, where Tyler's father was admitted after suffering a heart attack on Sunday. The photographer, who doesn't wish to be named, and is also a minor, was visiting a patient and observed Tyler and his unknown companion. He managed to obtain these photos using the camera on his mobile phone.

All attempts to reach Tyler for comment were futile as the Tyler family are in seclusion at the family home in Glenroy.

At present little is known about the mystery man in the photographs, but it has to be noted that this has been Tyler's worst season ever since he turned pro.

The AFL board, Devils' coach Scott Frasier, and team CEO Ed Wallace also have declined to respond at the time of printing.

A reticent star player... more on Page 4

From column "The Scene", *Reach Out, 3rd October*

NOT SO SHOCKING TO SOME
An editorial by Jasper Brunswick

It seems that the straight world is currently getting their knickers in a knot over the fact that Declan Tyler, one of the biggest stars in AFL, has been outed. This has led to an uproar over the belief that one of the best players in recent history can't possibly be a *fag*, after all, fags are better known for carrying a handbag than a ball, right?

At the moment it probably seems unimaginable to those who watch Tyler prowl upon the field like a modern gladiator that a sports star of his calibre could be queer, and there may be many who try to write off the recently published photos as fakes posed with look-alikes or excellent Photoshop jobs.

But what does this mean for Tyler's future in his chosen field? Is the AFL world ready for an openly gay player? Is Tyler himself ready for it? I would suggest he probably isn't, or else he would have come out of his own volition.

There have been whispers about Tyler for some time. And not only amongst the gay community. Tyler always has been loath to discuss his personal life and his relationship with frequent Brownlow attendee Jessica Wells. Privacy always automatically invites suspicion with the general public as well.

But who is the mystery man in the controversial photos?

He is no stranger to *Reach Out*. In fact, he has been profiled by us and was about to be interviewed again.

Simon Murray, 27, is the director of the Triple F film festival, which acts as a showcase for truly underground, independent filmmaking and also presents a large number of LGBTQ-related pieces in its programming each year. We have reprinted a previous interview we have had with him in this edition, highlighting the section where he talks about what it means to him personally to choose queer-friendly films.

You can rest assured that we will probably be hearing a lot about him in the mainstream press in the weeks to come as a new interest will be shown in his life, both with Declan Tyler and outside their relationship.

Only one thing is certain—life as they know it will never be the same again.

Interview with Simon Murray, page 6.

From the Herald Sun, 4th October

TYLER'S SECRET GAY LOVER REVEALED!

By Peter Van Niuewen

A local gay weekly has revealed the identity of the mystery man at the centre of the recent Declan Tyler photographs.

Simon Murray, 27, is the director of the Triple F film festival, which specialises in exhibiting independent cinema, usually with a large number of gay-friendly entrants. Attempts to contact Murray have been fruitless, and his assistant Nyssa Prati refuses to comment.

Gay columnist Jasper Brunswick, who has worked closely with Murray in the past, was the source who revealed the identity of Tyler's secret boyfriend. "We sat on this story for quite some time," Brunswick said in a phone interview, "as we are not in the habit of outing people. However, seeing as the Declan Tyler story became headline news in other media, it has now become newsworthy, and we couldn't ignore it."

All parties involved in this matter are remaining silent. Tyler remains in seclusion at his family's home in Glenroy while his father is under treatment at St. Vincent's Hospital; Murray has his answering service fielding his calls. Miss Jessica Wells isn't talking and her female "roommate" is maintaining silence as well. The AFL and the Tasmanian Devils Football Club have yet to release statements.

Calls to other players for comment have not been returned, leading to speculation that the club has issued a gag order.

"This is going to be huge for both the gay and the football communities," Brunswick says. "People are going to have to change their perceptions on all counts. We have never had a sports star this popular come out, and never at the height of their career. He *could* serve as a role model for so many people."

Meanwhile, this newly minted role model seems to be in hiding.

Your say... page 12

THIRD
QUARTER

CHAPTER TWENTY

THE world had gone crazy.

A full contingent of Australian media seemed to be camping out on my doorstep. I could only assume that they had partners-in-crime who would be doing the same on the Tyler house in Glenroy, and my suspicions were confirmed when I saw it on the news that night. I had started taking my car to work—the days I actually went—grimly battling through the journalists as I left my house each morning, wishing for the first time in my life I had one of those ugly new houses with a carport and a door that led directly to the kitchen so I could escape in relative privacy. I didn't answer the many questions thrown at me, not even to say no comment, the stock response given in many a news report by the hounded object of the item. It infuriated the pack, and their questions became more pointed and gradually even more insulting in order to provoke a response from me.

"Simon, do you have something to hide?"

"Simon, is your silence because you are ashamed?"

"Where's Declan? Have you two broken up already?"

I sang songs in my head to distract me. Eventually I barely heard them; I was too busy concentrating on whatever inane tune was working as a filter.

Nyssa had to hold them off at work and was now locking the doors so anybody couldn't just waltz in from off the street and demand to speak to me. It didn't help Nyssa was upset with me for having kept her in the dark.

"It's just that I thought we were friends," she said on the same day the newspaper had printed the photographs.

"We are," I told her earnestly.

"It doesn't feel like that to me right now."

"It's a difficult situation, Nyss. I couldn't tell everybody. Only Fran and Roger knew."

"Of course they did."

Her sunny disposition had all but evaporated.

As had mine. It took two days for Declan to call me.

"Are you okay?" he asked. No hello.

"I should be asking you that."

"I'm sorry I didn't call you straight away… you have no idea how crazy it's been here."

I didn't want to point out he had disappeared on me yet again, and it wasn't a habit of his I found endearing at all. "I can imagine. I had a journo from some trash rag trying to crawl in through the cat door."

"I've seen you on the news."

"I think *everyone's* seen me on the news. My mum's taping them for the show reel of shame, probably to be wheeled out in a few years for my thirtieth."

"How are your family taking it?"

"I think the better question is, how are yours?"

He took a long, deep breath. "Dammit, Simon, I can't talk to you over the phone like this. I want to see you."

"That's probably going to be real difficult."

"I know. Even Jess has people waiting outside her house."

"I know somewhere we can go."

"Where?" His voice had a soft note of hope in it.

"Fran and Roger's."

"But you're—"

"Roger and I are fine. Can you get there in an hour?"

"Of course." He paused. "Simon, just in case you've been worried… I love you."

I smiled for the first time in days. There was part of me wanting to castigate him for not being in contact, but I couldn't. At least not yet. "It hasn't changed on my end either, doofus."

OF COURSE, I hadn't been so convinced of that a couple of days ago. I was sure Declan hated me because only a short time after coming into his life, I had ruined it. Not hearing from him only seemed to cement that fear in my mind. Was he at home being berated by his family and pressured into saying that this was a temporary aberration which was all my fault? Was I being painted as the evil, gay predator who corrupted their innocent son?

As soon as I had gotten rid of Nyssa (which wasn't hard as she was trying to avoid me anyway to drive home just how upset with me she was), I tried Declan's mobile only to find it was switched off. I left work early, stupidly pulling my scarf over the lower half of my face in pretence of being cold but really to avoid detection as I could see my blurry profile on at least half a dozen newspapers being read on the tram.

I had been relatively safe the first day, as my name hadn't been leaked to the public yet. But as I got home, my mobile started ringing.

Surprisingly, it was my mother.

"What's up, Mum?"

"Where are you?"

"At home."

"Already?"

"I was… well, I'm not feeling very well."

"I hope you aren't coming down with that virus that's going around. Your Aunt Mary couldn't get off the toilet for three days!"

There was a vivid image which would do nothing to make me feel better. "Just a cold, I think, Mum."

"Well, I was just sitting here having a good old laugh. Guess why?"

I sat on the couch, falling heavily. "Why?"

"No, guess!"

Maggie jumped up onto my lap, and I scratched her behind the ears. "Dad accidentally ate the mull cake Tim made again?"

"No!"

"What, then?" I asked impatiently.

"I just got the paper—"

Oh fuck no—

"And apparently Declan Tyler from the Devils is a homosexual! Just like you!"

"Really?" I asked, one word being about all I could get out.

"And you'd never guess the funny thing!"

"That wasn't the funny thing?" I asked weakly.

"His boyfriend, well, I guess you would call them *partner*, wouldn't you?, looks kind of like you!"

"Uh—"

"I showed it to your father, and he said there was *no* way it could be you."

"What, he doesn't think I'm good enough for Declan Tyler?" I asked indignantly.

Mum laughed. "Well, it's just… he's a bit out of your league, isn't he? It would be like Tim dating, I don't know, a supermodel."

Wounded, I took a deep breath and said with as much dignity as I could muster, "Actually, Mum, it *is* me."

Mum burst out laughing. "Oh, Simon, stop it!"

"I'm not joking!"

"Just make sure you buy the paper and have a look, okay?"

"Mum—"

"Talk to you later, darling."

As I hung up, I looked down at Maggie. "The whole world has gone fucking insane."

I continued sitting there with a warm cat in my lap, staring at the wall before me. It seemed like a perfect moment to freeze time, to not have to deal with any further consequences. Archaeologists could find me in three centuries or so and never know my story nor the controversies attached to me. I would be dispassionately recorded in a museum log and rolled away into their archives section which would look something like the Pentagon basement in *The X Files*. And there we would be forgotten for eternity.

That seemed like bliss in comparison with my present reality.

The knock at my door made both Maggie and I jump.

As she fled for the safety of the bedroom, I cautiously moved towards the door, calling out, "Who is it?"

"Roger."

It *was* him. No journalist could fake that voice so well. I opened the door immediately, and there he stood. His hands were in his pockets, and he looked at me sheepishly.

"Hi."

That was as far as we got. He was shocked to find himself with an armful of me. Gradually he hugged me back.

"This… is quite a welcome. Hey, are you *crying*?"

"No," I sniffed. "Fuck off."

"Can I come in?" he asked. "Because if the press show up, tomorrow we'll be on the front page, and they'll be accusing you of two-timing Declan."

I laughed, and this time it didn't feel forced. "Come in."

It was like the past month had never happened, although Maggie was so surprised to hear his voice again she came back out to investigate and happily let him rub her belly.

"I saw the newspaper," he said.

I fetched us beers from the fridge. "Is that why you decided to forgive me?"

He shrugged. "I figured you needed me."

"You figured right," I admitted. "I'm sorry I was being such an arsehole about forgiving you."

"I'm sorry I was an arsehole in the first place. And then was an arsehole to you, when you stopped being an arsehole."

The perfect apology.

Now things were fine between us, I punched him on the shoulder. And not a playful one. "You watched the Grand Final without me!"

"Hey!" he rubbed the offended area. "If it's any consolation, I had a really bad time."

"I fell asleep," I admitted.

"Sacrilege!"

"It's true."

"Fran tried to watch it with me. She got bored and left into the second quarter and never came back."

"You should have called me. I would have been over in five minutes."

"I know. I should have." He finally got up from where he was crouching over Maggie and sat on the couch opposite me. "So, how are you feeling?"

"About the article? I have no fucking idea. I'm pretending it's not happening."

"What did Declan say?"

I shrugged. "Your guess is as good as mine."

"You haven't spoken to him?"

I shook my head. "His mobile's turned off. It's probably been ringing nonstop."

"I'm sure he'll call you."

"Yeah," I replied, although my tone indicated otherwise.

"You sad sack bastard," Roger sighed. "I'm calling Fran, getting her to come over here, and we'll have dinner and cheer you up."

"I don't need cheering up."

But the thought of all three of us being together again was about the only thing which *could* cheer me up at this juncture, although coming in a distant second to getting a call from Declan.

I would only have one day more of anonymity. But I lived it in dread of discovery, coupled with the very real fear Declan was choosing not to get in contact with me.

Nyssa unthawed slightly to me that day, her anger slowly subsiding into a low-level pity for my unfolding drama.

She crept into my office just after lunch and announced that Jasper Brunswick was on the phone. "Do you want me to get rid of him?" she asked. "I know you don't like talking to him at the best of times."

This was it. I knew what was coming. "No, I'll take it."

Nyssa nodded. "Line two."

I picked up the phone as she left. "Simon Murray."

"Simon, it's Jasper Brunswick."

"I've been expecting your call. You must love this."

"Wow, I know you hate me, but you've got me all wrong."

"Really," I scoffed.

"I did you a favour last time I spoke to you. And believe it or not, but I'm calling you to offer you a second one."

"And what's that?"

"Declan's little secret is out. So now we're going to be publishing some articles about it."

"Good for you."

"I'm naming you as his partner."

If I could have reached through the line to rip out his throat, I would have. It took all the power I had to restrain myself from answering.

"You're already out, Simon," he said quickly, to try and justify himself. "It's not like I'm outing you against your will. You've done interviews for the Triple F in which you haven't hidden your sexuality. And the other papers will find you eventually. We have to print the news too."

"And make sure you have the scoop, right?" I asked, finally able to speak again rather than simply emitting an outraged howl.

"If we have it, we'd be stupid not to take advantage of it. I'm calling to give you the opportunity to comment."

"You want a comment?" I asked. "*Fuck you.* That's my comment."

I hung up. It was childish and served no purpose, but it felt good.

I sat at my desk, trying to figure out what to do. The *Reach Out* would publish tonight and be on the streets tomorrow, which meant the word would spread quickly enough that the other newspapers and online journals would pick up on it by the afternoon. I was in Declan's position now, and I could understand why he had gone incommunicado.

Maybe I could try and beat Jasper at his own game, beat the scoop by outing myself to the press. But then I realised how that would look, as if I were trying to capitalise upon the story, selling it to the public. Declan Tyler's little fag gold digger. And what would Dec think, especially as we hadn't even talked to each other? Surely wherever we went from here should be a decision to make together, even if we were no longer *together.*

Like Declan was obviously doing with me.

I decided it would be classier to stay silent. Let Jasper have his scoop. I hoped he would choke on it.

With a twisted gut, I picked up the phone and called my parents. I hoped like hell nobody was home.

The gods were smiling upon me, at least in this instance. Their machine picked up.

"Hi, it's Simon. Look, I have something to tell you guys. What you thought was a joke, the whole Declan Tyler thing? Well, it isn't. And the press have found me out. So I just want to warn you guys in case they start calling or come to the house. Please don't say anything to them. Thanks."

I was amazed I managed to sound so calm.

I called Nyssa back into the office and told her basically the same thing. We were going from yellow to red alert.

The next morning dawned like any other. I peered out my window, but my lawn was free of any members of the media or other ferocious wildlife. I had done a large shopping expedition the night before so I could bunker down here if I had to without leaving for a few days. The street looked so peaceful it was surreal.

And it all went to hell about half past twelve.

I let the first call go through to my answering machine. It was that van Niuewen guy from the *Herald Sun*, requesting an interview. Then *Today Tonight* rang, followed by *A Current Affair* and *Who Weekly*. At that stage, I couldn't bear to hear their polite and measured voices offering their services in telling my story to the world at large, so I turned the answering machine off and unplugged my phone from the wall.

Just after four, probably the amount of time they had taken to track down my home address, they began arriving on my doorstep.

I was lying on the couch reading a book when the sound of slamming doors made me jump up with a start. My house was as silent as the grave, as I didn't want them to have any sign I was home. I crept across the room to peer out from behind the curtain. I recognised the journo, one of those ultra-serious types who still worshipped at the shrine of Jana Wendt. She signalled for her cameraman to follow her and strode briskly and importantly to my front door. She was here to get the news, dammit!

Even her knock was officious.

My heart was pounding; I drew back as if she had X-ray vision or Terminator-style heat sensors to pick up on my presence.

"Do you think he's home?" I heard her ask the cameraman, who only shrugged in reply.

She knocked again and stood there, silently fuming.

"We'll wait him out," she said, finally. "Huh, *out*, that's a good one."

Classy. I'd surely want *her* telling my story with that kind of real empathy. They walked back towards their van, pulling out folding chairs to sit upon.

Soon they were joined by other journalists from television, print and radio. Each time a new one turned up, they conferred with those already camping out on my lawn, all simultaneously relieved that nobody had spoken to me yet and all wondering where I was. They seemed practiced at arranging themselves in order of arrival. Their voices carried to me hiding within the house; they weren't bothered about keeping quiet.

"Do you think he's home?"

"He's probably either here or at the Tyler house."

"You think Tyler's family knows about him?"

"Well, they do now."

Laughter.

"He's not answering any of his phones."

"You can't even hear his phone ring."

"Probably has the jack pulled out."

At five o'clock I inserted my headphones into the telly and turned on the first news bulletin, shocked to see my house being reported from during a live cross. I realised I could see Maggie sitting in the window to the right of the journo's shoulder, staring out at the spectacle before her. I turned my head and saw her butt and tail poking out from behind the curtain. They then did *another* live cross, this time to the Tyler's household where they didn't even have a cat on the windowsill to indicate there was life within.

They couldn't camp out here all night, could they? When the only thing they could be guaranteed getting was some attention-whoring from my cat?

I imagined the headline the next edition of the *Reach Out* would probably use:

TYLER'S LOVER LIKES PUSSY AFTER ALL.

I turned the news off and drummed my fingers to try and catch Maggie's attention. She was still too distracted by the circus outside, which by the sound of slamming doors, had just welcomed another arrival.

I squinted around Maggie and realised it was worse than another pack of journalists turning up.

It was my parents.

"Are you friends of Simon Murray?" one journo asked.

"Are you his parents?" asked another.

My father remained silent, as usual, and pushed his way through them with a surly look on his face. My mother was gentler, and I could hear her singing out, "Excuse me! *Excuse* me!"

"Did you know your son was seeing Declan Tyler?"

"Did you know your son was gay?"

"Did you know Declan Tyler was gay?"

I rolled my eyes. Whoever asked that should have their degree stripped from them for not being able to follow a line of logical questioning.

I ran to the front door as soon as I heard them walking up the steps. I yanked it open, but kept myself hidden behind it. "Get in here quick!" I hissed.

I could hear the pack beginning to bray.

"He *is* home!"

"Bastard!"

As soon as my parents were in, I slammed the door shut. I expected to see the outlines of various journalists slammed into the wood like the hapless predators in the Loony Tunes, but they just milled about on my veranda.

"Well," my mother said. "May I have a cup of tea?"

"Uh, sure. Dad?"

"Do you have any beer?"

I nodded, and he looked vaguely surprised. Even though I *always* had beer in my fridge on the rare occasion he was over.

They followed me into the kitchen while I started preparing their drinks.

"You're a dark horse," Mum said, almost admiringly. "I thought you were joking about the whole Declan Tyler thing."

"How come you didn't call me yesterday, after I left the message?" I asked.

"Oh, you know us and that damn machine," Mum said. "We never know how to use it."

"So how did you know?" I asked.

"Well, darling, you *are* on the front pages of all the newspapers. And of course, they all started calling us."

Dad spoke up for the first time since entering. "Is Declan Tyler really... you know?"

"Yes, Dad, he is *really, you know*." I passed him his beer.

"He doesn't look it."

"We have a look?" I asked as I filled the kettle. "Do I have that look?"

"Don't start," Mum warned. "We came here to check up on you."

"I'm fine."

"Well, we're not," Dad fumed. "The phone's been ringing all bloody afternoon."

"Sorry," I said. "It will blow over soon."

"Where is he?" Mum asked.

"Who?" I lifted the kettle off its base.

"Declan Tyler, of course!"

"Did you come here to see him or me?"

"You're being shirty," Mum warned.

"Can you blame me?"

"You should have known this would happen." Dad huffed.

"You're blaming me for this?" I passed Mum her tea.

"Of course he's not," Mum said apologetically on his behalf.

"Is it serious?" Dad asked.

"What?"

"Your... *relationship*." He said it as if it was incomprehensible.

"Do you mean are we just fucking?" I said it to be cruel, to get the reaction I wanted. And I wasn't disappointed.

Dad coloured visibly.

"Simon!" Mum cried.

"That's what he wanted to hear."

"It bloody well wasn't," Dad said.

"Well, you're not comfortable with *relationship*, and you're not comfortable with *fucking*, so how are you going to feel when I tell you we *love* each other?"

Apparently that didn't go down too well either. Dad took a long gulp of his beer. "If he's in *love* with you, why isn't he here?"

"I'm expecting this shit from the general public," I replied as calmly as I could. "I guess it was stupid of me to expect support from my family."

"Stop it, both of you!" Mum said. "Your dad may say otherwise, Simon, but he *wanted* to come here and make sure you were okay. He worries about you."

Dad stared down at his beer.

I had to admit, it was pretty impressive he had come here. Before I could say anything though, we heard a commotion on the veranda. I told my parents to stay in the kitchen, and crossed into the lounge room to peek out of the window again. Roger was surrounded by journalists, who were demanding to know who he was and how he knew me, even speculating over whether he was an ex-boyfriend. I saw him reach back into the small crowd and pull Fran up next to him. She was fumbling in her purse and brought out my spare key.

They let themselves in and slammed the door shut. They stood there for a moment, shell-shocked and panting, before they spotted me in the lounge.

"We brought alcohol," Fran said, reaching into her bag and pulling out a bottle of gin.

"And that is why you're my best friends," I said.

Fran ran across the room to hug me. "You okay?"

"Yep, fine." Then I whispered, "My parents are here."

She pulled back and laughed. "I thought I saw a blood-red sky with fishes raining out of it on the way over here."

"Cute."

"Who is it?" my mother called from the kitchen.

"George Negus. He wants to interview you."

My mother came bustling into the lounge, patting her hair, and looked crestfallen. "Oh, hello, Roger, Fran."

"Mrs. Murray," they mumbled politely.

"Simon!" Mum protested. "You got me all excited."

Roger and Fran snickered amongst themselves.

"I don't know what *you're* laughing about," Mum said sternly to the two of them. "I'm sure you knew all about this while Simon kept his own family in the dark."

"Sorry, Mrs. Murray," they replied in unison.

Mum pursed her lips. "Cup of tea?"

I waved Fran's bottle of gin at her. "I think we're having something stronger."

"Gin and tonic, Mrs. M?" Fran asked.

"No, I'm happy with my tea, thank you."

"Roger," Fran gestured at the booze. "Hurry."

As Roger passed me, I handed him the bottle. I could hear him greeting my father, and they began talking about the Grand Final. Anything footy that didn't deal directly with Declan Tyler.

Mum wandered over to the window and looked out. "They're all still out there," she mused.

"Mum!" I hissed. "Get away from there! They'll see you."

"And what if they do?" she demanded. "It's your house! They can't make you hide in it!"

Fran gave me a sympathetic smile.

"You're going to have to face them sooner or later," Mum told me.

"I know," I sighed.

Luckily, Roger arrived with drinks, and I disposed of mine in one big gulp. "Do you mind making me another?" I asked.

Roger wordlessly handed me his own glass, handed the third to Fran, and disappeared back into the kitchen with the empty one.

"He's well-trained," Mum said approvingly.

"Like a puppy," Fran replied wryly.

"So how come you don't have any photos of him?" Mum asked, her eyes scanning around the lounge room.

I sipped steadily at my drink, wishing I would black out. "Wouldn't be much of a secret if I put stuff like that out, would it?"

I didn't want to tell her about the one photo I had hidden in my room, the only one in existence of the two of us together. At least as far as I knew. Lisa had taken it when I was in Hobart, of Declan and I together on his couch. It was a terrible photo of me; I was mid-laugh and braying like a donkey while Dec was looking at me in amusement. Great candid shot, but not that flattering. Of course, I loved it.

So I wasn't about to parade it before my mother as proof of our relationship.

"Were you expecting the tabloids to pass by?" Mum asked.

"Well, they *are* here now, aren't they?"

Roger walked back in, carrying a jug. "Saves making constant refills," he said.

I grabbed the jug and started on my third.

"You're not becoming an alcoholic, are you?" Mum asked.

I contemplated drinking straight from the jug.

Mum and Dad left not long afterwards, disappointed that they hadn't gotten much out of me and even more upset that they hadn't gotten to see Declan. I hoped such a meeting would be a long way down the track, and seeing as I hadn't heard from him in days, it could be even longer than I hoped.

Fran and Roger were the supportive friends they always were. And when I got stupidly drunk and ended up vomiting and sobbing over the toilet, they told me I only had one night in which I could let go like that and didn't leave until they sobered me up somewhat.

I woke up briefly around four in the morning and reached over to pull the photo of Declan and myself out of the book it was hiding in. I guessed there was no longer any reason to hide it and propped it up against the alarm clock. If all went well from here on, I would put it in a frame.

I WAS still fighting the resulting headache from the previous night's shenanigans as I drove to Roger and Fran's in order to meet Declan.

It was only the second time I had emerged from the house. Some of the media pack had subsided, but there were still enough of them that it was a struggle to get to my car. What felt like a thousand questions were fired at me, most of which I didn't even recognise as they all garbled into one unintelligible mess. Camera flashes blinded me as I tried to back the car down the driveway, and I wondered if my luck was so dire I would probably run over a journo as I tried to escape.

I kept one eye on my rear view mirror the whole time, trying to figure out if anyone had followed me. I was beginning to feel like I was trapped in some bad telemovie of my life and wondered which appalling soapie star they would bring in to play me.

But I managed to make it to Fran and Roger's unscathed. Neither of them were home, so I made myself comfortable on the couch nearest to the window so I could watch out for Declan.

He arrived about ten minutes after I did. I was opening the door for him before he even got to it, and I wasn't sure if I wanted to kiss him or hit him.

Once he got into the house and looked at me, I did both. I shoved him a little, but before he had time to react I was kissing him.

"Arsehole!" I mumbled before pulling away. "How is your dad doing?"

He grabbed me by the arm and brought me back to him. "I'm sorry. I did it all wrong, okay? I should have been on the phone to you first thing. But—"

Now he was here, in front of me, my anger was abating. "I know. Believe me, I know. But I was really fucking afraid you were blaming me."

Declan nodded.

"Did you, at any point?"

He took a deep breath. "Not you. But I'd be lying if I didn't admit I wish I had kept better control over myself that night."

I stared down at the carpet, too scared to look at his expression. "So what's been going on? What did your family say? Your coach?"

He led me over to the couch, and we sat down. "Mum wanted to try and keep it from Dad at first, just because of his health. But there was no way it could be done, I mean, he has a TV in his room and the newspaper guy goes round the wards every day. Dad knew by the time Mum went in to visit him that evening."

"And?"

"Do you know what sucks, Simon? I couldn't even go and see him at the hospital. They had reporters camped out there as well. A guy tried to sneak into his room to get a quote, but a nurse grabbed him before he managed to ask anything. Mum gets mobbed in the car park every time she goes to visit him. This is the first time I've left the house."

"Did you get to speak to him on the phone?"

"Yeah." Declan gave a short laugh. "He said I always got the limelight wherever I went and whatever I did."

"Doesn't sound like a ringing endorsement."

"He's my dad," Declan said simply. "He loves me. Just, being a dad, he won't ever say it. You have to read around it all."

I thought that was a nice way of putting it and remembered how my mum had claimed my father worried about me. Maybe Declan was a lot wiser than I was. "And your mum?"

"The same. But as I told you before, I thought she already knew. And now she wants to know who you are."

I instantly felt sick. "Oh."

Declan laughed. "I thought that would be how you would look. Anyway, my parents are coping. Or at least, they would cope better if the media backed down a bit. The bosses think if I release a statement it might help."

"A statement? They're really okay with you doing that?"

Declan grimaced, and I knew that everything wasn't as hunky dory as he was portraying it. "Let's not think about that for a minute. How are you?"

"I'm fine. I just want everything to be okay between us."

"I want that too."

"Do you think we'll survive this?" I asked.

"We better."

I knew there was a lot more to be talked about, but it didn't seem the right moment. We kissed, our bodies reacting against each other out of comfort and hurt, needing to be together to cement this bond that had been tenuous over the past few days.

As it always was when I was with Declan, I felt things were right and good and would be practically perfect if the world at large would leave us to it.

And for a little while, it did.

I started to pull at Dec's shirt, and he pushed my hand away.

"Not here," he panted. "We can't."

"They won't be home for a while," I assured him, lightly nipping at his ear.

"It'd be weird...."

But he was starting to slip. I pulled him up from the couch and led him to the spare room. We shed our clothes eagerly, hungering for each other. He watched me as I gently pushed him upon the bed. I lay him down by running the palms of my hands over his abs, up his chest, and applying pressure at his shoulders. He arched up to kiss me as I straddled him and brought his knees up to cradle me closer as we forgot about the outside world once again.

CHAPTER TWENTY-ONE

"DEC," I murmured. "Wake up."

He shifted groggily, trying to figure out where he was for a moment in the haze of sleep.

"Fran and Roger will be home soon," I told him. "Not exactly the best way to announce our presence."

Declan sat up. "Oh, shit, this *is* seedy," he agreed with a yawn.

"Roger can be a prude sometimes. Fran's brother made a joke once about his daughter being conceived in this room, and Roger practically called in an exorcist to cleanse the place." I couldn't resist cuddling in closer to him, trying to draw his warmth into my own body.

Declan snorted, and I smiled when his arm pulled me in even closer. "Isn't that what a guest room is for?"

"Conceiving children? No, I think they're just generally a place for friends and family to sleep in when they're too drunk to drive home."

"Come on, we better get up," Dec said regretfully, and he swung his legs out of the bed, searching for his boxers on the floor.

I threw myself over and hugged him from behind. "Maybe we can ask them if we can stay here. Maybe forever."

He leaned back and kissed me affectionately. "I think the press will still track us down eventually." He found my T-shirt next to his pants and threw it over his shoulder, hitting me in the face. "As much as I hate to say this, get dressed."

I reluctantly pulled my shirt on, reluctantly acknowledging that he wasn't going to lure me into getting back into bed, and jumped out to begin making it instead.

Dec laughed. "Put on some pants, you flasher."

"You want me to put my pants on, *find* them for me."

They came flying across the room along with my boxers.

"Good look, though," he said appreciatively.

I put my hands on my hips and slowly wiggled my hips in some bad imitation of sexy dancing. Declan began laughing, which wasn't exactly the response I was hoping for until he swooped in for a kiss with a gentle tease of tongue.

"Really good look," he murmured.

Shuffling into my boxers after that was slightly harder, and Declan sat on the bed to pull his sneakers back on.

I smoothed the bed down when he got back up and stood back to survey the room. "Looks reasonable, right?"

"They won't suspect a thing."

It was probably a lie, but I pushed him out the door and towards the kitchen. Declan started preparing coffee, and I slid onto the stool at the counter, happy to watch him as he moved comfortably around Fran's domain.

"They asked me what I wanted to do," Declan said suddenly.

I had been distracted, watching his hands and wishing they were on me again. "Who?"

"The bosses. They said they would support me with whatever I decided to do, but I think they were hoping I would agree to cover it up. For the time being, anyway."

"How could you cover it up?" I asked.

Declan slowly put his hands upon the counter and didn't look at me. He stared at the fake marble. It was the most interesting thing in the world to him right then, and I knew immediately.

"By blaming me," I replied, barely a whisper.

He still couldn't look at me. "Yeah."

"What, the predatory gay friend taking advantage of you in your hour of need?" My voice was starting to rise a little now.

"Something like that." His tone, however, was both bitter and flat.

"And what did you say?"

I could tell from his posture that he was feeling both defensive and ashamed.

"You thought about it, right?" I couldn't believe it. There he was on the phone, only a few hours ago, pledging his love to me, then *fucking* me; now he was basically admitting that he considered letting me fall on the sword for him.

"Of course I thought about it," Declan said softly. "I thought about every fucking possibility, every scenario. It's the way I am, Simon. I think things through. I don't just wing it like you do."

I wanted to throw something at him, but I stopped myself. "You think I wing it? Jesus, Declan, ever since I started going out with you I've been planning things down to the minutest detail! When to call you, how not to draw suspicion—"

"I know."

"So how is that winging it?"

"I just meant *naturally*, you wing things. If it wasn't for me, you'd be out battling the press and telling them to fuck off."

"Yeah, and I'm not doing that because when it comes down to it, I want to do everything to protect you."

He laughed. "I don't think that's going to be a problem now."

"What, you think that now, because we're exposed, I still won't have to do it? Or won't want to do it? If anything, the pressure will be worse now because before when I was only paranoid about the *possibility* of everyone watching us, they'll actually be doing it!"

"Simon...." He crossed around the counter and came over to me, but my body language warned him to back off slightly.

"I can't *believe* you considered it."

"Not seriously. And only for a minute."

I stared him down. "It was a minute too long."

He opened his mouth to defend himself, but closed it as he heard the door opening.

"Do we have visitors?" I heard Fran call out.

"It's us," I called back, not taking my eyes off Declan.

"Us who?" asked Roger.

They entered the kitchen, laughing. They tried to exchange greetings with us, but quickly cottoned onto the fact that high drama was unfolding. I excused myself and walked out the back to get some fresh air. I thought if I stayed in there any longer I could be sick.

It wasn't that long until I heard someone open the door and step up behind me. I was expecting Declan, but it was Roger.

"What's going on?" he asked.

"Trying to seek a bit of sanctuary," I said morosely. "But we just bring all the shit with us."

"It's early days yet," Roger said in an attempt to be comforting. "You have to expect it, really."

"Really?" I asked. "The bosses asked Dec if they should cover it up by saying I came onto him when he was upset about his dad, and that he wasn't reciprocating when the photos were taken. And you know what? He thought about it."

"And?" Roger asked.

I stared at him in complete shock. "You think that's okay?"

Roger shrugged. "I think it's human."

"Great."

"I think you'd consider everything if you were in his position, as well."

"I wouldn't."

"For fuck's sake, of course you would!" Roger scoffed. "I bet you *any* one of us would think about it for a bit. It would be a complete fantasy, this magic pill that could take your problem away, even if it's practically impossible." Roger sat down on the top step and pulled me down with him. "And I think that if you were to put yourself in his shoes for just a minute you *know* you would consider it as well, if you were honest enough to admit it. But what matters is that he *didn't* agree to it. Because that's not him."

"That's a lovely speech, Rog."

"Fuck off."

"Seriously, does Declan know you have a man crush on him?"

Roger shoved me. "Arsehole."

We sat in silence for a moment before I finally muttered, "Thank you."

"Simon, at the moment, you're going to have to choose your fights. And, of course, you being you, you're choosing the wrong ones."

What was it about friends that they could tell you the truth, no matter how painful, and you had to take it? I nodded. "I know. It just hurt, that's all."

"Girl."

I punched him in the shoulder, and we both sagged against each other, laughing.

"It's times like this I wish I smoked," I mused. "These moments need cigarettes."

"You hate the smell of smoke," came Declan's voice through the screen door. "You complain if the next door neighbour is in her yard and lights up."

Roger stood. "I'll let him take up the reins here and call you out for being a wanker. As usual." As he opened the door and stepped around Declan he asked, "Are you staying for dinner?"

"Sounds good," Declan said. "Thanks."

"Simon?" Roger asked.

I shrugged. "Might as well."

The two men in the doorway gave each other looks of commiseration, probably a shared feeling of wondering why they put up with me. Declan came out and sat beside me. I continued staring out past the Hills Hoist and to the dilapidated shed that was never used and was beginning to be swallowed up by junglelike grass. Declan reached for my hand, and I squeezed it, rubbing my thumb over the back of his, a silent gesture to let him know I wasn't really angry anymore.

"You know," he said, and cleared his throat because it sounded a little rusty, "I've always thought about this day and how I would act when it happened. And in my head I was always unbearably noble and accepted coming out with dignity."

I looked at him and tried to speak, but he cut me off.

"So how do you think I felt when it *did* happen, and they offer me this option, this way out that could make it all disappear? That could make it stop, for just a little while, all this fear and self-doubt, this worry that I'm not ready for it yet?"

I let him speak and brought my other hand over to rest upon his arm.

"How do you think I felt when I seriously considered, for one brief moment, letting the man I love take the fall for me? Believe me, no matter how angry you are with me, I hate myself even more for it."

Hearing him put his fears out there made what little remnants of the anger I was holding onto fade away. And Roger was right, Declan was not the kind of guy who would ever have *seriously* considered that course of action. It just wasn't him, after all.

"I'm not angry, Dec. You're right, it's a natural reaction to think about it. And I can be a fucking prig sometimes, expecting people to act better than they should, when I'm not in that position and would probably do the exact same thing if I were."

"I'm going to do it," he said. "I'm going to come out. And deal with whatever happens."

I nodded.

"Simon, you're part of this. Because whatever happens when I do this, you're a part of it. Are you okay with that?"

"Of course I am."

He sighed, and I knew he was feeling as uncertain about everything as I was. "So what do we do now?"

I stood up and yanked him up with me. I hugged him tight and said, "We go inside and help them with dinner."

He laughed. "If only everything else would be as easy."

Yep. If only.

A TRUER sentiment had never been spoken.

When I got home, my yard was empty. I knew it would be short-lived, however, and the reporters would probably be back in the morning. Declan had gone back to his parents', saying that he would probably be on the phone for the rest of the night in conference calls to his coach and the board as he convinced them of what he wanted to do and they figured out the logistics of it all.

I received a text as I was jumping in to bed later that read

Tomorrow is D-day.

I couldn't sleep, I felt so sick.

THE faithful pack had returned in the morning, and I resolutely ignored them as I got into my car and made my way into the city. When I walked into the office, Nyssa met me at the door and intoned theatrically, "The bosses are *here*, boss."

"What?" I asked. I think the only way to truly describe my expression was *aghast*. They *never* came to our office, Nyssa and I always had to drag our arses across town to meet with them. You would normally think that the consensus would be that as we were on our own territory we would have the advantage, but I didn't think this would be the case. They were showing how utterly serious this was, that they had to leave theirs.

"They're waiting for you in your office."

"How could they all fit?"

She shrugged. "Oh, and Alice Provotna has left you at least fifty messages."

"Alice Provotna is the least of my worries right now," I told her. "Wish me luck."

Nyssa crossed her fingers and waved them in front of me as if they could create a shield to protect me against the board members who were probably deciding my fate as we spoke. I took the long walk down the hall—had this hallway always been *this* long?

Seriously, it was normally three steps. I pushed open the door with as much confidence as I could muster.

As I swept my way grandly through my extremely small and now extremely cramped office, I tried to appear as nonchalant as possible. "Morning, all," I said casually, thanking them silently none had resorted to taking my chair in a show of superiority.

"Simon," Brian Emery nodded at me as I sat before him. "Been quite a few days for you, hasn't it?"

I didn't want them to start with accusing me of shirking my responsibilities in the workplace. "Well, the great thing about this job is that there's still a lot you can do from home. Especially when you have as good an assistant as Nyssa."

Lucie Andersson peered over at me through her thick-rimmed glasses. "So, the work's been getting done?"

I calmly counted to three in my head. "Of course. We're up to speed. We're exactly at the point we should be. Is there a problem?"

"Simon, don't be so defensive," Brian said, putting up his hands and warding me off. "We're not here to lecture about the way things have been handled lately. After all, your private life is *your* private life."

I nodded.

"As long as it doesn't affect the festival," Lucie made sure to point out as a friendly warning.

Jon Daintry finally spoke up. "Which is why we're here."

"I thought you just said you knew the festival hadn't been affected," I said.

Brian nodded. "We think, perhaps, we can use this to our advantage."

Why, hello, sinking feeling, my old friend. "How so?"

"Any publicity is good publicity," Brian said. "If we can get Declan Tyler to attend opening night and a few of the other festivities—"

"Hold on!" I interrupted. "You—"

"It's no time to get precious, Simon," Lucie said.

"Precious?" I asked. "This is my life, *his* life, you're talking about. He has enough to deal with without me having to parade him around like the ultimate PR accessory."

"It's not like we're asking you to do anything out of the ordinary," Lucie said. "I mean, you would normally bring your partner to events, wouldn't you?"

"I haven't the past couple of years," I pointed out.

"Were there any partners to bring?" Jon asked.

Actually, there had been, at least in my years as an assistant, but they were never interested enough to attend. I remained silent.

"You like your job, don't you, Simon?" Brian asked.

I glared at him. "Is that a threat?"

"Not a threat, no. But you can't deny that this is a perfect opportunity for you to cement your position with the festival. We took a risk hiring you—"

"And it's paid off," I said bitterly. "The past couple of years, promotion, sponsorship, and attendance have all increased."

"Now you have the opportunity to take it even further," Lucie suggested, not too gently.

The three of them stared me down, as if their combined presence could break me.

"If Nyssa's as good as you say she is," Jon said, "she could easily step into your shoes."

I guess they *were* going to break me.

THEY left me to "think about it", and "asked" me to have my decision ready by the afternoon.

I sat for the longest time in a funk, hating myself for having to mull it over. If it had been a couple of years ago, I would have told them to go fuck themselves. But since then, I had grown comfortable in a job I enjoyed, obtained a mortgage, and settled down into a false sense of security I couldn't bear to lose.

Nyssa came to the rescue with constant cups of coffee, and to try and cheer me up she supplied a Danish she had grabbed from the café downstairs. At twelve, she told me Declan had called in a rush, unable to get me on my line because I had had it diverted during my meeting with the bosses, and it was busy when he tried again later (I was relating my woes about the job on a conference call to a suitably appalled Roger and Fran). The press conference was going to be in an hour.

"He sounds sexy even on the phone," she said dreamily.

"You have *no* idea," I replied just as dreamily. Then I shook myself out of it and switched on the TV. The news breaks were already announcing that Declan Tyler and the Devils had called a press conference, and it was expected that Tyler would "come clean about his recent controversy."

They *wanted* to make it seedy. But I knew Declan would be nothing but classy as he stared them all down. Nyssa kept giving me worried glances until I sent her away, although I promised she could come in at one to watch the press conference. I would need the moral support.

It was like Melbourne Cup day, except it was the confirmation of a sports star's sexuality that would stop a nation rather than a horse race. Ian Roberts, an NRL player, had come out a couple of decades before, but that was rugby. *Nobody* had ever come out while playing AFL. This was history, and I was at the centre of it. Hiding under my desk all the way.

Should I have offered to face the press with him? Did he feel he couldn't ask me to? I felt like everything had been taken out of our hands at the moment; we barely had enough face time together to try and discuss these things, everything was going so fast.

Perhaps this was going to be Declan's first step at taking control of his own life and dictating the way he wanted things handled.

Nyssa rushed back into my office at five to one, brandishing rolls and drinks from downstairs for our lunch. "The press have left the premises for the moment," she told me. "They must have all run over to Etihad for the conference."

I took my roll off her eagerly. You would have thought I should have been too full of nervousness to eat, but I was starving. "Good for me at least, probably not for Declan."

"How are you feeling?" Nyssa asked, dragging a chair over to sit next to me.

"Hungry," I said through a mouthful of food.

Nyssa shrugged, accepting my answer readily. She seemed to be as well, the way she tore into her ham and salad baguette.

On the television screen, a reporter was talking to the anchor back in the studio. You could make out the long table set up with microphones to the right of his shoulder and the banners of the Devils unfurling from the ceiling. The hall was packed with possibly every form of the media and the usual interested members of the public who snuck into these events. Passes were hardly ever checked as long as you had some form of camera around your neck. Just ask Roger. But that's another story, for another time.

A hush fell over the hall as the curtains parted, and the more senior board members of the Devils emerged, followed by the coach, and finally by Declan. The room instantly became an epileptic's nightmare with constant camera flashes giving it a nightclub-like strobe effect.

"He is *so* hot," Nyssa said. Again. "I can't *believe* you're going out with him."

"Hey, I'm hot," I protested.

"No, you're not. Not Declan Tyler hot." She realised what she said, and in the manner of the best slapstick comedienne, clapped her hand over her mouth. "You know what I mean."

"Yeah. I know what you mean," I sighed.

She gave me an awkward one-armed hug, almost spilling the contents of her roll over me as she continued to watch the television.

Slightly embittered—really, what was it with *everybody* feeling the need to point out my boyfriend was so much better looking than me?—I tried to focus upon the situation at hand. Declan was standing and making his way over to the lectern, wearing his best serious face but also chewing at the inside of his cheek.

"Hello," he said, and he leaned back, probably spooked by the loudness of the microphone. "Thanks for coming today. I have a statement to read." He cleared his throat and scratched his neck nervously. "Ever since I was a kid, all I have wanted to do is play football. It turned out that, injuries aside, I was pretty good at it. I never expected to get into the official league; it was really just a dream. And I didn't know when it first happened at the age of eighteen just how much of a public figure you can become, and with that, how much interest there can be in your private life. For the most part, I have managed to keep it pretty private, but lately there have been articles and rumours I could ignore and deny, but would not be true to myself."

It seemed the press was now waiting with bated breath. Declan looked up, gave a hesitant smile, and consulted his notes again. Back in the office, Nyssa's hand suddenly slipped into mine, and I was grateful for it.

"So I come to you today to tell you my own story directly, rather than letting the misconceptions and rumourmongering of certain members of your otherwise fine profession continue to play out." He took a deep breath, and I hoped he was doing the right thing for himself, not because circumstances had forced him into it. "While I have always preferred to keep my personal life private, as that is the way I have been raised, right now questions are being asked and I will not hide away from them. I am proud to say I am gay—"

The room erupted in a low hum of excited chatter amongst the reporters, and the blinding flash of cameras desperate to capture the exact moment on film.

"—and I am very happy in my relationship, which has recently been the topic of discussion and pictorial spreads in the papers."

"Aww," Nyssa said, resting her head upon my shoulder. "He's talking about you."

"Unless he means his other, *hotter* boyfriend," I said.

She hit me; I winced.

"Neither my sexuality or my efforts, or lack of effort, on the football field make up the whole sum of me. I just hope by putting an end to this speculation I can continue on in all facets of my life with a respect for my privacy, and also of my partner's, whose life has been subjected to speculation and curiosity as well. Thank you."

Declan left the lectern as the press fired questions at him all at once. The coach of the Devils, Scott Frasier, patted him on the back as he passed him to take the microphone.

"I'm sure you can understand that Declan has said all he needs to say for the moment," Frasier said, looking more like a deer caught in the headlights than Declan had moments before. "I will take relevant questions from the floor. And I mean *relevant*," he said, with the glare that made him infamous *and* intimidating in the coaching box.

"Wow," Nyssa said. "That was quite a good speech."

"It was, wasn't it?" I smiled.

"Oh, listen to you, you sound so proud!"

"Of course I am. This is a huge thing he's done. I just hope he gets the respect for it he deserves."

"So, when do I get to meet him?"

My mobile rang, and I leapt out of my chair. "Hold that thought."

I was relieved to see it was Declan's number. "Hey."

"Did you see it?" He sounded excited, scared, and relieved.

"I did."

"What did you think?"

"You want to know what I think?"

"Of course I bloody do!" he laughed.

"I think…," I teased. "I love you."

"Sounds good to me," he couldn't resist teasing back. "Are you at work?"

"Yeah."

"I'm coming over before the media follows me."

When I hung up, Nyssa was looking at me in shock. "Did I just hear you right?"

"What?"

"You said you loved him!"

"Oh, Nyssa," I grinned madly. "That's old news."

TRUE to his word, Declan managed to beat the press to the office, probably because they were still detained at Etihad, trying unsuccessfully to get more details about his love life from the hapless Frasier.

He burst through the office doors, and Nyssa, who was still on red alert, locked them immediately after him and shyly hung back, suitably awestruck.

Declan crossed over to me; I was leaning against Nyssa's desk, and he pulled me up to him, taking my face in his hands and kissed me rather passionately. In public. With no fear. Still in front of the glass doors, where anybody passing by could have seen within. I liked it.

"Uh, hey, this is Nyssa," I said, fighting to gain my breath back.

Nyssa, her eyes wide as she had never seen her boss in any public display of affection, stepped forward and shook Declan's hand. "Hi, I'm Nyssa. Pleased to meet you. Nyssa. Nyssa Prati."

"Hi, Nyssa," Declan said warmly, taking her hand. "Simon has a lot of nice things to say about you."

"Really?" Nyssa asked suspiciously. "Simon? Saying nice things? *That* Simon?"

Declan turned back to me. "You really have people fooled with this whole pretend hate-the-world thing, don't you?"

I shrugged. "It works for me."

"Would you like a coffee, Declan?" Nyssa asked, all charm.

"Thanks, that would be great."

"I could even make it Irish." She smiled, looking rather like Fran and, I suspected, myself whenever any of us talked to Declan.

"Why not?" he winked. "Let's make it a celebration."

"Come into my office," I offered.

He nodded and took the few steps from Nyssa's desk to my tiny room.

"I have a good view—" I said.

"So do I," he growled, and before I knew it I was pressed up against the window with my arms full of lusty footballer.

"I'm pretty sure this is against office decorum," I panted.

His left hand had crept under my shirt and was stroking the skin of my stomach.

"You're probably right." Lips were now working against my neck. "And you *do* have a great view here."

"Told you."

We rested against each other, and it seemed that the weight of the past few days suddenly settled upon us. The afternoon sun lulled us into a silent reverie, just standing there and holding each other. Had I ever felt the sun upon us before as we did such a thing? I couldn't think properly, but I didn't believe so. It was a great feeling. Nyssa knocked on the door, and she smiled sweetly at the two of us. "Coffee," she announced, setting them upon my desk and discreetly leaving the room.

True to her word, there was a shot of whiskey in each mug.

"Making out and drinking on the job," Declan said. "Your bosses better not find out."

"I think they'd forgive me at the moment, as long as they got their way," I said, darkly.

Declan took his mug and sat beside me. I decided to beat him to the punch this time and dangled my hand down by the side of my chair to pick his up and hold it tight.

"What do you mean?" he asked.

"I basically got raked over the coals this morning by the big bosses," I said.

"What did you do?"

"Nothing. Which is why they're calling meetings with me."

"I don't get you."

"Don't tell the press that."

"Funny. What's wrong?"

"They want me to exploit our relationship by making sure you come to our premieres and guarantee us some major media attention." I tried to gauge his expression out of the corner of my eye, but he seemed unperturbed as he sipped at his coffee.

"And what, you were planning to take somebody else as your date?"

"Well—"

"You didn't think I would want to support my partner at a major work function?"

"No, but—"

"So what's the problem?"

"Just, I hadn't had the opportunity to talk to you first and make sure it was okay. Because I don't like the fact that I'm going out with you is going to be used for other peoples' nefarious purposes."

"What does it matter, if we're doing what we want anyway?"

"I guess?" I didn't sound so sure, as he could probably tell.

"Are you going to ask me for a date, then?" He grinned and tried to hide it by gulping at his coffee again. "Ask me nicely, and I *may* accept."

"Are you asking me to ask you on a date?"

"Yeah. But I would also like to go on a date that isn't a media event first."

"Huh. Maybe I'm waiting for you to ask me."

"I asked *you* on our first date!"

"Are you keeping score or something?"

"Something," he admitted.

"Fine. Hey, Declan?"

"Yes, Simon?"

"What are you doing this Friday night?"

"I don't know, I'll have to check my diary."

"Arsehole." I dropped his hand and cradled my mug like a baby.

"Stop sweet-talking me, you bastard," he murmured, reaching up to slowly stroke my neck. "What are you asking me?"

He almost had me purring. "Want to go out on Friday?"

"Sure. But my parents will probably chaperone."

That was it. I set my mug down, grabbed his and set it aside, and pulled him toward me by the collar of his jacket. "Shut up," I ordered, and I kissed him to ensure that he would.

CHAPTER
TWENTY-TWO

"SIMON," Dec murmured into my ear, "they're back."

On that ominous note, I opened my eyes and groaned. "It was too good to last."

While Scott Frasier was still dealing with the hordes at Etihad, I had left work early, and Declan and I had holed up in my house, determined not to answer the door or the phone in preparation of the second wave of attack.

After we had breakfast, we faced the media together in order to get to the car. They threw questions at us, but we pushed through until we unlocked the doors and Declan said, "You got your statement yesterday. That's enough for now."

It obviously *wasn't* enough for now, judging by the way they pressed against us and started yelling, hoping volume alone would make us respond.

Declan was meeting with members of his team at Etihad in some sort of preemptive get-together where everybody could air their feelings about how his coming out would affect them all. The rest of the team would be connected via video conference.

"They really push the psychology angle nowadays, don't they?" I asked as we turned out of my street, referring to the club's nicey-nice share-our-feelings approach.

"It's all very by the book," Dec agreed. "Sometimes I wonder if a few beers down at the local would get better results."

"Oh yeah, alcohol, extreme masculinity, and controversy. Can't see anything bad resulting from that."

"At least it would all come out. No pun intended."

We couldn't help but laugh at it anyway.

When he pulled over to let me off on Bourke Street, he surprised me by leaning in and kissing me. "I'll call you."

"Okay," I murmured, and I stumbled out the door.

It felt weird to have gone from hiding everything and being so careful to him suddenly being so cavalier. So far everything had gone really well for him; the backlash wasn't starting to appear (as it inevitably would), everybody that he dealt with personally had been supportive. There had been no reaction from Joe

Public he had seen yet. In his view at the moment everything was hunky-dory, and I felt shitty about waiting for the bubble to burst. I had been there before; I knew the pattern. I didn't want to be the one to burst it for him, but sooner or later he would hit his first of many walls.

I felt even more shitty when it only took a few hours. It was as if I had cursed him and made it become possible. Was I Cassandra reincarnated?

He appeared in the doorway of my office; Nyssa had told him to go straight through. She had gone in search of the office medkit and icepack even though the doctor at the Etihad's gym had already looked at him.

"Don't panic," he said, because my face must have already been showing what I myself hadn't even recognised as feeling yet.

I was out of my chair and across the room to him before he even took a step. "Who the hell did that to you?"

His jaw was bruised, the skin broken around the edge of his lip to show blood that was fresh even now, peeking out around the ends of the butterfly bandage attached to his skin. He winced as I gently inspected it, and he pulled my hands down.

"It was that bloody Geoff Hendricks, wasn't it?" I demanded.

I had never liked Hendricks; he always seemed too full of himself on the field, even by footballer standards.

"It wasn't Geoff." He looked at me, with what seemed like a new light in his eyes. "You look fucking mad."

"I *am* fucking mad!"

"What, are you going to go up there and defend my honour?"

"Give me a minute, and I will!" And I meant it. I was on fire, ready to let out all the frustration had been ebbing and flowing in me lately onto whoever had done this to him.

"That's very noble of you, but I really don't want you beating up Jess's dad."

"What?" *That* revelation forced me to sit down.

Nyssa appeared behind him with the icepack and handed it to me. "Is there anything else you need?" she asked.

"Thanks, Nyssa, this'll do," he told her, giving her a small smile.

Nyssa looked at me for confirmation; I gave her a grateful nod.

Declan took the pack off me and moved across the room to sink gratefully into one of the chairs. He held the pack against his jaw and gave a deep breath.

"Okay, you have to fill me in," I said, walking over to him.

"Can I just give you the abridged version?"

"No." I pulled my chair around my desk so I could sit beside him. I checked over his hands; no defensive wounds. He hadn't fought back. Whether that was good, I couldn't decide yet.

"The meeting actually went pretty well," he said finally. "I mean, the real test will be when we go back to training. You know, there were a few jokes, but it was all pretty easygoing. When we walked out, though, Jess's dad was there. And he just punched me. I didn't even see it coming, just heard him ranting about betraying his daughter, you know, that kind of stuff."

"Sounds like a bad soap opera."

"It was." He managed a smile, even though it was probably a bit painful. "I'm just glad it was inside Etihad's inner sanctum and the press wasn't around to capture it on film. I think he was actually about to come in for a second punch when Abe pulled him back. Then security came in and took him out."

"Took him out? With a gun?" I asked hopefully.

Declan looked at me like I had lost my mind. "No, took him *outside*, dick."

"Well, I don't care if he's Jess's dad. *I* want to take him out. And not outside."

Declan shook his head, trying not to laugh.

"Shit, Dec, it's not fair that he's singled you out when he doesn't know the full story."

"Of course he doesn't know the full story! So what else is he going to think?" Declan asked. "In his eyes, his poor daughter has been used and abused by the guy who would and could never love her. She's the victim, and I'm the bad guy. The evil, predatory fag breaking her heart to further his career."

"I thought predatory fag was my role," I said, trying to make him smile.

He didn't. "Don't."

I gingerly stroked his injured hand. "You're not a bad guy. It's just the way it was."

"Jess and I were stupid to think it could ever work."

"No offence, Dec," I said gently, "I'm surprised it lasted as long as it did."

He nodded. "Probably. I just wonder what Jess is going to do."

I kept my mouth shut. Wisely. I hoped Jess would have the courage not to let Declan take the fall for her actions as well as his own. The irony was not lost on me; this was an exact repeat of Dec's position only a few days before, where he had the choice to continue the charade or step up.

I don't think the irony was lost on him either, but he looked too exhausted to acknowledge it.

"Why don't you go back to my house?" I suggested. "I still have to work here for a while, but you should get some rest."

"It's not rest I need," Dec said tiredly.

"Well, go and see your folks or something. We can see each other later."

"You trying to get rid of me?"

"No. You can crash here if you want."

He stared down at his feet. "Is the floor comfortable?"

"I've never slept on it." I shrugged. "I only usually crumple on it in a ball when something goes wrong here."

"I'll go back to your place," Dec said. "Have a nap and a drink." He stood, for a moment seeming unsteady on his feet. "See you later."

"You okay?" I asked.

"Yeah," he said, because he felt he had to. And I had to accept it, because *I* had to.

But when he gave me a quick kiss, I could taste his blood on my lips, and it made me feel sick, vulnerable, and mad as hell.

THE sun had just about disappeared over the horizon when I got home, and my already troubled stomach fell into even further disrepute when I noticed the media presence on my street was even bigger than usual.

The scrummage for my attention started as soon as I pulled into my driveway. Yet the first person to get in my face was not from one of the major networks, but one of my neighbours.

Dale Watson. Somebody whom I avoided at the best of times.

"Simon, we need to have a word," she said firmly.

"Kinda busy, in case you haven't noticed," I replied.

"Have I noticed?" she fumed. "You can't help but notice!"

I couldn't help but notice that although the media were packed in tightly, they were being strangely silent. And I realised Dale was gearing up for a confrontation.

While courting the press at the same time.

"I'm sorry for the chaos around here lately," I said smoothly. "Believe me, it's not something I want either."

"And yet look at all this," Dale said grandly.

"It will blow over soon. Some soapie star or politician will get done for a DUI, and I'll be forgotten about."

I could hear some press members snicker at this; they knew it to be true.

"That's not good enough! Everybody on this street has been putting up with this crap for far too long!"

"There's nothing I can do about it," I repeated, just wanting to get inside.

"No," Dale said coldly. "The only time something could have been done was stopping the likes of you from moving here in the first place."

I was gratified to hear some astounded whispers from the press at her outburst.

Did she really think that would upset me, though? I've heard far worse directed at me during my life. There had been better insults when I was in primary school, for fuck's sake, and I wasn't even out then.

"If we could decide who could and couldn't move into our neighbourhoods," I said, "then I would have made sure we had an anti-old-nosey-bigots policy before *you* moved in."

More laughter from the peanut gallery.

It would have become even more heated, I could see the hate screwing up her face as she tried to think up a comeback, but everybody assembled around my car was distracted by the front door of my house opening and Declan stepping out onto the veranda.

The press immediately made a beeline for him, calling his name.

And then Jess stepped out behind him.

I groaned inwardly. They were going to have a field day with this.

"Oh, look," Dale said nastily, a satisfied smirk on her face. "It's your boyfriend's girlfriend."

I was stumped for a comeback; all I could do was roll my eyes.

The throng was also momentarily stumped by Jess's presence, but they were well practiced in responding to the unexpected scoop, calling her name and hurling cheeky questions at her.

"Jess! Are the rumours true that your father attacked Declan this afternoon?"

"Jess, how are you dealing with Declan's revelation?"

"Jess, did you know Declan was gay before he came out?"

Who *was* that journalist with the inane questions? Was it some high schooler on work experience? Because, crap, they needed to up their game if they wanted to survive in this profession.

Declan looked back at Jess; she nodded at him and moved around to take centre stage.

"I won't take up too much of your time," she said in a loud, clear voice. "And I'm not sure if I will be as eloquent as Dec was yesterday. But the truth is, I am not the victim as some of you seem to enjoy making me out to be."

Oh frig. Here it goes again. Did someone call a national coming out week and forget to tell me? At least they might have notified me it was taking place on my front doorstep. I would have gone round to the back entrance.

"Declan and I have always had an understanding; a marriage of convenience, if you will, without the marriage. We acted as support for each other when we needed it. I also am gay and happily living with my partner."

I thought Dale Watson was about to explode under the weight of her own prejudice. It would have been entertaining had it happened, for her to spontaneously combust like that shopkeeper from Dickens' *Bleak House*. Unfortunately she remained breathing, although heavily so.

Ignoring the hubbub that had erupted, Jess put up her hands. "I hope now that this is out in the open, there can be an end to the stories depicting Declan as some sort of coward or user. We both knew what we were doing, and now we're both happy to live our lives openly, as we should have always done."

Okay, that last line was a little sanctimonious, but it would play well to the public who claimed to feel "betrayed by the deception" even though they had no right to be.

"Declan, do you have anything else to add?" asked one of the reporters from the ABC.

"Nope, not today," Declan said cheerfully. He caught my eye and nodded for me to slip past the press into my own house and away from the madness.

As I made my way to the sound of cameras flashing yet again, I heard Dale Watson from behind me.

"This neighbourhood is going to the dogs!" she yelled uselessly and rather stupidly.

I grinned at Dec as he pulled me up the steps. I turned back to the press and faced Dale down.

"Woof bloody woof!" I said, unable to keep a straight face.

It was just as stupid a response as Dale's, but it was effective. We had the media on our side for the moment, and they laughed while Dale slunk away deflated.

Declan's hand snuck into mine, and this only made the cameras spring into action. "Good-bye, ladies and gentlemen of the press," he said warmly, but firmly. They understood what he meant. He had given them what they wanted, one hell of a show and one great photo opportunity. Now it was time for them to throw in the towel. Perhaps only just for now, because we couldn't expect them to give up entirely. But they all drifted away and started packing up their vans as we made our way into the house and closed the front door behind us.

"You are such a dork," Dec said with a laugh.

"Yeah, well look at you with your power trip," I countered.

"They're probably just moving onto my doorstep now," Jess sighed.

Not to be mean, but probably not. She wasn't in the public domain like Declan; interest in her would be short-lived. Just like I would always be in Dec's shadow. But apparently, as the song says, I would be the wind beneath his wings or some kind of crap like that.

"Anyway," she continued and turned to face me. "Sorry, Simon."

"Huh? You have nothing to apologise to me for."

"Well, I did kind of use your front lawn for my own press conference." She took a deep breath and shook slightly as she exhaled. "And I'm sure you weren't impressed with my father using Dec as a punching bag."

"It's still not your fault," I said honestly.

"Believe me, he's now pissed at me. He's embarrassed by the fact he went after Dec when he didn't know the full story."

"Jess," Dec said. "It's okay."

"Stop going for the fucking saint of the year, okay? You have enough awards."

He gave her the finger, and she laughed.

"Seriously, though. I'll make sure the old fart apologises to you at some point."

"Look," Declan replied, his face grave. "I'm sure he would rather just forget about it. And to tell you the truth, I would too. So just tell him that."

Jess reached up and kissed him. "Thanks, Dec."

She then surprised me by kissing me on the cheek. "Take care, Simon."

"Say hi to Robyn for me," Dec said, a tad evilly.

Jess gave him a sarcastic smile. "I will. Jesus, she always wanted me to come out, but I bet she didn't think it would involve the press in such a spectacular fashion."

"Maybe she can stop hating me now."

"Don't count on it." Jess opened the front door and peered out. "The coast is clear."

And it was. Jess walked to her car without disturbance, and we watched her drive off.

"So," Dec said slowly, as he closed the door and turned back to face me.

"So," I repeated back to him.

"What do you think happens now?" he asked.

Right now I had *some* idea, but for the short-term future? I looked blankly at him, and he grinned tiredly.

"Yeah, that's what I thought too."

IT'S funny what life can have in store for you, though.

"I used to worry about him," Mrs. Tyler said to me. "When he was going out with Jess, or what I *thought* was going out... they just didn't seem like a couple to me, although my husband told me I was being silly. I think deep down a mother knows, even if she doesn't admit it to herself." She took a deep breath and sipped from her cup of tea, making a face at its lame hospital-strength. "But I worried. I thought he was settling, even though I loved Jess. Just because they didn't have that connection. So when everything happened last week, and he finally told me, I wasn't as surprised as I might have been."

I was back at the scene of the crime: St. Vincent's Hospital. If you had told me I would be having tea (well, *I* was having coffee, of course) with Declan's mother this time last week, I would have thought you meant in some alternate universe. But here we were.

Declan was in his father's room, making sure all was okay before he brought me in for a formal introduction.

Yes. I was having the official meet-n-greet with the parents. And it seemed to be turning out okay so far. A lot better than the meeting I had had previously in the day with Alice Provotna, who was rather icy at the fact that I hadn't returned any of her calls and informed me that the angle of her documentary had now changed. Rather than just focus on the upcoming Triple F Festival, she would be including the behind-the-scenes drama of my relationship with "recently uncloseted AFL legend Declan Tyler." I hadn't told Dec yet; I was still hoping that I could talk her out of it. Her contract with us stated that she had artistic control, and I cursed myself for letting the lawyers slip it through. Of course, at the time I had no idea what was going to be happening a few months from the date of signing.

"Are you worried now?" I asked Mrs. Tyler, trying not to let my nervousness show.

She looked at me kindly, but I could tell her brain was ticking over as she tried to figure out how she could put her feelings tactfully. "Yes, I am."

I wished Nyssa was around to make my coffee Irish. I tried to keep my face blank.

"Not in the way you're probably thinking," Mrs. Tyler continued. "But a mother never stops worrying. It's just that now I have something new to worry about. Declan's found someone, but a whole new set of problems have come with it."

I wondered if she was referring to me as the major problem, but I remained silent to give her the benefit of the doubt.

"I'm not suggesting that my son's sexuality...." Here she faltered. "I don't like saying that word, it sounds so clinical. But you know what I mean. I don't care that Declan is gay. I just care it means life is going to be difficult for him in certain ways. No parent wants their child to suffer, especially at the hands of other people and what they may believe or not believe. I'd be lying if I said that I'm not dreading the first time he has to go out onto the field or when one of those bozos from the footy shows on the telly start doing their jokes."

"I worry about that too," I admitted.

"It doesn't help he's wearing a bloody nose and a cut lip from somebody who has been a friend of our family for over twenty years. You wonder what other people who *don't* know him are capable of."

"But if you're like all other mothers," I said gently, "then you're expecting the worse. You may be surprised by some good things as well."

She smiled at me. "You're very charming."

I smirked involuntarily. "Dec says that I can be, but only when I *want* to be."

"He says a lot of good things about you."

I was starting to squirm under her steady gaze. "He has to talk me up, you realise."

"Yes, one of the very first things he said was that you were self-deprecating. I see he's right."

I coloured. "Well...."

"My son thinks very highly of you, Simon. That's how I know despite everything else, he is happy. I can see it in him, in the way he never talked about Jess. You can see it in his eyes. You know, when you have a kid in the public eye, yet another thing you worry about is whether people will accept your child for himself, or whether they're just riding his coattails."

"You thought I could be doing that?"

"There was part of me wondering if *Jess* was doing that. Mothers can be the harshest judges of character, but it's only out of some misguided sense of love. But when Declan told me how you met—"

"Oh, he didn't, did he?" I wanted the floor to open up and swallow me and put an end to this torture.

"Yes, he told me you insulted him."

"It was the famous Murray charm you've heard about in action."

Mrs. Tyler smiled, and I could see it was where Declan's came from. "So I knew you weren't after him for his fame."

"No, there's a lot I love about Declan, and that's not it."

Oh crap. I had said the L-word. Slightly panicked, I coughed, my eyes watering.

She watched me with amusement, but looked slightly gratified at my slip of the tongue.

"Plus," she said, once I had settled down, "you gave up a lot to be with him. You didn't want the glory of *being* with him. You were... out... before you met Declan. And you had to stop being so in certain ways in order to protect him. That would have taken a certain amount of sacrifice."

I didn't say anything, because I feared it could sound self-serving.

"It's not going to be much easier from here on."

"Now you're sounding like a typical mother," I told her.

Declan walked out of his dad's room to find his mother laughing. He smiled nervously at me, and I could tell he was bursting with questions but they would have to wait until we were alone.

"Don't worry, honey," his mum said. "I'm saving all the embarrassing stories about you for another time."

"Just, please, hide the photos of me with the mullet."

"He never had a mullet," she told me. "I would never have let him out of the house if he had a *mullet!*"

"If there's a mullet in your past, we're over," I told him.

"That's quite a list you're compiling," he said, shoving his hands in his pockets.

"Don't worry. You're stuck with me for now."

"See what I have to put up with?" Dec asked his mother.

She didn't say anything, but looked at me and pointed to her eyes and then at her son.

I knew what she meant, although it confused Declan. "So are you ready to meet my dad?" he asked.

Hoping that this next family meeting would go as smoothly, I couldn't help but hear *The Imperial March* start in my head as I nodded and followed Dec into the room behind us.

Declan's father looked extremely hale for someone who had just suffered a heart attack. Like his son, he was in great shape. He had been a footy player as well, although he had never made it to the proper AFL, instead being in the higher echelons of the local clubs. Thankfully he had never been a stage father, though, trying to live his dreams vicariously through his son.

"Dad," Declan said softly, "this is Simon."

I stuck out my hand to shake his, and it was gripped with a fist of iron.

"So," Mr. Tyler said with a faint tone of bemusement, "you're the one who's turned my son's world upside down."

Dec looked about to object, but I was used to fathers with a healthy amount of snark.

"I guess I was a part of it, but I wasn't the catalyst."

He nodded. "Call me Barry."

The nurse entered at that moment with his meds. She gave a start when she saw Declan, and her eyes widened when she saw me in there as well. She had obviously been watching the news. Thankfully the Hippocratic Oath would stop her from running out the door and selling her story to *New Idea*: "Declan Tyler Brings Gay Lover To Meet Sick Father! Doctors on Standby!"

"Did Fred really do that to you, Dec?" Barry asked, sipping water to wash down the pills as the nurse left us alone again.

Dec fingered his jaw. "Uh, yeah."

"You didn't hit him back, did you?"

"No, of course not!"

"Did you, Simon?" Barry asked, amused.

"I wasn't there," I replied.

"Would you have?"

"I'm pretty much of a pacifist. Plus, logically, it just would have made things worse, and that's the last thing Dec needs."

Barry settled back against his pillows. "Good answer." He sighed. "I can't pretend I'm 100 percent dealing with this yet."

Dec remained silent; I could tell he was chewing on the inside of his cheek. Sometimes when kissing him, my tongue would sweep across the raw, constantly healing area, and I would feel a momentary pang of worry. But it wasn't the right place to be thinking about kissing Dec.

"I think you've got other things to worry about," I said. "Like recuperating."

"I don't mean I'm against it or anything," Barry said quickly. "Just… it *is* a bit of a shock. I mean, Sylvie said it was in the back of her mind for a while. I just haven't had the time to think about it."

"There isn't much to think about, Dad," Dec murmured. "It just *is*."

"You forget, Declan," Barry said, his tone swinging right into the tone of a father, "I've been on the field as well. Not at the level you are, but I know what the guys can be like. They can be the best people in the world, but if they have you in their sights, you can be in trouble. You don't think I'm going to be thinking about that the next game you play? Plus the fact you're still recovering and will have just had another op?"

Damn it, he was starting to make *me* worry again. And Declan knew it.

"They just have a different reason to now," Dec said. "It doesn't make much difference. Before they just went after me because I was apparently the top draw. If they're going after me for a personal vendetta, they'll probably fuck up because they'll be focused on the emotion."

"When did you get a psychology degree?" his father complained, and then he turned his sights on me. "What do you think, Simon?"

I gave a careful reply. "I think Dec will do whatever he wants to do and thinks is right. And we'll all have to support that. And be there for him."

Dec gave me a small smile.

"And if someone guns for him, then they better fucking watch out."

Dec's smile faltered, but Barry laughed.

"He seems all right, Dec."

I could tell Dec was perturbed by my last remark, but happy that his father approved. "Yeah," he said finally. "He's okay."

"THAT went better than I thought it would," I said to Dec as we walked out of the lift and made our way through the underground parking bays to his car. A couple of people stopped when they saw us and whispered amongst themselves, but we trudged on.

"Yeah, it did. I think Dad's accepting it better already than he thinks he is."

"Now you just have to get through meeting my family for the first time." I shuddered involuntarily.

"You still haven't met my siblings," Declan warned me. "My parents are *nothing* compared to them."

"Great."

"Don't worry. We'll all be fine."

I winced. "Don't jinx it."

He looked around for something wooden to knock upon, and when he couldn't find anything, went for the oldest joke in the world and grabbed me in a headlock to rap upon my head. By the time we reached his car, his arm had slipped down to encircle my waist, and it felt damn good.

I WONDERED when things would start to feel normal for Declan and myself or if this was going to be life as we knew it forevermore. It had to be the settling-in period, surely; the meeting of the parents, the first dealings with the press, being called into a meeting with the board of the Devils....

Which was where I found myself now, my arms crossed defensively. Declan sat beside me, slowly swinging from side to side in his chair.

"You're probably wondering why we wanted to meet with you, Simon," Scott Frasier said, deciding he would be the one to start things off.

"I have a pretty good idea," I said. I wondered when the pretty secretary who was meant to be getting me a coffee would be returning.

"Oh?" Ed Wallace, the Devils' CEO asked. "And what would that be?"

"You probably want to make sure I follow your rules so I'm not more of an embarrassment to the club than you already think I am. Maybe slap a gag order on me."

I heard Dec give a soft groan as he continued to swing slowly in his chair.

Ed grinned at me. "Bit paranoid, aren't you, Simon?"

"You tell me," I volleyed back.

"It's true we did want to discuss with you a course of action—"

"Hah." I don't know who switched the obnoxious button on me, but I knew I was making Dec uncomfortable so I tried to tone it down a little. "So what course of action?"

"The press and the public are expecting to hear your story," Wallace said. "So we want to try and put you out there to the friendliest outlets we can. We have some ideas, but we want to hear yours and Declan's as well."

I named one particularly bozo-ish footy show that aired during the week. "He's definitely not going on that, for a start. Exposing himself to that dickhead host—"

Declan gave another small groan, and I shot him a look.

"My friend, the dickhead host?" Wallace asked, and some of the other men in the room tried to conceal their smiles unsuccessfully.

"Then if he's your friend, you know his schtick," I said coolly. "With the act he puts on, you know Dec wouldn't get the friendliest welcome."

Wallace shrugged. "I'll give you that."

"Declan?" Scott asked.

"Oh, I can talk now?" Declan said pointedly, mainly to me, and he cleared his throat. "I was thinking anyone on the ABC, if they want to have me on."

Everybody in the room laughed, but not meanly.

"Declan," Wallace said amiably. "*Everybody* wants your story at the moment."

"Tracey," Scott said to a perfectly manicured woman sitting across from him. "Get onto the ABC after we finish here."

"You do know you don't get paid for going on the ABC?" Tracey asked of Declan.

"I think I get enough money to not have to worry about that," Declan told her.

"Just making sure you know that," she said, vaguely insulted.

"I think the ABC will probably the best," I said, sticking up for him.

"A lot of the gay rags are asking for interviews," Tracey continued. "You should at least do one of them. They'll probably want to talk to Simon as well."

"Huh?" I asked stupidly.

"You *are* part of this," Declan reminded me. "That's why you're here."

"I just thought I was going to be asked for my opinion," I said weakly.

"Don't be naïve," Wallace said, looking up as his secretary entered with a tray of mugs. "The public's hungry for both of you. They'll feel cheated if you don't figure into some of it."

I took a long sip of my coffee and placed the mug back upon the table. "Can I ask something?" I waited to hear Declan groan, but he only tensed slightly this time.

"Go ahead," Frasier nodded.

"You seem to be very accepting of all this. Call me cynical, but I thought you might be a little reserved instead of wanting to arrange photo ops and interviews to get the message out further."

Ed nodded. "I understand why you would think that. But we're a business as well. And our numbers are down, membership wise. Lower numbers of members means less money coming into the club and lower-tiered sponsorship deals. And you know what brings more sponsorship and more members?"

"Publicity," I replied. "Preferably positive."

"That's right," Wallace said.

"Do you know we've gotten more publicity in the past week than in the whole second half of last year?" Scott asked. "And it's all due to you two. Now everybody might not be down with the whole gay thing, but it makes us look good if we deal with it positively. Especially with the media on side."

"Well, that makes me feel so much better," I murmured.

"You don't know me real well, Simon," Scott said. "But I have always had Declan's best interests at heart, no matter what. And Declan would be the first to tell you that."

I looked at Declan; he nodded, and I could tell it wasn't just for show. I guess Scott was right; Declan had been out of commission for a while, the club hadn't pressured him beyond his capabilities, and although he was a commodity to the club both injured and at his best, I couldn't help but believe them.

"This could be a boon to the club, especially image-wise. So much media attention is put on the behind-the-scenes boozing or drug-taking that some of the players partake in. This is something positive affecting one of the players personally, and it is something everyone can get behind."

I waited for the tired *no pun intended* wisecrack to rear its head, but it didn't. Maybe they meant it.

"In that case, I should tell you that a documentary maker was already filming me for a piece about the festival," I told them. "Her name is Alice Provotna, and she now says she wants it to focus on Declan and me as well."

Ed entered her name into his Blackberry. "Can you send me her details? I would like to schedule a meeting with her."

I started to have visions of the highly artistic and temperamental Alice meeting with the business-minded Ed, and her inevitable accusations he was trying to control her project. "Uh, sure."

"She might like access to some of our stock footage of Declan. We can discuss that in the meeting. But Simon, I'd also be lying if I wasn't worried about your involvement in this. Declan has been dealing with the attention for years; he's used to it. You're not, so you need to be careful. Especially when we're trying to maintain a positive image."

"Is this the gag order?" I asked.

"It's the be careful order," Ed said, looking every part the businessman trying to protect his product.

"I THINK that went okay," Declan said as we headed back to the car. He was jiggling his keys in his hand.

I reached over and stole them away from him. "I'm driving."

"Hey!" he protested. "Do you know how to drive a SUV?"

"Can't be that hard," I scoffed.

"So you don't think it went well," Declan sighed.

"I feel like I'm on probation," I replied, activating the central locking.

Declan jumped into the passenger side as I opened my door. "You're not on *probation*. They just had a point. I'm used to both the press and the public needling me."

I slid in beside him. "You're forgetting I work in the media."

"Not personally, but as a representative of a business."

He had a point. "For you, I'll try to be careful."

"That's all I'm asking."

I turned the car over, threw it into gear, and we peeled out of the car park with Declan hanging on for dear life.

CHAPTER
TWENTY-THREE

THE ABC was quick to sign us on; we were scheduled to attend a taping the very next week.

"Now we're doing media," I told Declan, "you *have* to meet my parents."

He laughed at the expression on my face.

"I'm serious. As much as the thought of it scares the shit out of me, if they see us doing publicity and they haven't had the opportunity to slobber all over you they'll probably kill me."

"Well, I can't have you being killed." Declan grinned. "But do you have to try and scare me so much before I do it?"

"I'm just trying to prepare you," I reassured him.

Tim had been trying to get a hold of me for over a week. Well, in his own Tim-ish way. Which meant he tried once a day, while I was at work, and then sounded surprised on the machine every time he had to leave a message. It didn't occur to him to try my mobile or get my work number from my mother. When I finally did speak to him, I could hear the awe in his voice as he tried to accept that his weird wanker of a brother was going out with Declan Tyler™, who was a Gay Footballer Celebrity™ now.

"So, he's really a fruit?" he asked.

"A tropical one," I said, having promised my mother I wouldn't be too harsh on the dickhead.

"One of what?"

I sighed. "Fruit. A banana maybe?"

"Are you on drugs?"

"No, but I thought you were."

"Funny. No, seriously—"

"Well, he's either gay or *really* good at pretending he is."

"Gross. I don't want to hear about your sex life."

"And I don't want you to hear about my sex life."

"Glad that's sorted, then. So, he's *really* gay?"

I sighed heavily for his benefit.

Tim finally got the hint. "Anyway, I'm having a party this weekend."

"Really?" The hairs on my neck began to rise. Tim had never gone out of his way to invite me specifically to any of his parties before.

"Yeah. It's my engagement party."

"Don't you mean *our* engagement party?"

"What are you talking about?" he asked. "You're not engaged."

"Dickhead. I meant, it's not just *your*... oh, forget it."

"Anyway, are you coming?"

"Sure," I said, trying to sound happier than I felt about it. "Can I bring Roger and Fran?"

"Yeah, okay," he paused slightly. "But aren't you going to bring him?"

I played dumb. "I asked if I could bring Roger."

"Declan Tyler!"

"Oh, *him!* Do you want me to?"

"Well, he's your boyfriend or your *partner* or whatever is it you call them these days, isn't he?" That's Tim, sensitive to the last drop.

"I'm not bringing him just so you can show him off to your mates."

"Fine."

I knew all this would get back to my mother, and I didn't want the lecture which would result from it. Besides, it would be a public setting, Fran and Roger would be there for support, and we would only have to make an obligatory appearance for Dec to meet the family.

"I'll ask him," I said. Famous last words.

"Cool," Tim said nonchalantly, although I knew he would be bragging about the celebrity coming to his party to all his friends the second it was confirmed, if not before. I hung up after exchanging good-byes and thumped my head against the wall.

IT SEEMED my house was at peace again. The camp of journalists had been absent for a few days, although they still called from time to time hoping to get some comment from me. They were starting to sniff out Declan was signing up for interviews and wanted to get in on the action. Dale Watson, however, was still acting as Neighbourhood Watch and making sure to glare at me whenever our paths crossed.

Dec emerged from the kitchen, carrying fresh drinks. He sat next to me on the couch, and I immediately swung my feet over onto his lap.

"Are you nervous about the interview?" Fran asked.

"Me?" Declan asked. "Not really."

"Liar," I challenged him, and he scowled at me.

Roger reached for a beer. "That guy is really good at getting people to open up. He'll probably make you cry."

"He will not!" Declan protested.

"I don't know," I teased. "You've been holding in all your secrets for so long, it'll probably be like being on a therapist's couch. That's why he always has the box of tissues on set."

Declan groaned and buried his face under a cushion. "This is such a huge mistake."

"No," Roger said. "The huge mistake is all of us going to Tim's engagement party."

I felt that momentary stab of family loyalty that made me want to lean over and punch Roger. I know I bitched my family out all the time, but *I* was family. Nobody else was allowed to bitch them out. Even if Roger *was* the closest thing to family.

Fran not-so-subtly nudged him, and he looked suitably chastened.

"Is it going to be that bad?" Declan asked.

Fran and Roger remained conspicuously silent. I sighed and took a swig of my beer.

"One, it's my family, who can be trying at the best of times," I told Declan. "Two, my brother's friends will be there. Three, so will his fiancée's family. Gabby, if you remember me telling you, asked me if I was 'the gay one'. Four—"

"How long *is* this list?" Declan asked.

I ground my heel a little too savagely into his lap, and he yelped. Fran almost spat her beer across the room.

"Go on," Declan said through gritted teeth.

"Four," I continued. "Fuck… now I've lost my train of thought."

"Stick another drink in him and shut him up," Roger suggested.

"You're just lucky his feet aren't in your crotch," Declan told him. Roger blanched at the thought.

"Four," I said, ignoring them both. "Putting two and three together, combined with one, probably means that the apocalypse will finally occur, and we will be in the centre of it all. Nothing will save you, Declan Tyler. Which leads me to five."

"Stop it!" Fran groaned.

"Five," I said grandly. "Declan Tyler™ will be the focus of everybody's attention. And even though he wants you there so he can show off his connection to you, my brother will probably end up resenting it if everybody there starts watching your every move. Tim hates not being the centre of attention."

"It runs in the family," Roger muttered, and Fran was unable to stop a second explosion.

"There isn't a six, is there?" Declan asked.

"I'm sure I can think of one."

"Don't," Fran pleaded.

"Fine," I grumbled. "Don't say I didn't warn you."

I WAS trying to affect an air of grandiose nonchalance about it all and being pretty unsuccessful at it. As usual, my friends were quick to catch me out on it. Declan had already experienced his first exposure to backlash against his lifestyle through Jess's father, and although I wasn't expecting fisticuffs at Tim and Gabby's engagement party, I wasn't thinking it was going to be a barrel of laughs either.

Which I guess meant he *did* love me. He would have to, to put himself out like that. But I guess we were all going outside our comfort zones.

The interview on the ABC went perfectly, actually. The host of the program put Declan at ease and was compassionate, charming, funny, and extremely successful at managing to extract all the details the public was dying to know. Declan and I at times appeared awkward on camera discussing our private lives and our relationship, but this seemed to work for us as the media the next morning were all positive in their reports about the interview. Such is the power of media in being able to deflect the darker side of public opinion, because it meant Declan was still fooling himself slightly thinking it would always be like this.

Buoyed by the success of the interview, Declan agreed to do a couple of more, although I warned him not to overexpose himself. Too much of a glut in the media, and he could fall prey to tall poppy syndrome. He was already in the press enough before he came out, just because of his footballing. When the season started up again there would be double the attention on his return, both because of his playing and his recent revelations.

I didn't want to be particularly overexposed in the media myself, despite the fact that my bosses would have loved it. I agreed to do one more interview with Dec in the meantime, as part of the *Weekend Australian Magazine*'s regular "Two of Us" feature, where they profile a couple about their relationship. We wouldn't be the first gay twosome to be featured, but we were the most "famous." The photographer made us pose in the stands of the MCG with the field stretching out behind, empty and unyielding. I'm not sure what he was trying to say, but I know Declan was stressing about the pose he wanted us to take, that we should look casual but affectionate, but not affectionate enough to scare the general public off their Saturday breakfast. In the end it was best smiles forward, and our hands firmly clasped between us.

The interview and photo session was practically all we got to see of each other that week. Nyssa and I were at battle stations, for the festival began the week after. Alice Provotna was pissed Declan didn't seem to be around as much as she expected him to be; I had to remind her repeatedly that Declan didn't work for the Triple F and he had his own life and job. I could tell on opening night she wouldn't stray at all from our sides, desperate to capture us on every last frame of film she had in her camera.

Declan was still spending time with his family and shuttling back and forth between them and Etihad as his bosses were still figuring out a game plan for his media blitz and getting his career back on track.

"This operation better fix you," I threatened him one day. "Otherwise everybody will be blaming me for your decline."

"I'll make sure I play well," he said dryly, "just so you can save face."

"Thanks."

"Making you look good is what I live for."

When Friday came around I was feeling burnt out, even more than usual, and the last thing I wanted to do was go to the damned engagement party. What I wanted was to fall asleep on the couch with Declan and wake up to a blissful Saturday morning of breakfast and sex. In any order.

Nyssa was upset the traditional Bog-off-to-the-Pub excursion was cancelled, and could only be mollified when I told her that the rest of us would all be firmly ensconced in the first circle of hell. I told her she could come along if she wanted to, but she was smarter than the rest of us.

"You look exhausted," Declan told me when I came home and collapsed on the couch.

"Just prop me up if I pass out," I replied.

He studied me worriedly. "Did you look like this in the lead-up to the festival last year?"

"Probably worse." I closed my eyes, even though I knew it could mean I would fall asleep within seconds.

I felt the warmth and pressure of Declan's lips, which was the only thing at that moment of time that could rouse me out of my wannabe coma.

"Come on, Sleeping Beauty." He grinned as I opened my eyes to find him standing over me.

"Funny."

"Seriously, you were snoring enough to shake the walls."

"I was *asleep*?" I jerked into a fully upright position.

"It's eight o'clock, we've got to go and pick up Fran and Roger."

"What the hell? You let me sleep?"

"I didn't *let* you do anything. But you looked like you needed it."

I pulled him on top of me and began kissing him again. He gently levered me up, even though I tried to resist.

"Wouldn't it be nicer to stay here?" I asked.

"You know we have to go."

"I'll let you do anything to me you want."

"Nice, prostituting yourself to get out of seeing your family."

"You're not tempted?"

"Nope."

"Liar. Not even a little bit?"

"You have dried drool on your chin," he said, matter-of-factly. "It's pretty gross."

I pushed him away, and he laughed, watching me as I stomped off to the bathroom. I would have preferred to have a shower, but I had to make do with washing the drool off my face and putting on fresh deodorant and cologne. It was only my family, anyway.

Declan was being so cheerfully annoying it wasn't like I had to make a true Friday night effort for him. Although truthfully, what I was doing now wasn't that far removed from my usual effort.

"Shame you couldn't wash that grimace off your face," he remarked as I walked back into the lounge room.

I threw a cushion at him. He caught it easily and handballed it back to me. I, of course, missed, and it flew into the study.

"Nice," Declan said. "You're a natural."

I headed straight out the door and left Dec to lock up as he continued guffawing at my expense.

THE four of us stood outside my parents' house like we were about to storm the castle gates, battle-weary as we were.

Music was blasting away, some generic rock I didn't recognise. Man, was I getting out of touch with the youth of today? Maybe I was, especially if I used phrases like "youth of today." There was also a lot of yelling over the music, the clinking of beer bottles, and general rabblerousing. The smell of barbecued meat floated about, and Roger's stomach grumbled in anticipation.

"Do you smell that?" I asked. "It smells like teen spirit."

"Even Tim's too old for teen spirit," Fran said, burrowing herself further into her coat. "Can we go in? I'm fucking freezing."

"There's still time to run for our lives," I pleaded.

"He's like this before every party," Roger told Declan.

"Yeah, Simon," Fran butted in. "Remember that last party we forced you to? Where would you be now if we hadn't done that?"

"Desperately lonely and unhappy," Roger answered for me.

"Too right," Declan said smugly.

"All of you… *suck*," I said lamely, and I trudged off ahead of them, probably to my doom.

A few people milling in the hallway stared at me as I walked in, probably trying to figure out which side of the engagement party I belonged to. Like I said,

Tim and I didn't tend to hang out much. But when Roger, Fran and Declan appeared behind me there was an instant look of recognition in their eyes. Well, only in regards to Declan.

We pushed through into the kitchen, where Mum was bossing Gabby and some of her friends around. Mum squealed when she saw me, showing more excitement about my appearance than social etiquette would have normally allowed.

"Hi, Mum," I said, dealing awkwardly with her exuberant hugging. "You been into the sherry already?"

"Only a nip or two," she replied, eyes glistening. "Hello, Roger, Fran."

"Hey, Mrs. M," they replied in unison.

"And who's your friend?" she asked me, playing dumb.

Squirming with embarrassment that she was trying to pull *that* worn ploy off, I replied, "This is my friend, Vincent van Gogh."

She glowered. "Very funny."

Declan stepped forward to rescue the situation, his hand extended. "Pleased to meet you, Mrs. Murray. I'm Declan."

"Of course you are," she practically purred. "Let me tell you, Declan, you have your hands full with this one."

Fran snorted; Roger dug her in the ribs.

"I think I can handle him," Declan said pleasantly.

This time, Roger snorted and tried to cover it up with a coughing fit when he saw me eyeing the ashtray on the table as if I were going to pick it up and belt him with it.

Gabby and her friends rushed forward now, and I was shoved aside as Declan was surrounded with those wanting to make his acquaintance. Fran and Roger looked horrified and scuttled over to join me just as Mum pulled me into a deeper corner of the kitchen.

"He's lovely," she said approvingly.

"Uh, thanks."

"Really lovely."

"Um, okay."

"Have you two—"

"Simon!" Fran interrupted. "Drinks!"

I wanted to kiss her, I was so thankful. "Coming right up!"

Roger began to make small talk with my mother while I crossed to the fridge, opened it, and wondered if I could fit inside. If it weren't for all the people who would be opening it looking for drinks, it could have been an option.

Mum was distracted by the microwave beeping. "Your brother's out the back," she announced as she sailed past me.

I handed Roger and Fran their drinks; Declan was still surrounded so I held onto his.

"Shouldn't you rescue him?" Roger asked.

"I think he's used to being accosted on a regular basis," I replied with a shrug.

"You are the *worst* boyfriend," Fran admonished me.

"Yep." At the moment all I was thinking about was my own skin.

Gabby broke off from the group and ran outside. She hadn't said hello to me yet. Fran raised her eyebrows and calmly swigged beer from her bottle.

My future sister-in-law ran back in with her fiancé in tow. They swept past me to rejoin the Declan brigade.

"Nice to see you, Tim," I sang out, receiving no answer.

"Nice," Roger commented.

I pulled the engagement present the four of us had sprung for out of my bag and placed it upon the kitchen table with the others. With Declan and most of my family preoccupied, I slipped away to my old bedroom to put my bag down and hang my coat up for the brief amount of time we would be staying here.

You couldn't tell that I had once lived here; I managed to strip away most of my presence and take it with me when I had moved out. It wasn't that I was trying to cut myself out of the house; I just liked my stuff being with me. The room was now more of a storage area, although an old single bed stood in the corner for anybody who might happen to stay over.

The door opened, and Declan slipped in. "You hiding already?"

"I would have thought *you* had more reason to hide than anybody else."

He shrugged. "I'm used to it." He looked around. "This is really your bedroom?"

"My bedroom's in *my* house," I said pointedly.

"You know what I mean. I just can't really imagine you living here. There seems to be nothing of you left in here."

"Yeah, because it's at my house."

He opened his mouth to say something, but seemed to think better of it. He moved over to me and slid an arm through the crook of mine. "You're really not comfortable here, are you?"

I sighed and let myself become more malleable against him. "I can handle it."

"So it's me you're so tense about, then?"

I nodded reluctantly. "I just don't want anybody to be a fuckwit to you."

"If they are, they are." He shrugged. "But you can't give yourself an ulcer stressing about something that hasn't happened."

"I guess not."

"You're a prime candidate for a heart attack before you're forty, Simon," he murmured. "In case you haven't noticed I've had enough worry with my dad, and I don't want to have to start looking for warning signals in you."

Great. A guilt trip on top of everything. "You don't have to worry."

"But I will, because you will."

"So I'll put you in an early grave as well?"

He laughed, but gave me a kiss as an answer. I responded a bit more enthusiastically than I should have, but I guess I wanted to feel reassured.

And, of course, Tim walked in.

"Oh, gross!" he cried and childishly slapped his hands over his eyes. "The goggles, they do nothing!" he said in a heavy Austrian accent, mimicking Radiation Man from *The Simpsons*.

Dec gave me a sympathetic look.

Tim peeked out between his fingers. "If you're finished, Declan, I want you to meet some of my friends."

I would have been tempted to tell him to fuck off after that display, but Declan nodded with much more effort than I would have given.

"Hi, brother," I said pointedly.

"Yeah, hi," he said dismissively. "Come on, Declan. Haven't got all night."

Now it was my turn to give an apologetic look. But Declan didn't even have a chance to see it as Tim whisked him away.

I stood in my empty room and slowly gathered up the courage to brave the maelstrom once more.

I BARELY got to see Declan over the next hour. Any attendees of the party would have been hard pressed to believe we were a couple, as we were hardly seen in the same circles. Especially as my circle consisted of Fran and Roger, hiding in a dark corner. It wasn't like I thought couples should be glued to the hip, but let's face it, my date was more popular than I was, even amongst people *I* knew.

Declan's presence was certainly the talk of the party, but I got my share of unabashed stares and certain whispers as well. At one point when Roger disappeared to get more drinks and Fran followed him to go the loo, I was left standing stupidly in the corner by myself, hoping the shadows hid me well enough. Basically, it was my usual position in any large social situation (unless it was work and I was forced to sally forth in order to earn my pay check), and believe me, it brought back memories of the party where I first met Declan. Once again, I was hiding, and he was in the limelight, uncomfortable in the middle of people who laid claim to him but didn't know him at all.

A small group of Tim's friends, who I vaguely recognised, sauntered up to me. The usual small talk pleasantries about the engagement and the party were exchanged, but they soon got around to what they had really wanted to know.

"I know I've seen it all over the TV," one said. "But are you really going out with Declan Tyler?"

It really was that difficult to believe, it seemed.

"If it's on television, it must be true," I said, forcefully cheerful.

"Really?" number two asked.

I sighed. "Yep."

They giggled, and the hairs on the back of my neck rose. I had the feeling they weren't secret slashers of RPF let loose from the Internet for a night out.

The guy with them, whose name I hazily remembered as being Brian, eyed me narrowly. "So are you responsible for the fact that his playing's gone to shit?"

Apparently I was Yoko-freaking-Ono now. "He had his knee injury long before I came along."

"Are you sure it's not a *groin* injury?" girl number one giggled.

I shook my head sadly. She was the dumbest thing on earth. "Yeah, that was funnier last week when they said it on *The Footy Show*, and even then it wasn't that funny."

You would have thought they might have gotten the message after that, but they didn't. They mustn't have gotten enough out of the interviews we had done with the media or didn't think we were asked the pertinent questions.

Girl number two sized me up and asked slowly. "So, you know how Declan is like this really hot, good, footballer player?"

"Yeah, I've heard something about it," I replied, hoping I looked as bored as I sounded.

"And you're like some guy in theatre or something."

"Film."

"Same thing."

Well, no, not at all. But I let that slide.

"Does that make you, like, the woman?"

You know, you kind of forget every now and again that people can be so dumb. Or if not dumb, just ignorant. And then you get slapped in the face with it, just to remind you. And I know you're meant to turn the other cheek and try to be the helpful educator or whatever, to let them see in a kind way the utter stupidity that they spew, but it was beyond me tonight.

"Are you for real?" I asked.

"What?" she replied, her eyes wide.

"Seriously, how old are you? You must be the same age, or round about, as my brother, right?"

"Twenty-six."

"Okay. Then you're old enough to have gained some life experience by now to know that was the stupidest fucking question you could have asked me. Maybe you should know what you're talking about before you go shooting your mouth off." With my cheeks burning and definitely no sense of class, I stormed into the house.

But I could still hear her saying to the others, "Fags can be so bitchy."

Yeah. We sure can.

Fran was still in the line for the loo, and I pushed through it to get to my room. I put on my coat, grabbed my bag, and left to push back through the line as I made my way out the front of the house. I heard Fran calling after me, but I ignored her. I also ignored Roger as I passed by the kitchen, where he had been waylaid by my mother.

Out on the front lawn, I took a deep breath and ended up inhaling a mouthful of secondhand smoke. I turned around to see my father hiding away and sneaking a cigarette.

"Dad?"

"You caught me," he admitted.

"Hey, they're your lungs," I said.

"I talked to your...." He trailed off, unable to say the word. "Declan. He seems like a good guy."

It must have killed him to say that about a footy player who wasn't from Essendon.

"Yeah. He is."

"He always seemed kind of stuck up in the press and in the games. But he's not."

"No. He's not."

Dad finally noticed my bag. "Are you going already?"

This was the most we had spoken in quite a while, so I suddenly found myself not that eager to leave. "I was thinking about it."

"They haven't served the cake. And either your brother or mother will make some speech that will embarrass us all."

"All the more reason to leave, then."

"Why do you think I'm hiding out here?" My father laughed, and began coughing.

I tactfully avoided the smoking lecture, and I could sense he was grateful for it. "So why aren't your friends leaving with you?" he asked.

"I don't think they knew I was going. I just had to get out."

"Why?"

"Some of Tim's idiot friends."

"What did they say?" Dad sprang up immediately, ready to go to my defence.

Funny how family can be so funny about something themselves, but if anybody else showed it they got their dander up.

"Nothing, really. I just wasn't in the mood to hear that crap."

"You sound rattled. That's not like you."

"Well, Declan's in there and they're all over him, which is fine. But I'm fair game, so they think they can ask me all the stuff they're too scared to ask him."

"Like?"

I sighed. I wasn't even sure if my dad would understand. "They just asked me if I was the woman."

My dad was quiet. He cleared his throat. "Are you?"

I couldn't believe he was doing the exact same thing. My dad was usually gruff, but pretty smart. I would have thought he would know better. "Yes, Dad. I'm the woman. When we go home I hand Declan his pipe and slippers, put on my apron, and bake biscuits for him to take to training the next day."

"I'm only asking a question," Dad said, sounding genuinely puzzled.

"And it's a dumb one. I'm a man, and he's a man. We're gay because we like men. Neither of us is 'the woman'."

It was the most I had ever said to him about the issue since I had first come out. At least I hadn't used the word "cock." But I didn't get to hear what his response would have been, because Fran came out of the house.

"There you are," she said. "What's going on?"

"Can you go and get Declan for me?" I asked. "I'm going."

"Roger's already doing that," she replied, wanting to ask me more but being restrained by the presence of my father.

"See ya, Dad," I said casually.

"Bye, son," he replied, equally casually.

I began walking down the street to where Declan had parked his car. I knew it would be a few moments before Declan and Roger got out of the house and then say good-bye to my father, as they were infinitely more polite than I. And I found myself thinking of Declan's father, and how his heart attack had come out of the blue, and how I was a prick to leave while being in a shit with him, because how would I feel if something happened to him? But my eyes stung, and my throat was sore, the usual trademarks of someone upset trying to keep it all in. I leaned against Dec's SUV and waited for them to join me.

"ARE you going to tell me what's wrong?" Dec murmured.

We had just dropped Fran and Roger off. I had given Fran a short rundown when she had joined me at the car, but since then I had been pretty quiet.

Declan pulled his shirt over his head, and as usual I couldn't help but stare, glad that even after months of going out he could still have that effect on me. And be pissed off at myself that when I had this hot, kind, funny, patient, and smart man wanting to be part of my life I could still obsess over people who really shouldn't even be a blip on my radar.

"Was it the party?" Declan continued, turning down the covers and jumping into bed. "I thought it went pretty well myself."

I couldn't help but snort derisively. "Of course it did. For you."

"What?"

"Everyone was in awe of you. They wouldn't dare say anything to *you*."

Annoyed with the fact that he left his pants and shirt lying on the floor, I scooped them up and put them on top of the chest of drawers—even though I was always guilty of doing the same thing myself.

He scratched at the bottom of his lip. "I take it someone said something to you?"

"Quite a few things."

"Will you stop doing that and get into bed?"

I threw my clothes on top of his and did so. Declan tried to spoon into me, but I lay rigid.

"What did they say to you?"

"Nothing," I murmured. "I don't want to talk about it."

"Yeah, well, I don't like it that you're upset about something and you won't tell me."

"Just, they got to me, and I hate they did."

"How did they?"

"By insinuating that because you're the big footballer man, I must be the woman."

He breathed deeply and tried unsuccessfully to bring me in closer to him again. "People can be fuckwits."

"They just don't get it, I guess."

"You shouldn't get upset, Simon."

"I know I shouldn't. But I still did. Because of what you do, it's like you get this free pass."

"I'm not getting a free pass," Declan said heavily.

"You know what I mean. See, this is why I didn't want to talk about it."

"Simon...," he murmured.

I finally let myself relax against him.

"You're my man, Simon."

"Yeah?"

"You know that, I know that. All the rest can go to hell."

Calmed, I closed my eyes. Sleep came quickly.

AT SOME point during the night I stirred awake and realised by his breathing that Declan was as well.

"What's the matter?" I asked groggily.

"Just thinking," he replied, sounding more alert than me.

"About?"

"Everything."

"That doesn't sound good."

"Well, more specifically about you meeting my siblings, now that I've met yours."

"Should *I* be worried now?"

"I don't think so. I mean, they might give you a bit of shit, but they won't mean anything by it."

"Then why are you wide awake, thinking about it?"

"Just because."

I yawned. "Makes sense." I rolled over to face him and draped my arm over his waist. "Do you ever wish you could swap with them?"

"Swap what?"

"Lives."

"Like *Freaky Friday*?"

"The Jodie Foster version, yeah."

"No. I like my life. Everybody has their problems."

"Sometimes it seems that others' problems aren't as tough."

"It's all relative," Declan replied. "You can't dismiss someone else's pain so easily."

"I guess."

"Are you telling me you would want to swap lives with Tim?"

I shuddered. "No. But I can't help but think about it sometimes."

"You?"

I swallowed hard, finding it difficult to admit the next thing I would say. "It's just that sometimes I *envy* Tim."

"And you don't think he envies you sometimes?"

"Come off it."

"Seriously. He'd look at you and see university educated, working in a job with a lot of responsibility, in the media, supporting himself—to him, you're probably some superconfident guy who gets everything he wants in life. And now you have the hot celebrity boyfriend—"

I shook my head. "Now, seriously, get your hand off it."

He laughed. "I'm just saying it can go both ways. Why do you envy him?"

I sighed. "Because he knows what he wants, and he never seems to question it. It's like he's known all along what he's destined to do, and he just does it. And now he's about to get married, and sooner or later they'll pop out some kids—"

"So it's the traditional dream you want?"

"No," I retorted. But I had to be honest. "Maybe. Well, the thought crosses my mind sometimes. Doesn't it with you?"

"Of course. I always think about the future."

"But it's not so easy with us."

"Which explains probably why *you* don't like to think about the future."

"It's scary enough dealing with life day to day without taking into consideration the hugeness of the future."

"There's nothing to say we can't have that kind of life. Just it will come differently."

"How much *do* you think about it?" I asked.

"As much as anybody else does."

"The home in the suburbs? The kids?"

"Yeah."

"With me?"

"No, with the guy I'm going to dump you for."

I yawned, sleep wanting to take me again. "Do you think about the logistics?"

"Dreams aren't meant to include logistics. This is where you think too much."

"Somebody has to in a relationship. For example, how do we get kids? Do you and Jess enter an arrangement where she has a kid for us and then a kid for herself?" Lost in trying to imagine such an arrangement, I continued, "but then if she's using your soldiers, that means the kids are split up, which isn't fair on them."

Humouring me, Declan grinned. "We'll use your soldiers, then."

"Same problem. Or to try and ensure we get something resembling a child from both of us, maybe your sister can bear us a kid."

"*Now* you're making me scared."

"See, this is why you should think day to day."

"You've convinced me for now."

"I guess we could always buy a baby."

Declan winced and tried not to laugh. "I'm so glad you've never said anything like this in your interviews."

"What?"

"Well, your humour is pretty selective."

"It's what most celebrities or rich people do, isn't it? We could buy a little African toddler and call him Senze-tonguecluck-niña."

"Simon, shut up!" Declan was now holding his stomach.

I rested one of my hands over his and whispered, "I'd love to have a family with you one day. One day far away. Far, far, away. But one day."

"Got it," Declan said. "It's good to hear, though."

It sounded good to me too.

CHAPTER
TWENTY-FOUR

"I'M THE fifth wheel now," Nyssa complained, having to yell slightly to be heard above the music as we sat in the back room at the Napier. "I liked Simon better when he was desperate and dateless."

I threw a beer coaster at her, and she screamed as it hit her in the forehead. "For your information," I told her, "I was *never* desperate and dateless. You have to actually *want* a date in order to be desperate and dateless."

"You *wanted* it," Fran accused me. "You just didn't know it then."

"Bullshit," I countered brilliantly.

"She's right," Roger said maddeningly.

"Of course *you'd* agree with her."

"I have to. She wrote it into our vows." He received a punch in the arm from his gracious wife for that one. "Ow. Anyway, we can tell you wanted it because of how quickly you've settled into coupled bliss."

"I'm not sunk in coupled bliss," I lied.

The three of them cackled and jeered in an unintelligible cacophony.

"What are you, then?" Nyssa asked.

"I am now… quite content." I grinned.

Roger made heaving noises.

The beer coaster I had thrown at Nyssa now boomeranged off the end of my nose, and I rubbed it with an injured air. While the others continued to laugh at me, I swung slightly in my chair to see where Declan had gotten to. As I suspected, he was holed up at the bar with fans surrounding him. He had his polite public face on even though he was trying to juggle five drinks and a large packet of barbecue chips.

"Do you think he needs a hand?" Fran asked, looking too comfortable to get up.

I lazily waved my hand. "Nah, he's with his adoring public. We'd only cramp his style."

It was something I had to get used to; being the invisible half of a semipublic couple. I know, play the violins, right? It wasn't like I cared; I didn't want any publicity myself, but I didn't enjoy being shoved unceremoniously aside whenever some unknown person would target Declan and fawn over him until they got his autograph or made some comment about his career he'd heard a thousand times before. In a way, it was gratifying that Declan was having his fears assuaged that the public were generally accepting of him. I was just glad he tended to keep off the Internet; I was learning to stay away from certain forums myself.

"Sorry about that," Declan said, sliding back into his seat. The beers sloshed slightly onto the table and soaked the packet of chips. Fran picked it up distastefully before wiping the wrapper down and opening them up for everyone.

"The beer's probably warm by now, mate," Roger chided him.

"Stick it outside for three minutes, it'll be fine," Declan shot back.

"I'll take it whatever way it comes," I said, reaching for my pot.

"Isn't that what they're saying about you in the press?" Roger asked innocently.

We all stared at him, and he took a nervous gulp of his beer.

Declan shook his head and grinned at me.

Things were pretty good at the moment. Even though Nyssa and I were working full steam at the moment, and we had to fit our family and friends into our schedule in short bursts, thankfully I now had Declan to hand me a coffee in the mornings and feed Maggie when I didn't get home in time. Unfortunately it also meant I had very little time for him either. But hopefully it would get back on track within a couple of weeks as the festival was starting tomorrow night and previous experience had taught me it would pass all too quickly after the buildup.

"Have you heard from your parents yet?" Fran asked.

"You know my parents have never believed in the concept of RSVP," I reminded her.

I had sent Mum and Dad an invitation to the opening night. I called during the week and found out that Dad was apparently upset with the way I had "stormed off" from the party and how I had apparently slighted him as well. I had tried to explain to her how I had been upset myself and gave her the details of our conversation. Mum wasn't that sympathetic.

"He asked you a question," she said.

"It was a dumb question."

"How are people meant to know things if they never ask?"

She had me there. But she wouldn't have understood if I had tried to tell her that after a lifetime of getting snide accusations posed as innocent questions, sometimes it was hard to tell when somebody meant it in good faith (although perhaps worded badly).

Maybe I should have told her that, after all how *are* people meant to know? But I was tired and not ready for a deep and meaningful conversation when I was currently surviving on four hours of sleep a night. And not for a nice, fun reason like being distracted by Dec.

So I sent them the invite instead, hoping that it would show them there were no hard feelings and they would take it in the good faith it was intended. And like I told Roger, my parents never responded to RSVPs.

"You could just call them," Fran said.

Declan held his hands up in the recognised international symbol for *Why yes, that would be the most obvious thing to do, but that's not the way my dickhead boyfriend does things.* Fran caught it and smiled.

"Ball's in their court," I said shortly.

"'Ball's in their court,'" Roger mimicked. "Where have I heard that before?"

I ignored him by munching on a chip.

"Poor baby," Declan said sweetly, "are we all ganging up on you?"

"Fuck off," I told him.

"Mr. Congeniality strikes back." Nyssa giggled. "Speaking of which, boss, isn't it time for us to get back to work?"

Unfortunately, it was.

"Don't worry, we'll take care of your boy," Fran told me.

"He can take care of himself," I said. Out of force of habit, I found myself leaning in for a kiss, and then I remembered where I was and pulled away. Declan grabbed me by the zipper of my jacket and pulled me back in for a peck on my lips.

"Idiot," he whispered.

Nobody had seemed to notice; our usual corner was kind of darkish. I shook my head slightly and said, "Call you when I'm on my way home."

Roger and Fran watched me sombrely as they said their good-byes in unison like the creepy kids from *The Shining*. It freaked me out how couples did that, and I hoped Dec and I would never do the same.

Nyssa and I unwillingly left the warmth of the pub and walked out onto Napier Street, heading for my car. I had fallen into the habit of driving to work ever since the media barrage had started, and even though that had now fallen off, my reliance upon the car and sheer laziness had won out. Plus, I just didn't feel as anonymous on public transport that I used to.

"What was all that about?" Nyssa asked, pulling her gloves on as we walked through the brisk night air.

"What?"

"You know what." Nyssa stuck her gloved hands into her pockets; it was that cold.

"It's nothing."

"I've never known you to be so funny about being out in public with someone before."

"Yeah, well, I've never gone out with someone who came with their own press officer before either."

"Well, Declan seemed pretty okay about it."

It was getting quieter the further we got away from the pub, and I dropped my tone accordingly. "Declan doesn't quite get the enormity of it. It's just too new for him."

"What's too new? Stop being so vague."

"Being out. It's different for him than it is for the rest of us."

We had reached my car; Nyssa walked over to the passenger side and draped her arms over the roof while she waited for me to open the doors. "What, he got some special pass?"

"Kind of." I settled into my seat, put the keys in the ignition, but didn't start the car. "He's a celebrity, Nyss. People treat him differently. They're in awe of him. He might get some lighthearted ribbing but he doesn't get the other shit."

"Didn't he turn up at the office with the effects of some lighthearted ribbing on his face?" Nyssa pointed out.

She had me on that one. It was too hard to explain to those who didn't have to live it.

"It seems to me Declan's handling it well, and you're the one who's acting like you want to lock yourself back in the closet."

I turned the ignition and threw the car into gear. "Shut up with your perception and your insightful judgements. We have a festival to run."

I TRIED not to wake Declan as I crawled into bed in the early hours of the morning. He stirred anyway and groaned as he rolled over to turn on the banker's lamp.

"Go back to sleep," I told him.

"Why didn't you want to kiss me?" he asked.

Direct and to the point. "Dec, I'm exhausted."

"Is that your reason?"

"I'll kiss you now, if you want."

He closed his eyes, and I hoped he would fall asleep again. But his eyes sprang open, now clear and piercingly alert. "Don't try the cute act, even though you do it so well."

"I'm cute?" I turned on the bashful smile for him.

"I said *can it*," he growled.

"Fine." It was a tiring act, anyway.

"So what was it all about then?"

He remained propped up against his pillows while I lay beside him. "You just have to be more careful, that's all. You're still… adjusting. There are rules to public conduct."

"Oh." Declan clicked his fingers sarcastically. "I didn't know, because I wasn't given the queer handbook when I came out. Is there a number I can call to get one sent to me?"

"It's like cats and hunting. It's intuitive."

"So you're saying I'm a lousy cat?"

I tried not to smile on this woeful analogy I had started. "Yeah, you're missing some kind of generational chromosome."

"In case you haven't noticed, Simon, it's like I have an invisible sign over my head announcing my sexuality to everybody. I don't feel like I have to hide it anymore. Why the fuck can't I kiss my boyfriend good-bye, like any other guy would with his girlfriend?"

"Because it's not safe! You have to choose your moments."

"You didn't feel safe in the Napier?"

I sighed. "Not when I'm walking out into the dark street immediately afterward with only Nyssa to protect me. You know, *Charlie's Angels: Full Throttle* may be one of her favourite movies, but I really don't think she can fight like Drew Barrymore if it came down to it."

"That may be the gayest thing I've ever heard you say."

"No, the gayest thing you've probably heard me say is *ooh Declan yes yes*."

Declan tried not to laugh. "Stop the cute act!"

I gave him my cutest smile. "But it comes so naturally."

He traced his hand down my side, stopping at the hem of my boxers. "Okay, I get it. There's a time and a place."

"I hate thinking this way, you know."

Concern crossed his eyes. "Have you ever been…?"

"No. But you always know someone who did. It happens. Jesus, Dec, it's already happened to you. I guess it scares me more than I like to think it does."

He kissed me. "Hey, it was different with me."

"Yeah, it was someone you *knew*."

"I don't think it was so much to do with me being gay, though. It was more to do with him thinking I had betrayed Jess."

"Doesn't matter. You don't think I worry about when you first go back on the field next year?"

"Hey," he said gently. "You're forgetting I'll have eighteen other guys to back me up if anything happens."

"I guess that's something."

"You know, I could always call them in to walk you to your car next time I'm stupid enough to kiss you in a crowded pub."

"Goodnight, Declan," I said grumpily.

But I think I fell asleep with a smile on my face anyway.

"ABE and Lisa are meeting us there, right?"

"Yep. They're catching a taxi in. Same with Roger and Fran."

I walked into the bedroom, fresh from brushing my teeth. Declan was looking resplendent in a deep red shirt and black pants.

"Do I look respectable enough as the partner of the festival director?" Declan asked.

"All that and a bag of chips," I said approvingly. "That red will show up well on the cameras. Especially Alice Provotna's."

"Shit, should I change?"

"Nope."

"I see you're wearing your usual uniform," he said dryly.

I was all in black, although I was wearing a short-sleeved T-shirt over my shirt.

"There's a colour on the back," I told him.

Declan peered around me and shook his head at the print of Patty Hearst. "You making some kind of statement?"

"Yes. Chicks with guns are hot."

"Nice."

"But not as hot as you."

"Don't get frisky. You can't be late."

"Fucking spoilsport." I whacked him on the chest, and he rubbed at it with an injured air. "You know you don't have to come so early, you're going to be bored shitless by all the last minute stuff Nyssa and I have to do."

"What kind of supportive partner would I be if I didn't arrive with you?" he asked mockingly. "Besides, you threatened me."

"Oh, that's right," I said. "Come on, then."

The taxi driver was thrilled to have Declan Tyler™ in his cab, so he talked with him the whole way into the city, and I sat staring out the window letting the talk of statistics and injuries turn into a background drone.

"He seemed nice," Declan said as we jumped out near Flinders Street Station. "He also said he didn't care if I was 'one of those homosexuals'."

"He did?" I asked.

"I knew you weren't paying attention, because you didn't jump in all offended."

"I must have been distracted by the cheesestick."

Declan snorted.

"What did you say?"

"I thanked him?"

"What?"

"What else was I going to say?"

"'I hope you're not expecting a tip.'"

Declan grabbed me by the arm as I was about to step in front of a tram.

"I could have made it."

"Dickhead, *I* couldn't have made that, and I'm a professional athlete."

We bickered good-naturedly to the steps in front of Federation Square, where the Australian Centre for the Moving Image had graciously allowed us to hold our opening night in one of their underground galleries. Nyssa was waiting for us, sitting on the stairs that led to the lobby. "I could hear you two from a mile away."

"Simon's nervous," Declan told her.

"He always is on opening nights."

"No, I'm not," I protested.

"He's grumpy—" Declan continued, and then he grinned. "Grump*ier*. That's how you can tell."

"Has the wine arrived?" I asked Nyssa.

"You're going to start already?" she asked.

"I'm doing a checklist," I protested. "Although I think we should all take a glass now just to settle in."

Declan snorted again.

"The caterers?" I asked Nyssa, ignoring him.

"Setting up."

"Projectionist?"

"On his way."

"I am here also."

At this stern, new voice we all turned around to see Alice Provotna standing behind us, her camera bag hanging over her shoulder and her mouth set in a dour line as imposing as the clichéd beret upon her head.

"Hey, Alice," I said.

"Declan," she said, giving me the frostiest of nods before focusing upon the true object of her attention. "You will have time later on for a one-on-one interview?"

Nyssa and I quickly looked away so we wouldn't burst into laughter.

"Uh, sure," Declan said. He turned to me. "Did you say something about wine?"

LISA grabbed me in a bear hug and at the same time Abe knocked fists with me in what was a great show of multitasking.

"Are we too early?" Lisa asked.

"No," I said as the light mounted on Alice's camera hit me in the face. Lisa and Abe regarded the woman invading our personal space with polite curiosity.

"We're not going to end up in some dodgy behind-the-scenes thing, are we?" Abe asked.

"Are you insulting my work?" Alice asked, her voice rising into the semihysterical tone self-proclaimed geniuses take when they feel their art is being questioned.

"No, no, not at all," Abe replied hurriedly.

"Good," she said, and stalked off.

"Wow, she's... interesting," Abe murmured, looking somewhat stamped-upon.

"Abe," said a young man, approaching him. "Frank Jason, *The Age*. Can I get a photo of you with Declan?"

Abe nodded, and they disappeared further into the crowd.

Still hanging off me, Lisa gave a short laugh. "Welcome to the life of the football player's ignored girlfr... partner."

Her short slip of the tongue made us both laugh.

"Sorry," Lisa said.

"Not at all," I replied. "So this is pretty much what it's like, huh?"

"Oh, they'll probably grab us at some point to make sure they get a photo of us together. I'm surprised they haven't made you and Declan pose yet, you're pretty much the media darlings of the moment."

"Against our wills."

Lisa nodded. "Yeah, but you're always going to have a certain cachet."

"You mean the freak factor."

She whacked me across the head.

"Ow!"

"You deserved that," she chided me.

We became aware of Alice's presence again.

"You didn't get that on film?" I asked, with a sinking feeling.

"Of course," Alice replied tersely.

I groaned, thinking how my family would probably love to rewind again and again a scene of me being hit across the head. "Of course you did."

Satisfied, Alice melted away again.

"Seriously, she's like Nosferatu." I shuddered.

Lisa laughed, and I was happy to see Roger push his way through the crowd. I hugged him happily, and he asked if I was drunk already.

"Only with happiness."

"Then you should be fine that Fran's behind me with your parents."

"They came?" I asked.

Roger nodded. "Oh, shit, you're not going to cry, are you?"

Dry-eyed, I whacked him. "Are *you* drunk? Although I *am* slightly touched."

"You're telling me," Lisa and Roger muttered in unison. They laughed at their own wit, and I left them to it.

Fran was still struggling through the densely packed auditorium, hanging onto a glass of wine for dear life. She protested as I took it off her and had a healthy swig, but I needed it to fortify myself.

"Mum, Dad, you came."

"Why wouldn't we?" Mum asked.

"Well, I didn't know, because you didn't RSVP," I reminded her.

She leaned in to kiss me on the cheek. "Nobody does in this day and age, dear."

"Funny, everybody else here did," I murmured as I offered Dad my hand to shake.

"Hey, Dad."

"Big crowd," Dad said approvingly.

"Yeah," was my stunningly brilliant reply. "Well, it's bigger than last year's at least. That's always a good thing."

"Let's go and get a drink, honey," Mum told Dad, and they headed off in search of the free bar.

"Are you still starting with that doco on the cannibal who became a famous painter?" Fran asked.

"*Dinner with Frankie?* Yeah, why?"

"I'm just making sure to get seats near your parents so I can see their reaction."

"Take pictures, just in case I miss it."

We went in search of our various partners. And, of course, more alcohol.

DECLAN and I had to suffer through what seemed like a thousand photographs being taken of us and Nyssa and I stammered through the opening-night speeches we had to make before the crowd finally shuffled into the theatre to begin watching the premiere screenings. Thankful the intros between the short films would be handled by the guest speakers, Nyssa and I decided to go back out into the lobby and toast to our success. We were soon joined by our friends, and we found a dark corner to hide in, although the ever-present Bluetooth earpieces Nyssa and I wore made their presences known whenever one of the assistants called with an emergency.

"One night down," I announced grandly. "Twelve more to go!"

We clinked our glasses together and then owlishly blinked in confusion as we realised one of the newspaper photographers had ambushed us.

"That reminds me," Declan muttered as I tried to regain a sense of my surroundings. "Your little friend cornered me earlier. I just didn't get to tell you before."

"Who?"

"Jasper Brunswick."

"That bastard!" I hissed. "I didn't see him, I just thought I was lucky and he hadn't oozed in."

"No, he's here. He cornered Abe and me and wanted to get a quote from me."

"That guy?" Abe asked. "Oh, yeah, he was *great*."

"You didn't say anything, did you?" I asked Declan.

"Not a word."

"You're so clever," I gushed.

"And if you drink anymore, I'm going to have to carry you to the cab."

"You'll do that?"

"Fuck, no! Switch to Coke!"

I began to protest, and Abe regaled us with a story of how Declan had to carry him from Crown Casino to the St Kilda tram line in order to get him back to Lisa's house after a lost game last season.

My Bluetooth squawked in my ear. "Simon?"

I fumbled with the piece to answer it. "Yeah, Bron?"

"We're into the last ten minutes, so intermission's coming up."

I thanked her and alerted the catering staff to start pouring drinks. The crowd surged out of the theatre, and we were drowned in the white noise of their hubbub. Mum and Dad approached me, and I could tell from their expressions that they had had enough of avant-garde cinema for the year.

"Your dad's tired, love," Mum lied sweetly. "We're going to call it a night. We're old, you know."

"Thanks for coming," I told them, and I actually was thankful. Mum gave me a quick kiss, and I shook Dad's hand; I turned to watch them leave and saw Declan grab them by the door. They conversed comfortably together; in fact, Declan looked more like their son than I did through the ease he showed with them. Declan laughed, shook my father's hand, and caught sight of me.

"You're such a good son-in-law," I said as he joined me.

"I have to make up for you," he lobbed back.

We turned to head back to the table our crowd had adopted and ran straight into Jasper Brunswick. There was no escape, although I looked all around for one.

"We have to stop bumping into each other, Declan," Jasper purred.

"Oh, you have to be *shitting* me," I said.

Jasper acknowledged my presence by rolling his eyes. "Simon."

I felt Declan take my elbow, a warning to keep myself in check.

"Enjoying the films, Jasper?" Declan asked politely.

"It seems that the quality diminishes each year," Jasper replied. "No wonder you're becoming more desperate for sponsorship, Simon."

Declan's grip on my elbow increased, and I made some noncommittal noise as I grabbed another glass of wine off the passing plate of a waiter.

"I know you two feel that you have reason to blame me for some of the press you got," Jasper continued. "Especially you, Simon. I haven't forgotten how rude you were to me on the phone, but luckily I never hold a grudge."

I wondered why, with the strength of his fingers, Declan didn't accidentally crush the footballs whenever he caught one on the field. I was going to have bruises in the morning.

Jasper decided to appeal directly to Declan as I was being unrelenting. "I had nothing to do with your outing. I don't *out* people. Do you know how long I knew about you before I wrote about it?"

Declan's mouth was firmly set, and he remained silent.

"I seem to remember you saying that he's fair game now, though," I couldn't resist reminding him.

"All I want is an interview," Jasper admitted.

"I've already done interviews," Declan said firmly. "There's such a thing as overexposure."

"You're nowhere near overexposure," Jasper reassured him, and I tried to analyse his last sentence for any possible intended dirtiness.

"Precisely because I'm not doing interviews at the moment." Declan nodded.

"You two owe me."

"We owe you nothing," I said.

"You don't want the local gay press to get negative, do you?"

"Is that a threat?" I asked.

Jasper laughed. "So the footballer has the brains out of the two of you? Yes, Simon, it's a threat."

"Okay, *Jon*, that's it," I spat. "Outside!"

At the sound of his real name, Jasper grimaced. "Yeah, right, like I'm going to fight you."

I didn't really want to fight either. Mainly because the both of us would have looked absurd.

"I'll think about it and get back to you," Declan said, starting to pull me away before I could do any more damage.

"No, you won't! He just insulted you!" I argued as he pushed me into a booth and slid in beside me so I couldn't escape.

"Actually, he insulted *you*," Declan reminded me.

"You can't do an interview with him!"

"Maybe he's right. Local press would be happy, and it would keep them on side. We need their support."

"I think we're doing pretty well."

Declan sighed. "Yeah, at the moment. We need to think long-term."

"This isn't a football season. You can't think that far ahead."

"We should." He shrugged.

I started ripping a coaster apart and piled the pieces in the ashtray before me. "I don't like him thinking he's won."

"Jesus, Simon, stop acting like a brat. It's not about winning."

I glared at him. "You just called me a brat."

"Yeah. Because you're acting like one."

I couldn't say anything else, because I thought I would explode and say something far worse. Despite being flushed with alcohol, I was still somewhat sensible.

Declan reached for my hand. "Sulking isn't going to make you look like less of a brat."

I pulled my hand out of his. He sighed.

"You know what?" I asked.

"What?"

"There are two of us in this relationship. That means I also get a say in decisions that affect us. At the moment you're taking it upon yourself to make them all."

His tone was measured. *"Because* you're so goddamned pigheaded sometimes. Jasper Brunswick may be a tool, and I like him about as little as you do, but there are pros and cons to everything."

I went back to the silent method of avoiding a fight.

This pissed Declan off more. "Okay, I'm going to get a beer."

I nodded.

Declan sat for a few more moments, the silence between us thick and uncomfortable. He then got up without a word and headed to the bar. The bell sounded for intermission, and people started heading back into the theatre. Declan, with a beer in his hand, turned to look at me, but I remained seated. I saw his shoulders sag slightly, and he followed everybody else.

I patched through to an assistant. "Bron? They're all in now. You can start the second program."

The lobby was deserted, and now I felt weird and alone it had all the atmosphere of the hotel in *The Shining.* I seemed to be comparing my life to that movie a lot lately.

But for the moment I still couldn't move.

I'M NOT sure how long exactly I sat there, but I eventually got myself together enough for an idea to form. I headed over to the ticket box. A collection of postcards of Australian films were for sale on the counter, and although there was nobody around to take my money, I selected a card and left the two dollars next to the locked till.

It was a picture of international hit *Babe,* with the titular pig standing in the farmyard and its annoying but somewhat-charming refrain of *la la la* coming out of its mouth. On the back I scrawled, *I know I can be a stubborn pig, but hopefully I'm as cute as this one, and like him, worth keeping around. Keep this to remind yourself of that.*

Smiling at my own self-perceived cuteness, I flagged down a waitress and asked her if she could take it in to Declan. He would be easy to find; I had assigned him a seat in the handicapped row so he could stretch out his impossibly long legs.

She grinned at the picture on the card, but promised not to read it. I headed back to the booth, a sudden wave of fatigue overcoming me. The premiere and the final nights were always the worst, but the good thing was knowing it would all be over in two weeks.

I rested my head against the plush lining of the booth and closed my eyes. I could hear the muted sounds of cinema coming from the theatre doors as they opened and reduce as they closed again.

"Should I pull up a trough for you?" a voice asked.

I opened my eyes again and smiled up at Declan. "I'm sorry."

He slid in beside me. "Yeah, me too."

"Oink," I murmured.

He laughed. "Have I been a control freak lately?"

"Not a control freak, no."

"But something like it?"

"Hey, you know what? Let's not bring it up. Let's just be perfect together from now on and the envy of all our friends."

"Sounds good." He dug into his pocket and brought out the postcard. "I'm going to laminate this though, so that it lasts throughout eternity."

I tried to snatch it away from him, but of course, he was too quick. I relented. "That card's going to come back to haunt me."

"I hope so." Declan laughed and pinned me up against the wall of the booth. "Oh wait," he said evilly, "Is this a safe place for me to kiss you?"

"We're at an avant-garde film festival," I reminded him. "The only safer place would be Oxford Street during Mardi Gras."

He laughed, and his eyes were electric despite the muted atmosphere of the booth. I wrapped my arms around him and crushed him against me as we kissed.

The booth flooded with light as we heard a camera flash sound. Bewildered, we turned to see Jasper Brunswick standing over us.

"Thanks for the exclusive!" he crowed, and he ran off before we could disentangle ourselves from each other.

"That *shit*," I breathed.

Declan butted his head against my shoulder. "I guess that solves *that* problem."

I wanted to be angry, but amusement hit me instead. How could I be mad when my arms were full with Declan, and I was where I wanted to be more than anywhere else in the world?

"So this is what our life is," I mused.

"Pretty good, huh?" Declan asked.

I really couldn't disagree.

FOURTH
QUARTER

CHAPTER
TWENTY-FIVE

"WHERE'S Declan?"

Having had the life squeezed out of me, I managed to pull away from Fran and gain my breath enough to say, "He's in Hobart. It's a home game week. And it's good to see you too, Franny."

"Oh, you know that goes without saying," she chided me over the sounds of a flight from New Zealand being announced over the speakers.

Roger pushed her aside to have his turn at me. "Hey, mate."

"Jesus, is that a tan?" I asked in shock.

"The amount of time she made me go for walks in the sun, it's a good thing I didn't come back with a melanoma."

"Who's 'she'?" Fran protested. "The cat's mother?"

Fuck, I had missed them. It was the first Christmas I had ever had without Roger, and though you would have thought I would be distracted having my first Christmas with Declan, my best friend's absence was a sore spot.

"It's good to see you guys," I said sincerely.

"Oh God, he's getting sentimental," Fran said, hugging me again.

"We were only gone for ten weeks," Roger reminded me.

"It was eight weeks too long."

"You didn't miss us the first two?" Roger looked hurt.

Fran's lips brushed against my hairline. "For someone who missed us so much, you were shit at keeping in contact." She began ushering us down to the baggage carousel.

"I texted you!" I said defensively.

"*Text*," Fran muttered dismissively.

"I think I spoke to Dec more than I did you," Roger said.

"Yeah, well he's Mr. Perfect isn't he? You can make *him* your best friend."

"Someone's cranky."

I sighed, watching the bags start to spill out onto the rubber tracks. "I got jumped by the press in the car park."

Roger's eyes widened. "Was there a rumble?"

Fran hid her smile behind her hand.

"Yes, there was a rumble. Luckily this cute blonde girl came out of nowhere and staked them for me."

"Are they still following you guys around?" Fran asked.

I shrugged. "Sometimes. And sometimes they're just lucky and catch us out and about. But it's kind of increasing at the moment now that the preseason has started."

"But Declan isn't playing, right?" asked Roger.

"*That's* only increasing the interest," I grumbled. "Everybody's like 'when's he gonna play', 'why are they keeping him off the field', 'has he not recovered from the operation', blah blah blah."

"You were playing his nursemaid." Fran grinned. "I'm sure he recovered well enough."

"He was a shit to deal with, though."

"You must have *hated* having the competition, then," Roger laughed.

I whacked him, but missed as he moved off to grab one of their bags.

Fran grabbed my arm and squeezed it affectionately. "So when do we get to see his new apartment?"

They had left before Declan had gotten to move in properly. "He's already talking about dinner as soon as he next gets up from Hobart."

"You know me," Fran said. "Wherever there's food, I'll be there."

"Did someone say food?" Roger reappeared, a bag in his hand. "Only one of them so far."

"There better be presents in that," I warned him.

"There might be a snow globe." Roger shrugged.

"So *is* Declan really better?" Fran asked. "There's only so much information one can get via text from you, he was being a bit secretive about it whenever I spoke to him, and I didn't want to believe anything the nets were saying."

I grimaced as I remembered how often I'd had to help him change his gross and bloody bandages. Along with mopping his fevered brow and feeding him chicken soup.

"He's getting there," I said in a low tone, looking suspiciously at the other disembarked passengers and their greeters around us. "But the real test will be when he gets into a game. Especially because the other players won't be easy on him."

"What, because he came out?"

I shrugged. "It's the game. Could be a factor, but—"

"Go hard, or go home!" Roger said, a bit too enthusiastically, causing everybody around us to stare.

I automatically shrank back against Fran as my paranoia led me to believe that a glimmer of recognition began to register collectively in the group's eyes. "Yes," I said. "That."

"Bloody stupid game," Fran muttered.

"You just don't get it," Roger countered.

"Go look for the bags!" she ordered, and he skulked off. "Honestly." She turned her attention back to me. "And his family? How are they dealing with everything?"

"This is starting to feel like the start of one of those show starters. *Previously, on Simon and Declan....*"

"Give me a break. I haven't seen you for ages. You have to tell me everything. And then later on you'll have to tell me in greater detail."

That last few months had flown by in a barely discernible blur. Just after Fran and Roger left and I was feeling lonely, Declan introduced me to the scary reality of his overprotective siblings. They had all been eager to let me know just how much they cared about their brother and how I was a threat to his safety and happiness.

"They threatened to bury me where I would never be found if I did Dec wrong."

Fran giggled. "Did they speak in country song cliché all the time?"

I smiled. "They're actually pretty cool. They love him."

"What's not to love?"

"Careful," I growled.

"I'm married!" She laughed. "Not dead."

"What?" Roger asked suspiciously, dragging another bag behind him.

We just smiled. "Nothing."

"She's going on about how hot she thinks Declan is, isn't she?" Roger demanded. "Sure, *she's* allowed to do that kind of thing, but if *I* look at one girl on an Italian beach then you're suddenly capable of having an affair."

"He's overreacting," Fran told me apologetically.

"You kicked me in the balls!"

"I kicked you in the shin, you big baby!" Fran scowled. "And the difference is there's no chance of me getting with Declan."

"I don't know," I drawled, loving to add fuel to this little fire. "I think he *has* got a little crush on you."

"Really?" Fran asked, giving Roger a huge sickly sweet smile. Her eyes widened as she noticed one of their bags sailing by. "Be right back!"

Roger sidled up to me. "That's not really true, is it?"

"What?" I asked innocently.

"Declan having a crush on Fran."

"Who *wouldn't* have a crush on Fran?" I asked rhetorically.

Roger turned to watch his wife hoist a large bag off the carousel with ease. "Yeah." He smiled. "She's pretty cool."

"The coolest," I agreed.

"That's it!" Fran cried as she joined us. "Let's go!"

I was glad to get back out into the open air as we crossed over the bridge that led to the car park. The photographers who had jumped out at me earlier were nowhere to be seen. They had probably spotted far more newsworthy prey within the airport getting off another flight. On the other hand, if Dec had been with us....

"Are Dec's folks treating you like the son they never had?" Roger asked as we loaded the bags into my car.

"Isn't it about time I got some stories about your trip?" I tried to deflect.

"It's not as interesting as this," Fran said sweetly.

I sighed and unlocked the car. We got in and automatically groaned at the heat.

"Dude, it's about time you got a grownup car with air conditioning," Roger grumbled.

"'Dude'?" I asked.

"Get your sugar daddy to buy you a new car," Roger pushed.

"Shut up," I seethed. "I like my car." And I didn't want to admit that Declan *had* offered to buy me a new car, but I refused.

"So, Declan's parents?" Fran repeated.

I pretended to concentrate on the road as we merged onto the freeway.

"Simon!" Fran whined.

There was no fighting them. Just like it had been hard to fight off Dec's family when he finally took ownership of his apartment at the Docklands (unfortunately Cate Blanchett was not his neighbour as I had hoped), even more so when he had his operation just before Christmas and was holed up within it. You would have thought he had been left to fend for himself on an ice floe in the Antarctica the number of times they showed up unannounced, despite the fact I had moved myself in there with Maggie in tow during his convalescence.

Christmas had been a strange time, as it was the first where I had a partner I wanted to share the season with properly as a couple; before, if I had had a boyfriend around the festive season, I avoided any possibility of doing the family thing with them. But there was no escape this time round; my family had adopted Declan, in spite of what he may have wanted, and Declan's family made every effort to include me as well. I found myself in the strange new position of having in-laws and also having to watch my parents put in that position as well. Declan was surprised by the fact this seemed so foreign to me and that I tried to resist it; he was extremely close to his family, although you could question the irony of that fact because he had never told them about his being gay until he was splashed on the front cover of the *Herald Sun* kissing his boyfriend.

"It's kind of weird," I admitted. "It still doesn't seem real yet, like everybody's still on their best behaviour. They're always really nice to me, but I feel like I'm waiting for the real family drama to begin."

"You always have to be the pessimist," Fran said. "They probably can see how serious you guys are. After all you went from dancing around each other in the throes of early love to old married couple in only a couple of months."

"Is that a compliment?" I asked.

"Well, you think *we* rock," Roger pointed out. "And we're an old married couple."

"Like I said, is that a compliment?"

"If you weren't driving, I'd hit you."

"And VicRoads salutes you for responsible motor vehicle management," I said in all seriousness.

Fran groaned from the back seat. "Is it too late to go back to Italy?"

I ACTUALLY *did* take it as a compliment, because Declan and I were so comfortable with each other. It was new for both of us, and I think we were being careful in protecting it because we didn't know a relationship could be that way. It was true it was also because of an us-against-the-world attitude resulting from the continual intrusion of the press into our personal lives, although it was nowhere near the fever pitch it had been when Dec had first come out.

Looking back, I think we were just living in a state of suspended bliss that came to an end when Dec had to start shuttling back and forth between Melbourne and Hobart in order to start preseason training. The honeymoon period was over, what with interest in him ramping up again as the press, the club bosses, and the fans waited to see how his knee worked in anticipation of the season to come. Dec tried to stay out of the limelight as much as possible, but he couldn't. Even though he wasn't speaking to the press, *they* couldn't stop talking about him.

His coach had decided to make him sit out the preseason, which only intensified the speculation about his eventual return. Whenever I spoke to him on the phone, me at home in Melbourne and him in his apartment in Hobart, he sounded pretty miserable. I flew over a couple of times when I could get away from work, but it really didn't cheer him up any. He was itching to get back out onto the field.

The first game of the season was an away one for the Devils. They would be playing against Carlton at Etihad, and it was at a press conference leading up to the game that Scott Frasier finally gave the press and the public what they were waiting for: The Return of Declan Tyler™. Sitting beside his coach on the podium, Declan looked as unflappable as he always did. Nobody would have ever guessed how petrified he was.

"They kept me away for too long," he told me, when I met him at his apartment on the Docklands later in the afternoon.

"We've been over this before," I told him. "They haven't. The minute you get out onto the grounds, it will be like you've never been away."

"You don't know that," he said grumpily. "You have no idea."

It was true. I didn't. I mean, I could relate what he was feeling to the way I felt in situations in my own life, but Declan's would always be different. I would never know what it felt like to be a player; I would only ever have the fan's perspective of the game.

I didn't know what it was to be thought of as the team god, its saviour, and also its scapegoat if anything went wrong. Throw into that the whole rigmarole that went with being a celebrity, a role model, and the new poster child for gay rights, I guess the man was entitled to be a little bit emo every now and again. Frig knows he did the same for me a hell of a lot of the time.

I pulled him down onto the couch beside me and tried to hold him. He sat rigidly, like he was passively resisting a cop at an antiglobalisation rally. Eventually he sagged into me, and I held him tighter.

"I want to ask you something," I said.

"What?" His voice was muffled against my T-shirt.

"Do you mind if I came to the match?"

He sat up and looked at me earnestly. "You would?"

"Of course I would! I wanted to tell you I was coming for ages, but I thought maybe you didn't want me to."

"Why wouldn't I want you to?"

"Why didn't you ask me?"

He groaned. "I thought we were going to get *better* at communicating."

"Okay, so communicate. I'll tell you why I didn't, if you go first."

"Chickenshit." Declan grinned. "But okay. I want you to come to the game. But I thought maybe with me being such a stressed-out prick lately that it would be the last thing you would want to do. Plus the press attention will be huge. And they'll probably focus on you as well if you came. I didn't want to put pressure on you. Your turn."

"Almost the same," I replied. "I figured you had enough to deal with without me being there. Especially if the media got involved. I thought all of it would distract you and put you off your game." I brushed my lips against his hairline. "I want to be there and support you."

"This is why we should talk," Dec said, gently rubbing his thumb against my cheek.

"We're a team. The team of us."

"You schmaltzy bastard." He laughed. "I love it. And I love you."

"Now who's being schmaltzy?"

We kissed, and it was one of those moments where I felt perfectly assured that even though at times it seemed to be us against the world—*the team of us*—we would prevail.

"You're going to need someone to show you the ropes though," Dec said.

"The ropes?"

"Yeah. Someone who has been through all of this before and knows how to handle being the football wife."

"You did *not* just call me a football wife," I said, punching him in the gut. "Never do it again!"

He grabbed my fist, uncurled it, and fitted his own inside it. "You know what I mean."

"So, someone to be my Yoda?"

"Yeah. Or, your Yoda someone should be. And I know who."

"I'M SO glad I have a fellow freak to hang out with," Lisa declared, hugging me madly.

"Freak?" I echoed.

She kissed me on the cheek. "Don't take it personally. But that's what the WAGs think we are. In fact, you've probably taken my crown away."

The WAGs were the Wives And Girlfriends. Bad acronym I know. And not very gender-inclusive, now that I was around.

"Oh," I said, and then I asked in surprise, "Why would they think *you're* a freak?"

Lisa stared at me, trying to figure out if I was being serious or just merely dumb. "Uh, because I'm the only Asian in a swarm of Anglos? Any time I first introduce myself to one of them, they have trouble hiding the fact they're surprised I can speak English."

Lisa sounded more Aussie than even Roger and could drink Abe under the table; I thought it was much more likely the other girls were *intimidated* by her.

"They're that cliquey?" I asked.

I must have looked worried, because Lisa immediately began to backtrack. "No, not really. Well, a little bit. They're scared of difference. But then, so am I. I don't feel comfortable around—"

"Normal people?"

Lisa laughed. "Normal? They're hardly normal themselves."

"Most people would think they were."

"Let's just say that we got on the wrong foot with each other. I was already nervous about dealing with them; they made a couple of stupid, but probably well-intentioned comments, and I got pissy."

"That doesn't sound like anything *I* would do at all."

Lisa had seen me in social situations too many times to be able to treat that as a joke. "Don't worry. Once they've associated you with me, you'll be a social pariah. They're probably expecting some guy who can discuss shoes and *Sex and the City* with them, not someone who wants to discuss the meta-existentialism of David Lynch."

"Is *Sex and the City* still popular?"

"With them, yes. And *you* don't know a wedge heel from a stiletto."

"I know stilettos are good for stabbing people with."

Lisa grinned. "Be sure to slip *that* into the conversation."

We began crossing over from Harbour Esplanade towards Etihad, where a crowd was already milling for the game.

"We should have gone for a drink first," I moaned.

"You can buy me a beer once we get inside."

"Are you kidding? I have a mortgage. I can't afford game-price beer."

I wasn't sure if I was being paranoid, but I felt like I was being recognised as Lisa and I walked through the throng of people. Not by everybody, but there seemed to be a few people who nudged each other and looked in our direction. I had been the subject of more articles (and the press liked to slip in a mention of me whenever Declan was being discussed) than any normal person would have liked. I had never in my life wanted to be a celebrity, much less a celebrity by default.

At the gate, Lisa showed our passes, and we were whisked through to the players' box. There was already a small group of who I guess were the WAGs in there who stopped talking as soon as we entered. It was as comfortable as it sounds.

"Well, girls," Lisa said cheerily, but with a tone of falseness that I had never heard in her before. "Here we are, the start of a new season."

"And not all girls," one woman said, pointedly staring at me.

"I know! There's a penis amongst us!" Lisa said in mock horror, linking her arm through mine. "I'm sure you already know, but this is Simon." She made sure that all attention was on her before unnecessarily adding, "Declan's *partner.*"

That word and all its connotations, provoked a reaction of repressed smirks and sideways glances between the Aussie remake of the *Footballers' Wives.*

"Howdy," I said, sounding far more confident than I felt, although there was a part of me who was also enjoying it purely from a sadomasochistic viewpoint.

There were some faint murmurs of greeting, and Lisa's grip on me tightened. "They're being shy, Simon. Don't worry, they'll get used to you. Why don't you grab us some seats, and I'll get some beer."

It was the equivalent of throwing me into the lion's den. I squeezed past some of women in the second row and grabbed two at the end. I lowered the seat and sank into it, wishing it would swallow me whole. I looked up and offered a faint smile to the woman sitting closest to me; she just stared back.

"Are you enjoying the attention, then, are you?" she suddenly demanded, and once again, silence fell between everybody.

"What?" I asked, my tone edgier than I would have liked.

"You seem to like getting your face in the papers," she accused me.

I stared her down. "I don't invite it, if that's what you're getting at."

"I bet you like it, though."

"Well, no, I don't." And I didn't know why I was attempting to justify myself to her.

She snorted. "You could've fooled me."

"Are you playing nice, Rachel?"

I breathed with relief and hated myself for it when Lisa appeared at the end of the aisle with two plastic cups of beer.

"Just getting to know our new friend here," Rachel lied through gritted teeth.

"It sounded to me like you were accusing him of being a fame whore," Lisa said as she made her way around the other women in the seats, who were of course drinking in every word said between us.

"Not at all—"

Rachel screamed and leapt out of her seat as some beer sloshed out of one of the cups and landed on the front of her blouse.

"Sorry," Lisa said, sounding anything but.

"You bitch!" Rachel spat, wiping at herself. "You did that deliberately!"

"Nah," Lisa said dismissively, "I'm just clumsy. But I'll make it up to you, and give you the ten bucks so you can go to Supré and get a replacement."

If we had been in a film, someone would be snapping their fingers and drawling "oh no she di'n't!", but everybody stared at their feet so as not to provoke the beast. Rachel glared at Lisa one more time and then stormed off in the direction of the toilets. Or at least stormed off as best as she could while having to navigate between rows of crammed-in seats.

Lisa sat beside me and handed me one of the cups. "Waste of good beer," she fumed.

I smushed my cup against hers in celebration. "Nah, I think it was sacrificed for a worthy cause."

"I'll drink to that."

One of the girls in front of us turned around in a gesture of friendliness and said, "I can't believe she called you an attention whore when she was the one who went to the Brownlow in a backless low-cut gown with a diamante thong!"

Lisa snorted. "Glass houses, Jackie. Your boobs fell out of your dress when they were serving dessert."

Jackie smiled fondly, lost in memory. "Yeah, that was a *great* dress. So, Simon, what will you be wearing to the Brownlow if you and Declan are still together by then?"

Lisa and I both stared at her for her lack of tact, and I slowly said, "I don't know. Clothes, I guess."

Jackie laughed politely, but looked bewildered. "Sure." She seemed glad that the whistle blew and the players from Carlton began running onto the field so that she could start ignoring us with the best excuse in the world.

Lisa nudged my thigh with her own and smushed our cups together again. "You're one of us now. There's no escape."

I gulped down my beer and hoped Rachel would fall down the loo so I wouldn't have to see her again.

UNFORTUNATELY the toilet didn't eat Rachel, but she seemed happy to pretend we didn't exist from that moment on. The feeling was more than mutual. Some of the other girls thawed to us, but Lisa assured me that was about as good as it was going to get so I didn't expect anything more. It seemed like it was going to remain Lisa and me in one camp and everybody else in another. Unless, of course, someone deemed just as freaky as one of us infiltrated the group, hence supplanting my role as newbie and thereby doomed to come and increase the numbers of the dark side.

It was only six minutes into the first quarter when all hell broke out on the field.

Declan had just had a handball delivered to him, and he was making his way towards the Devils' goal posts when he was tackled by Fraser Johnson of the opposing side. They went down in a flurry of legs and arms, tumbling over each other, and when they got to their feet Declan immediately shoved Johnson away from him. I watched the action play out on the big screen; Declan looked furious. Johnson was obviously mouthing off at him because Declan came in a second time, and Johnson immediately shoved him back. It was only seconds before both teams came pouring in to the centre of the field, anxious to start blueing with one another. The panicked referees threw themselves into the fray, calling for calm as Lisa and I grimaced while watching from above. She pointed out Abe pulling Declan back from another confrontation with Johnson; he was almost foaming at the mouth. Their coach called for a suspension of play and brought Declan back into their camp for a debrief. After a few heated moments it appeared he wasn't getting anywhere, and the coach sent on another player to go back on instead. The whistle blew, and one of the referees threw the ball back into play.

"Shit," Lisa groaned. "What do you think that was all about?"

I didn't want to say, although I had my suspicions. Luckily Rachel was there to take it upon herself to clear it all up for us.

"Are you dense, or has that beer already gone to your head?" Rachel drawled. "Johnson obviously slagged off the boy toy here."

"I'm not this team's fucking Yoko Ono, so can it," I growled.

Rachel snorted. I'm not even sure if she got the reference, although she got the intent.

"They'll be fine," Lisa said, although whether she was saying it to reassure me or herself I couldn't tell.

"If he gets reported, he'll have blown his chances for a Brownlow on his first game back," Rachel said.

"Shut the fuck up, or I'll shut you up," Lisa threatened her.

"Hey!" I yelled. "We don't need a brawl in here as well!"

Lisa rolled her eyes but patted me on the knee.

"Is it always this entertaining in here?" I whispered as we all drew our attention back to the game.

"Only if Rachel's around," Lisa replied.

"Is she ever *not* around?" I asked hopefully.

Lisa shook her head.

"Great. Maybe we should just buy our own tickets next time."

"We can't. The media would love it if they could publish stories about infighting amongst the partners, and us not sitting here would only fuel them further. We're here to support Abe and Dec, that's all we can think about."

"Man, you're such a good footballer's wife," I said mockingly. "Did you get that from the guidebook?"

"Shut up, you're one of us now."

I shuddered. "They better not think I'm turning up to the Brownlows in a dress."

"I'll go in pants if you go in a dress," she challenged me.

I laughed. "No way. I'm not *that* stupid."

Lisa sighed. "Pity."

THE rest of the game passed without incident, although there seemed to be a tense atmosphere to the whole thing. Once the Devils left the field, all of the WAGs rose as one entity and exited the box.

"Stepford, party of one," Lisa murmured. She slapped me on the thigh. "Well, you survived. How do you feel?"

"Fine. Just wanting to know how Dec is after all that."

She nodded. "Yeah. I'm just glad Abe didn't throw a punch."

"Well, he's mellowed in the past couple of years," I said, remembering vaguely that he used to be known for being a wee bit volatile.

"Only because Dec and I made him. We're pretty convincing when we gang up."

"I bet."

We watched the crowds below us trickle out of the stadium, and when there seemed to be less of a crush, we made our way downstairs.

Which was when I *really* started feeling nervous. Meeting the footballers' wives had been enough of a frightening prospect, so coming across the footballers themselves seemed even more daunting. I would have tried to escape and meet up with Declan later if Lisa hadn't kept a tight rein on me.

Down in the bowels of the stadium we found a seat a little way from the WAGs and waited for the footballers to emerge. When they did, they were a sorry-looking group. A fight on the field that involved both their captain and the vice captain plus a loss to the other team meant that they were sullen and silent. No cooing from their supportive partners lifted their spirits as they left in pairs like a Prozac-ridden Noah's Ark. As they filed past where I was sitting with Lisa some of them looked stony-faced at me, obviously recognising me. Although a couple nodded, the rest ignored my presence.

Except for Rachel, of course, who couldn't help but smirk.

"Man, I hate her," Lisa said confidentially. Redundantly.

"Really?" I asked, just as redundantly. "I couldn't tell."

"You hate her too," she continued in a singsong voice.

"She's not my favourite person, no."

The door to the change rooms swung open again, and Declan and Abe emerged.

They looked even more drained than the rest of the team. Lisa jumped up and immediately hugged Abe. I hung back, not knowing what to do, and unconsciously jammed my hands in my pockets.

Abe nodded at me and turned to Declan. "Drink?"

Declan shook his head, and it looked as if it took too much effort for him to do so. "I'll give it a miss tonight, mate."

Abe nodded again, knowing not to press it. "I'll call you tomorrow."

"Sure."

Lisa looked at me sympathetically, knowing we were in the same boat. She gave me a quick hug good-bye, and then she and Abe were gone, leaving Declan and me alone in the concourse.

I moved towards him and gave him a hug.

He stood still against me, unresponsive, and I pulled back.

"Oh, now you'll hug me?" he asked.

"Sorry, I didn't know what—"

He sighed. "It was only Abe and Lisa. You haven't worried before."

The same old argument again. I remained silent.

Declan stared at me, then realising he wasn't going to get an answer from me he started walking towards the car park.

I followed him. Even though Declan only lived a short distance away, walking distance, really, during games he had decided it was better to drive home than risk having to put up with fans milling around the Docklands area afterwards. Especially as they would have had time to drink between their exit and the players'. It was just common sense for any footballer.

"Are you going to tell me what happened out there?" I asked, referring to the fracas at the beginning of the game.

He looked at me briefly, but continued walking. "Nothing to say."

"Ah, so that was just a friendly bustup, then?"

"Just drop it, Simon, okay?"

Wow, I had been *told*. Starting to fume a little myself, I kept quiet so I wouldn't explode.

We didn't say a word until we pulled into the car park at his complex. Declan turned the ignition off and sat there for a moment.

"Look," I said, my voice sounding a little rusty ever since I had forcibly kept it shut. "I'm just going to let you stew and go home tonight."

Declan turned and looked at me. "Don't. Just come up."

"You're pissed, and you're not talking to me."

"I'm not pissed, and I *will* talk to you."

"Wow, that sounds really inviting."

"Simon, please," Declan said tiredly.

I took his hand and squeezed it. He squeezed back.

We were silent in the elevator, but there wasn't the weird tension between us this time. As the doors opened upon his floor, I surprised him by taking his hand.

His grip was strong but comfortable as we slowly walked hand in hand to his door.

Inside, Declan threw his bag in a corner and slumped upon the couch.

"Okay," I said, sitting beside him. "Talk to me."

He groaned.

"Come on, you know what my imagination's like. I'm probably thinking it's something ten times worse than it actually was."

"What do you think it was?"

I lightly scratched behind his ears like I did for Maggie and was rewarded with a smile. "Doesn't take a genius to guess you were sledged."

"Yeah."

"What did he say?"

"The usual. Well, not the usual. It was all new." He took a deep breath. "I mean, I've been sledged before. It's just that this time there was new ammunition to use against me."

A little niggling thought began to form at the back of my mind, influenced by Rachel's little dig at me before. "Like you said, sledging isn't new, and you've probably been sledged a hundred times before."

"More, probably."

"Okay, you've been so calm about everything that's happened to you since you came out. Why did it get to you today?"

"It just did, that's all."

Again, that niggling feeling, combined with the fact that he wouldn't look at me. "It was something about me, wasn't it?"

"Christ, Simon. Not everything's about you!" he snapped.

I let my hand drop away. "Okay."

Declan covered his face with his hands and rubbed at it tiredly. "I'm sorry."

"Just tell me, Dec."

"Yes!" he admitted finally. "He sledged you."

I reached over and pulled his hands down so he would have to look at me. "You should have ignored him."

"You don't get it. There's an etiquette. You don't sledge the family or the girlfriends."

"Well, that's it, then," I said, trying to make light of it. "He didn't think he was doing anything wrong, because I'm not your girlfriend. A technicality, sure—"

"You know what I mean," he growled. "And you're family."

That made me kiss him madly. And he responded, finally seeming like Declan again.

"Wow, I've never had anybody defending my honour before," I teased.

"He knew what he was doing."

"Dec, you should have just let it go."

"I couldn't."

"You *don't* have to defend me. For fuck's sake, Dec, if they put you on an official reprimand you'll be out of Brownlow contention."

"Fuck the Brownlow," Dec muttered.

"*Fuck* the Brownlow?" I asked in shock. "What kind of footballer are you?"

He studied me and grinned when he realised I was mocking him. "One with integrity."

"A true white knight," I admitted.

"What would you have done?" Dec asked. "If it had been you on the field?"

"If they had sledged you?" I asked. "I would have made them pay."

Declan laughed and flung himself upon me. Crushed, I fell back against the arm of the couch, and once again the team of us closed itself against the world.

CHAPTER
TWENTY-SIX

I COULD tell Dec was awake and had been for a few minutes longer than me as I struggled against the last vestiges of sleep and opened my eyes.

"Morning," he murmured.

"Hey," I grunted. "Were you watching me?"

"Maybe."

"Stalker."

"I can't help it; you're so pretty."

I moaned and buried my head back into the pillow.

"Especially when you drool."

"What were you doing, really?" I asked, muffled by the material.

His hand flattened the pillow puffing around my head so that I could see him. "I told you. Watching you. Thinking about how nice it would be to stay in bed forever."

"We would start to smell pretty quickly."

"I could live with that."

"And pretty soon we would be swimming in our own shit."

My world went dark as his pillow went over my head and pushed me down into my own. "You're so fucking romantic!" I heard him hiss.

"You love it," I choked.

I struggled out from beneath his grip for air and rolled over on top of him. He lay supine beneath me, and I drew my thumbs in opposite directions over his jaw. I kissed the bottom of his chin and arched up slightly to kiss him properly. His hands ran along my side, and I shivered as they came to rest on my back and held me against him.

"Is this better?" I breathed.

He gave some sort of strangled moan in reply.

I knew his body so well by now. I ran my finger along the five o'clock shadow that had formed overnight, and it came to rest on a small crescent moon scar caused by a Bulldogs player who had accidentally gouged his cheek two seasons ago.

"What are you doing?" Dec asked.

I inched down the length of his body, slipping out of his arms. He arched like a cat as my hand trailed down his chest, and I breathed in the smell of him as I worked my way down his boxers until I faced his infamous knee.

"Admiring you," I said. And I meant it. One knee was distinctly different from the other, because of the surgical scars. It looked knobbier, and the hair was more sparse than on the other one because the scarring left shiny trails along his skin.

"There's nothing to admire about that," Declan said shortly.

I looked up at him. "There is."

I began to massage the knee, as I had in the weeks after his surgery when he'd been able to stand it being touched. Declan closed his eyes and lay back. I worked it for a few minutes, feeling simple pleasure in doing this for him. His hand tenderly stroked my hair as I did it. We were like two cats in the sun stretching for each other. I lowered my head and kissed the scar.

Declan opened his eyes. "Come back up here."

When I was lying fully against him again, he kissed me on the forehead. "Don't want to leave here."

"We can probably push it for a while longer," I told him.

"Longer than longer," he breathed.

It sounded good to me.

But eventually even John and Yoko had to get out of bed, and so did we.

Had I known what the next away game for the Devils back in Melbourne would bring, I would have gladly stayed in the bed drowning in my own shit.

MY PICTURE had appeared in the papers after the last game. They had captured me standing out like a sore thumb against the WAGs; I might as well have been naked and showing my different genitalia in a game of "one of these things is not like the others" as it couldn't have been any less subtle. *The Easiest Game of Where's Wally?* Trumpeted the caption beneath the photo in the *Herald Sun*. It was about the only time they were actually funny.

"Don't stress about it," Declan had told me.

"I'm not," I lied.

He studied me carefully. "You can sit the next game out, if you want."

"I'm not going to give them the satisfaction."

"Who? The WAGs or the papers?"

"Both," I growled.

Dec grimaced. "I don't know whether to love your attitude or worry about it."

"It's all cool," I said reassuringly, although I secretly agreed with him. But I knew if I sat out the next game, which was being played in my own hometown, the papers would have even more of a field day over it.

Declan still didn't look too sure, and when the day itself arrived I wasn't feeling all that certain myself. I woke up with a bad feeling, which I tried to put down to paranoia, but I think the stars were lining up against me.

I had tried to convince Roger and Fran to come with me if I could get them tickets, but they had already heard my horror story of my previous experience with Rachel of the WAGs so they declined. Luckily I still had Lisa.

"We're either extremely loyal or gluttons for punishment," she told me as we met outside the members' gate at Etihad.

"Can I ask you something?"

"Shoot," she said, as she inspected the bottom of her shoe and grimaced at the bubblegum stuck to it. She was lucky it wasn't a syringe.

"Before I came along, didn't you have *anybody* else friendly in that box?"

Lisa's eyes were firmly glued to the sole of her shoe. "Uh, sometimes."

She sounded cagey.

"Who?"

"Oh, just a girl."

I folded my arms and stared down at her. I could see her peer out below her fringe and realised she was caught out. She sighed, straightened up, and looked somewhat guilty. "Jess came sometimes."

"Oh."

"Not all the time—" Lisa said hurriedly.

"Well, of course she would," I shrugged. "They had a story to maintain."

She seemed somewhat relieved I wasn't melodramatically tearing my hair out and wailing at the moon about the "ex."

"But did you like her more than me?" I teased.

Lisa tilted her head and sized me up. "I like you both in very different ways."

"Fucking fence-sitter," I muttered, and we began walking towards the barriers of the entrance.

"I heard that."

"You were meant to," I replied perkily.

At that stage it all still seemed pretty normal. When we got to the players' box we were given the once-over yet again, with Rachel glowering at the thought of me daring to be in there. She wisely kept her mouth shut for the moment, though.

"How are you feeling?" Lisa asked as we took our seats.

"Fine."

"Beer?" she asked.

Supporting my boyfriend was going to turn me into an alcoholic, and Lisa would be my enabler. "I'll go get them."

"No, you sit. Won't be long."

She was throwing me to the lions again, but I remained tight-lipped and slumped into my seat, as if I could hide from view.

It didn't take long for Rachel to lean over. "Saw you in the paper again."

I grunted some form of reply.

"Just can't help yourself, can you?"

"Jealous?" I asked. I don't know why I was responding to her. I should have known better.

"Hardly," she snorted.

"Jesus, Rachel," said one of the other women. I think her name was Anna. "Leave him alone."

"Looks like you have your supporters," Rachel sneered.

"Maybe because he doesn't seem like a psycho," Anna shot back. "Can we just watch the bloody game?"

I stared ahead of me. The field was still empty; the teams were in the change rooms.

This was shaping up to be a long day. If I closed my eyes I could almost swear to smelling blood in the air.

As the Devils ran out onto the field, I recognised Declan by his gait despite the distance between us. He ran with a casual confidence, but favoured his right leg, as that was the uninjured one. I had gotten to know Abe well enough now to pick him out running beside Dec, flanking him like a loyal bodyguard. It made me feel better to know Abe was out there watching his back, at least, as I was still pretty sure Dec didn't tell me half the things that happened during the game.

"He's limping slightly," Lisa said as she sat back beside me.

"He's fine," I said stoically, although her noticing it as well made me start to worry a little more.

She must have heard it in my voice, because she immediately tried to cover it up. "I'm sure Scott wouldn't be playing him if he wasn't able."

I nodded, just as much for her as for myself. "It's cold today. His knee plays up on cold days."

"Maybe he should try and switch to West Coast," Lisa said. "At least the weather would only be a problem on away games."

Horrified, I rapped on the wood underneath my seat. "As if him living in Tasmania isn't bad enough, you'd banish him to Perth?"

"I could see you living in Perth," Lisa teased. "All those beaches and sun... you'd probably burst into flames."

I wanted to protest, but I was distracted by the roar of the crowd. Lisa and I looked up, only to see ourselves being broadcast on the giant screens around the stadium. Fuck, I hated it when they did this. It usually gave the anonymous people in the crowd a thrill to see their own mug put up there for ten seconds of fame, all it did to me was make my stomach cramp.

Lisa wasn't too thrilled by it either. She turned her head so her lips were partly obscured and murmured to me, "Crap. Try to look happy."

Following her lead, I turned my head as well. "You aren't smiling either."

"On the count of three, you say something," Lisa said, "and I'll laugh like you're the funniest guy on earth."

It was generous of her to do that, so I said, "I'm saying something really funny right now."

Lisa burst out laughing. She should have been an actress, she was that convincing.

I could hear Rachel bitch behind me. "Definitely *not* an attention whore."

I made sure I was still grinning for the camera and then turned and was glad my face was hidden when I stared Rachel in the eye and said, "For fuck's sake, just shut up."

Suddenly, a small group of the WAGs burst out laughing, so glad someone other than Lisa had bitched out Rachel.

I must have looked like I was in control of that box, surrounded by laughing and adoring women. When I turned back in my chair, we were all still on the screen. Then we abruptly disappeared, replaced with another section of the crowd, who were all holding up signs.

Lisa managed to decipher what it was first, squinting against the glare. "Fuckers!" she hissed.

I still couldn't see it, but I could hear Rachel's nasty snigger blowing hot in my ear, so I knew it wasn't going to be good.

Looking up into the screen, I could see myself. About five of me. Except they all looked odd, because I seemed to be a paper doll with five different outfits on. Women's outfits. Short skirts, long dresses, boobs hanging out of a halter top. I felt a small trickle of sweat form near my temple. I realised it was a doctored poster from a TV series, as the headline below read "FOOTBALLER'S WIVES." The camera panned out, and I realised that there were about twenty people clustered in one group who were holding them all. I scanned the crowd and could make out quite a few similar-looking posters scattered within it.

Rachel, enjoying herself far too much, leaned down and whispered into my ear, "They printed it in a local footy rag. Looks good, huh?"

I swallowed, vowing I wasn't showing that I was upset. "Amazing what you can do with Photoshop these days. Wish my legs were that good." It was a lame comeback, but at least Rachel was disappointed by my lack of crying and storming off to the toilets.

Which I was almost ready to do when I saw the poster had been doctored further by some of the holders. These ones read *WAGs and FAGs*. Now I felt like I was going to throw up.

Anyway, Lisa was raging enough for me. "That's so fucked!" she yelled. And after what Rachel had said, I thought she was about to leap over the seats and tackle her in a catfight worthy of any soap.

"Lisa," I pleaded, "sit down."

She did so, recognising that I didn't want any more attention drawn to me. She sat down with a thud and linked her arm through mine. "Are you okay?"

I couldn't answer. She squeezed my arm.

"Do you want to go?"

I shook my head.

The footage on the screen switched back to the players, and Declan appeared amongst a scrum that had erupted on the field. I felt a cold déjà vu at this happening again. I could have railed against the world, and the injustices of it all, but I literally felt frozen. I numbly watched the action unfold on the screen. Lisa's grip on me tightened.

The scrum dissipated, and play resumed. Dec looked furious.

It was only two minutes before the siren went for the end of the first quarter, but it seemed like it had only begun. There was an uncomfortable silence in our box after the siren stopped sounding, and we watched the players head to their respective coaches.

"I wish you would say something," Lisa said.

"I'm fine," I mumbled.

My mobile buzzed in my pocket. I pulled it out, expecting Fran or Roger. The number was private. I had no idea if I should pick it up. The last thing I wanted to do was find myself speaking to some contingent from the media and denying them a comment on the situation.

I answered anyway. "Hello."

"Simon." It was Dec. His tone was restrained, like he was fighting screaming.

"Hey," I said, tonelessly. "Where are you calling from?"

He didn't have to answer me; the big screen flashed the image of Dec calling from the coaches' box, Scott beside him looking uncomfortable.

"Oh, there you are."

"Get out of here, Simon. You don't have to put up with this shit."

The cameramen had obviously picked up what was going on, because I was back on the screen. I noticed Lisa was scratching at her nose with her middle finger; such a high school action but one which would have made me laugh if I weren't so mad. "No."

"Simon!"

I used Lisa's trick again, tilting my head so my lips would be hard to read. "I'm not giving them the satisfaction, Dec. It's just a fucking poster."

"Did you read what one of them said?" Dec demanded.

"Yes. It's awful, what else can I say?"

"I can tell you're upset." Declan, however, had obviously never been taught the subtle art employed by Lisa, as I could see when he appeared on the screen again.

"Yeah? Well, I can tell you are too."

"It's not me they're targeting today."

"So? It will probably be your turn next game. And what was that fight about on the field, anyway?"

"It was nothing."

"Yeah, well, that poster's nothing as well," I said, sounding more honest than I felt. "Now, laugh like I said something funny."

I could see him oblige, even though his mouth was still rigid. I was actually surprised he did so, but it made me feel slightly better. "Speak to you later, Dec."

"Bye."

I snapped my mobile shut and gave Lisa a small smile. There was a tap on my shoulder. Anna was standing behind me, holding two cups of beer.

"I thought you could use this," she said, handing me one.

Wow. "Thanks," I said, taking it.

"Hang in there." She shrugged. "We all get the crap at some point. They'll get tired of it. Unless, of course, you're Rachel."

I heard Rachel make some comeback, but it got lost in translation. Lisa gave me a surprised look, but Anna hadn't finished. She handed the second beer over. "This one's for you, Lisa."

Now it was Lisa's turn to be surprised. "Uh, thanks, Anna."

"You're welcome." Anna turned and settled back into her seat.

"Holy fuck," Lisa said, "am I dreaming?"

"I think we're both officially accepted WAGs now," I said.

We smushed our cups together in bittersweet triumph.

But I was the only FAG. That was my own special club.

THE Devils lost the game. I fumed a little as the other WAGs left the box, wondering if I would be blamed for it in the papers tomorrow.

"You're more upset than you're letting on," Lisa said.

"I'll be fine," I told her.

She didn't look convinced.

"Let's just go, okay?"

As we exited the box, I saw one of the offending posters lying discarded on a seat. I heard Lisa mutter something, and she bent down to pick it up, probably meaning to throw it in the bin.

I stopped her, took the poster from her, rolled it up carefully, and put it in my messenger bag.

"Simon, what are you doing?"

"Nothing."

"Tormenting yourself, that's what you're doing."

"My mother's been making a scrapbook," I said with a dismissive shrug. "She might as well have everything."

Lisa stuffed her hands into the pockets of her jacket and pushed past me.

We made our way down to the change rooms in silence; the security guards nodded at us, although my paranoia turned their usual friendly greetings into sneers and smirks.

Most of the team were leaving already; it seemed that they wanted to get out of there as soon as possible. They stonily ignored me and, by default, Lisa. As we walked up, Abe stuck his head out of the change room doors. He jogged up to us, relief visible on his face.

"How is he?" I asked immediately.

Abe never lied. "Not good. He's going off his rocker at the bosses."

"Why them?" I asked stupidly.

I could tell Abe was afraid of my reaction to what he was going to tell us. "He wants security to try and examine all posters at the next game and confiscate any that are about you."

Yeah, that'd work. "Has he gone insane? That would be impossible!"

Abe didn't want to criticize his best friend by taking sides against him. "I told you. He was upset."

"Can I go in there?" I asked. "I have to stop this. It's crazy."

"Simon—"

"Abe," Lisa said, and that was all it took for him to capitulate.

"Come on, then," he sighed.

I had only ever seen the inside of a change room in the telecasts, when they would follow the players after the win to record them singing the team song in victorious harmony. Need it be said, as a Richmond supporter, I never got to see it that often. Abe led the way past the benches, and I could hear Declan before I saw him. He sounded ropable, and as we passed a collection of lockers I could see him in a small office, standing in front of the window with his coach and someone else that I recognised from my own meeting with the board.

"Oh crap," I whispered. Ed bloody Wallace.

"We'll just wait back outside," Lisa said, catching Abe's arm as she knew the fewer people in this situation the better.

I nodded and made my way over to the office while Lisa and Abe went back towards the exit.

Dec saw me before I got there, and if it was possible for him to look even unhappier, he did. My old friend Ed had his back to me. I felt my stomach drop. The last time I'd met him and Coach Scott hadn't exactly been the social soirée of the season, back when Dec was in the hospital recovering from his operation and his two bosses had looked upon me as some sort of interloper bothering their cash cow.

I knocked on the door, and the two other men turned to look at me.

"Hey," I said. Wow, there was an opening.

"Simon," Scott said politely.

Ed, however, glared at me. "Can we help you?"

"I was just wondering if I could steal Dec for a moment."

"We're kind of busy," Dec told me, his tone telling me to go away.

Which of course, I wouldn't do. "Look, Abe told me what you guys were talking about."

"This is game business, Simon," Ed told me.

I stood my ground. "It's my bloody face plastered over those posters, so I'd say it's my business too."

"You can't honestly expect us to search over sixty thousand people who attend the games!" Ed spat.

"Hey!" Dec warned. "Don't talk to him like that."

I glared at Dec, trying to tell him to back down through the powers of the mind. He didn't want to, and he folded his arms defensively over his chest.

"Well?" Ed demanded. "Look, we're going to do a public statement saying that the language is unacceptable but to search everyone is impossible!"

I could see Dec straining, waiting for my response.

"I know," I said, finally. "It's just not feasible."

Ed looked pleased, Scott anxiously awaited Dec's next explosion, and Dec shook his head at me.

"What do you suggest then?" Ed was suddenly very interested in my opinion now he thought I was on his side.

"There's nothing to do." I shrugged. "And I wouldn't want anyone doing that on my behalf either."

"But they shouldn't be targeting you," Declan said with gritted teeth. "You're not a player. They—"

Old argument, and one that was never going to be solved with continual rehashing.

"Dec," Scott said calmly. "You know sledging happens on the field. Sometimes it even involves family. Just because you choose not to do it, doesn't mean other people won't."

"But this isn't other players doing this," Dec argued. "This is the crowd. And they've never gone after anyone who isn't actually a player before. *That's* why this is different."

"Dec—"

"You shouldn't be in here, Simon," Dec said, glaring at me.

I had never seen him look at me that way before, with pure anger. Sure, we'd had tiffs and major disagreements, but he'd always tried to battle me with humour. He was beyond that approach at this moment.

"And you're not turning me into the poster boy for censorship," I said, my tone made of steel. "Think about how fucking ironic that would be. I may not be on that field like you are, but I can take shit when it's flung my way. And I can deal with it as well."

Dec and I continued to stare at each other, neither of us wanting to back down.

"Well," Ed interrupted, sounding much happier than he had when I first came in. "That's that, then."

"No, it's not," Dec said firmly.

"You're alone on this one, Declan," Ed told him with more than a hint of satisfaction. "You're asking the impossible."

"I'll wait outside," I told Declan.

He didn't answer me. Ed went to shake my hand, but I pointedly ignored it. I hated having to take sides against Dec, but he was upset and being more than irrational. I had hoped to calm him down, but it seemed I had made things worse.

Abe and Lisa were waiting outside the change room, and they jumped up as soon as they saw me emerge from it as if it were from the entrance to hell.

"What happened?" Lisa asked.

"It's not good," I said truthfully. "He's pissed, and now he thinks I'm against him too."

"I'd feel the same if I was him," Abe said, "and it was Lisa they were doing that shit to."

"Thanks, Abe. That's helpful."

Abe looked upset by my mild sniping.

"Yeah, and I'd be doing what Simon is doing," Lisa frowned, deciding that because everybody else was sharing their opinions she may as well jump in as well. "I wouldn't give those arseholes the satisfaction of thinking they got to me."

"You don't understand—" Abe started.

"Stop!" I interrupted him. "You two are not going to argue about this as well!"

"Okay," they said together, chastened.

"Look, Dec's really in a foul mood. You don't have to wait around if you don't want to."

"Are you sure?" Abe asked quickly. I didn't blame him; he'd had to handle Dec on the field for close to two hours.

"I don't need *protection*," I scoffed.

I was hugged good-bye by both of them, although they looked reluctant to leave.

Once they had disappeared behind the huge security doors, I sat down on one of the couches and dug my book out of my bag.

Two chapters had been devoured, although my mind really didn't process anything I read, before Declan silently stood beside me.

I shut my book and looked up at his stony visage. "How did it go?"

"You know how it went," Dec said in a dangerous monotone.

"You're mad at me." It was a statement, because I already knew the answer.

"I don't want to get into it here."

"Okay," I said, faux-cheerily. "Your place or mine?"

Dec's grip tightened on his bag. "Actually, I want to be left alone tonight."

I stuffed my book into my backpack. "Oh, come on."

"Don't start," Dec warned.

"It's stupid for us to fight about this," I tried to placate him. "You know they couldn't have done it. And when you calm down—"

"I'm calm!" he snapped.

"Yeah, you sound it."

"I told you not to start."

"And you're sounding like an arsehole," I fumed.

The anger flared in his eyes again. "Simon, goddammit—"

"Seriously, you can't go off mad. Let's talk about it."

"I'm not going to talk about it here. Do you remember, Simon, not that long ago, when you said you would make them pay if you were in my position, and they had sledged me?"

I did. But this wasn't vengeful fantasy. "Of course I would *feel* that way. But there are realistic ways to deal with it, and then there's trying to make your club pay for security to search people so they won't be mean to your boyfriend."

"Great way to reduce it, Simon. I'm going."

And he began to walk off.

"Hey!" I yelled.

Dec turned back and said hoarsely, "Don't *ever* do that to me again. Pull me aside if you have to, but don't make me look like a fucking idiot in front of my bosses."

"I tried to, if you recall, Dec, but you were doing that on your own," I said, and I meant it to burn.

He didn't say a word. He just walked off in the direction of the car park.

So I was left there. And I didn't have my car. I sat there stupidly for ten minutes, wondering if he would calm down and then come back to get me.

He didn't. In the end I stuck my book back in my bag and left Etihad, heading over the footbridge through the Southern Cross Station and down to Collins Street to catch my tram.

This wasn't the way I had imagined the rest of the day would go. By now Dec would already be at home, stomping around his apartment. I wondered how long it would take him to calm down. I wasn't looking forward to the inevitable conversation we would have to have in which we hashed over who said what and what do we do now.

I just wished the damn fight hadn't happened and he had listened to me from the start. Or had just let me go back home with him and sort it out straightaway. Time would just make it worse.

I tried to lose myself in my book again but couldn't concentrate and ended up resting my head against the cool glass of the window as the tram rattled its way past Parliament Station.

The girl opposite was staring at me, and I was starting to feel unnerved. Finally she leaned in and whispered, "Hey, are you that guy going out with Declan Tyler?"

I gave her a tired smile. "If I was, do you think I'd be catching this tram?"

She looked disappointed. "I guess not."

And she left me alone after that.

CHAPTER TWENTY-SEVEN

"SO, HAS he called you yet?" Fran asked.

"You know I would have told you by now if he had," I told her, nursing my beer.

She frowned and then her look turned sympathetic. "Simon, have you tried calling him, or are you being stubborn?"

I wanted to pretend that I was being my usual self, all aloof and confident despite the fact everybody close to me saw right through it anyway, but I was too tired. "I've tried. Too many times to even count, actually."

We sat in silence for a few minutes, letting the background noise of The Napier take over in lieu of conversation. Finally, I asked her what I had been wanting to ever since I sat down. "Have *you* spoken to him?"

She looked at me sadly and shook her head.

"Oh," I said, defeated. "He must still be... calming down... then." But I fired up again. "He's establishing an MO, you know? A sign of trouble, and he disappears on me. I'm fucking sick of it. I want him to stick around, for once."

"He's probably more embarrassed by the fact that he lost his cool for once," Fran said, trying to calm me. "He always keeps things pretty close to his chest. To be so open about it, and lose face... well, he *is* a man."

"On behalf of my sex, I say 'Hey!'"

"Come off it," Fran protested. "Stupid, bloody, men."

"Yeah," I agreed before I could stop myself.

We both laughed, and it was the first time I had done so in days. But the natural serotonin disappeared immediately, and I tried not to let my funk show.

I DRUNKENLY wove my way from the tram stop back to my house and saw that Dec's car was sitting in my driveway and the windows of my house were lit. Instead of being relieved, I was mad. Stupid, bloody alcohol, being in my system. I felt this wasn't a situation that should be fuelled by malt and hops.

I fumbled with my keys in the door and walked in to find him sitting calmly on my couch with Maggie in his lap.

"Maggie, you traitor," I slurred.

"I let myself in," Declan said unnecessarily.

"Then you should know the way out," I said grandly, kicking off my shoes.

"Simon...."

I stumbled into my bedroom, feeling sick to my stomach although it wasn't from the alcohol. I lay on my bed, as I could no longer stand. I heard Maggie's bell sound; Declan must have lifted her off him, because I heard him coming down the hall.

"You're going the wrong way," I called out.

The mattress dipped sickeningly as he sat next to me.

"Have you been drinking?"

"Amazing," I said. "How could you tell?"

He rested his hand upon my side, and I twisted out from under it.

"Simon, please."

I dragged myself up into a sitting position although the room was spinning uncontrollably. Declan was looking at me with concern. Maybe he thought I had turned alcoholic out of despair.

"'Please'," I snorted. "I think I said that in one of the hundreds of messages I left you. *Dec, please call me.*"

"Can't we talk?"

"I tried talking to you on Saturday. You didn't want to. Now I don't want to."

He didn't answer; he just sat there. And I could tell he was chewing on the inside of his cheek. And just that little thing made me collapse internally.

I gave him a quick hug. "I lied. I do want to talk to you. But I think I'm going to vomit." I lay back down, glad that the room stopped moving when I did so.

Declan lay beside me, and his arms pulled me in closer to him. And strangely enough, I began to feel better.

MERCIFULLY, I didn't have a hangover when I woke up hours later, but I was cold even though Declan was still holding me. So the recent dreamlike events *were* real. We had fallen asleep on top of the covers, and Maggie was nestled between our legs.

"I'm sorry," Dec murmured, sensing I was awake.

"Me too."

We decided not to press the issue. We both knew how we had stuffed up, and there was no need to rehash it. But I just had to let him know one thing.

"I'm a big boy, Dec."

"You have tickets on yourself," Dec smiled, not being able to resist.

"I mean it. I can deal. It won't stop you from worrying about me. It won't make me stop worrying about you. But we'll deal."

His lips found the crook of my neck. I turned so we were face to face, eager to feel his mouth against mine again. We kissed deeply, slowly, savouring each other. Making up for what had been missed over the past few days. Maggie, disturbed by the shifting bodies, took off for safer ground.

My doorbell rang.

"Who the hell is that this early on a Sunday morning?" I groaned.

"It's Monday," Dec reminded me.

"Public holiday," I corrected him. "It's a Sunday by another name."

I gave him another kiss, glad he was there to receive it, and made my way to the door. I heard Declan following me.

Fran and Roger stood on the doorstep. Roger looked slightly green; Fran was wearing sunglasses, despite the fact that it was overcast. She held up a couple of greasy brown paper bags, and Roger was holding one as well.

"Hangover cure," she announced. "Don't say we don't love you."

She then lifted her glasses to reveal two bloodshot eyes as she stared past my shoulder. Declan had just appeared behind me.

"Well," Fran said, lowering her glasses again. "Good thing we brought extra."

Roger tried to give me an intimidating stare as he walked in. It failed, so he tried it on Declan. It failed again.

I turned to follow Roger into the kitchen; behind me I heard a muffled thud, and Declan protesting. I looked back and saw him rubbing his shoulder.

"She hit me!" he said, an injured expression on his face.

Fran gave me a wink as she continued on into the kitchen. "You're lucky it wasn't your knee."

"It means she loves you," I told Declan.

He continued rubbing the inflicted area. "Doesn't *feel* like it."

"Can we *eat?*" Roger moaned from the kitchen. "I'm starving."

"You go first," Declan whispered. "I don't think my shoulder can take another hit."

Trying to hide my smile, but failing miserably, I led the way.

AND that was how it was for us. Ups and downs. Sometimes more downs than ups. It was funny, though, because we experienced everything differently. He got flak on the field, but none from the fans. I, however, got it all from the fans. The needling at the games maintained a steady level rather than dying down as I had hoped it would. Dec got to the point where he wanted me to stay away for my own sanity, but I stubbornly took my place in the players' box at every away game that took place in Melbourne.

Away from the field I had also become more recognisable in the public eye, and it meant certain members of it now thought they were well within their right to start calling me out whenever and wherever they saw me. I took to wearing my iPod every time I was out and about by myself, but sometimes I could still hear them above the music. If I was with Dec they never tried it. They wanted to be his friend, so by default I was treated to their politeness.

Fran and Roger got to see it every now and again, though.

"How can you stand it?" Roger asked.

"I just have to."

"I want to hit them for you," Fran snarled.

"If you want to go ahead, I didn't hear anything, so I can't be responsible," I said. I kind of meant it, even though it was unwise.

The only face-to-face negativity Declan experienced was on a radio interview when one of the DJs asked him if he was a top or a bottom. When Dec had asked him if he was serious, the DJ told him he didn't have a sense of humour. Declan walked out of the interview early, the managers of the Devils went ballistic at the radio station, and battle lines were drawn. The more bozo-ish of the footy shows on TV admonished him as being a sook, yet Dec knew if he had actually gone on their show they would have been kissing his arse.

He was almost glad when the Devils didn't make the finals, as it meant he could have a longer break away from it all. I don't even want to discuss how the Tigers did.

Dec and the rest of his team went on their end-of-season holiday early, but would be back in time for the Brownlow ceremony.

The Brownlow. That was another thing I didn't want to think about, being in the same room as a large group of people who would sledge me on the field to try and provoke my partner every week. I know sledging wasn't meant to be taken personally, but I still took it as such.

"You've lost weight," Fran told me critically, while Declan was away.

"Good, I can go shopping in the petite section for my Brownlow dress," I replied sourly.

Fran gave me a small smile. "I heard what they said on that show. I don't know why Roger watches that crap."

"He says it's just because he wants to know the in-house goss."

"It's not worth it. Especially when they make fun of your friends."

"They did say I would look good in a dress, though. Y'know, because I'm a *girl.*"

"There are worse things than being called a girl."

"That's true." I shrugged. "They also called me *the little lady.*"

"Wow, so they're misogynistic and homophobic. They're trying to tick every box, what else is new?"

"You're not helping."

"I could go dress shopping with you."

"Shut up, Fran."

"What are you wearing to the Brownlows, anyway?"

"Have you turned into Roger all of a sudden? I'm surprised you even know what they are."

She shrugged. "It's amazing what you can learn when you actually care about it."

"You care about the Brownlows?" I asked with surprise.

"Two of my friends are going," she pointed out. "It was a huge controversy last year. I'm not that forgetful."

I breathed deeply. "I hope it's not that controversial this year."

Fran looked at me; her expression was strangely indecipherable. "I hope so too."

"ARE you sure that's what you really want to wear?"

Practically the first thing Declan had made me do when he returned to Melbourne was to go shopping with him and finalise my wardrobe for the Brownlows. I had to laugh at Declan being so concerned about clothing, and wondered if he just wanted some dumb movie montage in which we paraded around with various costume changes to some sprightly music track.

"What's wrong with it?" I looked at his reflection in the mirror as he walked up behind me and rested his hand upon my shoulder.

"It's just—"

"What?" I asked, grumpy and tired. I had tried on about seven different outfits, and I hated shopping at the best of times. I was the kind of shopper who wouldn't try anything on and would just chuck clothes at the register and get out of there as soon as possible. I would then hope that they actually fit once I got them home.

"It's not very *you*."

Was that a twinkle in his eye? "What's *me*, anyway?"

"It's just so plain."

"It looks kind of like what you wore last year," I pointed out. It was a perfectly nice, traditional black suit with white shirt and bowtie combo.

"Exactly," Dec agreed.

"So it's good enough for you, but not for me?"

"Stop fighting me on this. Traditional suits me. I'm traditional."

"Says the gay footballer." I turned to face him properly.

Declan laughed. "Okay, you got me there. But I'm talking fashionwise."

"Just because the papers keep printing that picture of me in the lime-green suit—"

"You love that suit."

"It's not Brownlow material."

"Oh," Declan said, as if that explained everything. He moved to go back and sit on the couch and pulled me along with him.

"Weren't they meant to be bringing us coffee?" I grumbled. "They offered it. I've never been in an upscale store like this before. I want the perks."

Declan wisely ignored me to focus upon the real issue. "I want you to be comfortable at the Brownlows."

"And?"

"You're not going to be comfortable if you don't go as yourself."

I sagged against the back of the couch and into him slightly. "I'm not going to be comfortable if I go as myself either."

"You're never happy."

"I just mean, I know I'm going to be on edge. And to be truthful, I don't want to embarrass you. They're going to be watching us enough, even before I turn up looking like Maria von Trapp dressed me in the venue's curtains."

"Even *your* taste isn't that bad."

"You know what I mean."

"Simon, you don't embarrass me. You've got to get over it. I want you to go as you, because you're who I go out with." He realised how badly structured that last sentence was and shook his head. "See what you do to me?"

"How about we compromise?" I suggested.

"How?"

"That longer-style black jacket, and I'll wear one of my crappy band shirts under it."

"Still a bit understated for you, but at least it's better than what you're wearing."

"I look that bad in this?" I asked.

Declan sat back to fully take me in. "I don't think you do at all. I think you look brilliant."

"And yet you're making me wear something else?"

He kissed me. "Shut up, Simon."

"But...."

The coffee finally arrived, and it was now Declan's turn to play model.

LOOKING back, this might have been the moment when it all started turning to shit. Or maybe it was the *Footballers' Wives* and *WAGs and FAGs* posters that started it. Anyway, everything escalated so quickly there was hardly time to even recognise what was actually going on. Of course, with hindsight you can say that everything could have been handled better on all sides, but it had been building up for a while and a few experiences just made it explode.

But as I started getting ready for the Brownlow ceremony I still felt good, despite the expected nervousness. Declan and I were getting dressed together, and I was feeling a little bit of déjà vu from the year before except this time I wouldn't be watching Declan get into the limousine with someone other than me.

"Have you decided on your shirt yet?" Declan asked as he buttoned his over his chest.

I threw open the wardrobe again and pulled out a few. "Patty Hearst, Kimba the White Lion, or should I show my true allegiance and wear my Richmond shirt?"

Declan snatched the black and yellow shirt away from me and threw it back into the wardrobe with distaste.

"Okay," I drawled.

Declan pounced on me and started pulling at my clothes. "Get dressed!"

"You're actually undressing me," I pointed out. "But I like it."

I let myself be manipulated like a doll as he yanked my arms up and pulled my shirt off. I shivered slightly as it was cold in the bedroom, but kept my arms in the air as Dec chose the Kimba T-shirt and pulled it over my head.

"Well, we're halfway there." He grinned. "Think I can leave you to do the rest?"

"You can do my pants if you like."

"Piss off. Get ready."

He disappeared into the lounge room, and I opened up the robe again to pull out the new shirt I had bought especially for tonight. It was a plain button-down, federation green, and I thought it would look good with the black tie I had also bought. I never thought I would have owned a tie in my life, but there was a first time for everything.

Declan came back into the bedroom just as I was smoothing the jacket down, and he pointed at me. "That's not... wow. You look good."

So did he. I felt bizarrely like I was going to the school ball. Except finally I was going to the school ball the way I *wanted*, with a date. A *boy* date. Well, a man.

"You look *really* good," Declan said.

"Try not to sound so surprised."

"Don't be so surprised if you end up on the best-dressed list this year."

I laughed. "Flatterer *and* liar! I need to look good when I'm going with tonight's medallist."

"Don't jinx it," he winced. "I don't think I'll win. In fact, I hope I don't."

Anybody else, I wouldn't have believed it. But Declan hated the attention, even more so after the past six months. Before I could say anything, the sound of a horn came from outside.

"That'll be the limo," Dec said. "Ready?"

He held out his hand, and I took it. "Sure."

My voice sounded steadier than I was, though.

WE HAD agreed to share a limo with Abe and Lisa. Lisa was rather raucous when Dec and I climbed into the back of the car with them, and said we both looked delicious. She had already raided the minibar, and I was only too happy to help.

"Try and save some room for the open bar at the ceremony," Abe said affably.

"We're just steeling ourselves," Lisa said. "So, Simon, who are you wearing tonight?" She easily slid into the role of the blue-carpet presenter.

I leaned into the nonexistent microphone in her hand and said rakishly, "Well, I plan to be wearing Declan later, if you know what I mean."

Dec shook his head while Abe sniggered. "Don't encourage him."

My overexaggerated sense of bravado was quickly extinguished when the limo pulled up to the foyer of Crown Casino.

"We are *not* going after you," teased Lisa. "We'll be overshadowed."

I was glad they were getting out first, although I worried it gave me a few extra moments to consider jumping out the other door and taking off anonymously into the night.

My thoughts must have been transparent to Declan, as he watched me with concern.

"See you in there," Abe said jovially, although he knew we were shitting ourselves. Lisa gave us both supportive hand squeezes and then was helped out of the limo by Abe.

"You ready?" Dec asked.

"You don't need to help me out," I told him, before his chivalrous side took over.

He gave me a withering look. "Really?"

"But stay close."

He smiled. "We'll be okay."

And then I followed him out into the glare.

The photos the next day would show Declan, sleek and confident, ever the pro. And next to him, looking like a rabbit on a country road watching the headlights of an approaching car, me.

I honestly don't remember much of stumbling down the long blue carpet, watching the photographers jostle for the best angles of us or the fans behind the barriers yelling for Declan's autograph. Remembering his promise to stay close, Declan ushered me over to the barrier alongside him while he signed whatever Devils merchandise was thrust at him.

"Simon!"

There was no way in hell I could have stopped my instant grin. Fran and Roger were pushing their way to the front of the barrier. I moved over to them and was grabbed in a bear hug by both.

"What are you doing here?" I asked, surprised but pleased.

"Moral support, of course," Fran replied.

"Is it working?" Roger asked.

"Yes!" And I wasn't lying. The snakes in my stomach had settled somewhat.

Declan had now caught sight of them and come over for his own hug.

"I wish I could get you guys in," he said apologetically.

"Well...." Roger started to say, but he was elbowed by Fran.

"Have fun," she said, pointing behind us. "It looks like they're demanding to interview you."

Dec and I turned to see the blue-carpet hosts glaring at us for daring to hold them up.

"Catch up with you later," Declan nodded.

"Text us when you get out," Fran yelled after us.

Away from the comforting circle of friends I had to fight against the nausea again, but their presence had emboldened me and I kept a friendly but neutral smile on my face as Declan and I stepped up to the podium to be interviewed.

"Declan, what do you think your chances are for tonight?" the bland television personality asked.

"It's up for grabs among quite a few of us," Declan said modestly.

"Playing it nice," the host chuckled.

"Not at all."

"For the viewers at home," the co-host asked, falling neatly into her required gender-specific role, "who are you wearing tonight, Declan?"

Declan bit the inside of his cheek, suppressing a smile. "A local designer, Keith Ho."

She then turned to me. "And you, Simon?"

I leaned in to the microphone as if it was Lisa's hand and said, "The Savers on Sydney Road. Six dollar rack."

Of course, I had gotten my suit from the same store as Declan. The hosts didn't know what to make of my answer, so with a brief flash of panic that disappeared quickly beneath the professional façade, she decided to take a different tack. "It'll be no surprise who you're hoping will win tonight."

"Probably not," I said smoothly.

"Who?" She laughed merrily, pretending she wasn't in on a game.

"Stephen Burrows from Richmond, of course."

Declan couldn't keep the laughter in now, especially as both co-hosts' jaws dropped. "He's my biggest fan, really," he said quickly, and he moved us on into the venue.

"How did I do?" I asked innocently.

"You are *evil*," Declan replied with a straight face.

Abe and Lisa were waiting for us just within the doors.

"The two of you are going to be all over the news with that little performance," Lisa said with a smirk.

"How did you know?" I asked, bewildered.

Abe pointed above his head, where a giant screen was televising the blue carpet footage live. "Stephen Burrows will be glad of your support, I'm sure."

"Yeah," Declan poked me in the rib. "I could have used your vote."

"If I could vote, you would have it," I said grandly.

"Liar, but thanks," Dec laughed.

We were seated at the same table as many of the Devils players. Anna and a few more of the WAGs greeted us warmly, while Rachel and some of her cronies pretended we didn't exist. Dec's teammates were polite to me, but there was a distance I couldn't help but pick up on even if Declan appeared to be unaware of it – or pretended to be unaware of it.

If you think watching the Brownlows at home is boring, it's even worse when you're actually attending them. Especially if you're attending as one of the contender's dates, because the camera will be on them every time their name is mentioned, and you must look attentive and supportive. Nothing would be worse than the camera catching you yawning or staring into space with a glazed expression or picking your nose; it was expected that Declan's name would be coming up a lot. My boyfriend was a god of football. Everybody at our table expected him to win, and it wasn't just because they were his teammates. It seemed to be the general consensus of everybody in the theatre.

But a quarter of the way through the count we realised something wasn't quite right. Dec wasn't getting the votes that were expected of him for certain games, games where he had even been named player of the day. Dec remained stoic, but I heard Abe hiss beside me and a general rumbling throughout the ranks of the table.

During a commercial break Abe leaned over me and said to Declan, "This is bullshit."

"Cool it, Abe."

"Seriously, Dec!"

"What do you think's going on?" I asked Dec in a low voice.

"Nothing," was his short answer.

"It's obvious," said a voice from across the table. I looked up to see Geoff Hendricks staring at me with a snarl that seemed more suited to a villain tying Penelope Pittstop to the railway lines.

"What is?" I demanded.

"Shut up, Hendo," Dec warned.

"What's he going on about?" I asked Dec.

Dec shook his head, but Geoff continued on. "Notice it's certain games he isn't getting votes on?"

I looked at Dec for an answer of some sort, but there was an announcement that we were coming back from commercial break, so we had to put on our pleasantly interested facades again.

Now that Geoff had pointed it out, I began to take notice of the games that Declan neglected to get points for. And the pattern became recognisable very quickly.

They were games I had attended. Games where Declan was usually involved in some sort of scuffle.

By the halfway point of the counting, Declan was fifth when he should have at least been second, and it looked like he was going to slip even further down the ladder.

"Come on, boys," Declan said to the table, trying to lighten the mood. "We can't expect to win everything."

"That's the point," Geoff said. "We haven't won *anything* this year. This was the one thing we had in the bag."

"Well, we obviously didn't," Declan replied.

"Wonder why," Geoff muttered into his beer.

"You got something to say, Hendo?" Abe asked threateningly.

Declan cleared his throat, and Abe drank sullenly from his own beer.

The mood didn't improve, even though Declan managed to get back up to third place. A few more rounds saw him and the other players jump around positions, and in the final few Declan shot from fourth to second, with only one point between him and first.

"That's it," Declan whispered to me. "It's all over."

"There's two rounds to go," I reminded him.

He shook his head. He already knew.

Even though Dec had ended the final round with three goals and a spectacular mark that had given him Player of the Day, I remembered there had been another bust-up on the field. Declan didn't get any points for the round and remained in second place, losing by one point to Francis Bevan.

Declan clapped at the announcement. "He deserves it. He's a good player."

Hendricks scowled. "You were meant to win."

"Well, I didn't."

"I'm glad you can be so casual about it."

"You seem to care enough about it for the two of us," Dec fired back.

Any escalation of their sniping was halted when their coach, Scott Frasier, approached the table and nodded to Declan.

Dec pushed his chair out, muttered "Excuse me," and went off to the side to talk to his coach.

"I'll be back in a minute," I told Abe and Lisa.

"You okay?" she asked.

I nodded and made my way to the toilets. I didn't need to go, but I did need a semiprivate place where I could just hide for a moment and try to collect myself. There were only a couple of guys at the urinals when I entered; I locked myself in a stall and stared dismally at the door.

I heard the door swing open and shut again and assumed the other guys must have left. I unlocked the stall so I could go and splash water on my face and just try to cool down the sudden heat I felt building from my neck upwards.

I wasn't alone.

Geoff Hendricks stood near the door, with some of the other Devils players flanking him. I didn't want paranoia to instantly overwhelm me, so I nodded at them and continued on to the sinks.

"You happy with yourself?" Hendricks asked.

I took my time washing my hands and stared back at him through the mirror.

"About what?" I asked steadily.

"About costing Tyler his medal."

I turned off the tap and headed for the dryer. "I didn't cost him anything," I yelled over the sound of the blower.

"Keep telling yourself that," Hendricks yelled back, and his voice faltered as the dryer's cycle ended, and he had to lower it again. "But we all know you did."

"What, he's not allowed to have a social life like the rest of you?" It was funny how now I wasn't paranoid or feeling threatened, I was just angry. "It's okay for you lot to have girlfriends, but not for him to have someone?"

"Our girlfriends don't cause the shit you do," Jack Hanley piped up.

"I'm not causing shit, everybody around me is. Even now," I pointed out. "You followed me in here, not the other way around. What are you hoping to achieve? Do you think Declan is suddenly going to see the light if you do something to me?"

I noticed from the expressions on some of their faces they weren't actually planning to do anything to me; it was more than likely they just wanted to vent at me over the perceived injustice against their team. And now they were recognising just how bad it was looking for six men to gang up against one in a public toilet.

Hendricks opened his mouth to speak again, but the main door banged open. Abe barged through, and he erupted at the sight before him. "What the *fuck* is going on here?"

"Nothing," I said immediately. "We were just having a chat. Weren't we, boys?"

Too much time hanging around Declan meant I could take on his mannerisms easily. Nobody really answered me, so I continued. "Well, that's that, then."

They filed out, a couple mumbling apologies to me. Hendricks remained unrepentant. None of them could look Abe in the face.

"Simon, are you okay?" he asked, concerned, when we were alone.

I leaned against the sink, my legs finally becoming rubbery. "Yeah, cool."

"What happened?"

I looked up at him. "How did you know to come in here?"

"They weren't very subtle. They practically got up a minute after you did, and I saw them heading here. I would have been here sooner, but I got waylaid by Scott."

"It's okay. I think I had most of them shamed before you came in."

"You don't look so good now."

I felt like I was going to throw up. "I'll be fine."

Abe sighed. "Declan's going to lose it when he finds out."

I turned around so fast I felt like the walls continued spinning long after I had stopped. "You can't tell him!"

"Why not?"

"Because he *will* lose it. And he can't be on the outs with his whole fucking team."

"You can't expect me not to say anything. Because when you eventually tell him, he'll take it out on me, not you."

"No, he'll be pissed at both of us. You should have just let me handle it, Abe."

And it was then I knew why Declan was best friends with Abe. He drew himself up and gave me a look full of scorn. "You know, you might not care, Simon, but I think of you as my friend now. And friends look out for each other. I came in here to back you up, just like I would if it were Declan. And if it were Declan in this situation, you'd be fucking kissing my arse for coming in here after him."

We stared at each other for a long moment before I admitted, "You're right. And thank you."

But Abe wasn't done with me. "Just a bit of friendly advice. I know you're not telling Declan everything that is happening to you. And that's because Lisa tells me, and she's worried about it. It puts me in a fucked position because I know something Declan should. You have to be fair with him."

I nodded. "Okay. But I bet you hide things from Lisa sometimes because you don't want to hurt her. If the guys on the field use me being gay as sledging, I bet they use racism against her."

"Yeah, and Lisa knows it anyway. Which is why I eventually break and tell her. You should do the same for Dec."

I moved past him to the door. "Thanks, Abe."

"If you don't tell him soon, I will."

It wasn't something I wanted to happen, but I had to concede. As we left the toilet, I was reminded of something he had said before. "Hey, you said you were stopped by Scott earlier. I thought he was talking to Dec?"

Abe momentarily faltered, but quickly said, "Oh, by that stage Dec was talking to other people about the medal."

We stepped back into the venue, and by now I could sense something secret and alive, charging itself between us. I looked across to our table and could see a well-known footballer crouched beside Dec. Dec was laughing at something he had just said and then leaned in closer to him to say something.

"Oh," I said feebly to Abe as it dawned upon me.

"What?" Abe asked. Too fast.

"It's the ex."

Abe didn't say anything.

"Just say so, Abe."

"I—"

"Thanks a lot, after everything you said in there about secrets."

"Simon—"

"Don't tell him what happened." I walked off, and I could feel him watching me. I turned a corner and found a small alcove with a couch. I burrowed in my pockets for my mobile and called Roger.

He answered after a few rings, and I asked him where he was.

"We're still in the casino. Sorry about Dec losing." He sounded as aggrieved as if it were himself who had lost. "That was rigged!"

"I'm coming to meet you guys."

He told me which part of the complex they were in, and I said I would be there in five minutes. I then put on my best composed face and headed back to the table. The ex (I couldn't even bear to humanise him by thinking of him by name) saw me coming and left before I could be introduced; Dec didn't say anything about him as I sat down. Abe and Lisa watched me closely; from the look on Lisa's face I could tell she had already been briefed by him on the events in the toilet and my discovering the identity of my predecessor.

"Hey, where have you been?" Declan asked. He looked innocent enough, and I hated for a brief moment I couldn't stand the sight of him.

"The loo," I shrugged. "Look, Roger and Fran just called me. They're still in the casino. I thought I would go and meet them while you finish up here."

"Need a debriefing session, huh?" he laughed.

I couldn't believe he was acting like this when I knew what I did. "Something like that."

"I won't be much longer," he told me.

"Take your time."

I said a terse good-bye to Abe and Lisa. Lisa looked like she was going to come after me, but she probably didn't want Dec to catch onto something having happened.

I got out of the venue as quick as I could, not able to avoid the looks some of the players and WAGs at other tables were giving me. Before I hit the lobby I pulled off my tie, unbuttoned the top of my shirt and carried my jacket so I didn't stand out too much. I skirted around the assembled media and took the back way into the casino. I found Fran and Roger pretty quickly, and they could immediately tell the night had not been a success. At least I felt like I was back among my own people again.

ON THE way home, Declan was just as quiet as I was. Even though he had assumed the reasons he had lost out on vital points was because of the scuffles he had on and off during the season, he had never been suspended for it, and that should have really been the only reason for the exclusion of his votes for those rounds. I think it had finally hit him the whole night of scoring was unjust, but he was too tired to let himself care right now. And he probably assumed I was quiet because he was.

At least Roger and Fran were excited by the fact that they got a lift home in a limo.

Roger was quickly becoming jaded by the fact that he now hung out with celebrities and wasn't doing his star-struck routine anymore. And Fran and Lisa seemed to have found an initial bond in their affection for me, which had quickly gone beyond that into the beginnings of a proper friendship. I also think they had quickly figured out each knew the happenings of the night and conferred in a corner, claiming it was "secret women's business" whenever they were questioned about their conversation.

I just kept waiting for Dec to tell me about his reunion with his ex. Although I guess it was pretty stupid of me to assume their paths hadn't already crossed within the past year. It made me wonder how many times they *had* talked. But of course Dec couldn't say anything to me while the others were with us. When we were the final ones in the limo, I expected him to finally tell me. When he didn't, I expected him to tell me when we got back to my house.

We undressed for bed, and as usual, once we were beneath the sheets he reached for me to snuggle against. I lay stiffly beside him.

"Is anything wrong?" he asked.

"No. Is anything wrong with you?" I asked.

"I guess I am disappointed about the medal in a way." He shrugged. "But I can whine about it to you in the morning once we've slept on it."

I waited for him to bring up the other topic, but of course, he didn't. Eventually I heard his breath deepen, and knew he had fallen asleep. I stayed awake for ages.

CHAPTER
TWENTY-EIGHT

I AWOKE with a headache and sleep trying to chase me back down, but Declan must have been waiting for me to open my eyes.

"Morning."

I mumbled a reply. I may have been half asleep, but not enough to stop everything about last night come flooding back with stunning clarity.

"I need to talk to you about something."

"Can it wait for after coffee?" I groaned. I had a feeling only coffee or hard drugs could sustain me through whatever was coming.

"Nope. Otherwise I might lose the guts to tell you."

Okay. This definitely didn't sound good. I sat up, but Declan remained propped up on his side with his elbow. With his free hand he rubbed his thumb over my kneecap.

"Shoot," I told him unhappily.

Declan gave a small sigh and then bit the bullet. "My ex approached me last night."

I decided to put him out of his misery. "I know, I saw you with him."

His hand dropped away, and he shook his head. "I *knew* you were acting weird about something."

"Is that the only reason why you're telling me?"

"No!" he said with such vehemence I knew I couldn't doubt him.

"So why are you only telling me now?"

"It threw me, that's all. Plus, you didn't seem very talkative last night."

I had to give him that.

"I just… had to mull it over, that's all."

"What did he say? It looked pretty intense."

"It was," Declan admitted. He pulled himself up to sit next to me properly and rearranged the doona over us as it was cold. "He told me he wanted to say how much he admired me for coming out, and he wished he could have done it back when we were together."

That was what I dreaded hearing. But I couldn't say anything. My throat had seized up.

"Anyway, he's thinking about doing it now," Declan continued. "He's been miserable the past couple of years, and I guess he wanted to kind of apologise for everything. You know, without really saying sorry."

There was an edge of bitterness in his last sentence, and I wondered if you were ever really over someone if they still could cause you to have so strong an emotion.

"He wants to get back with you," I said woodenly.

"Maybe." Declan shrugged. "Doesn't matter if he does."

"Why?"

"Christ, Simon, don't be so dense."

"Just look at it logically, Dec. He broke your heart because he couldn't live the way you wanted to or at least try to compromise. Now he's seen the error of his ways and he's considering coming out—"

"Yeah, *considering*."

"—you said that when the board offered you that deal where you cover everything up and blame it on me, you thought about it. So don't tell me you didn't think about the possibility of getting back with him—"

"Are you just looking for a fight?"

"No, I just want to know the truth."

The words rang out in the space between us, and Declan reached for my hand.

"Of course it crossed my mind. And you should be glad I tell you the truth. Because even though it occurred to me, I also knew I wouldn't act upon it."

"But how do you know? He said he's only considering it, if he actually *did* it—"

"Because I'm with *you*, Simon! Because I love you! Not him. You wanted me in spite of who I was, and what you had to do in order to be with me. How many times do I have to fucking say it?"

Any therapist would have told you the obvious, that I couldn't accept it at times because I didn't understand why anybody would prefer me over the seemingly perfect football player who Dec would have much more in common with if the guy could get over his issues.

"I love you too," I said, hoping I didn't sound desperate. "And that's why it did my head in last night. I could just see the history between you... the way he looked so comfortable with you. Do you think I *want* to be paranoid about it?"

Declan shook his head. "But sometimes, I just think you push me away deliberately because you think I'm going to do it one day by my own choice. And it could just happen if you keep doing it."

I stared at the lumps my knees made under the doona.

Declan waited for me to say something, but I couldn't talk. Mostly because I thought I would break down there and then.

"I'm going to take a shower," he said finally.

When I heard the water start, I threw on a T-shirt to add some decency to my boxers and headed out into the kitchen to feed Maggie. Once she was munching away happily, I watched her for a while and wished I was a cat so that my biggest problem in life was whether my human was going to open a tin for me as promptly as I wished. I gave her one final scratch behind the ear, and she jerked away as if she thought I was going to steal her food. I smiled and walked out to get the paper from the front lawn.

As the paper unrolled from its plastic wrap, the photo on the front page caught my attention straightaway. It was Francis Bevan, holding his medal up for the camera. But next to it, in a separate box was a photo of Declan and I. I had the stunned-rabbit look, and Declan looked perfectly at ease; the headline above us read *DID HE COST TYLER THE MEDAL?* Of course, the article was by my old friend Peter van Niuewen, the man who had broken the story of the kiss in the hospital grounds.

That was the last fucking thing that I needed. I quickly skimmed the article; van Niuewen had to have been hanging out at our table last night and dictating everything Geoff Hendricks had said. I was a liability, a controversy, a distraction resulting in Declan losing his cool on the field and rendering himself ineligible for vital points that would have won him the Brownlow.

I turned to the Letters to the Editor page; fans had already e-mailed in their opinions on the subject. Not surprisingly, van Niuewen's opinion seemed to be the universally accepted one. I *was* the Devils' Yoko Ono.

I slammed the paper into the bin, thinking it was best not to let Declan know until I had had enough time to get over it and be able to act like I was unaffected by it all.

The shower had stopped running when I stepped back inside. Declan was towelling himself off in the bedroom.

"Where were you?" he asked.

"Feeding Maggie."

"I thought I heard the front door."

"I was putting the can in the bin."

"Oh."

I crossed over to him and kissed him. He was surprised, but kissed me back. I rested my forehead against his, and we stood holding each other.

"What's that for?" he asked.

"Because I wanted to."

"Good enough reason for me."

I wanted to hold onto this moment forever, but they can never last that long.

LUCKILY the thought of the newspaper didn't even cross Dec's mind, as he was meeting his brothers for lunch and had to rush in order to get there on time. I was invited, but I thought brotherly bonding should win out, and I had to go shopping for Nyssa's birthday present. Presciently, I had arranged a mental health day for the Tuesday after the Brownlow, so I had a pleasant feeling of wagging as I made my way down Brunswick Street. Fran and Roger were meeting me at The Hideaway for coffee after work, and I could almost convince myself that I wasn't Yoko for a few hours... at least until Dec read the papers or saw the news. More than likely his brothers were already telling him right this minute.

I stared in the window of a store where I knew Nyssa liked to shop. There was a pair of gaudy earrings in the shape of miniature bird cages with a tiny parrot hanging on a branch inside them. They were just on the right side of ironic kitsch; therefore, perfect for her. Five minutes later I was walking out of the store, sticking them in my bag, and I accidentally ran into a guy trying to enter.

"Sorry," I said automatically, and I made to swerve around him.

I was blocked by a hand on my chest, and I peered at the guy to see what the problem was.

"Hey, I know you," he said.

I stared at him, but he didn't seem familiar. "Really?"

"Yeah," he grinned nastily. "You're that poof in the papers."

Great. "Yep, that's me," I said, and I tried to move away.

Once again, the hand on my chest.

I tried to control my voice, but I said with a tone full of venom, "I would really move your hand if I were you."

He scoffed. "What are you going to do about it?"

I whacked his hand away. "Fuck off." I began walking off, but he was dogging me.

A couple of people on the street began to take notice of us. All I could think of was getting back to my car, which was only a block or so away. I had a feeling if I tried to seek refuge in a shop he would only follow me, and things would get worse in a confined area.

"Hey, tough guy," he said, "where are you running to?"

I could feel my face burning. Most people who were watching us had sympathetic looks on their faces; I think maybe I was more recognisable than I ever thought. Of course it didn't help I was on the front page of the paper today.

"I'm talking to you!"

Just don't fall into replying to him. You'll make it worse. Just get to your car and keep your trap shut.

"They should run your fucking faggot boyfriend out of the league! There's no place for people like him in it!"

Now, I was in no way the tough guy when I turned on him. It was a fluke, really, I just caught him by surprise when I pulled my fist back and landed it on his cheek. He stumbled and fell backwards onto his arse, while my fist pulsed with pain. Later, Roger would inform me only amateurs go for the face when in a fight. That was me, of course.

But my opponent returned the shock of surprise. He looked up at me and licked the small trickle of blood coming from the edge of his lip. With a grin, he reached into his pocket and pulled out his mobile. "That's assault, I'm calling the fucking police!"

By now a small crowd had formed around us. I felt a small surge of panic and pulled my wallet out of my bag. I had never thought I would have use for it, but I knew it was probably my best bet.

I called the number on Ed Wallace's business card. It was time to bring in the big guns, and there was none bigger than the CEO of the Devils.

"WHAT do you mean, it's all sorted?" Declan asked.

"I told you, Dec, we took care of it," Ed replied smoothly.

I sat silently across from Dec, staring at the surface of the table. We were in one of the boardrooms at Etihad. Ed had sent a lawyer down to the station for me, and talks had taken place between her and my "victim", whose name turned out to be Jason Terne.

"Simon?" Dec asked.

I continued to stare at the table.

My lawyer—fuck, I had a *lawyer* now—spoke up for me. "Declan, I'm Nancy Hersh. I met Simon at the station and managed to speak with Mr. Terne—"

"Who?" Declan asked.

"My victim," I told him. It was the first thing I had said to him since he came into the boardroom looking tense and worried.

"Don't use that word, Mr. Murray," Nancy instructed me.

I could feel Declan's gaze burning through my skin. I looked up and our eyes met. He had a thousand questions to ask, I could tell, but he wanted to ask them when we were alone.

Nancy turned to him. "There are six witnesses willing to come forward for Mr. Murray and state that he was harassed by Mr. Terne, and when the alleged punch was thrown—"

"Punch? There was a punch?" Dec asked.

I lifted my hand. The skin on a couple of knuckles had split, and there was a butterfly bandage covering them. There had been some worry that I might have fractured one of them, but one of the on-call doctors at the Etihad gym had looked at it and declared me fine.

"*You* punched *him*?" Declan demanded.

"Allegedly," Nancy said quickly.

"No *allegedly*," I said softly. "I did it."

"You can only say that in this room," Nancy reminded me.

Ed watched this with some amusement. "As soon as the guy heard the other witnesses would testify against him, he dropped any threat of making charges. And just to make sure it would stay that way... well—"

"You *bribed* him?" Dec asked.

"Not a bribe," Nancy jumped in. She always liked things to be worded her way so there was no chance for recriminations later on. "We paid him for the exclusive rights to his story. That way he can't tell it to anyone else."

I started staring back down at the table again.

Declan sighed. "Unbelievable."

"You can't afford the controversy, Declan," Ed told him. "There's been enough already. Have you seen the papers today?"

Still not looking up, I awaited Declan's response while forgetting to breathe.

"Yes."

"Then you understand."

"I guess."

I guess? No *they're wrong*? No denial of any kind? I looked up, but it was Declan who was now staring down the other end of the table at anything but me.

"The contracts have been signed," Nancy said, starting to pack her briefcase up. "So there'll probably be nothing more said of it. Thanks for calling me in, Ed."

"No, thank *you* for clearing this up." Ed rose to shake her hand. "I'll walk you out."

He nodded at Declan, but ignored me.

That was because he had taken me aside before Declan had arrived and asked me if I thought things had changed. When I was perplexed by his question, he reminded me I had assured him the first time we met I had Declan's best intentions at heart.

He then insinuated that I was becoming a liability, especially with my "reckless behaviour." Although I knew he had only arranged this to stop further bad press for Declan, he had still been the only way I could get out of the situation relatively unscathed. But now he had something over me. And I had no doubt he would probably use it against me at some point, maybe in an effort to try to make Declan see that what everybody else said about me was true.

And it seemed that Declan didn't need much convincing at the moment. "What the *fuck* were you thinking, Simon?"

It was the question I was dreading, but I really hadn't expected him to say it with such vehemence. I thought he would have been concerned about me first and *then* let me have it.

"I wasn't thinking," I murmured.

"That's for fucking sure."

"Dec—"

"All those times you had a go at me for fighting on the field—"

"And did *you* ever listen to *me*?" I reminded him.

"But at least I wasn't acting all holier-than-thou and then turning around and doing the same thing!"

I felt like I was going to throw up. Or hit him. "'Holier than thou'?"

"When you go on one of your superior rants—"

"'Superior'?" It seemed like all I could do was mimic him at the moment.

"Yes, superior! Because that's the way you act sometimes, like you're above everybody else. That you're right about everything, and everyone should act the way you think. Except you never do it yourself. You just do what you like—"

"Maybe I do, sometimes! But I make mistakes. And I did that today."

"Why couldn't you have just ignored him?" Declan was going red in the face; I had never seen him look so angry before. At least, not at me.

"The same reason why you couldn't ignore them when they sledged me on the field!" I yelled. "Because I can cope with getting shit about *me* from strangers on the street, but I hate hearing it said about *you*!"

Instead of telling me he understood, because I knew it was the same from his point of view, he was still too angry. "You just don't think things through!"

I was starting to feed off his mood, and I was on the defensive. "*I* don't think things through? Everything I think revolves around you and how it affects you. And it doesn't matter what I do, it's all my fault. I have enough people telling me that, and then when they're quiet I have the *media* saying it. Even your fucking boss today said I was a liability to you."

The last sentence didn't seem to register with him. "Then why did you hit that guy, if you knew all of that? You must have known it would only make things worse!"

I slumped back into my chair. "Because I'm tired. I'm sick of it. I want a break."

Those words were out of my mouth before I even realised it. In my head I was having this beautiful, romantic fantasy of Dec and I loading the car and running away for a month, holing up in some deserted cabin somewhere... maybe along the Great Ocean Road. Where we could just be us without everybody else sticking their oar in.

That's all I wanted for a while. I needed it. And I knew he did as well.

But Declan misinterpreted it. "That's what you want?" he asked coldly.

I nodded.

"Then you've got it."

I couldn't comprehend the link between what he was saying, and the expression on his face. They were completely different. "What?"

"Enjoy your break," Dec said. Standing before me, he looked like a totally different person. A cold, robotic man in shut-down mode.

I then realised what I had said, and how it could be misinterpreted. "Dec, that's not what I meant—"

He shook his head. "It is. Bye, Simon."

I called out his name, but he closed the door behind him. I sat there for a moment, my mind racing over everything that had just been said between us. Was this really how quickly things could end, over such a stupid and simple sentence? I got to my feet and ran to the door, about to yank it open, when the knob turned under my hand.

Thank fuck, Dec—

It was Ed. "Everything okay, Simon?"

"Thanks for today," I said hurriedly as I pushed past him.

"Remember our little talk," he called after me.

I didn't give a fuck about our little talk. I ran down the maze of hallways, trying to find my way to the car park. In my frenzied state I got myself lost, but even with such a diversion I should have been able to catch up with Declan easily. Unless he was running from me.

By the time I pushed open the big doors to the car park, the space reserved for the players was empty. I hurriedly pulled out my mobile and dialled his number. The other end of the line rang for ages and then diverted to his message-bank.

I think I called it about six times, and on the seventh it diverted straightaway. He had switched his phone off.

Slowly, I made my way back to my own car, which Nancy had driven me from the police station to collect on the way to Etihad.

I hoped my mobile would ring and show Dec's number.

But it didn't.

CHAPTER
TWENTY-NINE

I DON'T know how Nyssa did it, but she managed to keep pulling the festival together despite my absence. Opening night was less than three weeks away. She sounded panicked when I said I would be off work for a while, but I must have sounded awful enough for her not to doubt I was sick.

I still couldn't believe it had come to this. I couldn't even claim Declan and I were in relationship limbo, because I couldn't even speak to him to confirm it. There was such an air of finality to it all, like he had given up on me completely and had shut me out so he didn't even feel the need to give me any details.

Roger and Fran finally realised something was up on Wednesday when they hadn't been able to get in contact with me the day after the Brownlows. Nyssa told them I was sick, and when they still couldn't reach me at home, they tried calling Declan. And apparently Declan was unreachable and never returned the messages they left for him.

So they let themselves into my house with the spare key and found me catatonic in my bedroom, listening to every depressing song I owned over and over again.

Joni Mitchell was singing about how she made her baby say good-bye, and I was singing along with her about how I had lost the best baby I had ever had.

"Oh crap," Fran muttered to Roger. "This is breakup territory."

"You'd be better dealing with him," Roger said, panicked. "I'll go and make tea."

She waved him away. Joni stopped singing, and I realised she had switched the stereo off.

"Don't," I moaned.

"Hon, you can't keep listening to that. What happened?"

I buried my face deeper into my pillow. "You already guessed."

"No," she said firmly. "I don't believe it."

"Believe it," I said. And I waited until Roger returned, and we all sat on my bed as I told them the whole sorry story.

"So it's just a stupid miscommunication," Roger shrugged. "Nothing new between the two of you."

"It sounds different to me," said Fran, the smarter and more intuitive one of the partnership. "Declan won't even talk to *us*."

"I wonder if Abe and Lisa know." I pulled Maggie onto my lap, and she struggled to get free, but I wouldn't let her. I had already let Declan escape; Maggie was now my prisoner for life.

"Call them," Roger said.

"I don't think I could handle it if they ignored me as well."

Maggie sank her claws into my arm, and I yelped and let her go. Even my cat hated me.

"Well, you can't sit in here forever," Roger told me. "You have a festival to run. And Nyssa won't tell you this, but she's stressing out."

"She is?"

"She's got some of her friends in to help her, though," Fran said quickly. "She can probably handle you taking another few days off."

"This will all blow over," Roger said, trying to sound reassuring.

"You didn't see Declan's face," I reminded him.

"But we know how much he loves you," Fran reminded me.

"Love doesn't always win out," I sniffed.

Roger wrinkled his nose. "Are you quoting Joni Mitchell again? And what's up with Joni Mitchell, anyway? It's not like you're a fifty-year-old hippie."

I whacked him over the head with my pillow; it gave me a momentary satisfaction.

THE next day I decided that I couldn't leave Nyssa in the lurch for any longer and drove into work, reverting back to my old public transport-avoiding ways.

She was surprised to see me walk through the door, and she instantly ran up to me and gave me a huge hug.

"Fran told you," I said flatly.

"I don't believe it," she said. "Just wait and see. You'll hear from him soon."

I didn't answer. She pushed me back so she could have a good look at me. Her brave smile almost made me break down.

"I'm going to make you a coffee. Go and sit down, I'll bring it in to you."

I thanked her and dragged myself into my office. The glare coming in through the windows made me wince, and I pulled the blinds down.

There was a pile of messages and mail stacked on my desk. I knew there wouldn't be one from him, but I searched for Declan's name anyway. The new

Reach Out fell out from the pile; I couldn't face reading it so moved to bin it. But I saw there was a picture of Declan and me on the front page, taken at the Brownlows. The box beneath it crowed about how it was a defining moment in the history of gay sport. I wondered how long before the same photo would be used with a new caption once word got out about our breakup: the oft-used and clichéd *In happier times.*

In larger print to the side of the photo: *EXCLUSIVE: DECLAN TELLS US ABOUT HIS NIGHT. PAGE 2.*

I quickly flicked to the second page, and there was a photo of Declan by himself, beaming at the camera. It was taken the same night, but obviously when I wasn't around.

The byline for the article read *An exclusive by Jasper Brunswick.*

What the hell? When did Dec speak to Jasper? Jasper freaking Brunswick?

Nyssa entered the room silently and set a cup of coffee before me.

I held up the newspaper. "Have you seen this?"

Her eyes widened, and she shook her head. "No. What does it say?"

"I'm just about to read it."

"Do you think you should?"

I gave her a slight smile. "I'll be fine, Nyss."

"Okay. I'll leave you to it."

"Nyss?"

She turned back, a look of concern still in her eyes. "Yeah?"

"Thanks."

She nodded and closed the door behind her.

I turned my attention back to the paper. Jasper seemed to be trying to turn himself into a proper journalist now. His smarmy gossipy tone was almost completely gone as he wrote about how Declan was a groundbreaker and a role model, and what he was doing would make things so much easier for people in the same situation in the future.

It turned out Dec had done a phone interview with him on Tuesday afternoon, obviously before he had found out about my misadventures on Brunswick Street with Jason Terne.

I skimmed the article, hearing Declan's voice in my head as he responded to Jasper's questions about the past year. I felt an ache worse than any I had ever experienced, especially when he got asked about the Brownlow:

Jasper: Do you really think being gay, and having a partner openly, hurt your chances of getting a medal?

Declan: I don't think that in itself cost me the medal. It was just that I let go of my temper on the field sometimes during the year for various reasons, and I guess that went against me when it came to the voting. I mean, if the umpires themselves were being homophobic in that regard, I wouldn't have even come that close to winning. I just wouldn't have gotten any points.

The man was classy. I was so fucking stupid.

Jasper: How did you feel on the night?

Declan: It sounds stupid, but like a million bucks. When you don't have to live closeted, people don't realise how much they take for granted… just the privilege of being able to be out and about with the person you love. For so long, I've wanted that, and this year it happened. I got to share that night with Simon, and it was the best feeling.

Jasper: So if he "cost" you that medal…

Declan: Then I think the price was more than worth it.

Jasper: Thanks for your time, Declan.

Declan: Thank you.

I ripped the page out of the paper, folded it up, and put it inside my wallet. I knew I would torment myself thousands of times by rereading it, memorising the beautiful things Declan had said about me, and berating myself for fucking it all up.

Unless I *gave* up.

I collected all my things together again and ran out of my office to Nyssa's desk. "Are you okay?" she asked, standing up.

"Nyss, I have to go, sorry. Will you be okay here today?"

She nodded. "I didn't think you were coming in, so I have some friends coming in to help."

"Thanks," I said, giving her a quick kiss.

"Where are you going?" she yelled after me, but I was already too far gone to reply.

I CAUGHT the tram up to Spencer Street, fidgeting nervously. I was still getting looks from passengers who could flick between the front page of the paper and compare the man in the photograph with the one standing before them.

Once off the tram I ran through Southern Cross Station and across the Webb Bridge to Declan's apartment complex.

Declan's spare key still hung off my set, although I was only planning to let myself into the security door; but my courage faltered when I actually got there, so I pressed the intercom for his apartment.

It took a while, but a voice eventually answered. "Hello?"

A female voice. Bewildered, I just stood there.

"Simon?"

"Umm, yeah."

"It's Lisa."

"Oh!" Damn those intercoms could really disguise a voice. "Uh, hi. How did you know it was me?"

"Videophone up here," she reminded me. Yes, that's how flustered I was. The amount of times I had stayed here, I should have remembered.

"I'll buzz you up."

I pushed the door open when it clicked, and in the elevator I wondered what reception I was going to get when I walked in. Did Lisa even ask Declan if I could be brought up? Was he going to be pissed at her?

She met me at the door and gave me a big hug. "I've been wanting to call you."

"I have as well," I admitted. I nodded towards the door. "How is he?"

Lisa looked at me sadly. "He's not here."

"What?"

"Come in."

I shook my head. It would be too weird. "Not while he's not here."

She took me by the elbow and brought me into the apartment. It looked the same as it always did, except for the glaring omission of Declan himself. It was too normal; it shouldn't be this way when I felt like everything had changed.

"Where is he?"

"Tassie."

He wasn't even in the state? When I drove people away they had to go far, I guess.

"Both he and Abe had to go for training for a junior squad, recruiting new members who can start next year. It's kind of a PR, role model thing."

"Why are you here?"

She walked over to the balcony and slid the door open. We stood in the sunlight, which was warm although the air was cool. I leaned against the railing for support.

"I told Declan I'd pick up his messages and mail."

I stared at her, my stomach somewhere around my ankles. "You listened to the messages I left?"

"Sorry, I had to," she rested her hand over mine. "Hey, they broke *my* heart, so I can only imagine what they would have done to him."

"He still hasn't spoken to me," I said. "So he can't be that upset."

Lisa pulled her hand away. "Don't be a dick, Simon. Declan's devastated. He's gone into complete shut-down mode, which he does whenever he's upset. It's not living, it's existing."

I couldn't stand her being mad at me as well. "I know he would be upset. I just want him to talk to me again."

She nodded. "You're just going to have to let him come around on his own time."

"What if he doesn't?"

Lisa looked as if she wished she had a better answer for me. "I don't know."

I sat on one of the banana lounges. "I have to stop doing this."

"What?"

"It's not like I purposely seek melodrama out," I told her. "I just think I can handle things, and I make them worse. And every time I swear to myself that I won't do it again... but then I always convince myself that it's different this time, and I *can* handle it. I just keep doing it over and over again."

She sat on the other lounge. "Can I offer you a bit of friendly advice?"

"Yes, please," I said, truthfully and gratefully.

"You had the perfect person to speak to about this the other night, and you brushed him off. Abe was probably the only person who could understand what you've been going through recently."

"Abe?" I asked, confused.

"Yeah, Abe," she rolled her eyes. "You're really thick sometimes."

"No argument here." I was being serious.

"You think that Abe isn't getting shit from some arseholes because he's best friends with Declan? That he isn't being asked if they're more than friends? Except they word it worse than that. He gets sledged on the field as well. They make little cracks about him on all the shows as well, but he seriously doesn't care. Because Dec is his best friend, and he loves him. Except straight guys don't say that to each other. Stupid, I know."

Her speech got to me. "Has he told Declan that happens?"

"Dec's not stupid. He knows. But they get past it because they're so close. And you have to get past it, Simon. Jesus, you really need to open up to people instead of thinking you have to deal all by yourself."

"I know."

She gave an exasperated sigh. "You say that, but I still don't think you get it. You've been used to being single for so long that you've forgotten how to be part of a couple. It's not easy, but other people aren't as resistant to it as you are."

"I don't want to resist it," I said softly.

"Well, tell that to Declan," she paused. "When he lets you."

"You know what, though? I'm not the only one at fault here."

"Believe me, I know. Dec's a runner. He always has been. It's the only way he can cope."

"Yeah, well, I wish he was here."

"If it's any consolation, I bet you he does too."

"But does he wish *me* to be here as well?"

"I don't know."

I wish she could have been more sympathetic for me, but I guess I needed the tough love. I also wondered if she was just avoiding revealing Declan's feelings on his behalf. All I wanted was to talk to him, to stop feeling empty.

Lisa checked her watch. "Anyway, I've got to go. I have a meeting with the building co-op." She looked at my puzzled expression. "Didn't I tell you? Abe and I are buying in here."

"That's great," I told her. "Really."

We went back into the apartment and locked up, heading back towards the lift.

"Think about what I said," Lisa told me as she got off on the fourth floor.

I nodded. "Thanks. And Lisa?"

"What?"

"Abe doesn't hate me, does he?"

She smiled and shook her head. "But that might change if you truly break Dec's heart. You don't even want to know what he planned to do to the ex."

I truly didn't, but the thought of losing Dec was actually far scarier.

ALTHOUGH my mad dash to the Docklands hadn't exactly gotten me the results I had hoped for, I was in a slightly better frame of mind when I got back to the office. Nyssa and her friends were doing a ring-around, finalising catering and invitations for the opening night, and they all greeted me warmly when I walked in. Nyssa had the presence of mind not to ask me anything about what she already suspected caused my absence, although I knew she would grill me for details later. But she did stump me when she followed me into my office.

"Alice Provotna came in to see you."

It had actually been a while since I had seen Alice. She had decided to adapt the focus of her documentary to being a "one year in the life" piece on Declan and his first year of being out, but a family wedding had kept her away from the Brownlows for which I was thankful for even before the trouble between Declan and I had occurred.

"Oh," was all I could say.

"She said she was having some trouble getting the Devils to talk to her today about releasing some footage. In fact, she accused them of being cagey."

Oh, *shit*. All we needed was for *her* to scent something in her newly self-anointed role of documentary-auteur. This wasn't the ending I wanted depicted in her doco. I didn't even want it to be the final-act storyline before the hopeful happy ending.

"She wanted to know if you could use your contacts to pull some strings," Nyssa continued unhappily, knowing the effect it could have on me.

I nodded. "Okay. I'm going to go home, Nyss, but if she calls again just tell her I'll look into it."

It was a brush-off; we both knew it, but Nyssa nodded. "Sure."

"Thanks for your help, guys," I told her friends. "Keep a record of the hours you've worked, I'll make sure you get some kind of pay."

I left them happier than I was, because Alice's request had brought up all my fears again.

I DIDN'T hear from Declan at all, although I tried calling his mobile and his landline in Hobart again and again. I refused to give up.

Now Nyssa's friends had been promised pay for their services, they threw themselves into doing even more jobs for the festival, and I didn't go in for the rest of the week. I swore even if I had to end up paying them somehow out of my own pocket it would be worth it. All I wanted to do was slop around the house and feel sorry for myself and try to get hold of Dec. I avoided calls from my parents and Alice Provotna, too scared that they would be able to wheedle out of me that something was wrong.

On Friday an invitation for Tim and Gabby's wedding came in the post, addressed to both Declan and myself. It was to be held in the first week of December; I filled out the RSVP to send back to them, saying we would both be attending.

Doing stupid little things like that were the only thing to gave me hope. I wanted to imagine into reality the vision of Dec and I turning up at the ceremony in Fitzroy Gardens, bickering light-heartedly as I knew undoubtedly we would, more than likely because I would be wishing to be anywhere but there, and Declan would be having to keep me in line. Then later we would shock some of the more conservative guests at the reception when we slow-danced together as couples were invited to join the bridal waltz.

I let my message bank take calls from any number I didn't recognise on caller ID. Checking later, most of them were from media sources that wanted sound bites about the Brownlows. I ignored them. Jasper's article caused a little bit of a stir when it was picked up by the AAP and reprinted in other papers. I dreaded the thought of Declan being contacted for follow-ups by the press when I was probably the last thing he wanted to talk about.

Returning to work the following Monday, I was in what Lisa would probably call "shut-down mode." I threw myself into the festival, and Nyssa and I were lost in a crazy schedule again, where I only saw my own house when I crashed into bed and then left as soon as I got up again in the morning. I had to rely upon Roger and Fran again to feed Maggie, as there was no Declan to pick up the slack.

I don't know whether it was the insane amount of work I had to do or whether I had just resigned myself to it being over, but I didn't attempt calling Declan that week.

However, I did send an invite for opening night out to him. I scrawled across it desperately *Please come. I miss you.* I didn't know if it would work.

Just because we hadn't spoken didn't mean that I was in the dark about what he was up to. The news showed footage of him in Hobart one night, helping to coach the junior squad Lisa had told me about. Aware that the cameras were on him, he had his media-smile on. Or maybe I just wanted it to be his media-smile. The possibility he actually *was* happy was something I didn't want to consider, even though Lisa had made out he wasn't.

I received an RSVP from Lisa and Abe saying they were coming to the Triple F opening night; still no word from Dec. I was glad that they were making the effort, although it could be awkward on both ends. I didn't want them to be caught in the middle.

It was three days before the opening of the festival when I collapsed over the paper in exhaustion with a wilting salad roll to try and find fifteen minutes of peace and found a piece on Declan buried back in the social pages.

The subheading asked *TYLER'S NEW SQUEEZE?* and the picture showed Declan walking down a set of stairs, his hands in his pockets. He was in the process of turning back to look at the guy walking slightly behind him, and they were both laughing. The reporter commented that they had been hanging out together "quite a bit" in Hobart.

I choked on a mouthful of roll and had to spit it out into a napkin as there was no way I could get it down. I stared at the photo, unwilling to accept any other explanation.

It was in the paper, so of course it *must* be true. The logical part of my brain was saying *Declan isn't like that, there's no way he would be with someone else when he hasn't even sorted out once and for all what is happening with you;* my emotional and exhausted self was saying *You fucked him over, why should he show you any courtesy?*

And I really couldn't think of a reason. Except I knew Dec wouldn't do that.

But it still hurt when I got home at about midnight and found a message from my mother asking if we had broken up.

I deleted it halfway through.

I picked up the phone and punched in Dec's mobile number. It went straight to message bank again. "Dec," I said, knowing that I was dancing on a knife's edge between white-hot anger and melancholy insanity, "just put me out of my misery for fuck's sake. And you know what? You can stop running away. You've done it the whole time we've been together, and I'm sick of it. Maybe this is the last time I'll ever have to deal with it. I don't know. And I don't know because you haven't bloody talked to me. I still love you. It's time to let me know what you feel one way or the other."

I planned to say a few more things, but I ran out of time. I hung up, thinking I had probably made an even bigger mistake.

And then I put on some Joni Mitchell.

WE HAD arranged things to be a little bit different for the opening night of the Triple F this year, riding off the back of last year's success and what it did to boost our reputation. The Yarra City Council had allowed us to use the Studley Park amphitheatre, and we were going to be screening the films on a floating screen in the river itself; it was going to be even bigger than Federation Square the year before.

There had still been no word from Declan. I steeled myself for having to turn up with Roger and Fran, and when questioned about Declan I would just say he had other commitments. As he hadn't made an official statement, I wasn't going to either. There was plenty of speculation in the media, however. Declan had turned up in another picture in the social pages, standing out on his balcony with some guy I didn't know from a bar of soap. *MORNING COFFEE?* the caption asked sneakily.

I couldn't believe I was now accepting it; it had to be over. It had been over two weeks since I had last spoken to him, and you had to assume that anybody seeking some form of reconciliation would have been in contact by now.

I told Roger and Fran I would drive so they could drink; alcohol wouldn't be my friend tonight when there was so much to do and so much to hide. Loose lips sink (relation)ships.

My spirits were raised when we parked the car and walked down to the amphitheatre. The Chinese lanterns Nyssa and I had been stringing up all morning in the branches above the pathway filled the air with a festive glow, and the amount of people milling around already guaranteed that the night would be a success.

"It looks great," Fran said.

"Thanks." I grinned.

"Yeah," Roger said. "Where's the bar? It's open this year, right?"

"All class," Fran muttered.

"Just wait for the photos first, Rog," I laughed.

As soon as the photographers saw me, they surged forward. I knew it wasn't really for me, just they mistook Roger to be Declan from a distance. The flashes rapidly diminished in number as they realised he wasn't there, and they were just stuck with the nonfamous half of the couple and his doofus friends.

"Simon, where's Declan tonight?" one of them yelled out to me.

I kept my voice clear and light. "He had other commitments tonight."

"What about the reports that have been published in the papers lately?" asked a woman holding a microphone emblazoned with a radio station logo at the bottom.

I grinned; it looked far more easy and comfortable than I really was. "You should know not to believe anything—" and I gave an exaggerated *whoops* expression, "Sorry, I mean *everything* in the papers."

There were actually a few laughs at that one, and the three of us fled to relative safety.

"That was good," Fran said comfortingly. "You did well."

Nyssa swooped upon me, and Roger went off in search of the bar. "Quite a lot of people are looking for you," she said, frazzled and forgetting to even indulge in any greeting. "But the most persistent are Alice Provotna and Gigi Jones."

Alice, I had to avoid. But what did Gigi Jones want with me?

"Where is Gigi?" I asked.

"Near the projector."

Fran gave me a kiss. "Go. I'll find my husband."

As I followed Nyssa through the crowds, I couldn't help but look for Declan, hoping he would be here with Lisa and Abe, even if he was angry and would be difficult to talk to.

Because just him being here would mean *something*.

"I haven't seen him," Nyssa said quietly, unable to avoid seeing my transparency.

"I wasn't thinking about that," I lied. "I was just wondering what Gigi needs to see me about."

IT TURNED out that Nyssa's most paranoid fear turned out to be real.

I had been headhunted.

Gigi Jones ran another, bigger, slightly more mainstream film festival. And she wanted me as part of the team. I would be in charge of local and national entrants, while her other team would handle foreign acquisitions. I would be in charge of five people and get a rather substantial pay rise. As guilty as I felt about considering leaving the Triple F (especially on the opening night of their current festival), it was a great opportunity.

But there were two things I had to clear first.

"I can't leave without Nyssa," I told Gigi.

Gigi laughed. "I thought as much. You two are far too loyal to each other to survive in this business!"

I looked at her blankly. "You already asked her?"

"Yes, and despite the fact it would be a promotion for her, she said she couldn't leave you." Gigi gave a small, self-satisfied giggle. "She was very relieved when I said I was going to be offering you the local acquisition leader role."

Now I had to bring up what could be the deal breaker. "I'm not being offered this job because of... well, the fact I seem to turn up in the media quite a bit?" I had to know if Declan wasn't going to be on my arm for required social functions whether the offer would be rescinded.

Gigi looked at me over the rim of her glass. "I hire people because of what they can do with the job. I've seen your work for the past few years, Simon. I just had to wait and ascertain it wasn't a fluke and then make sure I snatched you up before somebody else did."

"Oh." Compliments didn't sit well with me.

"So, what do you think?"

"I'll have to talk to Nyssa."

Gigi smiled smugly. "I'll get your business cards made up on Monday."

NYSSA tackled me to the ground, and we rolled around on the grass quite unbecomingly for festival runners.

"This is brilliant!" she howled. "I knew you wouldn't leave me!"

I briefly wondered if I had ever shown as much loyalty to Declan as I did to Nyssa that night, but I did truly think that was one thing I couldn't doubt about myself.

I sat with my friends in a small copse of trees a little way from the amphitheatre, where our talking wouldn't disturb the festivalgoers who were now watching the first film of the evening.

A bottle of champagne had been lifted from the bar, and I was allowing myself one celebratory drink as Nyssa and I toasted to our new jobs.

"What are we celebrating?" came a voice from behind us.

I turned to see Lisa with Abe standing slightly behind her. Of course, I looked for Declan, and I don't think either of them missed my searching expression. Recovering quickly, I jumped up and hugged them both. "I'm really glad you came. Nyssa and I have been headhunted for another festival, we just found out ten minutes ago."

"You really want to leave the Triple F?" Lisa asked.

"Oh, you know," I said offhandedly, "new horizons, blah blah blah."

Lisa took me by the elbow and led me off a little way from the others, who pretended not to notice even though they knew exactly what we would be talking about.

But before Lisa could start, I turned to Abe.

"I just wanted to apologise about the Brownlows."

Abe shrugged with characteristic nonchalance. "It's okay."

"No, it's not. I was a dick."

Abe laughed. "Okay, you *were* a little bit. But I understand why. I was just trying to help."

"I know, and I'm trying to work on being more gracious when people help me." I held out my hand. Abe smirked, gave it a quick shake, and pulled me into a hug. His build reminded me of Declan's, and I pulled away quicker than I would with most friends. It felt familiar, but wrong. "Be careful. There's press about."

"Oh yeah," Abe said mockingly, and he soft-punched me in the shoulder. "That better?"

"That's the usual manly gesture of affection, yeah."

"We really thought he would be here tonight," Lisa said, returning to the subject we knew had to be brought up. The white elephant in the middle of the festival.

I loved her, but the words burned. "Lisa, please don't make me want to believe something that might not be true."

"Do you really think I would do that to you?" she asked.

"No," I said immediately, honestly. "But did he really say that?"

Abe stepped in. "He was thinking about it. But maybe he knew seeing you for the first time in a place where media would be wasn't the best idea."

"But he *did* think about it?" I asked hopefully.

"Yes!" they said in exasperated unison.

"What about that guy he's been photographed with?" I asked pathetically.

"Simon, what did I tell you about being stupid?" Lisa asked, looking like she wanted to whack me.

I nodded. "Is he home?"

"That's where we left him," Abe said.

They both looked at me expectantly.

"Do you think—"

"Do we have to fucking drive you there?" Abe asked.

I shook my head. "Can you take Roger and Fran home?"

With *that* sorted, I ran back to the others. I wasn't sure how things had suddenly changed, but Declan must have said something to them tonight he hadn't shared before. I knelt beside Nyssa and whispered into her ear. She broke into a huge smile and said, "Go. I'll handle everything."

I looked at Fran; Nyssa's smile was practically a reflection of her own.

"Gotta go."

"Where's he going?" I heard Roger ask. I didn't hear Fran's reply as I ran back past Abe and Lisa, but I'm sure it was probably a comment on how dense he could be sometimes.

BUT the surprises of the night were not done with me yet. As I raced towards the car park, someone called my name. I debated running on and pretending I hadn't heard them, but they called it again insistently.

I turned, only to find Jasper Brunswick.

"Hey, Jasper," I said breathlessly. "Catch up with you later, catering emergency—"

The fact I had been speaking to him for five seconds and hadn't insulted him yet immediately put him on alert. "I was just speaking to some of the press—"

I wondered if I could throw him off the scent. "You know, I just wanted to thank you for the interview you did with Declan."

He couldn't have been more surprised if I had dropped to one knee and offered him an engagement ring. "Excuse me?"

"Just, it was nice, that's all. Maybe you should do more stories like that rather than your gossip columns. Now, I really have to—"

His eyes narrowed. "Why isn't Declan here?"

"He had other commitments," I sighed.

"I've noticed you've both been a bit AWOL since the Brownlows."

"Well, we're trying to keep it low key lately. No oversaturation of the media, you know what I mean?"

He stared at me without any hint of mercy. "Not really. Anything you want to share, Simon?"

"Nope." I shook my head vehemently. "Except, don't eat the mushroom puffs. They may give you gastro."

I was lying; there weren't any mushroom puffs.

Jasper was relentless. "What about these reports of Declan with other guys?"

I tried to appear as casual and nonchalant as possible. "You would probably know better than anyone else what the media can be like. Anything to sell a story."

"Well, as you just pointed out, I'm trying to move past that now."

"Uh-huh."

"But getting back to you and Declan, it would be tough trying to make a relationship last in these circumstances. With all the pressure from the media."

"What, like being waylaid when trying to solve an epicurean crisis?" I laughed.

Jasper didn't laugh, however.

"Look, Jasper. We're fine."

And before he could say anything else, I ran. We *would* be fine, if someone would just let me get out of Fairfield.

In movies there is this rousing, emotional moment when the hero or heroine does something grand and stupid to get their love back at the last moment. I jumped into my car, determined to drive to the Docklands and see Declan. I would let myself into his complex, and because I was so desperate I would think the lift was taking too long to reach the ground floor, so I would have to run up the stairs (because my fitness levels magically increased in my fantasies). Declan would open his door, shocked but happy, because my presence, of course, is the thing he has desired most. We would kiss passionately, he would tell me he was waiting for me, and then we would go into the bedroom, undress each other feverishly, and white lace curtains would billow in the background before the scene faded to black.

Or something like that. Of course, if your film is more like a 1940s melodrama, there is the tragic happenstance that stops the planned reunion from taking place. And my life, it seems, is more like a 1940s melodrama. Driving while high on adrenaline and emotion is not the smartest thing to do. I was wired, anxious, and fearful. In that part of Fairfield, because it was a large parcel of natural bushland, there were few streetlights to guide my way. So when a dog ran across the road as I was getting closer to the more suburban part of the area, I swerved and managed to avoid it, but forgot that I was on an embankment which would have been easy to see in the daylight.

The ground seemed to tilt beneath me as my car slid sideways down the embankment, chucking up plumes of gravel. As the car hit the bottom on an angle, my seatbelt snapped, and I fell against the passenger door, the headlights showing how close I had come to ploughing into a tree.

"Oh fuck," I managed to grunt.

CHAPTER THIRTY

WHEN I tried to move, my shoulder screamed with pain. Actually, I screamed with pain as well. My forehead throbbed and felt sticky, and when I touched it with my good hand it came away bloody. I was strangely calm; whenever there wasn't anything really wrong with me I tended to panic and overact, but it seemed in the face of real injury I was remarkably resilient. I knew head wounds tended to bleed freely even if only a small one, so I was more concerned about the arm.

Trying not to move it as much as possible, I pulled myself upright with my good arm. It was like being in *The Poseidon Adventure*, although my car was sideways rather than upside down. I was going to have to get out through the driver window, which currently resembled a sun roof. My bag was lying at my feet, and I looped it around my neck and began wriggling out of the window, using my good shoulder to latch onto the opposite side of the roof and pull myself out.

I could hear voices above me. It turned out that people coming from the opposite direction had seen my car veer off the road, and they had stopped to investigate. An ambulance and the police had already been called, and my good Samaritans hoisted me out of the ditch and up onto the bitumen of the road.

By the time the ambulance arrived, the police had already breathalysed me; my three or four sips of champagne barely registered, and I was cleared to go to the hospital.

I felt stupid that an ambulance had been called as my injuries weren't that extreme, but as the officers explained, I couldn't drive because of my shoulder, and the minor fact of my car presently lying at an angle in a deep ditch. So I meekly hopped into the back and lay down on the stretcher; one of the ambos cleaned the blood from my head, immobilised my arm and applied a couple of stitches to stem the bleeding.

In the lobby of the emergency room at the hospital, I knew it would be a while before I was seen by a doctor. It was Saturday night, and although the night was still young, the department was full. I was glad I hadn't been injured a couple of hours later, or else I would have been here until Monday. I rang Roger's mobile; it was Fran who picked up.

"Well?" she answered happily. "Can you put Declan on to say hi?"

"Uh, I don't want you to panic, but I'm at the Austin."

"He put you in hospital?" she screamed.

It was then I realised that she had had a little too much to drink. "Get a grip, Fran. Put Roger on."

Even though Roger was more sober, he was still Roger. "Declan beat you up?"

"Is there anybody with a working brain still with you guys?" I asked, exasperated.

"We're home already."

"Already?"

"We were bored without you. Why are you in the hospital?"

"I didn't even make it to the Docklands. I ran off the road in Fairfield. I think my car is totalled."

Roger snorted. "About time somebody put it out of its misery."

"Thanks, Rog."

All of a sudden, he kick-started into panic. "Oh fuck, you really *are* in hospital! We're on our way!"

"Don't worry about it! I don't want you to even think of driving!" That was all I needed.

"We'll catch a taxi."

"I'm serious. I'm fine."

"Shut up. We're coming."

There was no further argument, because he hung up on me, and I knew it was useless to try and call back. I sat back, waiting for my name to be called out, and tried to shut out everybody else in the waiting room by concentrating on the blaring television above my head.

"BROKEN collarbone," the doctor told me.

"Is that it?" I asked, disappointed. "It hurts like hell!"

The doctor shrugged. "It's still a broken bone."

"I was hoping it would be something I could sucker more sympathy for. I mean, it's the kind of injury a kid gets at a rollerskating birthday party."

He grinned. "You're covered in blood from your scalp wound. That might get you something."

I winced as he fitted the sling over the opposite shoulder to the fractured one and manoeuvred my arm into it. "So I have to wear this thing for four weeks?"

"At least," he looked up. "Looks like your friends are here."

I turned, expecting to see Roger and Fran.

Declan was standing in the small sliver of light coming from the curtain surrounding my bed.

This was... interesting.

I swallowed heavily. "Hi."

"Hi," he replied, his tone neutral.

"The nurse will get your paperwork," the doctor said, and he moved off to the next patient.

I wanted him to stay, because I had no idea what to say to Declan. Except the obvious question; the only question I could think of.

"How did you know?"

"Roger called me in a panic. He made it sound as if you were at death's door."

"He's a panic merchant, and he's drunk. So he's prone to hyperbole."

"I came down here, expecting to find you in a coma."

I tried to bite down on the anger rising in me. "Is that the only way you would talk to me? If you thought I couldn't answer back?"

Declan's hands were defensively positioned on his hips as he towered over me. "Jesus, Simon. I came here because I was worried. And now I'm wondering if it was all just a ploy to get me down here to finally see you."

Even he must have known how ridiculous it sounded. "Yeah, I trashed my car on Yarra Boulevard and paid this doctor off to give me a sling just to get you to finally return my calls." I picked up my jacket and jumped off the bed, ignoring the sudden spinning of the room.

"Where are you going?" Declan demanded.

"To get the paperwork."

"He said the nurse would bring it. Sit down."

"Piss off," I told him.

"Real mature."

"Look who's talking."

He suddenly leaned across me and easily picked me up and placed me back on the bed. What was most amazing was how he managed to avoid my shoulder so it didn't hurt. My pride was, though.

"I'll go and look for the paperwork. Stay there."

I could only sit and fume as he disappeared. I couldn't even turn on my mobile and find out where Fran and Roger were as we were in the emergency department and urban legend reliably informed me I could make somebody's heart explode if I did so.

Declan came back and handed me some paperwork in a clipboard. I took it and started to fill it in.

"How long would it have taken?" I asked.

"What?"

"For you to talk to me."

He rubbed his hands against his face. "I don't know."

"If you'd just listened to me—"

"Yeah, well, that's always the problem, isn't it? We never listen to each other."

"I was on my way to see you."

He looked at me, and I thought I saw a softening of his features finally. "Yeah?"

"Lisa and Abe told me that you almost came to the festival."

"I thought about it."

"Would you have let me in, if I had made it to your place?"

He avoided the question. "Have you finished the paperwork?"

I tried to reach for his hand, but he pulled it away. "You say we don't listen, well, sometimes we don't talk either."

Declan looked at his watch, and my anger grew.

"Do you have to be somewhere, Declan?"

"No."

I thought when he turned up here, that it meant he was willing to try and sort things out. But he was closed off, distant. I suddenly found myself wishing he had never come.

"Won't your boyfriend be wondering where you are?"

Declan looked surprised. "What boyfriend?"

"That'd be right," I said snarkily. "You've had so many recently, you probably don't even know which one I'm talking about."

"The guys in the paper?" Dec scoffed. "You know what it's like. I can't even ask a guy the time without them speculating over whether I'm fucking him. They've published photos of me with my brother-in-law, possible new recruits for the team I've been involved in trying out. Even the bloody broadband guy when he came out to fix the cable in the apartment!"

"What, so it's the closeted ex, then?"

"You can be a real prick when you want to be."

"Tonight, you're making me one!" I cried. "Why did you come here? Why haven't you released a statement saying we've broken up? Why haven't you even told me if we have or not? Why can't you talk to me now?"

His lips were white, they were so taut. "I just can't handle it right now."

I pushed it. "Are you seeing anyone?"

"No."

"Oh." I was relieved, but I still didn't know what it meant for me. "Well, I'm not either."

"I didn't ask if you were," he said coldly.

"Oh." It was obvious he still wanted to punish me. I couldn't blame him, but I wondered when I would finally pay enough so that he could get past it.

Declan sighed. "Jesus, Simon." He looked like he wanted to say something else, but then he thought better of it. Without another word, he began to walk off. He stopped only a few feet off, turned back halfway, but before our eyes met he was off again.

I should have run after him, made him talk to me some more, or force him to say *anything* just to keep him there. But I was so tired. The meds were kicking in, and my knees were rubbery. I shuffled over to the nurses' desk and handed in my paperwork.

Discharged, I pushed through the emergency department doors and sat down in one of the hard plastic chairs in the waiting room. All I could do was stare at the white walls before me. My arm was now throbbing painfully, and any kind of movement in my face made me aware of the torn skin rubbing against the stitching holding it together. I think I would have cried if I hadn't known the damage it could cause, and stoicism won out.

I felt a hand upon my good shoulder. I looked up to see Fran and Roger staring sympathetically at me.

"We saw Declan in the distance, leaving," Fran said, confused. "He didn't stay?"

I shook my head.

"He sounded panicked on the phone when I called him," Roger said.

"Well, he had obviously had a huge change in temperament when he saw I was okay."

"Was it wrong for me to call him?" Roger asked worriedly.

"No," I reassured him. "I just… still don't know what's going on."

"Sorry we took so long. It was ages waiting for a taxi," Fran told me. "But Declan didn't offer to drive you home?"

"No, he didn't."

"That bastard," Roger fumed, looking as if he was going to go and hunt him down and bring him back.

"He's not the bastard," I said. "I am."

Fran and Roger immediately started trying to assure me I wasn't, but I shook their protestations off. "Can you please just take me home?"

They flanked me as we walked out into the cold night air to wait for another taxi. But as we sat in the rank a familiar SUV pulled up and Dec jumped out with the engine still running. By that stage the drugs were making me feel like I was flying, and I was pretty sure I was imagining it until he hovered over me and said, "Can I give you guys a lift?"

CHAPTER
THIRTY-ONE

I DOZED most of the way home, hearing in some back part of my brain Dec saying good-bye to Roger and Fran as he dropped them off at their house. If this was a dream, it was the best one I had had in a long time. I woke up again to Dec unbuckling my seat belt and helping me out of the car.

"Are those keys magic?" I slurred as he opened my door with his own set.

"I still have my own key for here," he said.

"That's pretty presumptuous of you," I replied, although I think presumptuous came out as garbled nonsense.

I heard him say hello to Maggie as he pulled me through the door and closed it behind us.

"She's mad at you," I said to him, and that was the last thing I remembered until I woke up in the morning and saw him across from me. He must have dragged the ratty old lazyboy in from the lounge, because it was at the foot of my bed and Dec was folded across it with Maggie curled up on his side.

"Traitor," I whispered.

Dec's eyes opened. "Don't be mad at her."

"I have to be mad at something."

"Then be mad at me."

I wanted to be. But I was just so glad to see him. "Why are you in that chair?"

"It would have been awkward to share the bed, wouldn't it?"

It would have been, although it seemed I had been comatose the whole night.

"Dec, what are you doing here?"

He sat up properly, and Maggie jumped over to the bed to get some affection from me. "I couldn't just leave you like this, could I?"

The night's events still seemed foggy, but there was one thing I remembered. "You did in the hospital."

"I was stupid."

"You were running away again."

He nodded slowly. "And that's why I came back."

Just when it seemed like we were getting somewhere, there was a knock at the door. Dec and I looked at each other quizzically, not knowing who to expect.

"Wait there," I told him.

"I'm not going anywhere," he said. "I promise."

They were just words, but they were comforting. I believed him. Didn't mean he was off the hook yet. My shoulder was throbbing with pain, and I knew I had to get more drugs in me but I wanted to stay lucid for as long as I could while Dec was still around.

It wasn't anyone that I recognised who was standing on my veranda. He pushed his sunglasses back into his hair and grinned at me. "You look like you've been in the wars!"

"Huh?" I asked stupidly.

"Can't tell which is in worse shape, you or the car!"

I peered past him to see a tow truck parked on my verge with my poor car hanging off the back like some grim hunting trophy.

"I didn't arrange for a pickup," I told him. Or had I?

"Well, it's either a pickup or a delivery elsewhere," he said, which made no sense to me. He showed me his clipboard, and I saw Dec's name under the caller information.

"That's not *the* Declan Tyler?" asked the man with interest.

"Uh, yeah, it is." And I was just as surprised as he was.

"Wow." The guy was impressed. He looked at me a little closer. "Of course! You're the boyfriend. Or were. Didn't you guys split up?"

His eyes widened, and I looked behind me to see Dec had emerged from the bedroom.

"I guess not," the tow truck driver whistled.

I didn't know whether to debate the point, so I wisely kept my mouth shut.

"Anyway, it's prepaid and your friend here said you had to choose whether to have it dropped here or taken on to this other address."

I looked at the clipboard. The address was for the garage that Declan's brother owned. "Might as well take it on to the garage, hey?"

The driver laughed. "You think that thing out there can be salvaged?"

"Hey," I told him. "You gotta have hope."

I closed the door. Dec was leaning against the wall, and smiling. "You have hope?"

"I do. About a lot of things. I hope."

He gave me that smile again, and it made me want to scream.

"Declan, I'm going fucking insane!" I cried, grabbing him by his collar with my good hand. "I just need to know, what is going on between us?"

He steered me over to the couch and tried to get me to sit down, but I was too antsy.

"Why did you arrange for my car to be picked up?"

"Because you love that piece of shit car, for some reason," he said, as if it was the most obvious answer to give. "So I wanted it to be rescued."

Was the car a metaphor? "Why now? Why were you willing to talk to me after all this time?"

"Because I was ready. I was sick of hiding."

"And I was sick of having no idea what was going on."

"I just didn't think the premiere was the best place to talk to you. And then I got that call from Roger, and I was so fucking scared. It was like going to the hospital when I got the phone call about my dad. So when I got there and saw that you were reasonably okay, it was like all that worry turned into relief... but instead of acting relieved I got all tense, and it came out as anger. Probably because I hadn't had the chance to talk to you properly."

"But you came back," I reminded him.

"I got your message." It was a grin that seemed more like a grimace stretched across his face. "You were right. And you sounded so hurt and angry that it made me run even more. But something had to give."

He was right. Something had to give. "Communication was never our strong point. But can we talk now?"

"Sure, if you'll sit down. You're making me nervous, standing over me."

I did as he asked, but there was a large gap between us on the couch. Ease around each other still had to come, but I started to talk. I told him everything about how I had felt with the crowds at the games, the hassles I had gotten from the public, what the internet forums had said about me, the talk with Ed, the event at the Brownlow, and how it had all built up and caused me to snap and fight back against Jason Terne on Brunswick Street as he had just happened to come along and represent all those issues in one tidy little package.

And then Declan told me about the things he had kept from me, the details of the sledging on the field, how he felt helpless in hearing those things said about me and unable to do little about it, his guilt in thinking that he exposed me to all of this and how he feared that I secretly blamed him for it, and how he had always admired me as he thought I was dealing with it well, but that it had all came crashing down with the Jason Terne issue.

"The break wasn't from us," I told him. "It sounds so stupid now, because of everything that happened afterwards, but all I meant was *us* getting away from it all for a while. Taking off, just you and me, away from all that shit."

He stared down at the floor, chewing on the inside of his cheek. It must have been a gaping hole by now.

"I could have explained myself a bit better," I said meekly.

Dec laughed. "Fuck. I could have asked you what you meant instead of jumping to the wrong conclusion."

"I would never have broken up with you," I said earnestly. "I'm more miserable without you than I am with you." As soon as that sentence came out I groaned, because I knew how bad it sounded.

But Declan laughed. "Vintage Simon Murray comment."

"You know I say things the wrong way, but you know what I *mean*."

He nodded. "I know."

"It's tough going out with you, Dec, I'm not going to lie about that. But I know I'm not easy to go out with either. I was stupid. I let all the negatives get to me when I should have reminded myself what was good about us. That I loved you, you loved me, and *that* should have been the most important thing. All that mattered."

His hand twitched to reach across and take mine, but he kept it on his knee.

"I fucking hate not being with you," I continued, not caring if I sounded like a screechy stereotype in the final moments of some abysmal romantic comedy. "I hate thinking I've turned you against me, when I love you. Because I do."

"I haven't turned against you. I never did. I was mad for a while, but I eventually realised I was mad at my own stupidity and not being able to face something when it happened. So instead, I just cut you out. I couldn't think, and I'm sorry I shut down. But I'm not used to it."

"Used to what?"

He paused for a long moment, and I knew that whatever he was going to say was taking a lot out of him. "Being in a relationship that's also a partnership. Something that's equal. Where the other person gives a shit and feels things passionately. Jesus, Simon, I was in a relationship for two years where he felt safest pretending not to care about anything. And I went along with it. So I didn't know how much it could affect me when I saw you getting hurt or being pissed off because you feel things so *strongly*."

"We're meant to feel things strongly, Dec. Even us manly men types."

Declan snorted. "Yeah, we just never talk about them when we should. And then we fuck things up even more."

"We seem to be doing okay now," I pointed out.

Finally, his hand lifted and grasped mine. It was awkward because my closest hand was in the sling, and my free one was stuck between my leg and the end of the couch. To make it slightly easier I moved in closer to him.

"When you said you needed a break, I just reverted to the way I used to be," Declan continued. "I had to. And I didn't really snap out of it until Abe pointed out to me I was acting just like the ex used to. And he's the last fucking person I want to be in a relationship."

"You're not him."

"Maybe not. But sometime he's still part of me when I act stupidly."

"Now you know, he doesn't have to be."

"When I saw you, bloody and in that sling—"

"It was only a head wound. They're dramatic with the blood."

"All I wanted to do was come home with you, if that's what you wanted."

"Of course it's what I wanted."

"I have to apologise to Fran and Roger. I ignored their calls."

"You're lucky they forgive easily."

"*Your* Fran and Roger?"

He had a point.

"Anyway," he continued. "I have some news. It's partly why I was also off in my own little world the past week or so. I wanted to get it all sorted."

"What?"

"I've told the Devils I'm not renewing my contract this year. As of December, I'm a free agent."

Wow, that was *huge*. "And?"

"I'm moving back here. Permanently. Preliminary talks have already started for me to sign with a Victorian club."

"But it would have been on the news!"

"Ed's pissed, and he wants it hush-hush at the minute. And you know Ed."

I did, having had firsthand experience with Ed's machinations.

"So no more semi long-distance relationship," Declan said happily. "One more troubling factor in our problems solved."

"You were doing all this while we were…." I couldn't even bring myself to say the words for fear it would happen again.

"I had hope," he said simply.

"I wish you had talked to me so I could have had some."

"Yeah, well, things are going to change on that front now, aren't they?"

I kissed him. "Fuck, yes. I'm not going through this again." My eyes widened as a thought occurred to me. "Who have you signed up with?"

Declan grinned.

"Please say it's Richmond!"

"Like Richmond could afford me," he scoffed.

My face fell. "Oh fuck, anyone but Collingwood!"

He silenced me by kissing me again. "You look ready to drop." He stood and reached down to help hoist me up, leading me towards the bedroom.

I was in a lot of pain. I let him give me my tablets and a glass of water and as I was ready to fall back asleep he propped himself back up in the lazyboy.

"Hey, doofus," I said. "Get over here."

"Yeah?"

"Don't ask stupid questions."

The bed shifted as he crawled in beside me. I awkwardly tried to spoon as close to him as I could, as much as the sling and the pain would allow. I had to see his face.

"I missed you," he murmured. "And I'm never leaving again."

"Let's not be this stupid again." I could feel the painkillers wanting to pull me under.

His lips were against my forehead as he spoke. "We probably will be stupid again, but I promise you, not *that* stupid."

I closed my eyes; I finally felt at peace again. Drowsy with Declan's warmth wrapped around me, it was easy to feel that he had never been away.

I heard him say, "I'm in this for the whole season, not the first round."

I groaned sleepily at the bad metaphor. "Cheesy, Dec, cheesy."

But I managed to tell him I was in it for the whole season as well. I finally fell asleep, knowing he would be there when I woke up.

OVERTIME

FEBRUARY. A new year, a new season of footy.

I sit in the stands with Fran, Roger, and Lisa. Below us, Declan and Abe run out onto the field in their new team colours. The anticipation for them this year is high; they refused to be parted in their negotiations when leaving the Devils, and although it took some time their contracts saw them remain teammates.

With Essendon. You can imagine how my parents reacted. Especially as it means they get seats in the Essendon box at home games. They are here with us now, gushing over the unearthly abilities of their new adopted son.

Alice Provotna is a row behind us in the WAGs box, filming it all. This is her last day of shooting, and then she will do her final edit on the documentary. Declan and I decided to tell the truth about everything, even our temporary split, so that the film can realistically depict the pressure that weighed upon us in our year in the spotlight. What's going to be odd is that it will premiere at this year's Triple F festival, and we will all have to attend even though Nyssa and I no longer work for them.

The interest in us hasn't exactly died down, but it doesn't seem so controversial now. People seem to be getting used to it, although you still get the occasional dickhead.

Declan and I still bicker, but wonder of wonders, actually talking to each other gets us through it.

The siren goes for the start of the game, and Lisa and I leap to our feet. I may be supporting Dec and his team today, but I will be wearing my Richmond scarf tomorrow when Dec, Roger, and I will be going to watch them play against Hawthorn. Fran, of course, is not coming. This game today will probably be enough for her for one year.

As I watch Declan soar to take a mark, I think about how much my life has changed over the past two years. In life, like football, you need a good team to support you. I have that.

And if you have that, no matter what happens, you'll always be okay.

SEAN KENNEDY lives in the second-most isolated city in the world, so it's just as well he has his imagination for company when real-life friends are otherwise occupied. He has far too many ideas and wishes he had the power to feed them directly from his brain into the laptop so they won't get lost in the ether.

Visit Sean's website at http://www.seankennedybooks.com/.

Romance from SEAN KENNEDY

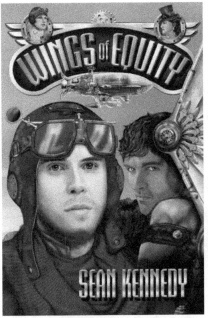

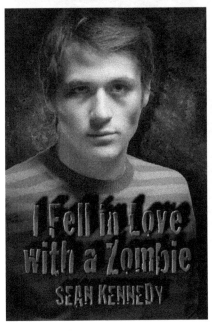

CPSIA information can be obtained
at www.ICGtesting.com
Printed in the USA
FFHW012319170119
50183026-55123FF